IN THE NICK OF TIME

Vesuvius had gone mad.

Great, surging waves of flame blasted upward and outward in a boiling seething mass a half-mile high.

First surge at midnight, fourth an hour after that—it'll kill Pompeii—fifth surge at 7:00 A.M., last surge 8:30, and it'll blast all the way to Misenum. . . .

Sibyl wouldn't have to worry about surges two through seven. Number one was going to kill her.

Four minutes. How much of that time is gone? How much is left? WHERE'S THE DAMNED TIME PORTAL?

A heavy man slammed into, then past her. More people crowded onto the beach. Lightning blazed, white faces lit with a hellish pink glow.

Sibyl shoved until she stumbled onto open beach again. The sea sucked back from the seawall, crashed forward. She whirled around, but the blinding white doorway in time was nowhere to be seen.

Then, shockingly, hands closed around her throat. She slashed at her attacker reflexively with the dirk she had forgotten she was holding. Too tall for a Roman . . . Lightning blazed. She found herself staring into Tony Bartlett's mad eyes.

Then it happened.

A brilliant crack of white light opened between them. *Oh, God, please . . . it's too late, it won't open fast enough . . .*

Baen Books by Linda Evans

Sleipnir
Far Edge of Darkness

Time Scout (with Robert Asprin)
Wagers of Sin (with Robert Asprin)

LINDA EVANS
Far Edge of
DARKNESS

BAEN

FAR EDGE OF DARKNESS

This is a work of fiction. All the characters and events portrayed in this book are fictional, and any resemblance to real people or incidents is purely coincidental.

A Baen Books Original

Baen Publishing Enterprises
P.O. Box 1403
Riverdale, NY 10471

ISBN: 0-671-87735-6

Cover art by Ken Tunnell

First printing, August 1996

Distributed by Simon & Schuster
1230 Avenue of the Americas
New York, NY 10020

Typeset by Windhaven Press: Editorial Services
Printed in the United States of America

Dedication

For Diana Hulsey, David Fletcher, and Dr. David C. Young for their incalculable help with ancient Rome (Dr. Young's knowledge of Roman circuses was priceless for this and previous novels); also for Dr. Jenny Land, for her support and encouragement; for Alan Hagan and Sandon Flowers for encouragement and willingness to share their libraries; and—as always—for Bob and Susan, for putting up with *everything*.

CHAPTER ONE

Sibyl Johnson didn't own a rifle.

She wouldn't have known how to shoot one, if she had. And Tony Bartlett had vanished, apparently right off the edge of the world.

None of which stopped Sibyl from wanting to center his face in the sights of an honest-to-God, high-powered varmint gun. Sibyl had spent her formative years increasingly disgusted with small-town drunken quarrels that led to knifings and shootings on Saturday nights. But if she *ever* saw Tony Bartlett again . . .

She'd do a whole lot more than *wish* for a gun.

Sibyl banged a fist against the steering wheel. *How could I have been so . . . so . . .*

Stupid?

Blind?

Naïve?

Any number of scathing put-downs would be appropriate.

Another lightning strike jerked Sibyl back into the present reality of creaking VW Beetle and steaming Florida heat. She tightened sweaty hands around the cracked plastic of the steering wheel. Another searing flash momentarily erased everything beyond her car: the rutted dirt road, the dust-white trees clinging to the hillside like forlorn mushrooms, the looming storm that had boiled up out of a clear sky the way storms always did on summer afternoons.

An aftershock of thunder, shaking the very frame of her battered car, was louder than the assorted groans,

1

screeches, and bangs issuing from the rear of the
decaying vehicle. "C'mon, Nuggie, you can do it," she
encouraged the faltering car.

Nuggie didn't want to climb the long, shallow grade.
She was glad the old car was running at all, given the
repairs it needed. If she'd lived in mountainous country, like West Virginia or Colorado, Nuggie would've gone
to slag-heap heaven years ago—although things might
have turned out very differently, if she *had* lived somewhere else. Tony Bartlett would've picked a different
victim, for one thing.

Sibyl punched the gas pedal savagely. Lightning flared
again, even closer. Thunder rattled side windows in their
loose frames. Sibyl winced and glanced through the
driver's window, the one that would roll neither up *nor*
down all the way. The air trickling through was cooler
than the inside of her car, but not much. Sweat dripped
down the back of her neck and prickled under her bra
strap. Hot as it was, it was little wonder the inevitable
afternoon storm promised to be a dilly. *The hotter the
day, the crazier the storm,* that's what Granny Johnson
had always said.

Industrial Light & Magic, Inc., would have been proud
to claim this storm. Greasy black clouds boiled across
the sky, just clear of the treetops. Nonstop lightning—
not bolts, but fantastic, sky-arching pink columns—jabbed
the blackness to strike beyond the hill crest. Nuggie's
headlights barely dented the gloom. Although it wasn't
yet four in the afternoon, cattle egrets had already started
to roost. Their wings flashed white against the backdrop
of black clouds and dusty, cringing trees.

Sibyl Johnson had lived through a lot of Florida thunderstorms. But she'd never seen one like this and she
still hadn't hit the worst of it. She hadn't even hit the
leading edge of rain yet.

Her car wheezed and lost acceleration. "C'mon,
Nuggie," she muttered again as she downshifted. Gears
clashed and groaned somewhere in the VW's battered
innards. The dying car wouldn't survive the summer. She

wasn't even certain it would survive the trip to campus. She growled under her breath. *Campus* ... Sibyl knew confronting those smug, lily-white fat cats wouldn't do any *good*. It was just something she had to do, to retain what was left of her battered self-respect. She would do it, get it over with, and leave the rest to fate.

Another sky-cracking column of lightning set roadside trees aflame, backlit with mad, pink light. She gripped the steering wheel harder and tried to ignore a frosty prickle of fear, left over from childhood tornadoes and the death of her parents. *I am not afraid of thunderstorms. I am not. Really, I'm not ...*

She tried to focus on practicalities to distract herself from unreasoning fear. Driving straight into the storm like this, she didn't have much hope of avoiding the rain. Once it cut in ... Nuggie's tires were balder than her department chairman. Eight-year-old tires just wouldn't cope with blinding rain on a washboarded dirt road. And there wasn't money—not *now*—to buy new ones or fix the roof on the house, either. She savaged her lower lip and blinked rapidly.

Car ... house ... career ... Sibyl wanted to bawl like a baby. But with a gullywasher in the making, she couldn't afford to cry about it now. So she pushed the Beetle as fast as she dared and eyed the storm for telltale funnel shapes. She found herself muttering a snatch of music that matched her mood. When *would* Rod Serling step out from wherever it was dead TV MCs went and say something appropriate about the mess her life was in? Maybe he could tell her the last three months had been a nothing more than a terrible delusion, caused by some foreign germ to which she had no resistance.

Yeah, right. And Tony Bartlett really is the answer to your dreams.

Another column of nightmarish pink slammed into the crest of the hill. Sibyl jumped, so badly the car swerved toward a ditch. Cattle egrets took wing in a blur of pink-edged white as she dragged Nuggie back on course. The storm grew madder with each shaky breath. *I'm not panicked, I'm not* . . .   But with the whole sky on fire like the edge of a Tesla ball, she could imagine driving over the top of this hill into anything at all: a black-sand beach beside an ammonia sea, even a stampeding herd of tyrannosaurs.

Come to think of it, a T. rex might be useful. One little enough to fit in Wilkins' office. *Yeah, that'd be just about right*.

Anger simmered to a boil again. Tony Bartlett's mocking grin floated in front of her eyes. She dragged the back of one hand over her cheek and said an ugly word aloud. At least her grandmother hadn't lived to see this. Had Sibyl not been Cora Johnson's granddaughter, the shattering end of everything she had worked for might have destroyed her. Granny not only would've understood, she probably would've been in Nuggie's passenger seat, ready, willing, and able to do battle.

And Granny Johnson would've had that rifle, too—the one Sibyl had sold right after the funeral so it wouldn't be in the house, the one she'd never understood the need for, propped so sinisterly in her grandmother's bedroom corner next to the quilt stand. She growled aloud another word which would've shocked her grandmother speechless. When Sibyl got to campus, there was going to be a storm in the chairman's office, one to match the gullywasher brewing overhead, and only an act of God would prevent it!

She gritted her teeth. *I'd have saved myself a lot of grief if I'd lived up to my ancient namesakes*. Rome's famous *sibyls*, priestesses of the Magna Mater—the Phrygian Great Goddess Cybele—had read portents that revealed the future.

"Some oracle I turned out to be." Sibyl wiped her cheek fiercely. "Displayed all the clairvoyance of a rock, didn't we, Sib?"

She should've seen through all that flattering swill Bartlett had fed her. She was a good student and motivated, but not brilliant—and overly eager. Her grip tightened down again on the steering wheel. Bartlett had set her up like the pro he was. And she'd walked right into his arms. Must be laughing himself sick, wherever he was by now. At the rate she was going, maybe life in the T. Zone *would* be a change for the better.

"Enough! First, you confront those tenured fat cats. Then, if they're stubborn, find a lawyer who works cheap and *sue* them."

Cora Johnson's granddaughter was not a quitter.

In point of fact, Cora Johnson hadn't been either, during those final, fatal months, of insulin-dependent diabetes when Sibyl had taken care of her.

The car finally chugged the last few yards to the crest of the hill, slipping gears and wheezing like a foundered racehorse. Sibyl took the VW out of gear to coast downhill in the vain hope her transmission might last just a few hundred miles more. A brilliant flash lit the whole interior of her car with a hellish pink glow. All she could see was afterimage. Sibyl swore, hastily shifting into first gear— in case she had to do some quick maneuvering around a downed tree—then tapped the brakes until she could see.

There was a hole in front of her. Not in the road.

In the air.

Sibyl stood on the brakes. Nuggie groaned a protest and fishtailed on the dusty road. The car lurched. She threw in the clutch to keep the engine running. Then she just stared, while the bottom fell out of her viscera and tried to crawl back up the hill without her.

A ragged puncture of brilliant white light was opening out of thin air. It was so bright she couldn't see anything: not through it, not around it, not beyond. Enormous columns of pink lightning crashed on all sides, arcing outward to strike the road, the trees, the clouds—

It widened, a doorway into hell. *"Ohmighod . . ."*

Her hand slipped on the gear shift. She fumbled with clutch and accelerator, hunted for reverse by feel. Like a rabbit trapped in a glare of headlights, Sibyl couldn't look away. The rupture splitting open in front of her gaped wider than her house. Where it touched the ground, there *wasn't* any ground. Pink lightning sizzled out of it. The whole world sizzled, while Nuggie's gears groaned and something inside the engine made a sickening, snapping sound. Sibyl jammed the accelerator pedal against the floor.

Impossibly, the car lurched *forward*.

The brilliant rupture swooped hungrily toward her, vast as the surface of the sun. Sibyl screamed and fought the gear shift. It was frozen in place, solid as a mountain. Lightning caught the VW and danced over the hood, spraying pink hell across the windshield.

Then blinding white light swallowed Nuggie whole.

Sibyl threw her arms across her face and screamed again, high, ragged. The brilliance was so intense it burned. A flash of disorienting nausea tore through her, along with the sensation of falling forever. The last thing she remembered was the vile smell of vomit.

Logan didn't outrun the storm.

Not that he really tried. He was enjoying the view across the lake and the clean, green scent of the wind far too much to seek shelter. He'd sat here since early morning, knitting more of that hideous sweater he'd begun several months ago, just to keep his restless hands occupied. While he knitted, Logan watched tall, ungainly wading birds stalk fish for their dinner—and 'gators stalk birds for theirs. So far the 'gators had gone hungry. Logan's belly rumbled in hollow sympathy.

All through the day a steady parade of college kids, outrageous in pink jeans and orange hair, had hiked down from main campus. Most ignored him, much as they might have ignored a lizard sunning on a log. That was all right. He ignored them, too. Others, though . . .

Logan glanced up as a foursome made their noisy approach down the wooded path to the observation deck where he sat. Nice-looking kids. Or they might have been, if their clothes hadn't been artistically ripped to shreds, their hair chopped off apparently by machetes, and their faces painted with inch-thick purple and orange makeup.

At least, the girls' were, if he was interpreting the bulges correctly. There wasn't much evidence on which to base a determination, since all four wore at least some makeup, a number of massive, unmatched earrings, and clothes loose enough to disguise even the most tell-tale anatomy. The cloying scent of clove cigarettes filled the air. The cloying sameness of their "rebellious look" blurred them into a whole generation with the same face, the same hair and clothes.

Had Logan's "Me-Generation" of Jim Morrison, LSD, and 'Nam Babies been just as indistinguishable?

"I can't believe he said that, I mean, *everybody* knows to activate a crystal you've got to bury it under an oak tree, not a stupid pine—"

"Syn, Jez, get a look at the crackerman!"

The girls (he assumed) obediently swiveled their heads to stare at Logan. One of them flipped ash from her cigarette in Logan's general direction. "You'd think the hospital wouldn't let those creeps out without an armed guard. I mean, Jeezus, they're all crazy, what are they doing running around loose?"

"They can't even dress themselves right! And they shuffle around and stare and drool on themselves every time a girl walks by." The other girl shuddered delicately. Her earrings jangled.

"God, one of them's going to pull a real crazy one of these days and kill another bunch of people. Let's get out of here."

They went. He listened as they disappeared back toward the road, still arguing the merits of keeping the "Ward Two" residents locked up. He sighed. He couldn't blame them, really, for being scared, not after the campus murders. Then he tightened his lips. Logan held no illusions, not about himself, at any rate. He knew perfectly well what that foursome saw when they looked at him.

He found, to his surprise, that he didn't really mind.

At first he was wryly amused. Logan Pfeiffer McKee overlooking an insult? Then, gradually, he felt a little lonelier. An osprey sailed out across the water. It dove, struck at a fish and missed, and lifted slowly into the air again. He watched until it disappeared into the woodline across the lake, then shook himself.

Logan couldn't hide from the truth, any more than he could hide from the plastic band on his wrist. He had become one of those grey old men in shabby clothes, the ones kids made fun of and parents watched with wary distrust. He felt old for the first time in his life. Somehow, he couldn't muster enough social consciousness to cut his greying hair or shave his scraggly cinnamon-and-salt beard every day, or even replace the twenty-year-old, olive-drab military "blouse" (aka, British Commando jacket), his t-shirt with time-worn holes through the soft cotton, and much-patched jeans that were his most comfortable clothes. A little hot, true, but he'd been trapped in hotter.

Much hotter. Logan shivered at memories crowding the forefront of his mind like teenagers trying to get seats at a rock concert. Facing the truth was bad enough. Even worse was the cold realization he had no one to jolly him out of his mood.

Growing old in a loony bin didn't do much for a man's self-esteem.

Hell, there were a lot of people who would have denied him even this one-day pass, after . . .

Logan shied away from those memories. What people thought or didn't think about him was no longer his concern. Legally he had been relieved of any further need to worry about such things. So he wouldn't. He glanced down and found he'd clenched his fingers into white-knuckled fists. He swore softly, then deliberately uncurled his fingers one by one until his hands lay still and dead on the rough wooden bench next to the "commando" jacket he'd shed earlier.

Slowly Logan emptied his mind. He watched the lake and the birds and the sky. The sweep of dark water beyond his bench reflected dark clouds scudding in low above the treetops from the west. Massive arches of lightning discharged through the clouds every few seconds. He smiled to himself, a bitter, wistful little smile, as the lake changed hue from sunny blue to algae green to slate and finally to the murky black of the lowering storm. A snowy egret launched itself from the shallows and flew off into the rising wind, its wings flashing starkly white against sky and water. Farther away, a flock of little cattle egrets or maybe white ibis settled earthward to escape the rising storm.

He drew a deep breath that smelled of dark water and rustling cattails and the thick, unmistakable scent of alligators and slowly allowed the furrows in his brow to smooth out. Dr. Brandon would lecture him on responsibility when he showed up soaking wet—Logan snorted wryly at the very idea—but he didn't consider moving from his seat. The wind was sharp and cool against his face, refreshing after the steaming heat of afternoon. The black lake began to froth as wind tore miniature whitecaps from its surface. Lightning blazed in the seething clouds, crackled through the wind like some living thing seeking its mate in the ground.

Logan breathed in the storm smell through dilated nostrils, through the very pores of his skin. Even plate glass windows closed a man in, if they were never opened to the sweet, living air.

He winced, inwardly, where no one could see. The temptation to start walking and never go back hurt him worse than any gunshots ever had. He shut his eyes, then sat listening to the storm's whistling, moaning descent. It came shrieking across the lake, driving a wall of water before it. Logan could hear the rain smash down into the black lake long before the first drops touched his skin. Lightning flashed starkly against the backs of his eyelids, blazing pink through the blood vessels in the thin membranes. A bull 'gator grunted in the reeds nearby.

Logan sighed as the rain burst over the observation platform. The deluge soaked him to the skin in a matter of seconds. Toadstranglers, he'd called them when he was a kid, these afternoon storms that swept across the land, sheeting down to flood the wet, low lands and fountain up through storm drains too choked with runoff to hold the excess. Wistfully, he wondered if bass still lurked in the deep, hidden holes along the Suwannee and Santa Fe, back under the overhanging cypresses. It had been too many years since he'd haunted those banks, cane pole in hand, his old reliable .22 propped nearby in case he surprised a water moccasin.

Reluctantly Logan opened his eyes. Hair streamed wetly into his face. He pushed it back onto his forehead. The very thought of going back left him physically ill. But lightning could be dangerous, out in the open like this. Well, he could always wander over to the state museum or take shelter at the student union. He didn't have to go back just yet. Slowly Logan hauled himself to his feet.

His leg felt stiffer than usual. He winced when his weight came down on it. Probably the rain and a whole day spent sitting in one place. God, he *was* getting old. Logan favored the old injury slightly as he reached for his rip-stop nylon satchel and the much-tattered jacket that had gone everywhere he had over the past couple of decades. That jacket had seen more combat than most soldiers saw in a lifetime. Like his leg, it was the worse for wear. He shrugged it on over his wet t-shirt and hoisted the pack onto one shoulder. Then, watching his footing, Logan started back along the winding path that led to the bus stop.

He didn't get far.

The dirt track was a slippery river of mud, made even slicker by last year's pine straw and decaying leaves. He was moving cautiously, head bent against the solid wall of water beating down on him, when the world erupted into a pink hell. Logan jerked his head upward. Great, sizzling fingers of lightning stabbed into an ancient, towering magnolia along the edge of the path. Gigawatts of electricity poured earthward like some demonic water-fall. Brilliance burned his eyes. Instinctively—uselessly— he threw up a shielding arm.

The tree's crown exploded forty feet above his head, then deadly rivers of raw lightning branched and slammed into the ground on all sides of him, trapping him inside a cage of crawling pink hellfire. Searing blue afterimages left him half blind. Logan felt a tremendous overpressure as thunder bruised his chest, bloodied his ears. He saw the tree begin its long, toppling crash to the ground, tried to hurl himself out of the way . . .

His bad leg twisted. He lurched sideways. Then started down, directly beneath the smashing weight of the tree. Time crawled like cold syrup and held him motionless. He could do nothing but watch the tree kill him. Logan felt the sizzling electric tingle of lightning as it crackled around him again. Blinding light shut out the image of the rushing tree trunk—

Then he was falling, faster than the magnolia. Faster than the rain. His stomach tried to meet his lungs, as though he'd stepped into an empty elevator shaft. Logan yelled and twisted in midair. He should have hit the ground by now—should have been crushed into bloody mud—

He got his eyes open. Icy cold mist had somehow formed beneath his feet and risen up to swallow him. He twisted backwards, then sideways through freezing air, and wondered why he hadn't felt the pain of dying.

Logan sprawled headlong into something cold and wet. He jarred every bone in his body, so hard he couldn't breathe. Instinctively he covered his head with both arms.

The tree didn't crush him.

In fact, he realized slowly, it hadn't even fallen. At least, not anywhere that Logan could hear. Cold, dead silence gripped the air. Which was curiously dry.

It wasn't raining.

Slowly Logan lifted his head.

He lay face down in a snowdrift.

—A *snowdrift*?

Logan blinked. Then picked up a freezing fistful of white wetness. Snow. In Florida? In July? At four o'clock in the afternoon? He looked up . . .

Towering, stark conifers rose blackly into a night sky. Millions of frozen stars glittered like ice chips tossed carelessly aside by a giant ice crusher. *God . . .* Logan hadn't seen so many stars since—

He winced, despite a heroic effort not to.

"Well, this sure as hell ain't Ethiopia, now, is it?"

The bite of air in his lungs convinced him the temperature was somewhere down around thirty degrees Fahrenheit. He lowered his gaze to the snow-covered ground. Creeping, ghostly white mist had formed in low-lying areas, obscuring tree trunks and blending in with the snow.

The silence was deafening.

Badly shaken, Logan sat up. Broken bits of magnolia branch lay scattered across crusted snow. Beneath him, Logan found the crushed body of an immature male skink. He picked up the little lizard. Its smooth skin was still faintly warm from the sun it had been basking in just before the rain hit. He stared at it, at his surroundings, for a long, impossible moment.

Then slowly began to wonder just where he *was*.

Logan snorted wryly. Given his luck, it would turn out to be one of the lower reaches of hell. He'd always figured hell for a Florida boy would be some godforsaken, frozen wasteland. Florida summers were generally hot enough to fry even Satan's ass.

Trouble was, Logan didn't really feel dead.

Which left him with some unpleasant alternatives. Either he was trapped under the tree, maybe bleeding to death or running out of air and hallucinating . . . or he was *elsewhere*. He'd never had much respect for those sci-fi transdimensional novels where the hero falls into another universe invariably peopled either with naked, big-breasted women who'd been waiting all their lives to be bedded by a real man, or crammed full of ghoulies and goblins anxious to oblige the hero in his task of proving a twentieth-century man could hack and hew with the best of the bloody barbarians, using weapons that hadn't been seen in centuries—if ever.

Logan snorted again. He didn't see any half-naked ladies *or* ghoulie-goblins lurking in the trees. All he saw was trees. And lots of snow. And since he didn't think dead men were supposed to get frostbite, Logan decided he didn't have the faintest idea what had happened to him.

That realization didn't bring much comfort.

He shivered violently. A little ruefully, Logan realized he was still soaking wet. The water in his hair and clothes was beginning to freeze. Wherever he was, he couldn't sit stupidly in a snowbank all night. He had to get warm and dry—and he hadn't exactly been dumped here with an abundance of survival gear. Logan spat a few choice oaths into the icy air.

"Now this is just a peachy goddamn mess, ain't it?"

He started searching pockets and backpack, knowing what he'd find, but making certain he hadn't overlooked anything. The doctors—and courts—hadn't allowed him to carry so much as a penknife. The most useful tool he currently possessed was the small pair of blunt plastic scissors in his pack, the kind kindergartners used to cut construction paper.

Plastic scissors were jim-dandy for therapeutic crafts projects, which even Logan had finally grown accustomed to carting around, but in a survival situation, kiddie scissors were about as helpful as a truckload of popsickles. Hell, with that many popsickle sticks, he could've at least built a roaring fire. Logan growled something incoherent in the Ethiopian dialect Marifa had taught him. Logan's breath steamed wetly, hanging on the air an instant before dissipating.

"Fat lot of good plastic scissors are going to do."

Well, he didn't have much choice, did he?

Gathering wood wasn't easy, since he had to dig to find deadwood. Snow stung his hands until the bite of cold vanished into dangerous numbness, but he finally had a respectable pile. Fortunately he seemed to have landed on the side of a mountain, with plenty of available cover among the massive boulders and cliff-faces that towered in the darkness behind his landing point.

He dragged the wood under the lip of an overhanging rockface he discovered nearby. The overhang didn't quite form a cave, but it sheltered him from the freezing wind. That alone would provide minimal warmth until he got a fire going. He used one edge of the scissor blade to scrape enough bark to provide tinder, having to pause now and again to blow on his fingers or beat them against his thighs to force warm blood into them until they would bend a little again. He'd begun shuddering so hard it was difficult to control his hands and arms.

Logan finally rummaged in his satchel for the matches he'd picked up at the cafe where he'd eaten breakfast. He didn't smoke, but old habits died hard. There'd been a time when he never went out without a minimum amount of survival gear. He grimaced as he struck the match with shaking fingers and lit the tinder. The heat from the match sent prickles of agony through his fingertips. What he really needed was a pair of gloves. And a heavy coat. Some GI boots, a good, sharp knife . . .

Goddamned doctors.

Within a relatively few minutes, Logan had a roaring fire under the overhang. He stripped off wet clothes and tennis shoes and all but crawled into the fire. The warmth, delicious against most of him, sent white-hot needles through his hands. *Bad sign.* Logan held his sodden garments over the fire as best he could and waited for the hot fire to work its life-saving magic. Bare rock, sharp and cold under his feet, warmed more slowly than he did. He huddled, shivering, with his toes practically touching the growing pile of embers, and fed the fire while waiting for his t-shirt and undershorts to dry.

He felt a little less vulnerable once he'd shucked on his underwear. Logan patiently scraped points on several sticks, which he jammed into loose gravel beneath the overhang, then tied cross-sticks in place with odd bits of yarn from his knitting. He grinned, then adjusted his jeans and jacket across the make-shift frame for more efficient drying. He warmed his hands again and reached for his satchel.

He'd started the sweater nearly three months earlier, just to give himself something to do. Even learning to knit beat vegetating in front of a TV set. He didn't know how people could sit and watch hours and hours of that stuff.

He shook his head. Some of the men on his floor might have sat in front of their TVs, but they hadn't seen anything but . . . memories. Grimly he had to acknowledge that being stranded in another universe, half-frozen to death, was better than *that*.

Thanks to three months of practice, followed by that long day at the lake, the sweater was nearly finished. All it lacked was most of a left sleeve. It was acrylic instead of wool, in a jumbled mess of scarlet, purple, and several shades of greeny and orangey yellow (he recalled with a grin how he'd stuck defiantly to his color choices, made specifically to piss off the hospital's crafts instructor), but regardless of color or fiber content, it was a *sweater*.

Any sweater would be warmer than what he had on now.

Logan pulled the garment out of his pack and rescued the remaining remnants of his yarn, then slipped thick plastic needles out of the sleeve and began knitting. A moment later Logan had to chuckle. He hoped nothing was watching. His old buddies would've razzed him for months if they'd seen Logan Pfeiffer McKee knitting in his skivvies, in the middle of somebody's winter.

Icy wind blasted under the overhang, sending a shower of sparks flying. A massive shudder caught him as the wind sucked away all warmth. Logan's laughter faded. He concentrated on the job at hand—survival—and worked as fast as his chilled fingers would move. Sooner than he expected, he had it finished. It wasn't pretty. And thanks to his basic lack of talent, it was miles too big; but the sweater was *warm*. He didn't mind at all that he had to roll up an improvised cuff on the right sleeve, or that the "hem" hung halfway to his knees. After a few moments, he even managed to stop shivering.

Who said crafts classes for mental cases were a complete waste of time? (He had a vague recollection that someone named Logan McKee had said so, forcefully and frequently, but dismissed the notion as the short-sighted nonsense it was.)

Logan put away knitting needles, scissors, and scrap balls of yarn, then checked his clothes. Socks, jeans, and jacket were dry. He pulled them on gratefully (jacket over the sweater), and checked the condition of his decaying Adidas. Nearly dry. Good. Not the best footgear he'd ever seen for hiking through snow, but a damn sight better than the sandals he'd almost worn instead.

Which reminded him how long it had been since he'd eaten. Breakfast was—subjectively, since he had no idea what "time" it was here—hours in the past. He'd skipped lunch in order to stay at the lake. And, of course, he hadn't stuffed a single, edible thing into his pack. *Stupid. . . .* He eyed the dead skink.

Logan didn't care what the experts said. He'd *seen* cats who'd survived eating them. Crazy he might be, but brain damaged he wasn't and didn't intend to be. He just hoped he could identify something here as safely edible.

Logan told his stomach to go to sleep and wished the rest of him could snooze, too. He was dead tired, but if he fell asleep, he was likely to be dead, period. God alone knew what kind of predators—two-legged, four-legged, or otherwise—might investigate his scent or his fire before dawn. Until he could risk exploring for a more sheltered place to hole up, Logan didn't dare fall asleep.

He sighed philosophically. This wouldn't be the first night he'd gone without sleep to preserve his skin. The odds of keeping body and soul together this time around were a little difficult to judge, considering his appalling lack of basic information, but he'd been in situations that were—on a scale of urgent immediacy—far deadlier. At least, so far. He'd come through *them* unscathed.

Relatively speaking.

His thoughts shied away from *that*, too.

Instead he peered skyward, trying to see constellations between tall treetops. The sky was familiar, although recognizable constellations had shifted considerably southward. High latitude, then. He felt a little less lonely, having placed the Dippers above him and Orion far down on the horizon. There wasn't any noticeable distortion in shape, so he probably hadn't been dumped fifty thousand years into the past, at least.

Logan hugged his knees to his chest and wondered if he'd ever manage to get home again. *Home. . . .* What the hell was home for a man nobody wanted walking the streets? And what would Dr. Brandon do when he failed to report back? Probably call the FBI.

Logan grinned into the darkness and wondered if the crackling firelight turned his expression as delightedly evil as it felt. His disappearance would cause panic in certain circles. Logan chuckled rustily and spat into the snow. He wasn't *genuinely* dangerous. Hell, he hadn't been *dangerous* when they'd locked him up, not really. He wasn't Ted Bundy or Charlie Manson or the Gainesville Campus Serial Killer. All he'd done was break the SOB's arms. And legs. And . . .

Well, he couldn't have just walked the other way, could he? That mealy-mouthed, silk-suited piece of slime would have killed her if Logan hadn't been there to stop him. And no seven-digit bank account or scowling judge would ever convince him otherwise.

Logan glared at his fire. Street people had no business playing knight-errant to rich men's wives. He'd been military long enough to know that survival was what counted. Dead heroes were just assholes too stupid to duck. Next time he saw a man beating his own wife to death in their own driveway, he'd just shuffle on by in the night and pretend he hadn't seen a thing.

Right. And birds flew north for the winter.

Logan grunted. It wasn't easy, being crazy.

CHAPTER TWO

Late afternoon sunlight glinted across the Tiber's murky surface, transforming it into a broad stream of painful golden sparks. River stench assaulted Charlie's nostrils well before he limped out through the gate behind the house. The stink of filthy mud, human waste, slaughterhouse reek, and dead fish permeated his life so completely, he'd almost grown accustomed to it.

Almost.

Charlie negotiated the path down to the dock slowly, using extreme caution on marble steps set here and there in the hillside. River yachts under sail and oar drifted past to a rhythmic creaking sound and the slap of water on wood. *Rich men, bound for unknown destinations.* Seaside villas, perhaps, where constant breezes made the summer heat bearable. Charlie wiped sweat from his face with the back of one arm and limped awkwardly down the next switchback of the path, leaning heavily against his crutch.

Downriver, wharves at the long, long reach of the Porticus Aemilia's warehouses attracted barges like flies. Some were heavily loaded with amphorae of oil, olives, wine. Others were empty, headed back downriver, their goods disgorged for the Emporia's marketplace. Rome didn't export much, except soldiers. They didn't even send back the empty amphorae.

A few thousand more broken jugs for the Mons Testae. An entire hill, made of nothing but broken clay amphorae. *Helluva trash heap. Somebody ought'a teach 'em about recycling.* The Mons Testae was nothing, of course, to the mountains of garbage that New Jersey seagulls covered in flocks thick enough to block the sunlight, but it was impressive nonetheless, for an entire hill made from just one kind of trash.

Charlie followed one of the empty barges with his gaze until it vanished around the river's bend, hating the men on it for their freedom to *leave*, then shook himself slightly and made the next turn of the path with a thump of crutch and a drag of his left foot. After a long two years (*after* two years of slavery in the Imperial Gladiatorial School), he'd grown accustomed to the sound, but not to the harsh reality of his crippling injury—which had, at least, ended the two previous years of forced "performance" in the games. To a Roman, the fight-and-die "game" was as addictive and enjoyable as playing dice.

The sole good he could find in having been crippled for life was that it *had* brought the slaughter to an end, at least for him. Every limping step he took, however, was a reminder of things he might have sold his soul to forget, had he been another sort of man.

Charlie Flynn didn't want to remember, but he wouldn't sell his soul to anyone—not to the devil and certainly not to the man who owned him. He'd come damn close, at that. An involuntary shiver caught him, unawares. At least the Aventine hillside's sprawl of noisy tenements, rich men's *villa urbae* and the imposing stone walls of public buildings hid from sight the monstrous shape of the Circus Maximus.

Memory chilled Charlie, despite the heat. The sunlight was blistering, the air sultry. Sweat clung to his skin, sullenly refusing to evaporate. A few cloud shadows raced ahead of the barges, their momentary chill passing across Charlie as he limped and hobbled down the last switchbacks of the path.

Raucous city noises, so alien from the scream of traffic and sirens he'd grown up with, all but drowned out the sound of slow-moving river craft. Barking dogs, the distant din of hammer on metal, rasping saws, chisels on marble and other clatter, much of it from a workshop district down the river, floated on the oddly quiet wind. No sirens, no choppers or jets, no blaring car horns, no sound of high-speed boats in Biscayne Bay, screaming past at nearly sixty miles per hour, despite "No Wake: Manatee Zone Maximum Speed 15 mph" signs posted every few yards.

No radios or boom boxes, either, or joggers in CD headphones, not even the distant rumble of a television left on as white noise to drown out the rest of the ruckus.

The only sounds floating on today's wind were the distant sound of hand-powered tools, dogs, and above it all, the sound of voices: arguing, shouting, endlessly yammering in a dozen foreign tongues.

Charlie Flynn could speak only one of those many languages—and not very well, at that, despite strenuous efforts to learn. He still made mistakes even the slaves laughed at. The eternal din of alien voices only underscored multiple, profound losses which came to him, sometimes, with wrenching suddenness.

He tightened one hand around the handle of the heavy bucket he carried and the other around his crutch. *Ancient history, Flynn. Forget it. You've got work to do.*

Charlie limped onto the dock, careful the tip of his crutch didn't slip on mossy stone. Xanthus' household steward had kept him so busy this past week, he hadn't found time to scrub the dock. If he didn't clean it before Xanthus Imbros Brutus—the Lycian Roman—returned, he'd probably catch another beating.

Charlie muttered under his breath and carried the smelly contents of the household's slop bucket to the end of the dock. Ordinarily, such waste would've gone straight into the house's privy; Xanthus' villa perched so near the river, it had its own sewage outflow, rather than connecting with a major branch of Rome's sewers. Unfortunately, the privy was clogged and had to be cleaned so that water could flow constantly through it again, the way it did in public privies. The steward hadn't assigned that job to any of the household slaves yet, but Charlie knew exactly who would draw that duty. For the moment, given the million impossible tasks Xanthus' steward had delighted in pouring onto him, it was easier to dump the stuff in the river than it was to open the privy and attempt unclogging it.

Most of Rome flung its filth into the street to be washed away by rains or Imperial slaves charged with street cleaning. Anything that ran into the great *cloacae* ended as raw sewage dumped straight into the Tiber. The huge Cloaca Maxima poured its filth into the river just a little ways upstream, between the Pons Sublicius and the Pons Aemilius farther upriver, just visible past the little round Temple of Hercules (the one all his childhood textbooks had called the Temple of Vesta) and the squarish Temple of Fortuna Virilis. And just hidden from sight behind them—

Charlie muttered under his breath and dumped the contents of his bucket. The sharp stink of ammonia and feces arced outward, then foul liquid splattered against the golden water and stained it dark, like ink. A passing yacht's wake caught the dark water and churned it into white froth, shot through with golden light. Charlie felt a grim kinship with the waste he'd thrown into the river. Out of place, swallowed up alive . . .

He adjusted his crutch so the fleecy wool padding rested a little more comfortably in his armpit, then set the bucket down and eased aching shoulders. Charlie wanted nothing more than to lie down in what remained of the sunlight and soak up rest like a dry sponge. So tired . . . He closed his eyes and leaned against the crutch, wondering how long he could get away with loafing on the dock.

Not long. Of that, Charlie was certain. Xanthus wasn't due to return until tomorrow, but any number of his master's household would delight in telling the merchant of Charlie's latest misconduct, simply to shunt the man's temper onto someone else. Charlie was afraid of another beating. Not only had he not healed completely from the last one, each new round of abuse brought him closer to the breaking point, where he would either give up and die or murder Xanthus—which amounted to the same thing.

And if he died . . .

Charlie muttered under his breath, just a few choice words in the language no one else in this godforsaken time could understand. *You can't even rescue your sorry self, Flynn. How the hell are you supposed to protect and defend anything now?*

Anything . . . or anyone.

Fierce emotion—he wasn't sure whether to call it longing or hatred—closed his throat. Entire weeks passed, now, when he didn't think of home—or other, nearer things—with this depth of pain. Mostly, he just tried to survive. That took most of what he had in him. Sometimes Charlie actually forgot what he'd once been in the endless struggle to stay alive, to earn the money it would take to buy freedom, to make plans for the future, rescue—

"Rufus!"

He grabbed at the crutch. Then swung around toward the river and the sound of a hated voice he hadn't expected to hear until tomorrow. A canopied, oar-propelled *phaseli* (a lightly built, bean-shaped boat) had turned course and was rapidly approaching the dock. A thick, swarthy man in an expensive, embroidered tunic stood in the pleasure yacht's bow.

His master.

Charlie's belly drew in so tautly it was hard to breathe. Xanthus Imbros Brutus, the Lycian Roman, glared at him across the open water. "Slave!"

Vicious little . . . Charlie forced the rage down, buried it under the need to stay alive.

"Yes, Domine?"

"Catch the line!"

Sailors who were part of Xanthus' household scrambled to ship oars and make ready the anchor. One tossed a heavy rope across. Charlie caught it awkwardly, then braced himself as best he could. Even so, the jerk nearly dragged him into the river. Charlie caught his balance

and hauled on the line. There certainly wasn't anything
wrong with his *arms*. The small yacht grounded against
the stone dock with a scraping sound that set his teeth
on edge. The anchor splashed into filthy Tiberian mud.

Sailors leaped nimbly across and relieved Charlie of
the line, which they made fast. They moved with unconscious ease, oblivious of the careless way they walked or
flexed leg muscles or jogged across the dock to retrieve
a wooden plank for the disembarking passengers.

Charlie watched through narrowed eyes and hated
them.

"Rufus, don't just stand there looking stupid! Help me
onto shore!"

Buried rage kicked him in the gut. He kicked it right
back. Charlie was nearly two feet taller than his master, but Xanthus had the might of Roman law on his
side. He was also one helluva lot stronger than he
looked—as Charlie'd had the misfortune to discover—
and owned plenty of other slaves to enforce his will.
Slaves who had amply demonstrated their willingness
to hold Charlie down, if necessary.

All Charlie had was a useless left leg, a body with too
many scars on it, and the will to get out of this alive.
Roman medicine being what it was . . .

Charlie swallowed pride and everything that went with
it and meekly assisted his master onto *terra firma*. He
then limped awkwardly out of the way. Charlie had not
given up the dream of being a *man* again, but for now,
he *must* obey the sadist who legally owned his body and
held the right to further maim or even kill him at will.
There was pride and there was stupidity.

Stupid and dead would help no one.

Most of the time, Charlie managed to remember that.
Just the memory of the few times he hadn't left him
chilled with sweat. For the moment, his master ignored
him. Xanthus had returned with a guest and, from the
look of it, new stock. The girl lying on a pallet under
the canopy had been drugged unconscious. Ropes bound
her wrists and ankles. Someone had already collared her.

The collar at Charlie's throat chafed over sweat and a prickly heat rash, but he would never again risk the punishment of breaking the lock.

Whoever the new girl was, she didn't look Roman. He wondered how she'd ended up a slave. Sold by her family? Confiscated for someone's back taxes? Maybe captured in a border skirmish somewhere. Or just possibly, she'd sold herself into slavery to keep starvation at bay.

Charlie frowned. No ... if she'd sold herself, they wouldn't have needed ropes and drugs to keep her secured. War captive, then, or maybe a kidnap victim from some coastal village. She was beautiful, in a wholesome way. About fifteen or sixteen, judging from her face and slender form under the shapeless *tunica*. She reminded him, oddly enough, of Florida summers. He thought about that for a moment. She was pale under a golden tan. Well, any provincial farm girl would be tanned. So would many a provincial town girl.

But she didn't have the defined musculature or visible calluses of a girl used to heavy labor, farm or urban. And her hair looked wrong. Shorter than it should have been, just about shoulder length, with dark brown curls that reminded him of something, or someone, he couldn't quite place what, or whom.

Whoever she was, this girl certainly didn't have the hard-edged, big-city look of Roman whores, the look that reminded him too vividly of wasted years in New Jersey. Charlie closed his hands until his fingers ached. In whatever godforsaken year this was—they didn't even use the same dates or calendar system—nobody had ever heard of Florida *or* New Jersey and wouldn't for another fifteen hundred or so years.

Thinking about time, Charlie shook his head—more than years were mixed up in this place. It had taken months for Charlie to learn enough Latin to figure out the system of reckoning days—the system that ruled Charlie's life for four terrifying years. Any given day, for example, was counted as being so many days *before* a major monthly event, of which there were quite of few. The *kalends* at the first of the month, the infamous *ides* at midmonth, the *nones* between the two, plus a sort of unofficial "work week" of eight days. Every ninth day was called a *nundinae*—farmer's market day. So, while not official, most people tended to talk in terms of so many days before the next *nundinae*. Then, of course, there were any number of official state and/or religious holidays, even days on which certain types of businesses were banned from opening.

Charlie thought the Roman calendar system was insane.

But, then, so had his life been, through four aching years.

Charlie turned his back and bent to retrieve the slop bucket. He tried to ignore the lump in his throat which sight of the young girl's tousled curls had brought. She was just another slave, a little shorter-haired than most, maybe, but just another slave all the same. She'd be sold probably before she even woke up.

"Careful!" an unknown voice chided, sending a prickle of irritation up Charlie's back. He glanced around as a dark-eyed, scowling man he'd never seen before back-handed the sailor carrying the girl. "Aelia is worth a great deal more than you are! Bruise her and I'll lay your back open!"

Asshole . . .

Then it happened.

Xanthus slipped on a patch of moss.

"Rufus!"

Charlie's insides cringed. "Yes, Master?"

The trader had regained his balance, but his face had flushed dangerously under a swarthy complexion. "A week ago, I told you to scrub this dock clean! What if my guest had slipped and fallen on this mess?"

Charlie tried to explain. "Master, your steward has kept me so busy—"

"I don't care what orders my steward left! *I'm* your master, boy. Never forget that. And *I* ordered this dock scrubbed."

"Yes, Master, I know that, Master, but Lucius—"

The Lycian Roman grabbed Charlie's shapeless tunic and jerked him off balance. Charlie went down hard, banging both knees on the stone dock. His crutch skittered away. He clenched his jaw shut and bit back any sound, waiting on his knees for his master to pronounce judgment.

Xanthus gazed at him silently for a long moment, evidently waiting for any sign of rebellion. Charlie offered none. His master finally spoke, in a deceptively soft voice Charlie had come to dread. "For two years, Rufus, you thrilled all Rome with your victories. But all through the next two years, you have done nothing but disappoint *me* again and again. You flout my authority, force me to punish you more harshly than I have wanted. How many times must I say it? Forget what you were. You are no longer Rufus the Champion. No longer a free barbarian, at liberty to do whatever you please. You are a slave, *my* slave. I had hoped you would prove valuable. You had a duty, boy, and you have failed in it every single time you have been put to the test."

Charlie bristled silently. It was *not* his fault that lead poisoning had done its work on nearly every child he'd been forced to sire, but lead-linked birth defects were simply unheard of in *this* time.

So Charlie's master blamed *him*, not the lead levels of the women they kept bringing to be bred. The one time Charlie had tried to explain, Xanthus had called him several filthy words and beaten him nearly senseless for blatantly attempting to foist off falsehoods as excuses. After all, who had ever heard of such a thing— simple *water* turning babies into monsters that *must* be exposed immediately to die.

Charlie knew how to hate, how to bide his time, but some days it was harder than others, knowing yet another child of his had been deliberately allowed to die.

Xanthus spoke again, soft-spoken voice a mockery of a concerned man who actually *gave* a damn about anything but the number of coins in his money chests. "It was my fondest hope to coddle and pamper you. Instead, you offer me treachery, laziness, constant disobedience. Do you *prefer* to be beaten into submission?"

Charlie, forced to huddle at his master's feet by the grip on his tunic—and by sure knowledge of the consequences of rebellion—remained silent.

"Answer me!"

Hating himself, Charlie whispered, "I do not, Domine."

"Then tell me, slave, what am I to do when you fail me in something as simple as cleaning the moss off my dock? Must I beat you yet again, in front of guests? Would that make you give me the respect and adoration I am owed as father of the household to which you now belong?"

Not goddamned likely, you pompous little bastard.

Evidently the answer, silent as it remained, was clearly visible even in his downturned face.

Xanthus sighed, a shade too theatrically. "I try to be a fair master. Really, I do. But you would try Jupiter's patience, boy, and mine is not nearly so great." The beating was mild, comparatively. All Xanthus did was bruise a few aching muscles with a folded-up bit of rope. Charlie compressed his lips and stood it. When it was over, Xanthus said, "I want every bit of moss gone from this dock by sunset. Is that clear?"

Charlie didn't point out that not enough daylight remained to complete the job by the deadline. He merely whispered, "Yes, Master," and crawled the hell out of Xanthus' way. He'd been lucky, this time. Xanthus hadn't wanted to seem too harsh a master in front of company—company which, ironically, had forced Xanthus to do *something* to punish dereliction of duty.

Charlie's back throbbed where the rope had thudded against old bruises and half-healed welts. He closed his hand around the fallen crutch, wishing bitterly it were a javelin. Xanthus' guest brushed past as though he didn't exist—which, in the eyes of *any* freeborn man, he *didn't*. The sailor followed, carrying Aelia.

Achivus, Xanthus' personal secretary, strolled off the

phaseli's shaded deck, holding a cylindrical leather case that would contain important business papers. Achivus' tunic was richer than most freedmen's. As the secretary disembarked, a boy of about ten came skipping hastily down the steps from the house, breathless from his run.

"Master," he cried, "they said you'd come back!"

Achivus handed the boy his leather case. "Be very certain you don't drop these, boy. Take them to Dominus Xanthus. Then be sure to have a basin of hot water ready for me. I reek of travel."

"Yes, Master!"

Achivus' slave ran ahead, leaving his master to follow at his leisure. Himself a collared slave, Achivus was not only well educated, he received a large enough monthly allowance to purchase slaves of his own to wait on him. Charlie's disgust ran all the deeper because of it, but Achivus was only one of many thousands of slaves who owned other human beings.

Over the last couple of years, with greater access to slaves who knew more than how to fight and kill, Charlie had managed to acquire a basic understanding of more of the seemingly endless insane situations life here provided. Thanks to the enormous influx of war captives and the lucrative kidnapping trade throughout the Empire—not to mention thousands of unwanted babies exposed on garbage heaps, free for the taking—most slaves were so cheap even extremely poor families owned a few. Not possessing even one slave was the mark of abject poverty.

Charlie—who'd once been popular in a way he tried desperately to forget—was universally looked down on by Xanthus' household for yet another reason: he'd never acquired slaves of his own, even when he *could* have. "Silly barbarian," people had said of him. "He'll come to no good in the end, just you see."

Well, it ain't over till the fat lady yodels. I might be down . . . but not completely out. Not of hope (or, at the very least), fighting spirit. Just now they amounted to the same thing—or as close as it came for accounting purposes. Achivus, who endured far less abuse in a month than Charlie did in the course of the average day, moved directly toward him. Charlie braced himself for the inevitable and wasn't disappointed.

"How's your back, gladiator? The welts were very bad when we left."

The question—and Achivus' dark eyes—were filled with genuine concern that only made Achivus seem more alien than ever. More alien, even, than Xanthus, and Charlie hadn't completely figured *him* out in a whole two years. Both men were as incomprehensible as any alien species in any science fiction movie he'd ever watched—and if Charlie Flynn were anything, he was a genuine, twentieth-century movie-holic.

Whenever he had wrangled off-duty time, he'd spent some of that leisure on getting women into bed—but mostly he watched movies. *Any* movies. Old, new, tragic, hilarious, musical, violent action-adventure, mystery: whatever it was, Charlie'd watch it, with rare exception, just to put out of mind for a few hours what he did for a living.

When Achivus reached out to pull aside the neckline of Charlie's loose tunic, Charlie shrugged out of his grip without putting either thought or effort into it. *Nobody* touched Charlie except Xanthus—the only man who gave him no opportunity to avoid unwanted physical contact— or anyone Xanthus *ordered* to touch him.

Irish hatred ran deep and lasted a lifetime.

It was often all he could do to control it, to stay alive rather than give in as everything he *was* demanded.

"Back's healing," Charlie told the slave–secretary shortly. "And Achivus? Don't *ever* touch me again. Got that? Now get out of my way. I have work to do."

"Yes. I heard. Rufus, *why* didn't you obey him? Cleaning the dock was such a small thing. Must you defy Master at every single order? He only wants you to love and obey him—"

Something in Charlie's expression must've gotten through, because Achivus paused without finishing.

The secretary sighed and looked away. "Please keep trying, Rufus. It isn't so difficult to be a good slave, you know. Just do whatever you can to make sure his fortunes rise. You might be surprised how well he'll treat you. He . . . wants to treat you well. If only you'd let him."

Charlie, who knew exactly what Xanthus wanted from him to "make his fortunes rise" held silent. That was one thing among many he simply could not give the Lycian Roman: lead poisoning was *not* his fault, nor could he change the way engineers constructed the aqueducts.

Achivus glanced the long way up into Charlie's face again. "Your trouble," he said with a touch of bitterness, "is your pride from being a champion. It galls to be just an ordinary slave. There is no shame, Rufus, in whatever the master orders. Pleasing him is our duty. Take pride in it. I certainly do. Master's whole household does. All except *you*. Rufus the Champion. Rufus the great, popular hero. Rufus the gladiator, the man even senators' wives wanted to sleep with, if their husbands would've looked the other way. Dammit, Rufus, stop pining away for the glory and—"

"Don't tell me what I feel about those years!"

Achivus backpedaled a step, eyes wide in sudden fright.

Charlie ground his fists until his hands ached, trying desperately to forget the sights, the sounds and stenches, the terror and the burning, red rage that caused even greater terror, it was so overpowering—

He thrust aside any attempt at explanation with a bitter, *Why try to explain anything to an alien?* Then, changing his mind just as quickly, desperate to connect with *someone*, try to make *someone* understand (and Achivus was the only person who'd ever seen him as something besides "Rufus the Champion"), he said a bit hoarsely, "Achivus, there is *nothing* about the arena that made me proud of what I did there. And there's nothing to be proud of in being a slave, either, good or bad."

Achivus swallowed a couple of times while the sultry evening breeze ruffled their hair.

Achivus' lips thinned, the household secretary still without the slightest comprehension of what Charlie was trying to explain. "Always, the stubborn fool. You will end a hopelessly bad slave, bringing death on yourself and disgrace on our master. Perhaps one day you will finally grow a brain to match those scarred muscles."

With that, Achivus headed toward the steep pathway and the marble steps Charlie had spent the past week cleaning with a scrub brush and a bucket of cold water. Charlie gripped his bucket for a moment, aware that in *his* hands, nearly anything was a lethal weapon. Then, forcing a deep breath, Charlie told himself hating Achivus was no answer. He might as well hate a beetle for the color of its carapace or the food it preferred. Achivus' beliefs were so far beyond anything Charlie had ever encountered, it was impossible to remain angry with him. Amazingly, very nearly *all* the slaves Charlie had encountered held the same insane attitudes about their masters.

Spartacus and his bunch were a minority.

Charlie watched the flow of the muddy Tiber for long moments. *Achivus, the educated Greek secretary. Achivus, the master's favorite.* Achivus was a *good* slave. Docile, obedient, devoted. Oh, to be sure, he gossiped about Master and Mistress—what slave didn't—but he actually *loved* that bastard and his harpy of a wife. Or claimed to, anyway. In reward, they treated him like a favored pet capable of particularly useful tricks.

The whole business made Charlie sick.

Charlie listened for a moment to the sailors as they finished securing the little yacht, but he didn't learn anything of importance. All they wanted was food in their bellies and a woman under their thighs. *Rutting pigs.* . . .

The nearest scrub brush was up at the house. Charlie held back a groan and limped painfully up the path toward the *villa urba* he had called "home" for slightly more than two years, now. The back wall, heartlessly plain, hid Xanthus' wealth from casual observation. It also deadened city noise, an important function, as close as they were to the wharves of the Porticus Aemelia. Charlie limped through the gate and made certain it was latched, then passed through the kitchen. Xanthus' cook screeched at him.

"Get that shit bucket out of my kitchen, cripple!"

Charlie flipped him a good old-fashioned American bird.

"And none of that barbarian filth, either!"

"Blow it out your ass," Charlie muttered in English. But he kept going.

Xanthus was in the *triclinium*, the Roman equivalent of a dining room. He and his guest had already reclined on couches. Household slaves were serving the evening meal, which would probably go on for hours. Some of Xanthus' banquets lasted up to a grueling ten hours of hard work for the slaves required to serve and entertain them.

Xanthus' wife, Adflicta, seated in the high-backed armchair only privileged ladies were permitted, remained silent and pale. Xanthus' sons, cowed by the terrifying formality of dinner with their parents—their one meal away from the comforting safety of *pedagogus* and nurse—also remained silent and pale. Charlie skirted the room, overhearing snatches of the conversation.

" . . . Caelerus, simply astonishing."

"Yes, the voyage from Iberia was well favored with good winds."

Iberia? Charlie frowned and tried to remember where that was supposed to be. Somewhere to the west? He hadn't been all that good at modern geography, never mind ancient Roman geography. The next comment brought him up short.

"Yes," Xanthus was saying, "Publius Bericus will be delighted with her. She's exactly as you described. I've already sent word. If we're fortunate, he won't have left yet for his *villa rustica*."

Publius Bericus? Hatred and terror detonated inside Charlie. Despite his crutch, Charlie's knees began to wobble. Publius Bericus was coming *here*?

"That would be excellent," said the man who'd slapped the sailor. "I want this business transacted quickly. A trade in goods is what I want, as you know."

Unable to move for the sudden tremors in his legs, Charlie studied this newcomer covertly from the shadows. He was thin-faced, surprisingly tall, with a look Charlie would once have identified as savvy street predator. He possessed the sharp, cold eyes of a vulture. When he smiled, Charlie repressed the instinctive urge to reach for his backup gun. He was a colonial, judging from his accent. Charlie's was much worse, of course.

Xanthus laughed. "Bericus will consider it a bargain, even *with* the gold you're asking in addition."

"If you would be so kind, Xanthus, perhaps you might handle the negotiations? For a . . . percentage?"

Xanthus' eyes gleamed. Adflicta compressed her lips. No Roman lady of quality wanted to have it whispered, "Her husband is in *trade*!"

"Of course. Say . . . ten percent?"

The conversation devolved into a haggling war over percentage points. Charlie regained control of his shuddering pulse and tried to inch past along the edge of the room, since the dining couches were between him and the storeroom where cleaning supplies were kept. The thump of the crutch, however, caught his master's attention.

"What are you doing in here?" Xanthus' brows had twitched down.

His guest glanced up. Judging by the pinched look around Caelerus' nostrils and mouth, Charlie's appearance and smell clearly disgusted him. Xanthus' sons squirmed in eager anticipation.

"I am returning this to the privy," he said carefully, to be sure he got the Latin verb tenses correct, "and I am searching for a brush to scrub the dock, Master, as you ordered."

"While I'm eating? Idiot! I want that bucket scrubbed out, slave, clean enough to drink from. It stinks. Then after you've scrubbed the dock, get to your other chores. Lucius tells me the privy is clogged. Clean it."

"Yes, Domine." He had to clench his teeth to keep from growling it out.

Xanthus eyed him suspiciously. "Use that tone again, slave . . ." He left the threat hanging.

Xanthus had decided shortly after acquiring him that Charlie was a "bad" slave who merited constant correction. Well, by Roman definitions, Charlie *was* a bad slave. Not even Charlie debated *that*.

Charlie forced himself to whisper humbly, "Yes, Domine."

"That's better. Proving even the stupidest of slaves *can* learn, under proper stimulation." The Lycian gave a short, hard bark of laughter before turning away. His guest grinned.

It would be so simple to break Xanthus' neck . . .

It took him fifteen minutes of cautious maneuvering through the villa to retrieve a coil of rope and a crude brush made of some kind of prickly plant fibers. He'd never been much of a botanist—hell, he'd never been much of anything, when it came to formal classroom learning—so he didn't have the slightest idea what it was made from. Whatever it was, it made a lousy scrub brush.

He hobbled out to the river again and lowered the bucket into it, then hauled it back up to the dock and used a lot of elbow grease to clean out the slime. *What I'd give for a lousy bar of soap. . . .* But soap—greasy stuff made from goat's fat and wood ashes in Pompeiian factories—was expensive. Slaves weren't allotted soap to scrub out shit buckets. When that chore was finally done, Charlie began dragging up bucketfuls of water. He sloshed them across the mossy dock and got down on hands and knees.

Xanthus' dock was a large one, built—as was Xanthus' villa—between the old Servian Wall and the frantic activity of the Porticus Aemilia. Not the *most* fashionable part of town, certainly, but close enough to holy places and luxury villas on the Aventine Hill that tongues still wagged.

Xanthus Imbros Brutus, although rich, was after all

a foreigner. A citizen, yes, but born in *Lycia*, which Charlie had finally gathered was somewhere in modern Turkey—hell and gone from the power center at Rome. Worse, it was whispered one of Xanthus' ancestors had helped murder the divine Julius Caesar.

Those whispers in high society galled Charlie's master, galled as much as the fact that some of the family had cowardly fled to Lycia in the aftermath of a murder that had occurred more than a century previously, rather than face the mobs. Romans were nothing if not incredible snobs. And Charlie—not just a slave, but a *barbarian* one—was on the very bottom of the pecking order. Xanthus' temper was infamous when some slight or insult from a social superior—or worse, an *inferior*—sent him into a towering rage.

Charlie dreaded those days.

On hands and knees in the gathering darkness of evening, Charlie paused for breath and eased aching shoulders. He glanced to the north, where the Bridge of Probus spanned the Tiber, then up the hillside, where the imposing edifice of the Temple of Juno Regina stood bathed in rust-colored light. Charlie had never seen the inside and had stopped wondering, long ago. He was just grateful both structures helped block the view of the great Circus beyond.

A feeling of relief touched him as the sun sank behind distant buildings, leaving Charlie in lengthening shadow. Not only was he just getting comfortable with the drop in temperature, twilight would hide many sins, like rest stops for breath. He set to work again and skinned knuckles on rough stone. Charlie cursed under his breath and kept going. He fiercely ignored aching pain that gradually made itself felt in his rope-bruised back and shoulders.

The smell of cooking food floated across the river from the elegant villas built on the Janiculum hill directly across the Tiber. The Janiculum wasn't precisely part of Rome proper, but a fashionable suburb for those who couldn't afford the *really* high-rent districts. Charlie's belly rumbled emptily. The scent of real food flooded his mouth with saliva. The scrub brush rasped against wet, mossy stone in a monotonous rhythm broken only when Charlie paused to slosh rinse water. Twilight deepened until Charlie scrubbed more by feel than by sight.

When he finally reached the end of the dock and the spine-cracking job, Charlie allowed himself to pause for breath. Stars speckled a velvet-black sky like a dusting of sugar on licorice. Charlie's belly rumbled again, demanding nourishment. He wiped sweat off his face with the back of one arm and swallowed down the saliva, telling his belly that was the best he could do at the moment. He stared into the night sky, captured by his own random thoughts. Sugar on licorice. . . . It'd been four years since he'd tasted sugar.

Four years was a long time to eat nothing but heartlessly plain gruel and whatever meat he managed to trap in snares along the riverbank. Over on the Janiculum, the black hulk of an amphitheater which could be flooded for mock naval battles blotted out the stars. The Colosseum—the Flavian amphitheater—(which Charlie bet was still under construction, as he'd heard no gossip about its opening) would shift the gladiatorial combats away from the Circus Maximus, but he was given to understand the "naval" battles would continue on the Janiculum hill. The old saw (even Charlie had heard it) about flooding the Colosseum had turned out to be just that: an old saw.

Charlie glared at the dark amphitheater on the Janiculum through narrowed eyes, remembering the stink of blood in the water and the crack of timbers as miniature warships rammed one another. He had fought *there*, too, and survived, sometimes only because he knew how to swim.

"Someday," he growled at the dark, murmuring river, "someday, I *will* kill you, Jésus Carreras."

He turned his back on the river, the Janiculum, his whole past. Carreras was so far beyond Charlie's revenge, it didn't bear thinking about. He hobbled back up the

path, so tired he couldn't even find strength to curse
at the thought of the rest of the chores waiting for him.
He skirted the dinner party, which was in full swing,
complete with musicians and a dancer. Xanthus' sons
listened, wide-eyed, to the off-color jokes and bawdy
songs. Adflicta had already retired for the night.

Charlie replaced the slop bucket in the privy, then
cleaned *that*, having to light a lamp to provide enough
light to unclog the water pipes. At last water from Rome's
aqueducts began to flow again. The accumulated mess
rinsed away, pouring down the outflow into the sewers.
Charlie knew he stank of shit and urine and his own
body sweat. There'd be no time tonight for a bath, either.
So he cleaned hands, arms, and body as best he could,
scrubbing with the brush he'd used on the dock.

He sniffed. *Better*, he allowed cautiously. The odor
was still there, faintly, but at least he could breathe without half-choking on the smell. He finished up his latrine
duties by checking the chamber pot in Adflicta's private
sleeping chamber, taking care not to disturb the *domina*
as her maidservants prepared her for bed. She was saying
bitterly, "It's bad enough he *works*, but to sell slaves to
that superstitious libertine, Publius Bericus . . ."

Charlie got the hell out. When Mistress was in *that*
mood, she was nearly as dangerous as Master. She'd once
had a hairdresser *crucified* for tugging too hard on a
tendril of hair. At least she hated Publius Bericus as
much as Charlie did. For any Roman to call another
Roman "superstitious" was the height of insult. Calling
him libertine paled by comparison. Many a Roman's
conduct earned him the name libertine. But no public
man wanted to be known as someone so superstitious,
he'd tremble before the gods like a slave before his
master.

Charlie emptied the chamber pot, which was no
longer needed, put it away with the brush and coil
of rope, and got busy with his main evening chore:
feeding those slaves valuable enough to be kept at
Xanthus' home while awaiting sale. They were housed

in the west wing, in tiny, dark rooms barred from the outside. Their doors opened onto an interior portico that bordered a pleasant *peristyle* garden, which made viewing by potential customers both simple and pleasant. Because they were valuable stock, Xanthus included cut-up figs in the wheat gruel which comprised the standard slave diet.

Before his crippling injury and sale to Xanthus, Charlie had eaten figs in his gruel, too, although back then it had been barley gruel, not wheat. The school which had owned him had wanted a man at top fighting form—but without the independent will to rebel. So they'd given him figs with his barley, a diet believed to give gladiators strength. Meat, of course, had been strictly forbidden. Rome still remembered Spartacus' rebellion as vividly as Charlie remembered the movie—and its ending. The school's barracks masters had talked of Spartacus often enough when beating him and the other gladiators into submission.

Charlie shivered and thrust aside memory of those tiny, windowless little rooms; of the cold-eyed, alert soldiers on guard during practice sessions; the whips and brands and chains and men driven to suicide . . .

Better to think of food. Memory of two years in that hell wouldn't keep him alive. Food—and thinking up new ways to get it—would. Charlie hadn't believed it would be possible to miss a handful of half-rotten figs so desperately. After a few months with Xanthus, he'd grown so desperate for a more balanced diet, he'd started setting snares for rats. Not only had he eaten them—raw—he'd been glad for the solid protein. A seemingly endless supply wandered into Charlie's snares along the river, which also hid the debris from his illicit meals.

But catching rats wasn't the only way to sneak food. Charlie entered the *peristyle* garden, empty at this hour, and pushed his cart toward the west wing, then paused in the darkness to bolt down five dipperfuls of fig-laden gruel as fast as he could swallow, not bothering even to chew. Food eased the hollow in his belly and the trembling in his limbs, enough that he could continue working, anyway. Charlie risked another quick couple of dipperfuls, then busied himself feeding his master's most valuable for-sale stock.

He stopped at each room in turn, made certain the occupant of each cell had water to drink, then dished out gruel from the bucket the cook had given him. None of the slaves ever offered to escape. Most seemed deeply grateful for the twice-a-day visits he made.

Most of what Charlie had learned about his new "home" he had learned from other slaves eager to talk to *someone*. Even gladiators trained to fight to the death had wanted someone to talk to on long, empty nights. Many of Xanthus' slaves openly pitied him. Charlie cordially hated them all. That didn't stop him from using them to improve his understanding of Latin. Learning the language of his masters was better than dwelling on the miracles of surgery which remained nearly two thousand years beyond his grasp.

The last door on the right was open. Lamplight flickered inside. Charlie frowned. That room had been empty for weeks. He limped to the doorway and found Sextus busily engaged bathing the new girl. Charlie glanced hastily away and retraced his steps. If Xanthus had Sextus watching her, she must be a virgin. She hadn't looked young enough. He was betting she hadn't seen her twelfth birthday for at least three years. But if Sextus were involved . . .

Charlie shivered and felt the icy hatred in his soul tighten down another notch. Xanthus and that other trader were going to sell that poor, untouched kid to *Publius Bericus*. Not only did they have no pity, clearly they had no souls.

Charlie returned the empty gruel bucket to the kitchen, then found his broom and a flint and pyrite. He lit lamps and torches in the garden so he could see what he was doing, then got busy sweeping the *peristyle* portico, a chore he was not permitted to shirk no matter how late other chores kept this one waiting. Dust coated the tile floor, along with leaves, twigs, and flower petals blown in from the garden by stray breezes.

He loathed the broom itself, which was difficult to use without propping his crutch against the wall, but the job was just about the least strenuous of his major daily tasks. Charlie took full advantage of his slowness of foot to stretch that job as long as humanly possible— without risking punishment, of course. Usually, he had the *peristyle* garden to himself.

He enjoyed the silence. Starlight fell across statuary that reminded Charlie of a trip his grade-school class had made into the City, to visit the Metropolitan Museum of Art. Even there, however, his new reality jarred unpleasantly with his old life. Unlike the museum statues, these had been painted in lifelike tints, which only underscored the *differentness* of the world into which he'd been dumped.

Charlie thrust away all memories of his former life and concentrated on the scent of the flowers and the splash of the courtyard fountain. Charlie enjoyed this garden more than anything else in his new life. It was very nearly the sole pleasure he managed to wring from his existence, which left him deeply jealous of the time he spent here. Thoughts of other fleeting pleasures brought a tremble to his torso.

Publius Bericus, not Xanthus, had possession of Charlie's only surviving, born-healthy-and-normal child, sired on a woman newly brought in from the frontier, where lead had not yet had its chance to creep into her blood. Charlie halted in the middle of a row of tiles, wondering with a helpless ache in his soul if Bericus had abused his little girl yet. Surely not?

Little Lucania wasn't even a year old, the very first child he'd been essentially forced into siring on a sweet but unfortunate slave girl who didn't particularly want to become pregnant with a killer's child. *Surely* Bericus hadn't hurt Lucania yet? Not even *Bericus* could be such a monstrous libertine as *that*. Could he?

Charlie closed his eyes as hurt throbbed through him.

He wondered what his one surviving little girl looked like. He would probably never know. He doubted Bericus would keep a girl who couldn't fight in the Circus Maximus. Not unless he really were into child rape.

Enough Romans were—he'd seen the girls on the auction blocks, sold into brothels—Charlie closed his hands on the wooden handle of his broom until his palms burned against rough wood. Charlie wanted to hurt Publius Bericus and Xanthus Imbros Brutus as desperately as they'd hurt him—and knew there would never be a way to do it. Not and survive. Not and protect Lucania's life, too.

He was a slave. That said it all.

At least Xanthus and Bericus had apparently given up their grandiose plans, convinced by the fact that he sired only girls and monsters, that breeding Rufus the Champion might not be such a good—

Voices close by jerked Charlie's attention back to the present. Xanthus and his guest had emerged from the main house. Charlie returned to sweeping with renewed haste. Loud laughter and drunken talk shattered the hush in the *peristyle* garden.

Dinner's over early tonight. That made him uneasy. Whenever his master broke routine, unpleasant things occurred. Charlie listened with only half an ear, just enough to know if his name were mentioned, and concentrated on cleaning the portico floor. The Lycian merchant and his guest drank wine and wandered through the torchlit garden, talking, while Charlie swept half of one long wing of the four which comprised Xanthus' house. He had just paused to retrieve his crutch for the next four rows of tile when the household steward entered the courtyard and bowed.

"Master, Publius Bericus."

Charlie went cold. He eased deeper into the shadows and narrowly studied the new arrival. Bericus was somewhere between thirty and thirty-five. He possessed the kind of nose that had earned "Roman noses" the name: it drooped at the end, just like a Clydesdale stallion's. His hairline had receded considerably since Charlie had last seen him. Bericus was, if anything, fleshier than ever. Gold jewelry glittered at his throat and on his hands.

As alienated as Charlie was in this world, even he had come to recognize the expensive tunics from the shoddy ones. An armed guard, collared as a slave, moved unobtrusively behind Bericus. If this had been Miami or Hoboken, Charlie would've pegged Bericus as a particularly vicious breed of pimp. Here . . .

Charlie slatted his eyes and gripped his broom.

Torchlight played over the white scar Bericus still sported on his chin. Hatred tightened through Charlie again, worse than before. It choked him into immobility. If he *ever* got hands on Jésus Carreras . . .

Across the courtyard, Bericus, Xanthus, and the trader Caelerus were moving toward the new girl's room. Charlie stayed well out of their way. He recognized Bericus' smile all too clearly. The wealthy Roman said something to which Xanthus Imbros Brutus responded with a polite laugh, then Bericus' glance fell directly on Charlie. For an instant, utter malice glinted in those cold eyes.

Then Bericus turned to Xanthus. A moment later, Charlie's master called sharply, "Rufus! Come here!"

Charlie gripped the broom so tightly he bruised his hands. Everything in him wanted to refuse. Instead, Charlie found his crutch, laid aside the broom, and limped toward the three men. Flickering torchlight caught the gold at Bericus' throat and emphasized the sallow pallor of his complexion. Too much wine and dissolved lead . . .

"Master?" Charlie managed, forcing his gaze to remain carefully on the ground.

"My dear friend has requested your company, Rufus."

He had to bite back a foul comment that seared his throat. A thick-fingered hand caught his chin. Charlie knew better than to break free of that grip. He was forced, instead, to content himself with meeting Bericus' gaze steadily. *If we were in Miami, asshole . . .*

But they weren't. Here, the crushing weight of law, Imperial law, was completely on Bericus' side. The Roman's eyes glinted, reflecting the dancing flame of a nearby oil-soaked torch. The corner of his mouth twitched.

"Still defiant, little barbarian?"

Charlie didn't bother to answer.

"I have not forgotten, you know. Two years isn't very long, Rufus."

Thick fingers caressed the burn scar on Charlie's throat. Charlie's stillness had once been infamous, a signal to gang members and street roughs that a deadly explosion was about to follow. He had no real weapons, beyond his crutch, but even a wooden crutch was a lethal weapon in the right hands. All questions of survival aside, he did not intend to be locked helpless into a room with Publius Bericus ever again.

Bericus chuckled. "Xanthus, it might amuse me to finally buy this one, as well as the girl. I'd like to watch his face when I sell the brat he got on Benigna."

The wooden crutch handle creaked ominously.

Xanthus' dark eyes darted a glance toward Charlie. The threat in them was unmistakable. *Do it, and you'll beg for death*. . . . The Lycian Roman coughed delicately. "I would advise you, Bericus, to keep him chained if you do. I've had to beat him nearly every week just to force decent drudge work out of him. He's not fit for your household."

The glint in Bericus' eyes sharpened. "Really? Let me see your back, slave."

To comply, he'd have to let go of the crutch. That would leave him effectively weaponless. The tilt of Bericus' mouth told him that was precisely the bastard's intention. He glanced back toward Xanthus and found no pity. "Obey or die" his master's eyes told him.

Charlie ground his teeth and let the crutch fall to the ground. He turned his back on the Roman and dragged off the coarse woolen tunic that was his only decent garment. Bericus sucked in his breath. Not in shock, but in perverse pleasure. Thick fingers touched scars on his back. Charlie started to jerk around, then forced himself to stand rock-still. Rage shook through him, until his muscles felt more like stone than flesh.

The other trader, Caelerus, laughed from Charlie's blind side. "You *have* had trouble with him."

Not as much trouble as you'll have if you sell me to that—

Publius Bericus patted Charlie's shoulder in a caress that brought unbearable memory. Charlie swallowed a snarl and endured it.

"I see you've at least beaten some restraint into him." Bericus laughed. He caressed Charlie's scarred back again, sensually.

Charlie clenched white-knuckled fists until his hands hurt—and *hated* with every fiber of his being.

"I'll consider him. Meanwhile I'd like a look at this girl you've brought me, Caelerus."

The three men moved off, leaving Charlie to stand semi-naked in the shivering torchlight. He found he'd tightened his fists through the woolen tunic so tightly the seams had given under one armhole. He didn't care. Charlie jerked the ripped tunic back on and stooped for his crutch. Xanthus had conducted his guests into the new girl's room. Bericus' voice drifted across the garden, asking questions in tones that strove not to sound eager.

Charlie narrowed his eyes. If Bericus bought the girl, it would be a tragedy. If the bastard bought *him* . . .

Then neither he nor the Roman would likely survive the week.

CHAPTER THREE

Up ... down ... sideways ... up and down again ... sideways with a gentle, sliding motion. ... Hot, sultry air reminded her of ... something. ... Wet wood, too, and the smell of dead fish ... and other things ...

A dim sense of pain slowly resolved into a raging headache, a prickly sunburn, and a throat raw from screaming. She stirred slightly and regretted the movement instantly. Pain, combined with the heaving surface on which she lay, brought bile to her throat.

She vomited before she was fully awake and lay in terror of choking to death—especially when she discovered she couldn't move her arms.

Blind hysteria seized her. She thrashed against ropes on her wrists and ankles. That made the nausea worse. She vomited again, then lay still, trembling. Voices rose and fell, much like the surface beneath her, but it was dark where she lay and the sound was dim, as though heard through a thick partition. The voices refused to resolve themselves into words. Like the voices, smells and sounds made no pattern she recognized.

The fear that crept over her this time was quieter.

—And far deeper.

She didn't know who she was.

Or where.

But she was someone's prisoner. ...

She tried to remember why. Pain stabbed deeply into her head, bringing on the nausea again. She doubled at the waist. Her empty stomach heaved. Her strangled cries brought heavy footsteps from somewhere above.

45

A loud scraping sound was followed by a shaft of painful light. She clenched her eyelids shut, helpless to stop the heaves still wracking her. The voices grew louder. Then someone thumped down beside her. She felt body heat near her skin just before firm hands took hold of her shoulders. She was lifted, rolled onto her back across a hard leg. She was held securely in that position; then someone pinched shut her nose. She gasped—

Bitter liquid filled her mouth. She choked and tried to twist aside. They held her, forced the stuff down her, clamped her jaws closed so she couldn't vomit it back up. She whimpered, half-mad with the pain in her head and the confusion in her whirling thoughts. The dizzy, whirlpool sensation worsened. Darkness slithered into the edges of her awareness. She was still fighting to remember who she was, and where, when blackness reached out with questing, powerful tentacles. They wrapped around her, irresistibly strong, and dragged her under.

She woke several times to sensations of movement, nausea, and confusion. Each time, people waiting in the light forced her to drink the bitter liquid that shoved her—reeling—back into unconsciousness. When she roused again, some impossible-to-judge time later, she tried to hold down the nausea long enough to gain some impression of where she was.

Silence wrapped darkly around her. She received the impression she was alone in a small, dark chamber—at least, if the thick, close air were any indication. She lay on her side. Her wrists and ankles were still tightly tied, but she wasn't gagged. When the significance of that sank in, alarm spread cold fingers through her. Wherever she was, her captors weren't worried about her screams.

The world had stopped lurching beneath her. The only light came from two pairs of narrow cracks, one vertical, one horizontal, that marked the location of a small door. She lay on a hard surface. When she moved her cheek, she felt the rough grain of wood. Judging from the angle of the lower slit of light, she was approximately two feet above the floor.

But *where*? And *who was she*?

Pain, unexpected and treacherous, stabbed through the center of her skull. She cried aloud and squeezed shut her eyes. Nausea tore her throat. Her stomach heaved, then she was thoroughly sick, onto herself, onto the platform on which she lay. She doubled up, whimpering, and was sick again. When she tried to roll sideways, to throw up over the edge, she slipped completely off. An involuntary yell of fear cut off when she hit the floor with a bone-jarring thud. The slithering fall brought more nausea and the sound of footfalls outside the door.

It opened abruptly. Light flooded the room. She flinched from it and shut her eyes. Someone knelt beside her. She tried to escape, fighting irrationally despite the crippling pain in her head and the knowledge that she was bound hand and foot.

"Shh," a masculine voice whispered, "shh, you've hurt yourself. . . ."

The monster behind her eyes broke loose again. The man turned her, gently, to lie on her stomach across a hard thigh while she was sick again. He smelled faintly of human excrement and a smelly soap that reminded her of petting zoos full of goats.

"It's all right. Go ahead and be sick, little one. Shh . . ."

She tried to regain control of herself sufficiently to ask him where she was, or *who* she was—and the agony in her head redoubled. She cried aloud and was disastrously ill again. He held her until the tremors eased away and the nausea with them. When she lay quietly, he brushed her face with gentle fingertips, working them in circles across her temples.

She flinched, despite the surprising tenderness in that brief contact. More footsteps approached from beyond the door.

"What are you doing in there?"

The new voice was also male, sharp with disapproval or anger. Instinctively she didn't like that voice.

An odd tremor ran through the leg under her belly. Then the man holding her said, "She woke up sick." His voice, now that he wasn't whispering, was deep and very easy on the ears, but the language sounded . . . wrong. . . . Or did it? She didn't know. "I heard her fall out of bed," he added to an unknown man in the doorway. "She is *very* ill, Domine Xanthus."

Domine Xanthus—what kind of name was that?— swore. His voice emanated from the nebulous region above her. "Well, you're in there, now. Get her cleaned up." Domine Xanthus' accent differed from the other man's in a way she couldn't define.

"I will need a bucket." The voice nearest her sounded far more patient than Domine Xanthus', or maybe just a great deal more tired. The leg she rested against was knotted with muscles and about as pliable as steel. But he was very gentle when he eased her down to her back.

A series of impossible-to-identify sounds reached her ears; then she heard a thump and the unmistakable slosh of water nearby. The tired man spoke softly, almost in a whisper again.

"Easy, little one, I will wash your face now. Lie still, no one will hurt you. . . ."

When he touched her face with a wet cloth, she flinched back.

"Can you understand me?"

She was too afraid of being ill again to move or try answering. He added wearily, almost to himself, "Well, little one, I wish you knew what I am saying. I will try to be gentle, all right? Poor child."

His accent was very strange. She received the fleeting impression he wasn't speaking his native language. Vaguely she wondered what language he *was* speaking . . . and decided she didn't really want to know badly enough to risk that agony again.

The wet cloth touched her face again. He cleaned her

mouth and cheeks very gently. The water was lukewarm. He rinsed her hair, then paused.

"Your clothes are soiled."

She heard a scrape and thumping footsteps, low voices. . . . He returned and knelt at her side again. She tried to get a look at him, but the bright light pouring through the open door triggered nausea again. She clamped shut her jaws and forcibly held it down. She kept her eyes closed.

What's wrong with me? she wondered desperately. *What have these people done to me?*

A knife sliced through the bonds at her wrists. Her benefactor—captor?—chafed her skin until circulation began to return. She whimpered at the pain of needles in her fingers and hands.

"Yes, I know it hurts, little one. Be easy, just lie still, easy. . . ."

Briefly a hand stroked her wet hair, then returned to her abused wrists. She tried again to get her eyes open and groaned. He'd knelt between her and the light, cutting off the worst of the bright ache in her head.

No . . . it was worse than an ache. Her brain felt out of kilter, as though something had kicked the world askew. She couldn't focus anything back on track again, and that frightened her more than captivity. Her head hurt too much to keep her eyes open.

The man reached inside the neck of whatever garment she wore, nudging aside a narrow metal collar she hadn't noticed, and grasped the edge of the cloth. The knife cut downwards with a soft ripping sound. She stiffened. His hands bared her naked breasts. She gasped and flinched, an ill-advised move. The sharp point of his blade nicked her. The pain in her head ballooned. She cried out and pulled her arms away, trying to grasp throbbing temples. His weight came down hard against her, pinning her to a cold, roughly tiled floor. His grip crushed her wrists.

"Be still!" he whispered forcefully, holding her immobile. The next moment his voice—if not his hands—was gentle again. "There is nowhere to run, child, and you are very, very ill. Please do not fight me. I do not want to see you hurt. Just lie still, let me help. . . ." He murmured to her in the same way she might have murmured to a whipped puppy. The pain kept her from understanding his misapprehension for long moments. Involuntary tears squeezed out from beneath her clenched eyelids. She knew her face had blanched white. She felt dangerously close to vomiting again.

But the lurching sickness was only the symptom of something far more deeply wrong. She had to communicate with this man.

"Please . . ." she whimpered. "It hurts. . . ." God, was that her voice? *What had happened to her?*

"You do speak La—" he began in surprise, and immediately eased his grip. "What hurts? Your wrists? I did not mean—"

"Head . . ." She didn't want to talk anymore.

Very gentle hands explored her skull. He parted the hair, pressed lightly. "I see no bruises, no swelled places. You cannot have struck your head with any force."

"No," she whispered. "It . . . hurts from inside. When I move, talk . . ."

There was a long silence. Then he said, "It must be the sleeping drug you were given, little one."

That might explain it. Somehow, it didn't sound right. And when she tried to deny the explanation, the pain worsened. She bit her lip and let him finish cutting her clothes away. He did not free her ankles, which reminded her forcefully that she was still his captive.

But he did wipe sour vomit and sweat from her, earning her gratitude. He rolled her carefully to one side and cleaned beneath her, then wiped down the bench she'd fallen from. Then, just as carefully, he dressed her once more in a lightweight sheath that felt incongruously like homespun linen. He pulled it over her head and arms and eased it down across her nakedness.

She tried again to get her eyes open and managed to keep them open this time.

He was younger than she had expected from the sound of his voice, although she had difficulty pinning down an exact age. Early thirties, maybe even late thirties; or, then again, as sunlight streamed across his face, maybe late twenties. She knew somehow that she'd never been very good at judging a person's age. She blinked slowly. He was not handsome. He was ugly, in fact, with curly red-orange hair cut very short. A hooked nose had been broken at least once. A lurid scar snaked across his jawline and down the side of his throat. Despite the red hair, he wasn't freckled. His skin was extremely fine-textured, just a tiny bit darker than the color of whipped cream. His whole face wavered under the steady pounding in her head.

"Could you tell me . . ." She hesitated as narrow lips, dry and bitten, with tiny lines of dried blood along the lower one, tightened briefly. Then he sighed and wordlessly encouraged her to continue.

She swallowed, bracing for worse pain in her head. "Who am I?"

His whole face flushed—with anger, she realized muzzily. It crackled in his eyes, deepened the furrows around eyelids and nostrils. Dry, bitten lips nearly vanished into a thin, compressed line. The anger surprised her. It was out of place. He should have said, "Don't you mean *where*?" She felt instinctively that most drugged captives knew *who* they were, at least.

He glanced once over his shoulder, as though hiding something. Then he bent cautiously over her. He examined her skull again, peered into her eyes, felt her neck and spine, and was ruthless in pulling aside her hair to examine her scalp in minute detail. She suffered and held back cries of pain. At length he grunted to himself. When he let go of her, she sensed he had reached a decision of some kind. She met his gaze, unable to read anything from it. He spoke, watching her carefully.

"Your name is Aelia."

Aelia?

She tried it again: Aelia.

Tried imagining her face and was faintly surprised when an image floated into her mind, showing her pale, small-boned features framed by reckless dark curls. She tried again, matching face to name.

Aelia.

No. It was wrong . . . somehow. She didn't know how, exactly, but wrong.

The pain in her head kicked her, as brutal as it was unexpected. She snapped into a fetal ball, gripping her head, trying to force the agony away.

"Gently, gently." His voice, as smooth as good Irish whiskey, soothed. He rubbed his fingertips in whispering circles across her scalp, kneaded her neck and shoulders. "Do not fight it, little one. Relax. Breathe. Again. And again. . . . Better."

Gradually the pain eased away. She lay still, eyes closed. She was too exhausted to move, mesmerized by the touch of his fingers. At length he lifted her chin. She opened her eyes.

"Better?" His gaze was concerned.

She took a ragged breath, deeply afraid. "My name is not Aelia."

This time was much worse. She tried to vomit, but there was nothing left to bring up. She trembled and wept and waited for the stabbing punishment in her head to go away. When she was finally able to meet his gaze again, his eyes were dark, his expression deeply troubled. The lurid scar that snaked downward from his jawline jumped under tension.

"I think, little one," he said very softly, "that for now, you must not ask who, or even why, but your name had best remain Aelia."

She wanted to rebel, then flinched and nodded slowly. Then she wondered how he had associated the pain in her head with her need to know her identity as rapidly as she had. Had he done this to her?

"Rufus!" The ugly voice she remembered interrupted.

The man beside her glanced up. A face swung across her vision, leaned down through the open rectangle of light. The movement made her dizzy. She closed her eyes.

"Yes, Domine?" Rufus didn't sound like the same person when he answered. His voice came out weary, afraid. . . . Her incipient dislike of Domine Xanthus intensified.

"Bloody balls, what's taking so long? Is the bitch dead? If you've touched her—"

"She's sick. And I mean *sick*, Domine Xanthus. Sextus gave her too much of the sleeping medicine." A heavy, sour scent she identified as fear sweat filled her nostrils. Rufus waited for the man's response.

She had never heard swearing quite as colorful as what now reached her ears. Domine Xanthus was inventive. And someone named Publius Bericus was going to be furious if she didn't get better fast. . . .

Who was Publius Bericus? Who were Xanthus and Rufus? More importantly, who was—no, her head had finally stopped throbbing and she didn't want it to start again. She couldn't remember ever hearing about an injury—or a drug reaction, since that's what Rufus was calling it—that caused pain only when the victim tried to remember things.

Of course, she couldn't remember anything, so how could she be certain what might or might not cause such agony? And despite his nice eyes and the genuine concern he'd shown for her, she decided she couldn't trust Rufus. Not to mention Domine Xanthus the inventive and Publius Bericus the unknown. They'd tied her up and done this to her and Rufus was one of them.

It hurt more than she expected to consider Rufus an enemy.

Xanthus' next words sank through her confusion to capture her full attention: "Listen and listen good, Rufus Mancus. We lose this piece of choice ass and I will hold you personally responsible! You were *not* supposed to be in here! Bericus is paying a fortune for her. More than you'll ever see. You were lucky once, got the thumbs down before they chopped you into little pieces. If she dies from something you've done to her, what I'll do to you will make that feel like a romp with a fat slut."

Rufus, the red-haired man, said nothing, but the terror in his sweat stank in the close confines of the hot room.

"Sextus! Get in here!"

A third individual arrived with a flurry of heavy footfalls. "Domine?"

The voice was . . . male? High, light, not quite female.

"I want you to keep her drugged. She's throwing up."

"But, Domine," Rufus protested, "the drug is what—"

"Defiant barbarian! Did I ask your opinion? *You* are not the man I put in charge of this girl! Sextus is! Now drug her, Sextus, and be quick about it!"

Rufus, sounding desperate, said, "Please, Domine, I beg forgiveness, but the drug is what is killing her! She can't even remember her name or where she comes from, you can't order this—"

A meaty smack jarred Rufus against her. *"Don't presume to tell me what I may order in my own household!"*

A malignant silence was broken by another meaty blow. Rufus sprawled onto the floor beside her, his mouth bleeding onto dirty, broken tiles.

Domine Xanthus, a dizzying apparition in the bright light from the doorway, stood breathing heavily for long moments. "I give you warnings. *Beg* you to behave. Curse it, Rufus, you force my hand. Fetch me the cat!"

Another terrible silence fell. Rufus didn't move.

"I said, fetch the cat!"

"Yes, Domine," Rufus choked out. Rage and dread trembled in those two, brief words. She got a look at his face and immediately wished she hadn't. Helplessness . . . a promise of murder . . .

Domine Xanthus vanished from her awareness. Rufus scraped himself from the floor and disappeared into the light after him. Aelia—she didn't know what else to call herself—tried to rise and fell back with a moan when her head spun traitorously. The voice Domine Xanthus had identified as Sextus' said, "Back to bed, Aelia."

Sextus was an enormous man. When he picked her up, Aelia received the impression he could have lifted her with one hand, but he used two in order to brace her head. When he pressed a cup to her lips, she struggled.

That high, light voice went steely. "You must drink it, girl."

"No ..."

Fighting was useless. It only brought on the pain and nausea again. Sextus forced the bitter stuff down her throat, then tied her wrists once more and left her alone in the hot little room. Aelia was still crying as she slid into unconsciousness.

When the phone shrilled in his ear, Francisco Valdez had been asleep for maybe ten minutes. He groaned and tried to ignore the insistent jangling. It kept ringing with the shrill of a vengeful harpy. He finally rolled over and glanced at the glowing clock face to confirm the time. Francisco muttered obscenities. Three-forty A.M. It had better not be another emergency surgery....

He groped for the receiver and promptly knocked it to the floor. The solid bang woke him up another millimeter or two. Francisco groped along the cold linoleum.

"Yeah?" he finally mumbled. Lieutenant Kominsky's voice boomed at him so forcefully he winced and held the receiver away from his ear.

"Major Valdez, we have a medical emergency, sir." Francisco bit back a groan. "The patrol just radioed in from the perimeter. They're bringing in an intruder. Said he's half dead from frostbite."

Francisco mumbled something about that not being surprising, considering how cold it was. Kominsky asked him to repeat himself. He grunted and managed to say clearly, "Davis is the doctor on call, Kominsky. Shuddup and lemme sleep."

Before he could recradle the receiver, Kominsky said,

"Colonel Collins requested you specifically, Major. I'm sorry, sir. I heard about Kruger's spleen."

Great. Kominsky was sorry. Well, so was he. And when he got his hands on Dan Collins—

"Send a hummer. I'm in no shape to drive." Not when he hadn't gotten out of surgery until 2:45.

"It's on the way, sir."

Francisco hung up, reflecting that if he couldn't drive, he certainly shouldn't be seeing patients. Stifling a whole series of groans, he dragged himself out of bed and into the bathroom. The mirror mocked him silently. He couldn't see any whites in his eyes, just red. He splashed cold water into his face until he felt semiconscious. That exercise in futility burned up nearly ten minutes.

"Uniform," he mumbled on the way out of the bathroom. He tripped over a chair. "Ow."

The uniform wasn't in the bedroom. He found it sprawled obscenely over the couch. By the time he'd struggled into it, the hummer had arrived and the driver was banging at the door. And Private Simms, bless his Anglo heart, had brought a thermos of coffee.

"The L-T said you'd need it, sir." Simms grinned sympathetically as Francisco prepared to deliver a few Hail Mary's into the steaming cup. He refused to budge from his living room until he'd finished the first cup and was glad he'd insisted when he finally stepped outside.

If it had been cold before, the air now was bitter. "How much has the temperature dropped?" he asked as he climbed into the hummer's passenger seat.

"Ten degrees this past hour, sir."

Francisco damned the bureaucratic idiot who'd sent them transport vehicles without *heaters* in them and huddled miserably into his parka.

Simms offered hesitantly, "It's supposed to be below zero by dawn, but I wish the sun would come up, anyway. It just *looks* warmer in the daytime."

"Yeah." Francisco was from southern California. Alaska's winter weather still left him feeling shell-shocked. One of his ward nurses had taken perverse delight in telling him this winter was much milder than the previous one—a veritable heat wave, she'd said. Francisco shivered. He didn't even want to *think* about weather colder than this.

Francisco stared glumly out the window toward a glitter of lights which marked the one building he hadn't ever been given access to, a squat concrete bunker of a structure which represented the reason this base existed. Francisco scowled at it and sipped at his second cup of coffee.

One of these days, maybe even later *today*, he was going to confront Dan Collins with a whole bellyful of questions. He was tired of his commanding officer dodging him while mystery after mystery piled up on this base. Like how Kruger had managed to rupture his spleen in the middle of the night, on guard, with injuries that looked more like a mauling than a fallen tree?

And whoever heard of thunderstorms in January? Yet Francisco had clearly heard the rumble of thunder, not only during that emergency surgery, but off and on again for the past several weeks. And now Collins dragged him out of bed to deal with an intruder, for God's sake. They were literally centered in the smack dab middle of nowhere, up here. Who could possibly be around to intrude?

The patrol beat them to the infirmary by less than a minute. Francisco gulped the last of the coffee, tossed the thermos cup to Simms with a heartfelt "Thanks," rolled up metaphoric sleeves, and waded in.

The patient was middle-aged, pushing fifty. He was unkempt-looking, with thinning, rusty grey hair and a scraggly cinnamon-and-salt beard. Francisco peeled back the thermal blanket the patrol had wrapped him in and frowned in surprise. He was dressed—except for a bizarrely ugly sweater—as though he'd planned an afternoon stroll down Long Beach, rather than a hike through the mountains of northern Alaska in the middle of January. No coat, no hat, no gloves. . . .

"Mother of God, what on earth was this guy *doing*?"

he muttered.

"Dying," was Jackson's laconic reply.

"No kidding? Let's take care of him, Jackson. Put him in the fridge." Francisco motioned for the patrol to carry the man into the treatment room which unhappy troopies had named "the fridge." The room's temperature was set considerably lower than the rest of the clinic, to deal with frostbite victims. Frozen flesh needed to be warmed slowly. Francisco had treated more frostbite in the past few months than during the rest of his cumulative medical career.

Francisco met Captain Davis, the duty physician, halfway there.

"Frank, what are you doing back?"

Francisco scowled. "Dan rousted me out. We've got another frostbite victim."

"Frostbite? I can handle simple frostbite, Frank."

He rubbed his eyes, yawned, and nodded. "I know. When I get my hands on Dan Collins, he'll wish he'd let me sleep. But this guy's an intruder. They caught him camping inside the perimeter."

"*Camping?* In this weather? Up *here*? Christ, Frank, not even reindeer go camping up here."

Francisco managed a tired grin. "Tell me about it. Let's see what we've got."

Captain Davis ordered thermal blankets and a blood workup as they passed the night nurse's duty station, then they stepped into the fridge. Davis took the intruder's vitals. The duty nurse arrived a moment later with a Mylar survival blanket and a blood kit.

Francisco wrapped the blanket around the victim's torso and legs, careful to leave the frozen extremities uncovered, then glanced at the vitals. Core body temp was 96.1; not too disastrous. He'd dealt with worse. Blood pressure good, heart rate good, nice and regular.

"He's dehydrated," Francisco said quietly, noting the condition of the man's skin. "How long were you out there, hmm?" he asked the unconscious patient. "Better start an IV, D5 one-half normal saline."

Davis nodded.

"How's that blood work coming along?" Francisco called through the open doorway.

"Low on oxygen. Still checking electrolytes, sir."

Francisco fitted the man with oxygen, then carefully examined the frozen extremities. Both hands were nicely frozen, one up to the wrist, the other to the knuckles. Both ears, too. . . . Fortunately, the frost hadn't bitten too deeply yet. He tugged off incredibly ancient shoes and socks, both pairs held together by the holes.

"Mmm . . . I've seen worse," he muttered, turning the feet up to peer at the soles, "but they're nicely bitten. He's not going to be running any marathons this week. Whoever you are, you are one lucky son," Francisco murmured to the unconscious man.

"Damned lucky," Davis agreed as he threaded the IV needle into the vein and taped it down.

The nurse came back with the blood work. Francisco glanced at it, then nodded. "Very good. We found him before things got critical. Prepare sixty milligrams of Toradol, John. Whoever he is, he's going to hurt like bloody fire when he comes around. And let's put a steam pad on his chest to help bring up his core temp."

The nurse nodded and vanished in search of the prescribed items. Francisco scribbled on his chart.

The mystery man groaned softly. Francisco glanced up just as his eyelids fluttered. His expression mirrored deep disorientation. He tried to sit up and mumbled something too confused to catch. Davis placed a restraining hand on the man's chest.

When the patient struggled, Francisco helped hold him down. "Hold on there, take it easy. We found you in time. You're going to be fine. Just lie quietly . . ."

The man appeared to think about that for a moment, then stopped struggling. He moaned again and shut his eyes. Given the fellow's dazed expression, Francisco wondered if he'd walked away from a light-plane crash.

"Let me take a look at your eyes," Francisco murmured.

His pupils responded normally to a pen light. No signs
of concussion. Francisco picked up the nearest hand
again to examine the webbing more carefully, then
noticed a plastic wristlet under the sweater cuff. He
tugged it down into view, turned it around—

"What the . . ."

Francisco glanced up to the man's face. Logan McKee
watched him quietly. Francisco stared at the wristband
again. VA hospital patient. Mental ward. . . .

"What'd you find?" Davis asked curiously, looking up
from the IV lead he was hooking into the needle.

"An ID bracelet. Mr. McKee," Francisco asked quietly, "can you understand me?"

McKee nodded.

"Good. You're suffering from exposure. Your hands
and feet are frozen, but we found you in time to prevent permanent damage, I think. In a few minutes, you're
going to start hurting like hell. We'll give you something
for pain as soon as we've finished examining you. Don't
be too alarmed if you feel a little dazed or confused.
Your body temperature has dropped several degrees, but
we'll be warming you up nicely in a couple of minutes."

"Okay." McKee's voice was a raw whisper. He shut
his eyes and lay still.

Francisco and Captain Davis eased McKee out of his
clothing and into a hospital gown. Their intruder couldn't
use his hands at all. McKee hissed when the sweater
came off over his ears. Further examination revealed no
other frostbitten areas. In fact, they found no trace of
injury anywhere.

"Is that steam pad ready?"

John was just walking in with it. They draped the
heated pad over McKee's torso, then wrapped the Mylar
around him again to hold in the heat, taking care not
to heat any frozen extremities. McKee started to hurt
sooner than Francisco expected.

"Where's that Toradol?"

John handed over a prepared hypo. As McKee's eyes closed under the influence of the drug, Francisco found his thoughts straying again and again to one question. Just how had this man ended up inside their perimeter, dressed for summer, with a VA hospital in-patient wristlet on his arm?

Francisco rubbed his eyes, then the back of his neck. Just one more little mystery to add to the list he'd been compiling over the last couple of months. If Dan Collins hadn't been base commander . . .

He shook his head. His job, at the moment, was to bring McKee out of danger. He'd tackle disturbing questions later. But he *would* tackle them. Something decidedly odd was going on. Francisco intended to find out what.

She woke with a vile taste in her mouth and a raging thirst that pulsed through her whole body. Queasiness lingered like ghostly nightmares, along with a half-memory of odd, thumping footsteps and an out-of-balance gait that made the queasiness worse. It took her long moments to remember why she couldn't move and even longer to recall that her name was supposed to be Aelia. A low scraping noise along the floor told her she was not alone. For an instant, all she could hear was a frantic knocking that she finally realized was her own pulse.

Then something splashed with a liquid sound. A moment after that, Aelia distinguished the faint wheeze of human lungs laboring in the muggy heat. She slitted her eyes just wide enough to see a familiar, red-haired man at her bedside. Rufus. Rufus Mancus. The name was eerily familiar, but slid away from her, into a dim, roaring pain in her head.

The door was open again. Pearl-grey light, clear as liquid and smelling sweeter than the air of her prison, slid along the tiled floor. Shadows lay like pencils on edge where broken, dirty brown tiles had tilted up. Other tiles were missing; the floor underneath was packed earth. The floor stank, or maybe the room did, of human waste and stale air. She focused her attention on Rufus. Maybe she could learn something while his back was turned.

Which it was, literally. He faced away from her, intent on emptying a ceramic pot into a wooden bucket. The stink of urine clung in the back of her throat. His coarse brown tunic, dark with sweat, lay molded to his back. Propped against the wall, she found the reason for the odd, thumping footsteps she'd half dreamed: a crude crutch, padded with a sweat-stained bit of fleece. Rufus moved awkwardly without it.

When he straightened, his breath caught a little too sharply. He halted and eased his shoulders under the tunic, then bent to finish filling the bucket. When he moved, nacreous light fell across a ghastly scar along the back of his left thigh, just above the knee. Another scar, lower down, cut across the calf. They were ragged, badly healed wounds, old enough that they'd whitened from the feverish red of new injuries to a sickly pink.

Something about the placement of those injuries tried to ooze its way past the blackness in her mind. She tried, and was at first unable, to grasp the implications of those scars; then cold horror spread through her. Aelia traced the plane of his thigh and saw where the ligaments had been severed, and lower down, along the Achilles tendon—

Her breath choked in her throat. He had been deliberately hamstrung.

Rufus Mancus turned quickly at the tiny sound she'd made. He lost his balance and caught himself against the wall. When he found her shocked gaze on him, a vertical line appeared between his brows. Open puzzlement darkened his eyes for just a moment. Then he said, in that Irish-whiskey voice she recalled so clearly, "I did not mean to wake you."

She licked her lips. "I don't mind." Then, hopefully: "Could I have water? Please?"

He nodded. "Just let me finish this and I will get Sextus." He bent to pick up the bucket.

"Wait—"

He paused.

"I'd . . . rather not be drugged again. And I don't like Sextus. Couldn't you bring it?"

Rufus' face went utterly still, an alien mask that left her chilled despite the close heat of the room. Deep furrows at the edges of his eyes aged him beyond his years.

"I am sorry," he said stiffly. "But it is not permitted. I should not be here, alone with you, while you are awake."

She tried to sit up and was faintly surprised when she managed it, although nausea in the pit of her stomach rumbled warningly. She rested bound hands awkwardly in her lap. "Why not?"

A film of sudden sweat shone on his battered face. His glance slid away from hers. "Because I am not a eunuch."

A eunuch?

"And I do not want to become one," he added with a low growl.

He left her sitting in darkness and took the bucket and crutch with him. Rufus shut the door with a solid thud. A bar outside dropped into place with a bang that made her jump.

A eunuch? Sextus had been *castrated?* Dear God . . . *Where am I?*

Aelia closed her fists—but her name, ill-fitting and wrong, galled some inner portion of herself, distracting her from Sextus' misfortune and the implied threat to Rufus. She gripped her temples awkwardly with bound hands, desperate to remember anything about herself. Immediately she felt a warning lurch of pain in the center of her skull.

She drew a ragged, foul breath—and felt a metal band at her throat rise and fall. She explored tentatively. The thing circled her throat completely. The back of it was fastened with a crude-seeming but effective lock. The breath she drew this time shuddered all the way down to the diaphragm.

"I want to go home!" But she didn't have a clue as to what, or where, home might be.

Sextus arrived with a deep wooden cup and an unglazed ceramic jug. She eyed him warily.

"I won't drink any more of that drug," she said with more conviction than the circumstances probably warranted.

Sextus eyed her sidelong while he poured. "If you keep down this water," he murmured in his light voice, "and if you behave yourself, you won't need any more of it."

She wanted to ask what constituted "behaving one's self" and discovered a sudden, sweating fear of the answer. Sextus set the jug beside her on the bench— except it wasn't really a bench, it was more a wooden daybed, without a mattress. Sextus turned toward her with a smile on his lips, but not in his eyes. He held the cup to her mouth. The water was warm and tasted metallic. Drinking while someone else held the cup was awkward. She was thankful when the liquid seemed content to stay in her stomach. Sextus released her wrists, but not her ankles. Then he called for Rufus.

Aelia winced at Rufus' halting, slow-footed approach. "Yes?"

The light where Rufus stood in an open corridor of some sort had strengthened to a clear, pale gold. Aelia heard the splash of water somewhere nearby. A fountain, she realized, somewhere inside this building. Farther away she could make out the muted sounds of civilization: voices, the rattle and clatter of workshops, barking dogs.

"Watch her while I prepare her breakfast."

Rufus held Sextus' gaze. "I am not supposed to stay with her."

The immensely overweight Sextus grinned. "Dominus is out looking at stock from an estate sale. He'll be gone for hours. Besides, if you don't, I'll tell him you tried to rape her."

Rufus flushed dark red, all the way to the base of his

throat. Scarred hands closed slowly into fists. Only his lips, drawn into a tight line, remained pale.

"You do remember how I came here? Don't you, Sextus?"

Aelia shivered at the gently delivered threat.

Laughter drained from Sextus' eyes. "Just guard her!"

Rufus limped aside to give him room to pass. Then he returned to the doorway without offering to enter her cell. During the time he'd been gone, he'd removed his sweat-soaked tunic. Except for a dirty, ragged loincloth and a thick metal collar around his throat, he was naked. Glistening moisture along his chest and in his hair suggested Sextus had interrupted his bath.

Rufus was scarred across most of his visible body: arms, legs, chest, and that hideous burn scar on the side of his neck. It pulsed lightly with the rhythm of his heart. The scar was shaped like the letter F. Something deep in her mind stirred again, but she couldn't grasp it solidly enough. It slipped away.

Despite the exhaustion she had heard in his voice, his body was neither starvation thin nor bowed. He rippled with muscle, every part of him she could see. Whatever had happened to his leg, he hadn't allowed himself to go soft. Given the little she'd gathered about the crazy world into which she'd awakened, he probably hadn't been given much choice.

He stood glaring down the corridor, in the direction Sextus had gone. Tension had tightened Rufus' body into hard knots of muscle. Pale eyes glinted in the early daylight. Aelia decided abruptly she would not want Rufus Mancus for an enemy, no matter how desperately he'd been injured. He turned abruptly toward her. She jumped, then bit her lip.

"I did not mean to frighten you," he said heavily. "And my anger does not lie with you. Dominus Xanthus is a fool to keep that slave. He's worse than I am, in his deceitful way. Cheats Master blind and—"

"Slave?" she echoed, Slow disbelief seeped out from beneath the blackness that held her mind captive.

He met her gaze. Bitterness stiffened the set of his mouth. "Did you not guess? Sextus and I are hardly dressed as freedmen." He gestured with one hand to his near-nakedness and the metal band around his throat. "Perhaps you do not welcome another slave's company?"

The implications—and the band at her own throat—left her suspended between broken thoughts, astonished at some basic level that couldn't quite comprehend slavery as a concept, never mind as a reality for herself.

When he turned his back on her, she forgot everything else. Rufus' back was a mass of criss-crossing scars and welts, some of them so recent they were still bloody. Old bruises discolored his ribs and shoulderblades.

"My God!" she choked out. "Who *did* that to you?"

He glanced over one shoulder. "Don't be stupid, girl."

The accusation stung, even as it deepened the sense of dislocation behind her eyes. "I'm not stupid!" When his glance begged to disagree, she felt compelled to add, "I'm sick and confused and . . . Why do you hate me?"

"Hate you?" That brought him around again to face her. Wary surprise colored amber-green eyes. "I do not hate you, child."

"I'm not a child," she said levelly.

At least, she didn't feel like a child. Her body, under the shapeless linen, was certainly more developed than childhood.

He frowned. "How old are you?"

She opened her lips—

And pain struck her down. She cried out and clutched her head. She heard a distant clatter; then he was beside her, catching and cradling her, rubbing her temples and whispering to her. His Irish-whiskey voice was gentle again, soothing. The pain gradually faded, leaving her limp and drained, with a wet face.

"I'm sorry," they said simultaneously.

She looked into his eyes and discovered a slow, cautious smile. That smile was almost beautiful. It lit his eyes until their color lightened into a clear amber with just a wash of green remaining. A moment later, the smile and the clear amber hue vanished without a trace, replaced by the darkness she'd seen there before. That darkness watched the world warily and didn't expect to find anything good in it.

She found herself wanting to trust those watchful eyes and the personality behind them. *Now there's an irrelevant thought*, she chided herself. Or was it? She needed help, information. And he'd been kind to her.

Rufus eased her back to a sitting position and braced her carefully against the wall, making certain she wouldn't topple to the floor the moment he let go. When he stood up and started to limp back toward the doorway, she lifted bound hands involuntarily and caught his arm.

"Wait—"

He didn't turn back, but he stopped. And waited while she marshaled her scattered thoughts.

"I . . . Rufus, I'm . . . I'm very confused," she finally managed. "I can't remember anything at all. Everything about myself, about . . . the very world, is black. Empty. Almost . . . It's like I came from nowhere, to a place I've never been. When I hear you, or that man you called Xanthus— When you talk about things that should be familiar, I just feel lost. And when I try to remember, even little things . . ." She swallowed too quickly. "You've seen what happens. Please help me, Rufus."

She tightened her fingers on his arm, felt the unyielding muscles knotted like so many steel cables. "At least tell me where I am. What I am. Where I'm going. Who Publius Bericus is. I need to know *something*."

His sigh was more shudder than exhalation. She felt the muscles beneath her fingers relax again into flesh. "Publius Bericus," he answered gruffly without turning to face her, "is the man who plans to buy you. He will be here again today, to . . . examine you."

She swallowed a little too sharply and discovered a lump of pain in her lungs that made breathing all but impossible. Examine her? How were . . . slaves . . . examined?

"A trader named Antonius Caelerus brought you in,

said you were from one of the colonies. Iberia. I think that's somewhere far to the west, but I—" His cheeks flushed, surprising her. "I don't really know where it is. Caelerus asked Xanthus to hold you for a special customer. The sale had already been arranged. Caelerus just needed someplace to keep you, to let you recover from the journey. You were . . . drugged."

He hesitated, then added woodenly, "And you were—are—beautiful. Yesterday, after Bericus and Caelerus left . . . Xanthus could not keep his hands off you. He wants to handle your training. Bericus may not permit that. I am sure whoever trains you will enjoy the work," he added bitterly.

She swallowed hard. "Training?" She had already guessed, didn't want it confirmed. But she had to know.

"Bericus owns quite a stable of beautiful women. And beautiful boys." A shudder contorted his shoulders; he visibly fought off some unfathomable memory.

He finally faced her. His jawline was set, his expression grim. "And if you are too ill to please him, Bericus will beat you. And Xanthus will probably kill me in a fit of anger. He has already threatened it. Xanthus can easily afford to replace me."

Her own predicament seemed curiously unreal. A side effect, perhaps, of whatever else was wrong with her mind. "What happened to you?"

His laugh was short and hard. "I'm told I killed a man. The close friend of someone important."

That struck her as an odd way of putting it.

Rufus glared at the wall, avoiding her eyes. "That was before Xanthus bought me, before the school bought me. Before many things . . ." She shivered, wondering what he was remembering. "Xanthus has uses for me, even though my leg does not work as it should. I can still fetch and carry and clean shit from his slop buckets." Abruptly he straightened and pulled his arm free. "And if I am caught alone in your room again, he will castrate me."

This time, she didn't try to detain him. He limped

to the door, dragging his left leg awkwardly, then bent to retrieve his crutch. Rufus leaned against the door jamb, facing out into the corridor, and settled himself to wait for Sextus' return. After several blank moments trying to assimilate everything he'd just said, Aelia finally regained control of her chaotic thoughts.

"Rufus?"

He eyed her from across the room, his expression closed.

She sighed. "I wish you wouldn't do that."

One shaggy, red eyebrow rose.

"I just wanted to say thank you."

He blinked. Started to speak, thought better, then shut his mouth again. Finally Rufus said, more gently than she'd expected, "No one thanks slaves, Aelia."

She stared at the filthy, broken floor, trying to sort through that. At length, she lifted her gaze again and found him staring at whatever lay beyond her prison. His jaw muscles had bunched up under the scar. He reminded her of a feral dog that's been shot at once too often for trust.

Even more gently than his last comment, she said, "You've helped me, Rufus. I owe you thanks for that."

He shook his head without looking at her. "No. I have merely done my job."

"Just your job?" The sharpness in her voice brought a dull flush to his cheeks. "There was no need for tenderness, Rufus. A bucket of water across my face would have cleaned up the mess. And you didn't need to say a single word. But you did. At considerable risk to yourself," she added pointedly.

He didn't answer. She pressed on. "Whoever you were, whatever you have or have not done . . ." She shrugged. "You didn't need to show me kindness, but you did. You can't know how grateful I am for that. I'm lost in a strange place. I have no memory at all, no idea what to expect. Perhaps it isn't much, but if the friendship of a slave counts, you have mine."

His hands clenched almost as tightly as his eyelids.

"May Bericus *rot* . . ." His breath came out as a harsh rasp. "You just don't know."

"Then tell me," she said quietly.

His head came up. His eyes had filled with angry denial. "No. It is too ugly—"

"Ugly or not, I'll be the one living in it!"

He blanched and turned away again.

She softened her tone. "If I am to be his . . . property"—the word was difficult to say, as though the concept itself were utterly alien—"then I have a right to know."

He actually flinched. Then said something in another language. The words seemed oddly familiar, yet brought no recognition. Worse, the warning lurch of pain started behind her eyes.

Rufus finally grated out, "You are right. I . . . I will tell you what I can." He still hadn't looked at her. "I am sorry, Aelia, but tell you is all I can do. I cannot help you escape what waits for you. No one can."

A chill crept up her spine. He finally looked up. The memory burning behind his eyes was so terrible, she wanted to flinch away. Aelia forced herself to sit still. She held his gaze only through a supreme effort of will.

"I have heard, from slaves who should know," he began heavily, "that Publicus Bericus craved more luxuries than his elderly father would permit him. It is strange, but under Roman law, no grown man with a living father can marry or choose a career or spend money without his father's permission."

His lips twisted. "It is their only real taste of slavery and they hate it. Bericus wanted to make his own career decisions, wanted to buy luxuries he could not afford to buy on the *peculum*—the allowance—his father gave him. It is said Publius Catellus Bericus murdered the old man to inherit his fortune. What he has done since that day . . ."

Aelia listened in growing horror.

The longer Rufus talked, the colder her little cell grew.

CHAPTER FOUR

Dan Collins was scared. Had *been* scared so long it had almost begun to feel normal. Every night when he went to bed—although usually not to sleep—fear haunted him. And every morning when he woke up (if he wasn't already awake), it was there waiting for him, like some monstrous housecat stalking a crippled rat. Only the habits of twenty-three long years in uniform got him out of bed and moving once he turned off the alarm clock. Now, as he faced his mirror, the silver bird pinned to one collar screamed, "Coward!"

He turned away, unable to look himself—or the silver bird—in the eye.

Dan was on the point of walking out the door without bothering to eat breakfast, when the phone shrilled. He stopped short. Acid burned his stomach. *If it's him . . .* Slowly he turned, crossed the room, picked up the receiver.

"Collins."

Kominsky's voice sounded like a reprieve from death. "Colonel, the intruder we picked up last night has been positively identified. St. Louis confirmed his records and faxed a copy. I also have faxes of FBI and police files on him."

Sour bile rose into his throat. Dan clenched his jaw and managed to swallow. God, nothing was uncomplicated anymore. . . .

"Good work, Kominsky. Send the reports over to my clerk. Have him put them on my desk. I'm on my way." He hoped that had come out sounding reasonably normal.

"Yes, sir." The phone line went dead.

Dan hung up and stared at the silent telephone. Then leaned his forehead against the wall. His knees shook; the house was too silent. Framed photographs the length of the short hallway tortured him. He swore softly and staggered toward the bedroom door. He shrugged on his parka, slowly settled gloves over his hands, made his way woodenly through the living room, on his feet and moving out of habit and nothing else.

The inevitable guard was waiting. Dan didn't even know this one's name. Dan charged past him. The slam of the front door was mild, compared to the slam he'd liked to have made.

The guard fell into step behind him without a word. The driver waiting outside took one look at his face and wisely threw him a silent salute. The driver—Dan thought he was genuinely Army, but couldn't be sure—held the door for him and his guard, then roared the hummer away without saying a word. The silent guard seated beside him smiled coldly. Dan ignored the man as best he could. In the distance, Table Mountain glittered in the early sunlight. Cold, remote . . .

By the time he reached his office, freezing Arctic air had cooled him down a little, but sight of the immense, squat concrete building hunkered down to the earth a quarter mile away was like salt in an open wound. The guard followed him out into the frozen morning. Dan hurried into his office, wanting nothing at the moment but to feel *warm* again—*inside* as well as out. He'd have to deal with what was in that building soon enough. First, he needed facts.

Dan's office was warmer than the outside air, but not by much. He kicked the thermostat up twenty degrees, bawled out his Spec-4 clerk, then slammed the inner office door shut. His guard, of course, simply opened the door, stepped inside, and closed it again, wordlessly. The man took up a vigilant stance between Dan and the room's only exit. Dan glared at him, but knew far better than to protest.

He told himself to ignore the unwelcome presence and sat down to read the reports Wilson had carefully placed on top of other stacked folders. Dan opened the first one and found faxed copies of the intruder's service records.

His name was McKee. Home of record *and* current address both listed in Florida, not too far apart, judging by zip codes.

McKee was one helluva long way from home.

He grunted as he read through the file. McKee's military record was spectacular. Up to a point. Dan wondered what had happened. He'd graduated with honors from the Citadel. Had entered the Army as a second lieutenant. Had attained the rank of captain at an impressively young age. Fought in Vietnam, received several commendations, including the Silver Star. Near the close of the war he'd been injured, badly enough to ship him stateside for "reconstructive surgery" on his leg. Dan winced at that innocuous-sounding phrase.

And then . . .

Shortly after his recovery, he'd received a medical discharge. But no disability rating was included and the code for the discharge gave no hint as to *what* medical condition had prompted the action. Dan frowned. Odd . . .

The next several years were a complete blank. No trace of him existed, as though he'd dropped completely out of sight. Then, nearly seven years ago, came another entry. Criminal court proceedings had ceased the moment McKee had been committed to a Veteran's Administration hospital psychiatric ward. He'd had no opportunity to fight either the charge of assault and battery with intent to kill, which had at least been reduced from attempted second-degree murder. He glanced through the police file. The description of injuries sustained by his victim were graphic and coldly horrifying. He set the police file aside and finished the army records.

Eight months after entering the hospital, reports on

his progress toward sanity had been extremely promising. A year later, he'd been approved for supervised excursions. Several months after that, with the permission of local law enforcement authorities, McKee had been approved for unsupervised excursions into town. On his second "pass" out of the hospital, nearly two years after the court had ordered him committed, Captain Logan Pfeiffer McKee had simply vanished. That had been five years ago.

A man could go a lot of places in five years.

Slowly Dan set the file aside, then picked up the FBI report. It was worse, even, than the police files. Suspected mercenary, suspected gunrunner (no charges brought), known affiliate with a number of foreign subversive groups, suspected mafia connections, known to be violent, finally adjudged insane by a board of army and civilian psychiatrists, thus avoiding trial for attempted murder. . . .

Dan whistled softly and settled back in his chair. He had a live one on his hands—and a bellyful of questions. The first of which was, where had McKee *been* for the past five years? The fact that he'd resurfaced just outside this particular post caused Dan's skin to crawl.

He picked up the police report again. A brief entry regarding McKee's disappearance stated the fugitive had last been seen wearing jeans, tennis shoes, an Airborne t-shirt, and an OD green British Commando jacket. He was believed to have been carrying a nylon satchel containing a small amount of cash and his knitting.

—*Knitting?*

Well, he was crazy. . . .

The last report on Dan's desk was from his own men, the patrol that had picked up McKee the previous night. He'd already heard their preliminary report from Kominsky, during the middle of the night. Now he wanted details. McKee had been camped half a mile from the southern perimeter: well within the ten-mile restricted zone. How had he gotten in so close without being detected? There were security devices all over the place.

At the time of his capture, McKee had been suffering from extreme exposure. He'd been only semiconscious. Unseasonably warm weather, a localized side-effect produced by their research—and Carreras' tinkering with it—had taken a turn for the worse after 2200, when a very cold air mass had moved inland from the Arctic Ocean. The mercury was still dropping like a brick through feathers. No wonder McKee had nearly frozen to death.

Dan read—and then reread—the patrol's description of McKee's clothing. Then he picked up the police report and compared the two. The sound of Wilson's typewriter in the outer office faded from his awareness. He stared. Except for an obviously handmade, *knitted* sweater, the two reports were identical. Right down to the plastic wristband that marked him a Ward Two patient. Five years after his disappearance, McKee resurfaced nearly four thousand miles away, wearing and carrying exactly the same items he'd possessed the day he vanished? Dan thought about the concrete building that squatted in the center of his post like some obscene, blood-sucking tick, and just managed to repress a shiver.

McKee's clothes had not been designed for twenty-five-degree weather. A man with his background would have planned a hit mission better than that. Unless something had gone wrong? No, there was still the too-coincidental coincidence. If nothing else, McKee would have removed that tell-tale wristband. Dan shook his head. There was already enough craziness in his life. He didn't need more.

The patrol had taken McKee directly to the infirmary, where Major Valdez had, at Dan's personal request, treated him for exposure. When Valdez had finally released him, McKee had been confined in the brig. The last notation indicated that Kominsky had held off interrogation, guessing correctly that Dan would want to conduct it himself. Dan glanced at his watch before he picked up the phone and punched the local line.

"Wilson, get Major Valdez on the line."

"Yes, sir."

A moment later the local buzzed. He picked up and punched line one. "Frank, good morning."

"Good morning, yourself. What the devil was the idea of dragging me out of bed at o-dark-thirty? I took out a busted spleen at 0100 this morning, dammit. I'd just gotten to bed again."

Dan grimaced. "Sorry, Frank, I didn't know. I'd have let the duty doctor handle it if I'd realized. I just wanted my best man on it."

Francisco Valdez grunted. "Right. Thanks for nothing. I assume this good-morning call is about our visitor? Damned fool, wandering around in January with nothing more substantial than a sweater."

"It's worse than that. We've made a positive ID. He's no fool, he's bad-news crazy. I want you to meet me in the brig. This guy's got a psych record you won't believe. He may get violent—hell, with this guy's record, I'd wager a month's pay on it."

Francisco whistled.

"I'd just as soon you were there with something to calm him down." After a moment's thought, Dan added, "And maybe something to get him talking, if necessary."

Francisco paused. "Come again?"

"I said, bring something to loosen his tongue. I want some answers. Chemicals may be the only way to get them."

The silence was even longer this time. Dan ground his teeth.

"Dan, are you sure—"

He forced himself to say it, already mourning the friendship he was destroying. "That's an order, Major. Do you have a problem following orders?"

The stiff, "No, sir," spoke volumes.

"Then pack whatever is required and meet me in Kominsky's office in half an hour."

"Yes, sir."

Those two words couldn't have been colder if Frank had bitten them off a glacier. The surgeon hung up, rather forcefully. Dan sat staring at the phone for a long moment. Hard as that call had been . . . he knew he ought to make the *other* one. His guard would expect him to do just that. Nor was Dan naïve enough to think he could hide something like this, not for long. *He* probably already knew of McKee's existence, probably knew as much at this point as Dan did. But Dan wanted— no, needed—more information before he made that call. Any edge he could possibly gain . . .

Dan shut his eyes for a tiny moment. He'd heard the doubt in Francisco's voice. Dan couldn't blame him. Not even a friendship as long as theirs had existed could explain away what was happening on this base. Somehow, he had to protect Francisco, as he'd failed to protect so many others. . . .

His palms had started to sweat. He wiped them on his uniform pants before he buzzed Wilson again.

"Yes, Colonel?"

"Call Lieutenant Kominsky. Tell him Major Valdez and I will be arriving at 0900 to interrogate his prisoner."

"Yes, sir."

Dan hung up, then sat slowly back. Only time would tell. . . .

Dan asked Kominsky to send a clerk in with coffee before he walked back to the interrogation room. Francisco was there ahead of him.

"Colonel." The only way to classify Francisco's greeting was frosty. The surgeon's cold, clear-eyed gaze scrutinized him, flicked briefly across his "bodyguard" then returned to pierce Dan with accusation, hurt, and worry.

"Morning, Frank." He sounded stilted, even to himself. He knew there were dark circles under his eyes. He was equally aware that his uniform had been fitted to a frame forty pounds heavier. He couldn't help that.

"So talk to me, Frank," he plunged ahead before the base's head surgeon could ask him what had been wrong with him for the past four months. "What kind of impression did you get from this guy last night?"

Francisco continued the narrow-eyed scrutiny for a moment longer than he should have, then shook his head. "Hard to say. He was in pretty bad shape. I wouldn't have suspected a mental history at all, if I hadn't spotted that ID band. Quiet, calm. Of course, he was nearly unconscious when they brought him in. And once he started coming around, I gave him something for pain. His hands and feet were frozen. Guy's lucky he won't lose fingers or toes. Or ears. If he hadn't had a fire going, you'd have a corpse on your hands instead of a prisoner."

Dan nodded. "Okay. Let's get this over with."

The coffee arrived just ahead of Kominsky and two more MPs. Dan returned quick salutes and gave the MPs permission to stand at ease. He took charge of the coffee first. Dan poured three cups, handed one to Francisco, another to Kominsky, and sipped from the third himself. The "bodyguard" glanced longingly at the coffeepot. Dan ignored him. Francisco didn't.

Frank never did miss much. Christ . . . Don't get curious, Frank. Gotta keep you out of the worst of this. . . .

But he needed the surgeon's help. No way around that. Nobody else had Frank's training or experience with what Dan needed.

"Gentlemen," he finally said, taking a seat behind a small metal table along one wall, "our unexpected visitor has quite a history. He's violent, unpredictable. Spent two years in a VA mental ward before he escaped and disappeared. He's an expert at hand-to-hand combat. I want him cuffed and, if necessary, hobbled." Kominsky nodded, expression grim despite the obvious attempt at neutrality.

"If the manacles won't handle him, Major Valdez will administer a little happy juice. Let's see if we can bring him in here quietly. Frank, go with Kominsky."

Francisco's answering nod was anything but congenial,

but he began preparing hypos. When the doctor was ready, Kominsky led the little party out. The MPs wheeled about smartly and fell into step behind the two officers. All spit and polish and regulations. He'd been that way, once. A long, long time ago. God, four months. . . . It felt more like four centuries. Dan's guard stayed right where he was. Dan sipped his coffee and tried to hide the tremor in his hands.

He hadn't yet finished his coffee when they returned in formation. Francisco shook his head slightly and set his bag beside the chair he'd vacated. The two MPs stationed themselves just inside the door, which they carefully closed. McKee's hands were cuffed in front of him with military-style bar cuffs which kept his hands separated yet immobile. Kominsky had also hobbled him. He wasn't, however, drugged.

Yet.

Kominsky shoved McKee to stand in front of Dan's table. The security officer took up an alert stance a few paces behind the prisoner. McKee glared at Kominsky, then shuffled awkwardly forward and faced Dan. McKee stood at attention—or as much as the hobbles and bar cuffs allowed. They'd put him in a mechanic's coverall.

The birthdate in his file put his age at forty-eight. The lines in his face would have caused Dan to add another five years to that figure. His hair was long, tangled, and badly needed to be washed. He needed a shave. Curiously, his expression seemed to waver between outrage and quiet confusion. A madman's expression. . . .

But when he finally looked directly at Dan, his eyes appeared to be as sane as any man's. Dan found that particularly disturbing.

McKee lifted his manacled wrists slightly. "This wasn't necessary." He sounded angry.

"The FBI would disagree."

For a moment McKee looked genuinely startled. Then his expression settled into hard lines of resignation. "Yeah. I guess they might, at that."

The admission was encouraging, if surprising. "Would

you mind telling me why you escaped from the VA Hospital in Gainesville?"

McKee's bark of laughter startled him. "Obviously, Colonel, you've never spent any time in a nuthouse." After a moment, he shrugged. "Besides, you wouldn't believe me if I did tell you. I'm crazy, right? My word's automatically suspect."

Dan started to shift his weight, then suppressed the urge and said, "What have you been doing since then? You disappear in Florida, nobody sees a trace of you for five years, then you just show up out of nowhere half frozen to death outside my base."

For some reason Dan couldn't determine, that information shook McKee, deeply. His gaze dropped and he seemed to withdraw into his own private little world. "Five years," Dan heard him mutter. "Five *years*? Jeezus H. Christ . . ." Abruptly McKee caught his eye. "Just where am I, anyway?"

"You know damned well where you are!" Dan snapped.

"Do I?" The question was phrased softly, nearly a whisper.

McKee's eyes looked haunted.

It was Dan's turn to feel shaken.

"Look, McKee," Dan said into the silence which followed, "before I decide whether to simply ship you back to Florida, or charge you with attempted espionage, attempted sabotage, and anything else I can think of, I'll need some answers. And I will get them, either with your cooperation or without it."

McKee stared at him coldly for a moment, then his glance flicked over to Francisco's medical kit. His cheeks lost color.

"You don't need that crap," he muttered. Then he looked directly into Dan's eyes. "But you'll use it anyway. Because you're not going to believe me. Not a word. Hell, *I* wouldn't believe me." His steady stare became the glare of a trapped animal. "Go ahead, damn you. Ask. Then have your Gestapo Major, there, fill me full of Pentothal so you can ask me again. Damn you to hell. . . ."

A tremor of barely suppressed fear quavered beneath the bitter bravado in McKee's voice.

"All right, McKee," he said quietly. "Let's begin with your escape."

"I didn't."

Dan blinked. "You didn't what?"

"Escape."

"What would you call it?"

McKee laughed. The sound scraped along Dan's nerves. "I don't know. Time travel?" he suggested darkly.

Dan's blood chilled. "Go on." He noticed Francisco's quick, curious glance, but ignored it.

McKee's voice, his whole manner, was distant, distracted. "I went for a walk during a thunderstorm. Lightning struck a tree, bounced off. It hit the ground where I was standing and probably me, too. The tree came down, just about crushed me. Would've killed me if I'd still been there when it landed. Fortunately for me"—his voice took on a deeply ironic note—"when I tried to jump out of the way, I fell smack underneath it. And kept falling. Right into somewhere else. Some*when* else. I landed in a snowbank, in the middle of the goddamned coldest night I've ever had the pleasure to spend. Thanks for hauling my frozen ass in out of the weather."

McKee fell silent.

Dan frowned. If he'd been struck by lightning, he might have experienced some memory loss. But that wouldn't account for the clothes, the wristband. Time travel? He shuddered.

"Frank," he said heavily, "I'd appreciate your assistance."

Francisco hesitated, clearly on the verge of arguing. His long-time friend searched Dan's eyes for some rational explanation for his behavior, for this particular order, for everything that had been happening on this base and was happening right now, in this horrible little room. Dan couldn't hold his friend's gaze.

When Dan let his eyes slide away, Francisco said heavily, "Right."

Dan fought the urge to wipe sweat off his face. He'd expected more resistance, maybe even a full-blown confrontation. That Francisco had capitulated, probably for old times' sake and long-standing trust, hurt more than any loud, angry argument would have.

Sweat had appeared on McKee's seamed cheeks, too. It dripped down the sides of his nose. Francisco had already prepared the hypo. McKee glued his gaze to the syringe as Francisco moved toward him. McKee stumbled backwards, *away* from that needle and its contents, only to trip himself up in the hobbles. He crashed backwards and landed hard. He yelped and swore, then tried to roll to his feet. Both MPs jumped on him. They pinned him— or tried to. They had a hard time holding him despite the restraints. Dan watched with difficulty as McKee struggled to free himself. Dan's guard watched with a glitter of intense enjoyment. Francisco looked a little white around the mouth. Dan felt sick. He looked away.

"Hold his head—don't let him jerk away—"

Dan glanced back as Francisco eased open the coverall. McKee's struggles intensified. The surgeon exposed the fleshy muscle on McKee's upper arm. He swabbed quickly. "Hold that arm still. I don't want him to break the needle off."

One of the MPs sat on McKee's shoulder. Francisco jabbed the needle in. McKee sobbed something inarticulate. Francisco rose heavily and turned away, facing neither McKee nor Dan directly.

"Give it a few minutes," Francisco advised. His voice had roughened slightly. "We ought to put him in a chair." As he spoke, he retrieved another preprepared hypo. This time, McKee didn't offer to struggle. He just lay quietly and barely flinched when the needle slid into his flesh.

Dan looked quickly away again as tears oozed down McKee's cheeks and vanished into his beard. Dan kept his gaze averted as Francisco stepped to the door and shouted for the clerk to bring a chair. Dan wanted to hide from the look that pierced him from the man lying drugged on the floor. Francisco wouldn't look at him at all.

The chair arrived. The MPs pulled McKee off the floor and sat him down. He nearly slid off again. Francisco jumped forward and held him in place.

"Easy . . ."

The MPs unmanacled his wrists and ankles, then remanacled him to the chair. McKee's eyes had glazed. His expression was dull, unfocused. His head drooped.

Francisco said quietly, "I've given him something more effective than Pentothal. One of our new mixes. It's very potent stuff," he added, voice heavy with warning. "One of the compounds is a hallucinogen. If you tell him you're his Aunt Agatha, he'll ask to feed your canary."

Dan saw the MPs stifle grins. Stupid bastards. Francisco was warning them to be damned careful with this man's mental condition and they thought he was making a dumb joke. Dan's guard didn't so much as blink.

"Use his first name," Francisco added quietly. "And start with easy questions, things that aren't threatening. Things we can verify."

Dan nodded. "When can I start?"

Francisco tilted McKee's head back. The man offered no resistance as Francisco peeled back his eyelids one at a time and peered at his pupils. "Mmm. He's hanging just at the edge of consciousness, right where you want him. Go ahead."

Dan checked the file to be sure of the name, then spoke. "Logan, can you hear me?"

"Mmmph," came a mumbled, indistinct reply.

"Can you hear me? Logan?"

"Uh-huh . . ."

"How old are you, Logan?"

The reply was blurred. Dan repeated the question.

"Forty-three," McKee said slowly.

Dan frowned. The report had said forty-eight. He was sure it had. "Hand me that top file, would you, Frank?"

The surgeon complied. Dan riffled through a couple

of sheets before finding it. There it was, birthdate and age. Logan McKee was forty-eight.

Dan frowned again, then tried once more. "Logan, I want you to think very carefully. What is your birthday?"

He answered slowly and correctly.

"How old are you?"

Dan read brief confusion in the man's eyes. McKee struggled unsuccessfully to focus his gaze on Dan's face. "Forty-three, I turned forty-three in June. Gettin' so old . . ."

"What is it, Dan?" Francisco asked quietly.

Dan glanced from McKee to his surgeon. "Why would he lie about his age?"

Francisco's eyes widened slightly. "He wouldn't. Or shouldn't, anyway. That's not something important enough to cover up with any kind of conditioning. And I don't think he's resistant to what I gave him. Not many people would be." Francisco frowned slightly. "It's just a hunch, but based on his reactions earlier . . . I'd be almost willing to bet he's been under truth drugs before and knew he'd sing like a nightingale. I don't think I care for the implications, Dan. I take it he's not forty-three?"

"No." Dan tried another question. "What is your name?"

"Logan."

"Your full name, Logan. What's your full name?"

"McKee. Logan Pfeiffer. Captain. Serial number RA three four nine dash seven seven dash two eight one one."

Dan pursed his lips. He still thought of himself as military.

"Notice his response," Francisco commented. "He's cast us as the enemy, himself as the prisoner of war."

"Yes, I caught that." Dan wondered if his prisoner had ever been captured by enemy forces. It wasn't mentioned in his records, if he had been. Dan shrugged slightly and plugged into McKee's hallucination, with a twist. "Captain McKee, this is your commanding officer. You've been in the field on a mission. It's time for me to debrief you on that mission, Captain. Do you understand, Captain McKee?"

"Sir . . . yessir." It came out slurred. He tried to stiffen to attention. *Citadel grad*, Dan sighed inwardly. They made the best—or worst—officers in the service. According to his records, Logan McKee had been one of the former, *not* the latter. But he didn't look much like a Citadel man anymore. He didn't look like much of anything, any longer, except a rag-bag of wasted training and potential. *And who are you to judge anyone, Dan Collins?*

"At ease, Captain." Dan sighed.

McKee slumped again.

"Now, McKee, tell me about your mission."

"Mission . . . mission, sir?" McKee was visibly struggling with the concept.

Dan paused and wondered about that, then continued on the same tack. "You left Florida. You were posted in Florida. Do you remember Florida, Captain? Gainesville, Florida."

McKee's face glistened under a sheen of sweat. "Hospital . . ."

"That's right, Captain. You were in the hospital. Then you left. Tell me what happened when you left."

"Had me a Asher Special, over to Skeeters', eggs 'n cheese, peppers 'n onions over hashbrowns, grits on the side . . . Can't get a decent breakfast inna damn hospital." His accent had become far more pronounced, reminding Dan of a Deep South drill sergeant he'd known several hundred years ago in ROTC basic camp. "Walked over, you know, not the bus. Felt good, stretching my legs again. Wonder'f Skeeters is still there. . . ."

"Captain, tell me about what you did afterward, please." At this rate, they'd be here all year.

"Went over to the lake, watched the birds 'n the 'gators. Tried to finish my sweater. Stupid sweater . . . ugly." Dan waited patiently for him to continue. "Storm come up. Always storms in summer, 'bout that time.

Damn near set your watch by it. I didn't leave, though. Nice, being in the rain again."

Abruptly McKee struggled against the manacles. "Tree! Ahhh—my leg—damn leg—can't get out of the damn way—"

Francisco jumped forward and caught his shoulder.

"Logan! Logan, it's all right. You're fine, Logan. There's no danger. . . . None at all. . . ." Francisco kept talking, almost whispering to the terrified man. McKee slowly relaxed.

Francisco took his pulse, then finally nodded toward Dan.

All right . . .

"Captain, tell me about the tree."

McKee drew a ragged breath. "Magnolia. Big. Real old. Get big like that, swamp trees. Real pretty, too. Used to fish on the Suwannee, lots of swamp magnolias. . . ."

"The tree, Captain. Tell me what happened to the tree."

McKee stiffened again. "Lightning . . . God—it's everywhere—" He jerked once, hard. The chair bounced. He gave a keening groan, then slumped. McKee began to tremble violently. Francisco murmured softly again until the man relaxed in his grip.

When he finally straightened, Francisco said, "I think he actually was struck by lightning. He may well have experienced some memory loss."

"Is it safe to continue?"

Francisco thinned his lips, then checked McKee's pulse and pupils again. "Yes." It came out grudgingly. "Just try to avoid asking him about the damned tree, would you? I don't want him slipping into shock."

Dan nodded. "Captain," Dan said quietly, "can you hear me, Captain?"

"Sir . . . yessir."

"Where are you now, Captain?"

"Sir?" Complete confusion overtook McKee's face.

Dan tried a different approach. "After the tree fell, where did you go, Captain?"

McKee sighed. He appeared momentarily baffled. "Don't know, sir. Stars are funny, though. Too far south. Snow everywhere, but there's a skink, musta crushed the poor little fella when I fell. Magnolia leaves in the snow ... Shouldn't be night, sir. Where'n hell am I? Can't figure out where I am. ..."

Francisco shook his head. "Revise that to significant memory loss. We seem to have skipped a substantial amount of time."

That word again.

Dan wondered if some other clue hidden in McKee's mind might end up linking him to—

Dan stood up. "Gentlemen, I'll conduct the rest of this interrogation alone. Frank"—Francisco had already begun to protest—"I need to ask him questions about classified material. You don't have the proper clearance to hear this. None of you do. I'll yell the second I think he's in trouble."

"Yes, sir." Francisco still didn't look happy, but he left. Kominsky and his MPs followed. Dan glared down the guard. When the man didn't offer to leave, Dan said tightly, "Either get out, or I'll have Kominsky toss you in the brig. I'll answer to your boss for it later."

The man narrowed his eyes slightly, then shrugged as if to say, "It's your funeral, buddy," and followed the others.

Dan locked the door behind them.

"Now, Captain McKee—" He barely recognized the voice as his own. Dan grasped McKee hard by the shoulders, until the man's eyelids fluttered open again. "I want to know how long you've worked for the mob. Which family do you represent? Or are you with the FBI? Or NSA?"

"Sir?" McKee tried to get his eyes focused.

"Who is your contact? What source of information led you to this base? What the hell do you know about Project Gallivant?"

CHAPTER FIVE

Bericus—oh, God—had come and gone.

Aelia huddled in near darkness, waiting for . . .

What?

The bill of sale to be finalized? The door to open again into horror? The sale was made. Gold for Xanthus, more gold and some sort of trade in goods for Caelerus. She'd heard them talking outside the room, afterward, through numb shock and pain. Bericus was already on his way home to some rustic country retreat, accompanied by Caelerus. Xanthus was supposed to deliver her there tomorrow.

Tomorrow . . .

She scrubbed tears fiercely, grateful they'd at least left her untied. She muttered words that would have shocked . . . whom? . . . into disbelief. Someone important to her, but Aelia couldn't place a name or even a face. All she had was a brief, intense feeling of kinship, followed by a profound sense of loss.

Who're my parents? Am I married? Just how old am I?

The bottomless pit inside her head hid its secrets well. *All right* . . . If she couldn't remember anything, she'd try to get at this logically. She knew the dominant language here. Languages, she felt certain, weren't learned overnight. Yet everything about this place seemed alien and the muttered, half-heard words Rufus had spoken in another language had set up a tremor of near recognition all through her.

Were she and Rufus natives of the same country? He didn't seem to know her and she didn't recognize him.

Of course, she didn't recognize *anything*. Aelia was certain the language she shared with Rufus, Xanthus, and the others was not Rufus' native tongue and she was fairly certain it wasn't hers, either. Her accent was better than his, but not as pure as Bericus'—which was slightly different from Xanthus'.

"Very well," she decided. "I'm no more a native of this place than Rufus. We just both happen to speak the language here."

What else?

Certain concepts—like slavery—seemed to shock her beyond rational expectation. Yet slavery was clearly well entrenched. So she must be from somewhere considerably different. A colony, Rufus had said, far to the west. A colony, though, implied strong ties with this place. If that were the case, she ought not to have felt so shocked at what was clearly a dominant culture trait.

Could Rufus be lying? She didn't think so. That left only one viable alternative: someone had lied to Rufus. Which brought into question her whole supposed background, including her current status as a slave. Somehow, Aelia didn't think either Bericus or Xanthus would take the word of an amnesiac awaiting final sale that she wasn't supposed to be a slave at all. . . .

The bar outside her cell rattled and lifted. Aelia clenched her fists and braced for the worst. When the door creaked open, a flood of hot golden light swept into the room, bringing the scent of flowers and clean sunshine. She strained to see who stood silhouetted in the doorway. A scrape and thump gave her the answer before she could actually see him.

Her relief was so intense, she actually sagged back against the wall.

"I've brought some supper," Rufus said.

"Where's Sextus?"

He grimaced. "Who knows? Master's gone again and so's he. Mistress tries to pretend this wing of the house doesn't exist at all. She keeps herself too busy supervising the spinning and the weaving," he gestured to his crude, handwoven tunic, "to remind herself that her husband is in trade, with stock that must be fed. I just didn't want you to starve."

His face flushed slightly. He wouldn't quite meet her eyes. Aelia didn't care. He'd come, hadn't he? With food . . . Unbelievably, her stomach rumbled. After Bericus' *examination*, she hadn't thought she could *ever* be hungry again. He set down a wooden bucket that looked heavy and hobbled outside again, then returned with a wooden bowl and spoon.

"You are lucky. Master ordered figs with the gruel."

He dished up a generous serving and handed over the bowl. Aelia took one look, swallowed heavily, then forced herself to eat. The taste was tolerable—barely.

"How is your back?" she asked before he could pick up the bucket again.

Rufus glanced up, then over his shoulder toward the open doorway. Slowly, he straightened up. Then, with another wary glance over his shoulder, leaned against the wall. "Terrible. But thank you." He tried a smile and nearly succeeded. "We may see more of each other than I had thought."

She ignored the tasteless gruel to study his face. "What do you mean?"

The second smile was less successful than the first. "Bericus is threatening to buy me."

"But . . . *why*?"

Rufus shrugged and glanced away. "I gave him cause to hate me about thirteen months ago."

Aelia narrowed her eyes. "How did you manage that?"

Unidentifiable emotion flickered briefly in his eyes, then was gone. "That scar on his chin?" he asked. "You noticed it?"

She nodded.

"Well, among other things, I put it there."

Oh. "I thought you belonged to Xanthus?"

Jaw muscles knotted. "I do. But Bericus is a very good customer. He . . . Well, never mind."

"Rufus, who did you kill?"

For an instant, all she saw in his eyes was rage. Then he spat out something that sounded ugly. Again, the words in that other language he used set up flickers of near recognition.

"Honestly? No one. Except a bunch of men whose names I barely knew. That's why I'm still alive."

She just looked at him. When he lifted a brow, consigning her to the realm of mental defectives, she frowned. "What do you mean? Was that supposed to make sense?"

Wary distrust crept back into his eyes. "Haven't been to the arena much, have you?"

Something twinged in her mind, nearly breaking loose. She frowned again, but it was gone. Impatiently, Aelia shook her head. "No, I suppose not."

He sighed. "I was condemned to death for murder. I have no idea who I was supposed to have killed. I, er, was something of a stranger in town. Didn't speak the language, even."

"I see. It's a little hard to argue your case if you can't even talk to the judge."

A brief glint of amusement lit amber-green eyes. "You have an astonishing grasp of the situation, Aelia, for someone with no memory."

She felt herself flush. "I can't help it, Rufus. Sometimes, things bubble up out of the darkness before I'm really aware of them. Other times, I *almost* remember something, but it gets away before I can grab it."

He nodded. "I've heard amnesia is like that."

She studied him again. "If you were condemned to death, what happened?"

He adjusted his position against the wall. His face, its stillness, reminded her of cold, white statues she'd seen . . . somewhere. "They sent me out with a sword. No shield, no armor. Just a badly made sword, with a loose hilt, and my bare skin. Against leopards . . . Clawed me damn near to shreds, but I killed them. I don't remember exactly what I did. I just hacked and rolled. Slashed and ran. When it was over . . ."

He shivered. "When it was over and the cats were dead, they sent out three of their favorites to finish me off. Gladiators," he added, with a faint quirk of his lips. "Professionally trained ones. One thing I *did* know was fighting. I used moves the crowd had never seen."

A sigh shuddered out of him. "When *that* was over, all three of their damned favorites were dead. I was still alive. The Emperor was so impressed he had me sold to a gladiatorial school instead of executed. About two years later, I finally lost a fight." He glanced down at the terrible scars on his leg. So did Aelia. The sunlight slanting through the doorway caught the damage cruelly. "But I was lucky again. The crowd was impressed with my performance. The Emperor let me live. The school had no further use for me, so while I was recovering, Xanthus bought me."

He looked up, met her gaze. She didn't know what to say, knew she ought to say something. When she sat staring stupidly into his eyes, aware of tears that had begun to prickle, he shrugged. He let his gaze slide away again. "I'm not asking for pity, Aelia. You asked what happened. I told you." In a roughened voice, he muttered, "I have work to do."

He lifted the heavy bucket and started toward the door. His left foot scraped along the floor with a sound like something out of a bad horror movie: thump, scrape, thump, scrape. . . .

The tears she'd tried to suppress spilled down her cheeks. What Bericus had done to her—what he would do to her—paled, by comparison. Now Bericus was threatening to buy him, just to inflict further torture?

"Rufus?" It came out sounding watery.

He paused in the doorway without turning around.

"I . . . I hope, for your sake, I'll miss you like hell after tomorrow."

The stiffness in his shoulders abruptly disappeared. In a voice made rougher than ever by exhaustion and pain, he said, "Thanks a bunch. I don't want your pity, Aelia. So just forget it. I—just forget it. And me."

He closed the door with a soft thud. A moment later the bar dropped, locking her into darkness with her forgotten meal growing cold in her lap.

She grew queasy at the thought of finishing, so she set the gruel on the floor and left it for the roaches. She *hoped* there weren't any pests larger than roaches in the room. For a long time after the faint thump of his crutch had faded down the corridor outside, Aelia sat with her back against the wall, thinking about what Rufus had said.

He'd killed leopards and three trained gladiators even before receiving training at a school, had said the one thing he'd known was *fighting*. That hinted at quite a bit of training of his own, but he hadn't mentioned what it was. She wondered what he'd been, before the murder accusation had landed him in the arena. Why had he been in this particular city in the first place, if he couldn't speak the language?

He'd said nothing to indicate he'd been anything but a free man until the arena. Try as she could, Aelia couldn't come up with a good reason for a man who couldn't speak the native language to have traveled voluntarily to a place like this. He couldn't have been a merchant, not without the ability to negotiate trade terms.

A soldier? That made more sense than anything else she could come up with. A mercenary might not need significant language skills to make a living. Of course, after what had happened, Rufus didn't have many career options open to him, even if he did manage to obtain his freedom.

Something about that statement reverberated oddly through her. She closed her eyes and chewed her lower lip thoughtfully. Career options . . . Something about loss of career options . . . Instead of chasing it down, she tried letting her mind go blank. The first thing that came into her head was a voice.

"In light of this scandal, you will be dropped from the degree program."

Degree program? That almost made sense.

She swallowed against reflexive nausea, trying just to clear her thoughts again, and waited to see what might bubble out of her dark memory. Her own voice replied to the half-remembered statement.

"You *can't*! I didn't do anything wrong!"

Whoever had spoken, he wasn't present. At least, she couldn't see him. But she could hear his voice, over the instrument she held. Something familiar about that instrument. The chill in the man's voice reminded her of something hideously unpleasant that had happened to her—recently, if the impression were correct.

The disembodied voice said, "Just because there was insufficient evidence to convict does not mean this department absolves you of guilt. The reputation of this university must be maintained. You have seriously jeopardized it."

"What happened to innocent until proven guilty?" She was angry. So angry, she trembled all the way to her boot soles. Except she wasn't wearing boots. The anger was part of the memory, same as the boots. So was hating the fact that her voice sounded like she was about to burst into tears. She didn't *feel* like she was about to cry. She was just angry, clear through. "What about that bastard, Bartlett? He's missing—"

The voice said icily, "You are out of the degree program."

A faint, remembered click told her he was gone.

So was the memory, except for a lingering impression she'd discovered something terribly important about the man called Bartlett. Whoever *he* was. Just thinking his name caused pain to mushroom inside her head and sickness to rise like a tidal wave toward her throat.

In the dark cell, Aelia wrapped arms around herself and shivered. For long moments, she did nothing but breathe and blank her thoughts. Nausea rumbled, then reluctantly subsided. Clearly, she had enemies, dangerous ones, who had smashed up her life even before . . . *this*.

"Who am I?" she whispered in the darkness.

And who had hated—or feared—her enough to damage her mind and sell her into slavery? Aelia had no answers, not to that question or to any of the others buzzing angrily through her numbed brain.

She realized with a sinking sensation that *getting* those answers might be the most important thing she ever did.

Logan woke up in a cell.

The first thing he did was groan. The second thing he did was wish he hadn't. His mouth tasted vile and his head throbbed. A raging thirst drove him to try and sit up. For a moment he swayed drunkenly and nearly toppled off a narrow bunk. He stared at it for a moment, wondering who had dumped him on it and when, then managed to put out hands to steady himself. The room still lurched in front of his eyes. He shook his head, which only made matters worse.

Drugged . . .

Logan dug fingers into a rough wool blanket and mumbled an oath around thick fuzz on his tongue. He remembered needles, sweating dark faces . . . No, that was wrong, he wasn't in Ethiopia, hadn't been there for a long, blurry span of years.

"Gotta think . . ."

Someone else had ordered him drugged this time. He scrubbed at his eyes with the heels of his hands and tried to remember. A face hovered just beyond the edge of consciousness, a face with an implacable, angry voice attached to it. An American, a uniformed colonel . . .

Collins. The man's face swam more clearly into his memory. Then he remembered the needles, the struggle to escape, the questions and his helpless, babbling answers. . . .

Logan snarled softly and shoved himself to his feet. At least they'd taken off the manacles. He rubbed his wrists, which ached and throbbed all the way to his fingertips. His feet were swollen inside his tennis shoes. The cell contained a bed plus a combination toilet and sink.

He relieved himself first and fumbled awkwardly with the buttons on the coverall. His fingers were so swollen and painful, they didn't want to function properly. He slaked his thirst at the sink and doused his whole head in an effort to clear away the lingering fuzziness in his mind. Slowly he wrung water from his hair and beard, then just as slowly straightened and leaned against the wall. His legs wobbled. He wondered if his captors intended to feed him, or planned on starving him to death.

He dragged a dry sleeve across his wet face and worked on ignoring the emptiness in his belly. It was one fine mess he'd gotten himself into this time, that was for sure. From a Florida thunderstorm to a military lockup somewhere in the Arctic, and not even a halfway lucid explanation as to why.

No, things weren't looking good at all. He wondered with a flush of dull anger what they'd learned while he was under the Pentothal. Not much, he'd wager. He couldn't divulge secrets he didn't possess. Which brought him to the logical question of how he had gotten here. And where was "here"? Obviously some sort of high-security installation. Collins had threatened to charge him with espionage and attempted sabotage. Somebody had one helluva secret to hide.

Logan wondered if his little accident could somehow be tied to it, then shook his head. Not likely. He'd just as soon believe Martians had taken over the U.S. military as believe the government—any government, for that matter—had access to something powerful enough to scoop him up and dump him through both space *and* time.

Which brought him back to the question of where he was. Greenland? Alaska? There weren't very many other places the U.S. could put a military base as far north as he suspected this place was. And Logan didn't think the terrain in Greenland matched what little he'd seen of his "landing zone." Too mountainous and too wooded. Greenland was mostly just one big glacier.

Logan swore and lurched back to bed. There had to be some sort of explanation for all this. He had a sinking feeling that unless he came up with one, he was in for more sessions with the needles. And since he might never come up with the answer. . . . He rubbed the lingering ache in his biceps and the crook of his arm, where the needles had gone in, and fought a shudder that wanted to crawl up his spine. The very best he could hope for was a return to the hospital. He shut his eyes and leaned back against the wall. Bleakness tasting of death settled over him, heavy and shroud-like.

Once they put him back in, they'd *never* let him out again.

He was only marginally aware of the harshness of his breathing as he struggled with memories of straitjackets, isolation cells, drug therapy. . . . Unconsciously Logan wrapped arms around himself and squeezed his eyes more tightly shut. Why had he been allowed to taste freedom, if he had to give it up all over again? He'd almost adjusted to . . . that . . . once. He didn't think he could do it a second time.

Logan clenched his fists. He'd kill himself and every soul within reach before he let them do that to him again.

The sound of the lock on his door being unbolted brought Logan instantly to combat readiness. He was on his feet and crouched in a defensive stance before the door began to swing open. Colonel Collins stood in the opening. Logan's snarl was instantaneous, uncontrollable. Then he checked an impulsive lunge forward. Two seriously armed MPs flanked Collins. Behind *them* stood a man with the dark, sinuous features of a mixed-blood Hispanic. That guy was dressed as a civilian, in a silk suit that cost six thousand dollars if it cost a cent.

Logan gave the civilian a long, clear-eyed stare and didn't like anything he saw: expensive taste in clothes and watches, ugly face, dead eyes. Big-time hood, his intuition suggested. If anything, the sight of him made Logan feel more than ever like a caged cat.

"Subdue him," Collins snapped. The MPs started

forward, but Logan kept his attention on the civilian. *He* watched the proceedings with a cold, inhumanly detached expression.

And people called Logan crazy. . . .

"Just come along quietly, buster," the MP corporal said. Logan let him get close, deciding to cooperate for now. Then the man seized Logan's arm and twisted it brutally behind him.

About four seconds later, both MPs lay stretched out on the floor of Logan's tiny cell, too unconscious to moan about bruises and broken bones.

Logan flexed his sore shoulder slightly as he straightened. He knew Collins would have him covered. He turned around slowly, hands carefully out to his sides, and faced the deadly black eye of the colonel's drawn Beretta M-92-F pistol. Logan glanced from the unwavering automatic to Collins' eyes and tried to strike a reasonable tone.

"Why don't you teach those goons some manners, Collins? They damn near dislocated my shoulder. And I hadn't *done* anything. I keep telling you, Collins, you don't need the rough stuff." He eased sore muscles as best he could without reaching up to rub them.

"I'll be the judge of what's needed, McKee," Collins snapped. "And I don't need advice from a madman. Sit down on that bed, nice and slow."

Logan noticed a slight tremor in the colonel's hands. The man's face was tense, the muscles along jaw and neck knotted too tightly. It came as a shock like winter ice that Collins was terrified and trying not to show it.

Terrified? Of *him*?

Somehow, he didn't get that impression. His glance flicked back to the silent civilian.

Bingo.

Logan caught and held the civilian's gaze. "Tell your whipping boy, there, to call off the dogs, will you? Even if I made a break, I wouldn't likely get far. Besides, it's too damn cold outside to try it."

The man's eyes widened almost imperceptibly. Then

narrowed again. Collins' hands began to tremble visibly. The colonel swore and took an angry step forward. The civilian, however, gave Logan a tight little smile, showing perfect white teeth. They reminded Logan of a vampire's fangs. The smile did not touch his eyes. Before the colonel could move forward more than one pace, the man in the silk suit placed a restraining hand on his arm.

"Colonel Collins"—yep, that accent confirmed Logan's guess—"I believe our . . . guest . . . has made a valid point. And he is most perceptive." That was delivered softly, sounding almost like a threat.

Logan studied the glacial eyes and was sure it had been. In the terse silence that followed, Logan was intensely aware of a turbulent internal struggle taking place in the colonel's mind. Collins' face showed signs of prolonged strain. His eyes were a mute testament to some kind of waking nightmare. Logan realized too late that Collins was on the ragged edge of shooting him out of hand.

His rash behavior might well have gotten him killed. Given Collins' white-knuckled grip on his Beretta, it still might. Gradually that grip eased, however, and some of the terrible strain left the man's face. The barrel of the pistol didn't waver, but the crisis had passed. Belatedly Logan resumed breathing.

Whatever was rotten in Denmark—and for all he knew, he was *in* Denmark—it smelled to Logan like death. *His*, to be specific. *But why?*

The MP closest to Logan's feet began to groan, moving toward consciousness.

With a bravado he wasn't even close to feeling, Logan sat down on his bed, stretched his legs in front of him and crossed his ankles, leaned back with his hands behind his head—fingers interlaced—and said, "Shall we chat, then?"

Collins looked shocked.

The silk-suited Hispanic just chuckled. A chill crawled up Logan's spine from the cold wall.

"Indeed, Captain McKee," he said, "let us chat. Colonel Collins." His voice turned cold. McKee saw Collins barely control a flinch. "Get these fools out of here. I will call for you when I'm through."

Collins yelled down the corridor. "Kominsky! Get an ambulance over here, stat! Two men with multiple injuries, broken bones! Tell 'em I want that ambulance here yesterday!"

Nobody spoke or moved into the long, ensuing silence. Eventually the ambulance crew arrived with two gurneys. Each semiconscious, battered MP was lifted on a gurney, strapped down, and wheeled away.

"Collins." Silk suit and Rolex barely glanced Collins' way. "Get out. And keep a *very* tight mouth about all of this."

Once again, Logan's guess had hit right on the money. He didn't want to know what the prize might be, but had a sinking feeling he'd find out all too soon. Whatever was going on, the base commander was definitely not in command of the base. And he obviously knew that fact all too well. Question was, who *was* the nameless Hispanic, and what was *his* game? Collins threw Logan a murderous glance, then stalked out and slammed the cell door shut.

Which left Logan alone with the Hispanic. Unconsciously, Logan straightened his spine. All trace of humor had vanished from the Hispanic's expression.

"Now, Captain McKee," he said softly, "I have a few questions for you."

"Ask away. My answers may not make sense." He forced a grin. "They did tell you I'm crazy as a rabid raccoon, didn't they?"

His interrogator's response came back as dry as the Ethiopian desert. "Colonel Collins did mention the fact, yes. Your files were, shall we say, entertaining reading? Tell me something, McKee. What were you, exactly, during those missing years after Vietnam?"

"Well-l-l, I was lots of things. In lots of places. Anything in particular?"

The man's eyes glinted briefly. "Indulge yourself. Anything at all, I am sure, will prove to be quite interesting."

Logan expelled air through his teeth. "Okay. Ever been to Australia? They've got birds down there you wouldn't believe. Black parrots and other amazing winged thingies. People all over the world crazy to own 'em. Hell, I made enough money smuggling birds to buy a whole closet full of suits like yours."

"Go on." The man inclined his head slightly in acknowledgment of the compliment.

"Then there was Ethiopia. Did you know they've been fighting a nice, bloody little civil war in Ethiopia? Least they used to be." The man's expression shifted almost imperceptibly. Logan snorted. "Thought you might know something about that. *Are* they still fighting that little brushfire?"

The brief flicker of a smile across the man's face told him very little. Damn . . . His nameless interrogator asked mildly, "You were there in what capacity?"

"Supplier. To the rebels," he added, probably unnecessarily. The commie government had gotten plenty of aid from Mother Bear. "The rebels are a nice bunch of guys. Pretty ruthless, of course, but what would you expect? They've even got women in the ranks, did you know that? Some of them real pretty, too." He shrugged. "The rebels let 'em fight and don't treat 'em like some man's private property. I might have married Marifa if she hadn't—" He stopped abruptly.

"You do not like to remember Ethiopia." It wasn't a question.

Logan stared at a spot on the floor which reminded him of a squashed cockroach. "Nobody likes to remember a war," he growled.

"Ah. Then you were . . . captured?"

Now who was perceptive? "Yeah. I was captured." He wouldn't give the stranger the satisfaction of seeing him shiver, but he couldn't help the rigid clenching of his muscles from jawline to toes. "I caught some artillery frags during a big government offensive." He shrugged in feigned nonchalance. "When I came to, there were government troops crawling all over us. I was questioned. The interrogators who did the job learned their techniques from Soviet advisors."

He snorted and kept his gaze on the floor. "Needle-happy bastards, and real good at their job. When they got what they wanted, the Ethiopian commander ordered me shot. The guerrillas counterattacked before they could carry out the order and I got rescued. End of story."

End of Marifa, too. . . .

The Hispanic pursed his lips. "I see. And then?"

"I went home. Lived on the streets, mostly. Money was gone, health wasn't so good anymore, and," he shrugged again, "there just wasn't a lot of demand for my kind of skills in the States."

"Surely a man with your . . . connections could have found work suitable to your credentials?"

Logan eyed his interrogator suspiciously. Was the guy a lousy FBI agent? "Tell you what, Mister Silk Suit and Rolex watch. You spend twenty years getting shot, blown up, and tortured, then come talk to me again. I hurt, man, all the frigging time. Let the kids sell crack on the street corners or run guns to Nicaragua if that's what gets their rocks off. You find me a job where I can put my skills to use without some effin' black-eyed fourteen-year-old trying to shove a bayonet through my ribs, and maybe I'll talk to you."

"Ah, security is what you seek, then?"

Logan shut his eyes. "You tell me, mister. I'm crazy, remember? How should I know what I want?"

A brief silence fell between them.

"Captain McKee?"

"Yeah?" He didn't bother to open his eyes.

"Describe for me, please, the thunderstorm."

Logan blinked. Then stared. "You're serious?"

The Hispanic didn't bother to answer. His expression was closed, patient. He reminded Logan of an alligator waiting for a fish to swim just that little bit closer. . . .

Logan told him. In detail. Twice. (The second time prompted by a barrage of questions which made no sense at all.) When he finished, the man muttered something in Spanish. Then he nodded sharply to himself and banged a fist against the door to get the guard's attention. The door swung obediently open to reveal Collins who wore a sullen, bruised expression.

"Captain McKee." His still-nameless interrogator's voice sent involuntary chills up Logan's spine. "I regret it, but you will not see me again. I have enjoyed our little chat."

He turned and strode out, ignoring Collins completely. The cell door swung shut. The sound of the lock clicking into place echoed in Logan's ears.

The chirp of crickets and the lonely sound of a nightingale in the garden were among the first sounds to greet him, well before the first hint of grey had touched the sky. The dawn smelled wet. Maybe it would rain. Charlie was tempted to pull his too-thin blanket over his head and worm his way back to sleep. He hadn't gotten much rest last night.

Xanthus' personal astrologer had advised him to give a lavish farewell banquet for his friends before setting out on the sea journey that would take him to Bericus' country villa. Accordingly, the household had been up until nearly 2:00 A.M. as calculated by Xanthus' water clock. Afterward, Charlie and other household slaves had worked another two hours cleaning up the considerable mess, without the benefit of their own suppers until the work was finished.

Charlie, slow of foot and trembling with hunger and exhaustion, had been carrying a pail of refuse through the house to dump into the river when he stumbled and fell—as luck would have it, almost directly in the household steward's path. Lucius had slipped and fallen in it—and taken out his rage by ordering that Charlie be given no supper. No amount of pleading—he *needed* that meal—had done any good. And their Master had been in bed two hours already.

From the steward's judgment, Charlie had no appeal.

So he finished his chores in a fog of exhaustion and hunger, trying to sneak bites from the refuse being thrown out, but was so closely watched by other slaves, he didn't have the chance to sneak much.

When Charlie finally dragged his sleeping cot out, he accidentally set it up near Achivus'. The secretary was busy screwing one of the slave girls. *She* had an unfortunate tendency to shriek during orgasm, which she did repeatedly.

Clearly, Achivus was a good lay.

Charlie, too exhausted to get up and move his cot someplace else, simply dragged the blanket over his head and spent what little remained of the night hating both of them. He had no more than dozed off when the household steward's voice rumbled through the predawn blackness over the sound of crickets and nightingale song, ordering the household slaves out of bed.

Charlie groaned in the predawn cool and swung around to sit up. *There's gotta be a faster way out of this. There's just gotta be.* Sure there was. And money really did grow on trees. Charlie groped for a flint and pyrite and tried to find the lamp he'd blown out last night. He managed to light the wick on the third try.

I'm actually getting better at this. About the only preparation Charlie'd had for his current life was the movies. And no movie he'd ever watched had bothered to show some poor slave trying to light a wick with flint and pyrite. Charlie groped for his crutch. *Everything* ached. His back still burned with each pull of half-healed skin. Charlie didn't want to drag on a dirty tunic over his injuries, but he owned only one garment. If he asked Mistress for another, *she* would order a beating, for insolence as well as for giving her more work to do.

He desperately needed a bath and his sole—now

ripped—tunic needed laundering worse than he did. He wasn't likely to accomplish either chore today. Not with Xanthus leaving by the second hour for Ostia. Maybe the astrologer would give him bad omens for a voyage and he'd postpone leaving?

Well, maybe infection wouldn't set in between now and the time he could scrub himself and his tunic clean. He settled the grubby garment gingerly over his shoulders and shrugged it cautiously into position. At least he wasn't allergic to wool.

Charlie could already hear sounds from the kitchen, despite the early hour. Xanthus had ordered breakfast—leftovers from the previous night's banquet—by first light. For once, Charlie wasn't the only slave in the household getting out of bed seriously sleep-deprived.

Charlie's stomach screamed for nourishment. His belly felt glued to his backbone. He'd rarely been *this* hungry. Xanthus fed his slaves two meals a day. Yesterday's thin breakfast of watered gruel seemed a long, long time ago. Charlie told his stomach to be patient. He wouldn't be able to check his snares until after the *phaseli* had left the dock.

Provided, of course, he remained behind. His gut tightened painfully, driving away hunger and leaving only nausea. Whether or not he, too, would make the trip, Charlie had no idea. If Bericus had decided, Xanthus hadn't bothered to inform him. Of course, keeping him in the dark was probably a smart move on Xanthus' part. If Bericus *had* bought him, not even a mangled leg would prevent Charlie from bolting.

Charlie muttered under his breath, then picked up the lamp and carried it with him for a brief stop at the newly repaired privy. From there, he headed into the kitchen. Chores were waiting and the sun waited for no slave, tired or not. The cook bellowed at him to fetch wood and be quick on his feet.

He ignored the jab and made his halting way to the woodpile. He had to move without the crutch in order to carry a useful amount, which was a dangerously tricky proposition. His balance was far better than it had been even six months ago. He'd worked hard at that, doing calisthenics after the slaves were dismissed from their chores for the night, even when he was too tired to eat. Xanthus had forbidden him to manufacture even a crude leg brace for himself, hoping to keep Charlie helpless enough to turn him into a properly loyal, devoted slave.

A kind word would have gone a whole lot further.

Five trips to the woodpile later, the cook was marginally satisfied. Faint pink light had begun to touch the eastern sky. What was it his grandfather had said, a lifetime ago? *Red sky in morning, sailors take warning . . . ?*

Charlie shied away from the images in his memory. For too many years, whenever Charlie had thought of his grandfather, he had no longer seen the seamed, laughing face of childhood bedtime stories and kites built and mended together. He saw instead the shock of pain and betrayal, the terrible, pumping bloodstains against dirty city snow. . . .

Charlie straightened his back against the pull of barely healed scabs and closed his hand around the crutch as though it were a javelin. *Someday, you bastard, someday I'll get my hands on you. And when I do, Jésus Carreras, you'd better pray you kill me first.*

"Rufus!"

The cook, bellowing for help with some other chore.

Maybe, if Charlie were very lucky, Xanthus' ship would go down at sea. Then he flushed, realizing Aelia would be struck down by any disaster that befell Xanthus on the Mediterranean. *Okay, scratch that wish. Maybe he'll get sunk by a storm on the way back.*

Charlie limped into the kitchen. "Yeah?"

The cook scowled at him. "Feed the stock!" The inevitable bucket of gruel and figs waited. "You're late. Loafing as usual. I'd tell Master, except you'd be even slower after he beat you. I'm far enough behind as it is, waiting for you. Get moving, cripple."

"Fuck you," Charlie growled in English.

"Move it! I've told you, none of that barbarian filth!" The cook waved a sharp knife threateningly.

Charlie repeated the crude curse under his breath and loaded the little pushcart with bowls and spoons. Then he hoisted the heavy bucket and started his rounds. As soon as he was safely out of sight from the kitchen, he used the cover of darkness to bolt down several brimming mouthfuls of hot gruel. Charlie scalded his tongue, but felt better within minutes of downing the stolen meal. Of course, he needed about ten times that amount to really be caught up. . . .

Deeper in the house, Xanthus bellowed at some hapless body servant. A cry of pain floated to him. Nearer at hand, the *pedagogus* assigned to Xanthus' sons chided them to wake up and be on their way to school.

Huh. Another morning in paradise. Charlie woke up the first of his charges. By the time he'd worked his way down the portico to Aelia's cell, Charlie could make out the garden fountain by sight as well as sound. The nightingale had fallen silent, leaving Charlie alone with the crickets, the gruel, and the *slap-scrape* of his bare feet against the tile.

Sextus—as usual—was missing from his duty post. Where the hell that man had slipped off to, this time of morning . . . Charlie glanced around the garden, but saw no trace of the eunuch. He hoped Xanthus caught him on the way back from wherever he'd gone. It was about time Sextus' back started looking like Charlie's. More than once, Charlie had caught punishment for something that was Sextus' fault.

He glared at the closed door to Aelia's cell. Did he dare risk feeding her? Xanthus might swoop down at any moment to check on her condition. On the other hand, it wasn't fair to let her starve just because Sextus, the lazy sod, was not there to chaperon.

He lifted the bar and pushed the door gingerly open. It creaked softly on iron hinges. Silvery-pink dawn light flooded the room. She lay tucked on her side, with her hands buried under dark curls. An odd sensation touched his gut. Vulnerable didn't begin to describe the way she looked, huddled there with last night's supper on the floor, hardly touched.

Her cries of pain yesterday had caused an ache to tighten through his chest. He didn't know why, really. He'd heard worse screams from Xanthus' slaves. Maybe it was just that she was so lost, without any memory, even. The ache returned, now, as he gazed at her. Bericus wouldn't have raped her yet, not until the deal was finalized. But physical examinations could be brutal enough and Bericus was not the kind of man to be gentle with *anyone*. Given the bruises visible on her wrists, they'd held her down for it.

He wished bitterly for just one moment with a Colt .45 Government Model and Bericus balanced over the sights.

Charlie had no more than finished the thought than Aelia's eyelids fluttered. The odd sensation in his gut left him gripping the doorframe and swallowing far too hard. She focused her gaze, then lifted it. The smile that touched her lips made him go hot all over.

"Good morning," she said a little huskily.

He found himself unable to speak. To hide his embarrassment, Charlie dipped up her breakfast and hobbled into the room. She took one look into the bowl and pulled a face.

"I'd rather not, thank you."

He nudged the bowl on the floor with his crutch and ignored roaches that ran across his bare toes. Aelia shuddered.

"You need to eat," he managed to say fairly steadily.

"Sure. Give me some food and I will."

Charlie found himself smiling. "If you think this is terrible, try it without the figs."

"Is that a threat?" She spooned up a mouthful. From the deliberate way she chewed, she'd rather have eaten rat poison. "How did you get used to this stuff?"

Charlie stared at the wall. "I get mine without, Aelia. When I get any at all."

She swallowed. "Oh." Then she held out the bowl. "Want mine?"

Charlie surprised himself with a rusty chuckle, then paused to wonder how long it had been since he'd laughed. "No, thank you. I'll wander down to the riverbank later, after Xanthus is gone, and check my snares."

A look of utter horror crept into her eyes. "What in God's name do you set snares for down there? *Rats?*"

He shrugged, grimaced, nodded. Aelia went a shade more green than white. She set the bowl aside.

"I'll . . . finish later."

Charlie bent awkwardly. He shook straggling roaches off the remains of her supper and stood up again. "Don't wait too long. Master means to leave within the hour."

"I . . . see." She looked like a little girl, ready to cry, but she didn't quite break. The set of her jaw tightened in a way Charlie had come to recognize in himself. He hated seeing it in her.

Impulse led Charlie to foolhardiness. He hesitated, then touched her cheek. She glanced up, eyes startled. Then she tried to smile.

"Thank you. I—I'll finish it." She picked up the bowl again, took a determined bite, chewed, swallowed. "You'd better go," she said in a near whisper. "They beat you once already because of me. I—I don't want them to do that again."

Her concern—Charlie decided it was *not* pity—touched him.

"I wish—" He halted. "I wish you good fortune, Aelia." He didn't add, *You're gonna need it.*

A shadow darkened the doorway. "Well, now. How cosy."

Charlie spun around and nearly went to the floor, only saving himself from a nasty fall by dropping the bowl of cold gruel and using both hands on the crutch. He caught his breath, terrified of looking up, knowing he had to, anyway.

Xanthus.

Stormclouds had already built in his dark eyes.

"So," Xanthus glanced at Aelia, "was that little caress a farewell to a new lover? *Did you climb onto her belly and plant your seed?*"

Charlie's face went cold. "No, Domine, I swear it—"

A hard hand slapped his face hard enough to split a lip. Charlie stumbled off balance, but retained his footing.

Xanthus glanced at Aelia. "Wanton little slut. Your taste in men is common as a street whore's."

She paled, whether from anger, insult, or fear, Charlie couldn't tell.

"As for you, Rufus, you have disobeyed me once too often."

Charlie expected to be beaten within an inch of his life. Instead, Xanthus did far worse. And the first thing he did was force Charlie at swordpoint to drug Aelia for the trip.

CHAPTER SIX

Xanthus didn't beat him.

He put Charlie in the special chains the gladiatorial school had needed to forge to fit his greater-sized ankles, wrists, and height. While another slave carried Aelia, Xanthus hauled Charlie out to the *phaseli*. Which could mean only one thing. Charlie struggled just once, then dazedly allowed Xanthus to drag him down the marble steps and across the dock.

"Maybe," Xanthus panted, shoving Charlie into the bottom of the boat, "Bericus *will* pay enough for your worthless ass to cover all you've cost me."

Achivus, carrying the inevitable case of important papers, bit his lips silently. Charlie, chained to an iron ring on the gunwale, glared at nothing and said nothing. He was light-headed and short of breath from simple terror.

Charlie refused—desperately—to think about Bericus or the last time he'd visited the Roman's country house. Given half a chance, he vowed he'd jump overboard and swim for it. Drowning with rusted iron locked around ankles and wrists beat . . . *that*. He shut his eyes as the yacht shoved away from shore. *I will survive this. I will. Carreras, I swear to God . . .*

The trip downriver passed in a queasy blur. Empty as his belly was, Charlie should have been ravenous. All he felt was a deep, cold nausea. Achivus sat under the awning at Xanthus' feet. His master, fanned by a young boy to keep him cool, sipped wine and played dice—a game to which the Lycian Roman was utterly addicted.

111

As near as Charlie could figure, it was semi-religious. Romans at the games were mad on the subject: gambling, odds, fate, risking—and cheating—death, the whole schmeer.

While his master tossed the dice again and again, Charlie sweltered in the hot sun. He'd cheerfully have slit Xanthus' throat just for a drink of the blood. Thirst crippled him, left him weak and hopeless against the side of the yacht.

A structure that could only have been the Claudian harbor he'd heard slaves gossiping about slipped into view, with the slowly dying city of Ostia visible a couple of miles away across densely silted marshlands. And beyond Ostia, bright sunlight winked off wavelets in the Mediterranean. Charlie, sweltering in the bottom of the yacht, felt woozy every time he tried to adjust his position. *Too little protein, too little sleep, too little of everything.* He sagged back against the gunwale and waited.

The low-slung yacht swung about smartly and headed for the massive harbor where two curving breakwaters had been constructed across the entrance. Between the two breakwaters, Roman engineers had built an artificial island. A tall, four-story lighthouse rose toward the bright sky, essential for nighttime dockings or arrivals in dense fog, as every ship had to pass that artificial island safely.

Charlie wasn't certain in his blurred state of mind whether the walls of the artificial basin were stone or concrete, but the piers themselves were solid stone. He wondered dully how they'd hauled some of those blocks into place. Slaves swarmed across the massive docks, hauling heavy cargo bales, loading and unloading sturdy ships. Furled sails hung limp, like dead birds in the hot light. The stink of the river, of human refuse, of malarial salt marsh filled his lungs.

Great place to die in. . . .

Beyond the two-mile stretch of marsh, Charlie could see the old port city of Ostia, still alive and struggling with its much-reduced commerce.

In the distance, at the city he'd heard gossiping slaves call Ostia, he could make out single- and double-story villas, three- and four-story apartments, and a few taller structures that looked like public buildings. They stretched away from the water front in disordered confusion, their baked-clay tiles rusty in the harsh summer sun.

The town reminded Charlie of Eastern Mediterranean cities he'd seen on the six o'clock news: dirty, sprawling, and crowded. Its only saving grace was a lack of TV antennas, battered cars, and power lines.

As Rome's once-primary port city, Ostia left Charlie vastly unimpressed. The Mediterranean beyond, at least, fulfilled his expectations. Charlie had discovered, after the move from New Jersey to Miami, that he liked the sea. Unlike the Atlantic off Miami, which was often slate grey or odd, dark shades of green, the Mediterranean off Ostia *did* look like a postcard of paradise. He shifted his weight and grunted softly against pain throughout his whole body.

Trouble was, paradise had too many rats in it.

Just like Miami.

Xanthus' yacht grounded against a solid stone pier. Sailors made lines fast and jumped ashore. Xanthus and Achivus disembarked, followed by a sailor who carried Aelia. She slept in drugged oblivion. Poor kid. He'd whispered, "I'm sorry," before forcing the drug down her. He didn't think he'd ever forget the look in her eyes.

Other sailors unloaded luggage and hauled it aboard the nearest *naves oneraria*, a sturdy, seagoing merchantman. It was a small ship, compared to some at the dock. A single bank of oars bristled along her sides, sticking straight out, parallel to the water. A striped sail in cheerful red and bleached white completely failed to lighten Charlie's spirits. He glared at the little ship and thought black thoughts.

Someone eventually remembered the cripple had been chained to the deck. A sailor with foul breath and rotted teeth unlocked him and stepped back. Charlie groped for his crutch and struggled to his feet. The world swung unsteadily, but he managed to keep his balance. Getting off the *phaseli*, however, proved impossible. The first step he took, Charlie lurched. He went to one knee, then caught himself awkwardly with chained hands. He heard a snicker. Charlie ignored it and tried to regain his feet.

After the second nasty fall, Xanthus shouted, "Get that cripple up here! Now!"

The sailor grunted and hauled Charlie onto the pier, then half carried him aboard Xanthus' ship. He then dumped Charlie unceremoniously at their master's feet. The crutch clattered to the deck beside his ear.

"Get up," Xanthus growled.

Charlie braced himself and tried. He was still too light-headed. "I cannot," he said in a low voice, desperately afraid of Xanthus' temper. "I have not eaten since—"

"Crawl, then. Get below with the rest of the cargo. Achivus, make sure he finds the hold."

Wordlessly the secretary hoisted Charlie to his feet and supported him across the deck. A square hatch led into the belly of the ship. A ladder of sorts descended into the gloom, less substantial than stairs, more sturdy than an ordinary wooden ladder. The stench wafting upward was worse than the stench on Charlie's skin.

"Phew . . ." Achivus wrinkled his nose. Then, very quietly, "I'm so sorry this has happened. I did try to warn you, Rufus. I really did. And I'm sorry you're too stubborn to listen. Or learn."

Achivus was, as always, completely incomprehensible.

At the moment, Charlie didn't care. He moved cautiously down. He managed to gain the bottom without quite falling. The chains hampered him badly. His crutch caught sideways in the hatch. Achivus tossed it down, then left him to his fate. A sailor slid down the ladder and took a place at one of the rowing benches.

Charlie was so exhausted he half slid, half fell to the rough wood, then just sat where he'd fallen. He spent long moments fighting for breath and trying not to tremble. Memory battered the backs of his eyelids, fanged and cruel. *Why'd I do it? Why'd I come down here? Without even fighting?* The answer was almost too much: *Because I need to stay alive.*

When he finally did look up, the sight jolted him.

Every Easter after his grandfather's death, he'd made it a tradition to watch *Ben Hur* on his VCR—just so he wouldn't forget. Charlie had bought copies of both versions, Charlton Heston's and the 1920's silent film. He watched them every Easter season, usually more than once. Angie Fitzsimmons—the latest ditz in a whole series of bad relationships—had complained he liked movies better than her.

Yeah, well, movies don't bitch at you to take them sailing or buy them fancy dinners. Leaving out the sex, Chuck Heston had frankly proven more entertaining.

The little he'd known about Romans had come from those two films and an occasional rerun of *Spartacus* or *The Last Days of Pompeii.* Hollywood Romans didn't bear much resemblance to the real thing. He'd long ago made himself a promise that if he ever got back, he'd track down the Hollywood geniuses who made "historical" films and set them straight on a point or twenty.

But the inside of this ship almost matched Hollywood. Almost.

Chuck Heston's galley had supported three ranks of rowers. Here, there were only two ranks per side, rigged to form a single rank outside the ship. The movie rowers had relied solely on a time-keeper to stay synchronized. Here, Charlie found rigid bars of wood connecting the oars. *Must be to keep 'em from tangling oars with their neighbors.* A wooden sounding box, much battered from use, and two heavy mauls could have come straight from the movie set.

The rowers nearest the center aisle sat on "benches" the thickness of telephone poles. The second rank sort of knelt, half standing and half crouched, at a higher elevation on their own "benches." Charlie estimated a hundred rowers; he pursed his lips in a silent whistle.

Galley slaves must be cheaper than he'd thought. But then, convicts generally *were* dirt cheap.

Looking at the heavy oars, Charlie shivered. A man didn't need *two* functional legs to row a Roman ship. Charlie knew he was lucky—damned lucky—he hadn't ended in the belly of a ship, dying slowly. Then he thought of Bericus again and wondered if maybe he wasn't so lucky, after all.

No point sweating about it now. Save your strength and try to stay alive, Flynn. . . .

"Get moving, cripple!" An overseer stood near the stern, fingering the frayed tip of a knotted cat-'o-nine-tails. "Get to your place!"

Charlie eyed the rowing benches with deep misgiving.

Did Xanthus expect him to row? He could hardly keep his feet. And the gentle motion of the ship at anchor left his inner ears dancing a rhumba. Xanthus hadn't specifically ordered him to do any rowing. All he'd said was, "Get below with the rest of the cargo." So Charlie looked for it.

Wet wood and dirty seawater smells blended with a locker-room reek of sweat and the filthier stink of human excrement. The benches took up most of the hold's width. The *hortator*'s platform in the stern was surrounded by huge amphorae, sealed shut and labelled in scrawled Latin script. Charlie couldn't actually read Latin, but he could detect the faint scent of wine above the stench permeating the hold.

There wasn't room for him in the stern.

More rowers coming down the ladder shoved him impatiently aside.

"Get out of the way, cripple!"

"Lazy, useless fool! Move!"

"Get up in the bow, where you belong!"

All right, already . . .

Charlie struggled to his feet and stood swaying for several moments, bracing himself with his crutch and with one hand against the nearest wooden support. Then, dragging in a deep breath, he hobbled awkwardly down the narrow center aisle. Dizziness and the shackles around his ankles threatened to topple him. Maneuvering awkwardly around heavy oar handles, he headed for the prow.

The most difficult part was negotiating the support beams which ran from the upper deck to the "floor." The space between the rowing benches and the thick beams was cramped. Chains ran through iron rings the length of the central aisle. In the movies, rowers were chained in preparation for battle so they couldn't bolt their posts at a crucial moment.

Did Xanthus chain his rowers? Maybe to prevent them bolting if the ship were attacked by pirates? A glance at the rowers' ankles confirmed it. They wore ankle shackles, with rings for cross-tie chains. *Helluva way to die, chained to a sinking ship.* Charlie shivered, aware that if the ship went down, he'd be among those who drowned. He already *had* chains around his ankles.

He finally gained the front of the cramped hold. A tiny cubicle had been built into the bow. *Wonder what's in there?* Couldn't be room for much more than a few stacked crates—or a single cot. A clumsy-looking, box-type lock held the door closed, but there were ventilation holes cut into the walls. Maybe Aelia was in there. Or was she up on deck, with Xanthus?

Wherever she was, clearly Charlie couldn't take refuge in a locked cubicle. He found a bundle shoved up against the curving side of the ship and prodded it with his crutch. It proved to be a spare sail, folded and stored out of the way. He collapsed onto it. Rough sailcloth scratched bare legs and arms, but it was considerably softer than the wooden planks that formed the ship's lower decking.

Charlie closed his eyes. His inner ears persisted in doing spins and he was thirsty enough to kill. Daydreams of icy lemonade, of foaming, cold draft beer, tantalized him. Charlie heard someone overhead shouting to hoist anchor. A few moments later, a loud boom brought him straight upright.

Under motion, with the *hortator* beating time and the rowers straining at their benches, reality came damned close to Hollywood. The heavily muscled *hortator* pounded time, while the sailors overhead bellowed to one another. The ship began to creak and roll. The rattle of the sail going up reached his ears above the rhythmic groan and slap of oars in their oarlocks.

A loud bang and an abrupt darkening of the hold marked someone on deck closing the hatch. Little squares of light fell through the open grillwork and caught the glint of sweat on rowers' shoulders and chests. The overseer began chaining their ankles. Charlie watched long enough to determine that nobody planned to chain *him* any further, then lay back down.

No one offered to feed him or give him water. That didn't really surprise him. With a little luck, Charlie would be dead of thirst before Xanthus had a chance to finalize the upcoming sale. Charlie clenched both fists to accompaniment of rattling chains at his wrists. *I should be so lucky*. He wondered, with acid burning his belly, what he would have to endure before Bericus killed him.

Aelia never quite lost consciousness, but disorientation and a deadly lethargy she couldn't fight kept her paralyzed for an unknown length of time. She received impressions of rolling motion, the cries of seabirds, sounds and smells that reminded her dimly of summer days spent watching shrimp trawlers unload their haul. . . .

She wondered hazily what a shrimp trawler might be. That only brought on the pain and nausea, so she let the image go again. Gradually, a booming sound that punctuated the darkness every few breaths reached through the disorientation. Whatever it was, it brought her more fully aware of her surroundings. Even then, long moments passed before she identified her whereabouts. *Ship* . . .

Memory returned, then, cuttingly. Rufus had drugged her. She turned her head on a soft surface. She lay on a down-filled featherbed that nearly filled the cubicle into which she'd been placed. She closed her hands until her fingers hurt. She couldn't blame Rufus. Not really. He'd tried to apologize, while Xanthus stood over him, enormous knife in hand . . .

They'd dragged him away afterward and locked her into her cubicle again. She distinctly recalled poking a finger down her throat, but she hadn't been able to throw up enough of the drug. She wondered what Xanthus had done to Rufus.

She tried sitting up. She could see, after a fashion. Dim light poked like dirty soda straws through a series of small holes cut into her prison walls. For a moment, Aelia frowned, trying to grasp the image in her mind. . . . But it was gone. As always. And the pain in her head threatened again.

She swore softly and explored her prison, instead. Her fingertips encountered smooth-planed wood on all sides, the bottom third lined with some kind of feather-stuffed bolster to keep the occupant from falling against wood, so long as said occupant remained sitting or lying flat on the featherbed. There was no blanket, but that was all right—the heat in here was stifling.

A dim crack revealed the location of a narrow door. Further exploration led her fingertips to the metal fasteners of some sort of locking device. *All right. I'm locked in. No surprise, there. Now what?* In the closeness of her prison, she could smell her own rank sweat. She stank of fear and helplessness. Aelia leaned against the nearest wall and tried to breathe fresher air through one of the holes.

The stench *beyond* her prison was worse. She coughed and sagged against the cushioned bolsters. At least they hadn't tied her. They doubtless counted on the drug, the locked door, and the sea itself to keep her secure. *You're not going anywhere, kid. That's clear enough.* She rubbed her bare arm absently and bit her lower lip. How long before *he* took possession of her? Aelia shuddered. There had to be some way to escape. There *had* to be!

Bericus' brief "examination" had been humiliating and somewhat painful. What rape would feel like, with Bericus grunting and sweating over her . . .

Aelia dragged her thoughts away from the upcoming ordeal. She tried to peer out through the one of the holes in the wall, instead, to get an idea of where in the ship she was. She focused gradually on an oddly surreal sight. At some deep level of herself, she was certain she'd never seen anything quite like this, outside of illustrations. Sweating men sat in a long row that stretched away into the gloom. They groaned over long-handled oars to the booming rhythm of a drum she couldn't quite see. That explained the odd, rolling noise she'd heard on waking. They were propelling the ship, with someone beating time.

She peered through a different ventilation hole on the other side, expecting to see the same view—and froze in shock. A scarred, red-haired man lay curled up on a bundle of cloth, right outside her cell. He'd been chained hand and foot . . .

Rufus!

She hadn't realized she'd said it aloud until he stirred and glanced around.

"Wha—?"

Her tongue glued itself to the roof of her mouth. For a long, terrible moment, she was afraid she would burst into tears. She bit down hard on her lower lip to prevent it. Then she swallowed and whispered, "Rufus! It's me! Aelia."

He stared at her prison wall, then presented his back. Her eyes burned. He was afraid to talk with her. She closed her fists. *Well, it is your fault he's here.* If he hadn't been caught in her cell, attempting to show her a little parting kindness, Xanthus would never have had a reason to punish him. Rufus' presence could mean only one thing. She shut her eyes, overcome by horror. Rufus must hate her desperately.

She heard him swear under his breath, then, astonishingly, he scooted closer to the hole where she crouched. Without quite turning his face to look at her, he murmured, "I thought you might be on deck, with Xanthus."

She could just make out his face. He didn't *look* angry. That didn't seem possible. "Oh, Rufus, I'm so sorry . . ."

"For what?" He swung around to stare.

She started to cry and silently raged at herself for it. Somehow, she received the deep-seated impression she *hated* snively women. He must have heard her, because scarred fingertips poked through the hole to touch her cheek.

"Haaeee, doaant . . ."

The words weren't Latin, but they made strange sense. She frowned, trying desperately to think *why* they should, but it was too late. Whatever had briefly slipped out from beneath the darkness in her mind, it was gone now.

"I'm not crying," she lied.

He actually smiled. The motion crinkled the corners of his eyes and tugged on the hideous burn scar. "Good."

"Rufus, I—" She halted, trying to find the right words. "If there's any way I can help . . ."

The smile vanished. Skin along his temples tightened. "That wouldn't be very wise."

"I'm not afraid to escape. First chance I get. I mean that."

His eyes flashed in the dim light. Then he turned his face away, deliberately baring his scarred throat. "Aelia, that's what they do to slaves who run away. *If* they're lucky. Lots of poor bastards they kill as an example to the others." He paused. "The brand was supposed to be on my face. I lunged aside at the last instant or it would've been."

"I don't care." Her voice came out low and hard. "I'd rather die, than be raped again and again."

His breath caught. Anger flushed his face. He turned away and swore.

"Don't be stupid. What you're saying is plain crazy. Slaves don't escape their Roman masters, Aelia. Not for long. Too many available patrols and citizens on the watch for runaways. Wouldn't ever work. Just get me killed and . . . and God knows *what* he'd do to you. Just . . . just forget it, please."

"So you're just giving up?"

Eyes flashed like burning emeralds in the dim light. *"I've been through what they do to runaways!"* He visibly grabbed hold of his temper. "You're so damned delicate, it'd kill you. So just shut up about escape, would you?"

Aelia compressed her lips. *All right. I'll drop it for now. But not forever, Rufus Mancus. Nowhere nearly forever.*

Charlie was whispering again, head averted. "And . . . and I don't want them to . . . I don't want to watch them hurt you, the way they hurt me, knowing there's nothing I can do to stop them. Besides, there are other reasons I *can't* run."

How long had he been a slave, enduring this?

"What reasons?" she asked quietly.

He was silent so long, she didn't think he would speak again. Then, finally: "There's . . ." He had to stop. His throat moved sharply. "There's more to it than that. A whole lot more."

His face was ashen, his gaze determinedly avoiding hers. She studied him for a long time. She *knew* he was no coward. Not stupid enough to fight a hopeless fight, but no coward, either. Maybe he was afraid of spoiling *her* chances by coming along? No, he'd called her stupid for even thinking it and she supposed he knew a great deal more about it than she did. Aelia finally asked, very softly, "What is it, Rufus? What else is there?"

"If I run . . ." Again, the long pause, the hard swallow. "Bericus has my daughter."

Oh, God . . .

He was speaking again, bitterly. "Before I was crippled, I was a 'great' Circus champion. Curses on 'em all. . . . Popular as winged Mercury himself, for a while. Xanthus . . . he and Bericus had this idea they would . . ." Rufus looked away. "They wanted to breed me and sell my sons for huge profits."

It was so simple. And explained so much. She didn't know why she hadn't seen it sooner.

"I didn't catch on quite fast enough," he was saying. "When I tried to refuse . . ."

"Yes," she whispered, voice choked down by horror. "Oh, Rufus . . ."

"Don't. Please."

A man's pride'll make him push you away when he needs you most. Never let on, if you pity him. . . . She didn't have a face to match the half-remembered voice, but knew the unknown woman was important to her. Important and very, very wise. Again, an overwhelming sense of loss crushed her spirits.

Outside her cell, Rufus was turning away, closing her out of his own private hell. She had to draw him back before it was too late. "You're afraid he'll kill her if you run?" She managed that in an almost normal whisper.

He nodded mutely. Then, driving pain straight through her heart, he muttered, "He's already had six of the children he forced me to sire exposed to die. Deformed," he choked out. "Lead poisoning, I think. Most of 'em . . . most of 'em were born months too early, anyway."

There wasn't a single thing Aelia could say in answer to that. He seemed to understand her shaken silence.

She finally found her voice, although she scarcely recognized it. "Rufus? How . . . how old is she? Your little girl?"

"Lucania?" His already scarred features twisted in pain. "Not even a year old yet. She was the first one born."

Four years since he's been enslaved, then.

Rufus managed to choke out. "He's threatening to sell Lucania. Just to watch my face when she goes. He—"

Rufus halted. Aelia thought she knew why. Bericus was a *monster.* But she had no answers to give him. With her entire past a great, black void, there was nothing she could even *think* to say.

Without looking at Aelia through the ventilation hole, Rufus growled (voice deadly), "I think I'd almost rather kill her myself than watch what Bericus is capable of doing to her."

Aelia shivered. She didn't know what would drive a man to that kind of desperation—and was terrified Bericus was going to educate her, all too quickly.

The chains at his wrists clanked faintly. He glanced up, trying to catch her eye through the air hole. "You must realize, not only can I not save her, I can't possibly stop him from raping you. Or even me," he added bitterly, "if he decides that would whet his appetite."

Somehow, the idea of Rufus being held down and buggered was worse, even, than the thought that Bericus would rape *her*. She wanted to hurt Bericus, badly, for what he planned to do to her; what she'd do if he raped Rufus, she didn't know. Slip some poison into his cup, maybe. Slavery, Aelia was rapidly discovering, led to an ugly sort of pragmatism. She closed her hands and longed for a weapon, then frowned.

An image had come into her mind of a long, narrow shape propped in a bedroom corner, next to a wooden rack over which colorful quilts had been draped. *Grandmother's room.* . . . Her fingers twitched, wanting the rifle. . . .

Then the memory was gone. Only a throbbing headache lingered in its wake. She groaned aloud and scrubbed at her brow with the heels of both hands. "I've *got* to remember!"

Outside her cell, Rufus swung around unexpectedly. "I must go," he whispered. "Xanthus is yelling for me."

The strain in his voice came through despite the thick wooden panels separating them.

"Rufus—"

He paused without looking in her direction.

"Be careful."

He lifted his head a fraction, indicating agreement, then levered himself awkwardly to his feet and hobbled beyond her line of sight. The chains at his ankles rattled above the low groans of rowers and creak of oars in ungreased oarlocks. She sagged back against the wall and shut her eyes.

Please, don't let that bastard hurt him again. . . .

Whatever Xanthus had in store for Rufus, it would be mild compared with what *Bericus* would do to him. She thumped a fist against the planks and did some swearing of her own.

Somehow, they would survive this.

They *had* to. Rufus' fear was understandable, but Aelia would never give up on the hope of escape—for both of them. And neither could escape without help from the other. She would bide her time as long as she must.

But she was going to get out of this.

And Rufus and his kid were coming with her, whether they liked it or not.

Francisco's dissatisfaction came to a boil after watching Dan interrogate their intruder. The whole affair disturbed him, particularly Dan's order to drug McKee—and his insistence on finishing the interrogation alone. Francisco had trusted Dan Collins for a lot of years—ever since that rainy night in high school ROTC, multiple years and a seeming lifetime ago, when Dan had saved Francisco from drowning during a flash flood. He'd been more than pleased when their careers had brought them together again, after years spent in different parts of the world.

Francisco had never disobeyed a commander's orders. And Dan Collins was an extremely able commanding officer. *Had* been, anyway, during their first several months up here. But during the last three or four months, Francisco had grown more and more uneasy. The McKee affair brought home just how sharply Dan had changed. The Dan Collins he'd known would never have chained a man to a chair and tortured him.

All day it had gnawed at him, during his entire duty shift, afterward at the officer's club, where he found faces he didn't know and missed others that should have been there. Some of those new faces had dark, watchful eyes. He'd found himself wanting to glance over his shoulder, as though a two-way mirror had been slipped in without his noticing it. Francisco had left early, aware that the officers he *did* know were also subdued, not quite themselves, prone to fits of silence and uneasy glances at the strangers.

The whole day left a taste like skunk oil in his mouth. He didn't want more mysteries. He wanted answers. So, after staring at the dark ceiling in his quarters for about six hours, Francisco gave up. He got dressed and drove back to his office to start finding them. He started by pulling medical records on base personnel. The first thing he discovered was a discrepancy in the number of personnel supposedly assigned to the base. According to payroll records—he checked those by computer, to be sure—there were 527 people stationed here.

He had medical records for only 359. Who were the others? And why didn't he have files on them? A hundred sixty-eight discrepancies? That was more than a few too many to explain away by clerical error.

Then there was the very odd matter of several officers who had failed to report back to duty after weekend leaves. Wilkie and Gugliano had been killed in traffic accidents. Under ordinary circumstances, that wouldn't have aroused his suspicions. But two hit-and-runs in an area with a human population density lower than that of bald eagles . . . They'd occurred less than a month apart, too. That had started more sinister alarms ringing in the back of Francisco's head.

Another young officer, Jack Tozer, had supposedly rotated out to Korea. Again, nothing untoward in that simple fact. Except Francisco still had Tozer's medical records. That had merited further checking into. He'd searched everywhere, but had discovered no trace of a request to transfer them. He'd been so busy with a rash of illnesses and injuries, he hadn't found time, before, to find that odd.

He did now.

Francisco leaned back in his chair and frowned at Lieutenant Tozer's medical history, then dug through the piles until he found the phone book. St. Louis, where officers' records were kept, should be able to confirm Tozer's transfer and let him know where to forward the records.

When he dialed to send out a fax request, Francisco got a recording. "All circuits are busy. Please hang up and try your call again later. If you need assistance . . ."

Thoughtfully, he cradled the receiver and leaned back once more in his chair. It creaked slightly, gunshot loud in the stillness of early morning. Who could be tying up all the circuits at this hour? Francisco checked his watch. It was barely 5:00 A.M. He tried an intrabase call, dialing at random. It went through without difficulty.

"Gate Three."

"Just checking my phone. Thanks." He hung up without bothering to identify himself, then muttered half aloud, "Odd. And I'm tired of things around here being odd."

Francisco tapped Tozer's file with one dissatisfied fingertip, then set the file aside and considered Dan's file. The chair creaked again. He frowned at the innocuous sheaf of papers which represented Dan Collins' medical history since ROTC. There wasn't much in it. Dan was healthier than most horses. Francisco crossed his arms and pursed his lips, trying to puzzle through this. He'd stood up as Dan's best man when the lucky stiff had finally convinced Lucille to marry him. He'd managed to wrangle leave when their son, Danny, Jr., had been born.

Their kid was . . . what? Fifteen, now? The years had passed so quickly, he'd hardly noticed. A smile played at the edges of his lips as he recalled his arrival at the base. Lucille had remembered his passion for schnitzel. Danny's astonishing growth had called for a complete reevaluation of how he'd spent his own life during the past fifteen years. Maybe it *was* time to put down some roots, start a family. He'd found himself deeply envious of Dan's quiet happiness.

Then, four months ago, Dan had simply stopped talking to him.

In the ensuing weeks, his commanding officer had made a heroic effort to behave normally, but the quiet evenings spent chewing over politics and plans for the future had come to an abrupt end. And Dan's warm, comfortable way with others had turned cold as ice. New arrivals Francisco treated at the "fridge" referred to him as Old Man Winter.

Having been on the receiving end of Dan's inexplicable new personality a few times, himself, Francisco couldn't blame them.

Lucille and Danny had supposedly fled to Juneau for the winter. He hadn't seen them since Labor Day weekend, at the base picnic. Francisco sucked air soundlessly across his teeth and narrowed his eyes. Labor Day weekend. . . . The trouble had started shortly afterward. Danny and Lucille hadn't even told Francisco good-bye. When he'd said as much, expressing hurt and concern, Dan had nearly taken his head off.

And now Dan was losing weight, avoiding him, and— judging by the smell—drinking pretty heavily.

Was Lucille having an affair? Was *Dan*? Or maybe Danny, Jr., was in some sort of trouble or seriously ill. . . . He couldn't credit that; if he were, Francisco would have been the *first* person Dan and Lucille would have consulted. Drugs, maybe? Up *here*?

Yeah. Right. He'd as soon believe Frosty the Snowman wintered in Miami to catch a glowing tan.

When Francisco tried to call Juneau, he got the same recorded message.

"That's nuts," he muttered. "Who the hell lives up here to tie up all the circuits? Nobody for miles but the caribou and grizzlies. And the bears are asleep."

He picked up a pen and tapped it absently against the desk. All right. What else? He glanced surreptitiously toward a featureless wall, in the direction of the ugly, squat building at the far edge of the base. Francisco had no idea what went on inside that building. He didn't have the security clearance to know. He'd never crossed the threshold, never mind taken a gander at what was inside. All he knew was, a pack of civilian physicists with security clearance far higher than *his* had been holed up in there for months.

They'd arrived shortly after Francisco had, many of them with families. Francisco frowned. What about *them*? He hadn't seen some of them in weeks. That was *more* than odd; it was downright unsettling. He decided to check his file on Sue Firelli, out of curiosity. She'd come to him complaining of stomach pains. He'd diagnosed ulcers and put her on Tagamet and had been seeing her every couple of weeks since. But he hadn't seen her in a while and her prescription ought to have run out by now. He wanted to check the file, see what the date of her last visit was. But he couldn't find it.

Where in blazes was her file?

He double-checked the cabinet, then the scattered stacks and waterfalls of paper, but it was gone.

Francisco closed a lateral file drawer thoughtfully. He hesitated to go to Dan with his concerns. He shrank even further from talking to base Security. Francisco didn't like Kominsky. And most of the men he'd seen working Security details were strangers. The longer he thought about them, the more his back crawled. Those Security "officers" could well be some of the hundred sixty-eight people for whom he had no military medical records.

Who the hell *were* those hundred sixty-eight men? More to the point, did Dan Collins know who they were? And why—given the fact they were literally in the middle of nowhere, up here—why did Dan Collins have a twenty-four hour personal guard? Francisco hadn't missed the unpleasant little interplay between Dan and his bodyguard in the interrogation room, waiting for McKee.

Despite Francisco's bone-weariness, he paced the narrow floor restively. He liked to walk when he was puzzling out things and it was far too cold to walk outside. The sounds drifting in from the infirmary ward were completely normal. The night nurse was talking to the duty physician about Kruger's recovery. The familiar smells of antiseptic and illness soothed the sense of not-quite-rightness he couldn't shake.

He knew how to deal with patients recovering from emergency surgery. Francisco didn't have the faintest idea what to do about his questions or the genuine worries that had begun to plague him.

And what about that intruder, McKee? Francisco muttered under his breath. The man was clearly insane. Babbling about time travel and lightning strikes . . .

But Dan's reaction . . .

Dan Collins had taken Logan McKee very seriously, indeed. Nor could Francisco explain away the very disturbing questions Logan McKee represented. How had he gotten onto the base in the condition in which they'd found him? His story made no sense, but neither did the facts.

Time travel?

Absurd.

But Francisco had been watching Dan's face when McKee had suggested it. For just an instant, panic had utterly stricken his old friend. Francisco swore under his breath again. He would have given a great deal to know just what Dan had asked McKee after they were alone.

"Well, there's one way to find out. Isn't there? Just march in and *ask* him." He wasn't thinking about Dan. He needed to check McKee's hands and feet, anyway, to be sure no complications had set in from the frostbite.

Francisco abandoned the stacked files and put together a medical bag, then headed across base. As chief medical officer, not even Kominsky could deny Francisco access to the prisoner. One way or another, Francisco was getting to the bottom of this mess. As he stepped out into murderous cold, he had a sinking feeling no one else on base *wanted* him to get to the bottom of it.

And that frightened him.

He ducked his head against the wind. Wonderful. He'd signed on as surgeon, not hero. His idea of national defense service was stitching up the hides of the *real* soldiers, the ones who got themselves shot in the line of duty, not solving mysteries that piled up like freeway accidents. Life, Francisco Valdez reflected sourly, was seldom fair.

CHAPTER SEVEN

To Charlie's vast surprise, Xanthus was actually kind to him. As kind as he'd been since Charlie's initial purchase. He even allowed Charlie to crawl up the ladder onto the deck, where the clean scent of fresh air revived him at once.

"You're no value dead," the trader muttered. "Here. Drink all the water you want."

He handed Charlie a waterskin.

Charlie slaked his thirst frantically. He closed his eyes, lost in the ecstasy of life-giving fluid soaking into parched tissues. He would have given anything to drain the whole water bag, but Xanthus said, "Share the rest with Aelia."

Reluctantly he lowered the waterskin. "Thank you, Master," he whispered.

Xanthus' lips twitched. "Still trying to avoid the sale, eh? Should have thought of that before you took liberties with another man's virgin slave."

"Master, I didn't do *anything* to her—"

"Don't lie to me again, boy. I *saw* the look on your face—and hers." He scowled, then let it go with a dramatic sigh. "I suppose I'd better feed you. Bericus will want you reasonably healthy. I suspect he'll find ways of getting the healthy brats he wants out of you. I've been too lax with you, I suppose. Adflicta tells me I'm much too soft to try what would really work."

Charlie shivered. He didn't even want to *think* about what Bericus might try to turn his children from lead-poisoned, pitiful little things into healthy, strong sons to be sold to the Imperial gladiatorial school. Most

Roman medical treatments quacked like a whole flock of ducks.

Xanthus sighed, seeming almost human in that moment. "If only you would submit to my orders . . ."

His doom already sealed, Charlie saw no sense in pulling his punches. "I might have, if you'd been charitable with kind words now and then. But you had to be tough, beating me into submission. Would you want *your* sons put through what you've put *me* through these past two years?"

Xanthus' eyes flashed, then a slow glint of respect appeared. "No. But I'm a patrician of an old family. You're a slave. Does my horse care if I geld its foal? What concern is it of yours what I do with my property? Mithras' pity, most slaves could care less what happens to their brats. They sleep with whatever woman they can get to open their legs and enjoy life where they can." Xanthus' brows twitched down. "But then, you always were an odd one. Even in the arena. I'm tempted . . ."

Charlie waited, wondering what his master was considering.

"No." Xanthus sighed. "Bericus tried that and you put a gash in his chin trying to kill him."

Charlie shuddered involuntarily, remembering.

"I'll let *him* deal with you. And with your incorrigible temper. Too bad. I couldn't feel more disappointed if one of my own sons had failed me. Achivus!"

"Master?"

"Give him enough food for himself and that girl of Caelerus'. Rufus, feed yourself and Aelia, too, when she wakes up." He tossed Charlie a heavy iron key, which he caught awkwardly.

Charlie considered only for a few seconds leaping overboard and trying to swim for it. He *might* make it to shore. But that would leave Aelia trapped below and Lucania trapped with Bericus. So he crawled meekly back into the hold as ordered. One of the sailors handed down a bucket of gruel, two bowls, and two spoons. Then, astonishing him, the sailor tossed down a limp wineskin and a couple of rough-hewn wooden cups.

"Maybe if she's drunk," Xanthus muttered, "we won't need as much of the drug. Can't have her fighting Bericus again. . . ."

Charlie had to make two trips and nearly went down several times as the ship rolled through the swells. The motion compounded the light-headedness that swept through him every few moments. What wine would do on an empty stomach . . . It'd been four years since he'd tasted *anything* alcoholic. Wine ought to taste wonderful. And if he couldn't avoid being sold to Bericus, alcohol might deaden nerve endings enough to endure his first night.

He set everything down beside the locked door, then fished out the key Xanthus had given him. Iron grated rustily, then the lock gave and came open in his hand. He swung open the door. When it threatened to slam shut again, he braced it with his crutch.

Aelia had flattened herself into one corner, a she-wolf at bay. Her gaze came up, focused on him . . .

Tension drained visibly from her body.

"What's up?" she asked.

The phrasing, so un-Latin-like, reminded Charlie painfully of home. A brief supposition crossed his mind, but he dismissed it immediately. That would be stretching odds just a little too far.

"Xanthus told me to feed you when you woke up."

She looked hopeful. "Is it edible?"

He grinned. "Edible as the last meal I brought you."

"Faugh . . ."

"But there's wine." He couldn't help sounding smug.

"Wine? Great heavens, has Xanthus discovered a sense of mercy?"

"No," he answered honestly. "He thought if you're drunk, he might not need as much of the drug next time. Just what *did* you do to Bericus?"

She slipped past him into the hold, then pulled a face

at the stench. "I hit him in the balls," she said crudely. The flash in her eyes betrayed intense satisfaction.

Charlie just groaned. "Dear God, Aelia. He'll *kill* you on your first night with him."

"Oh, no." She shook her head emphatically—in the manner of Americans, not Latin fashion. Just where *was* Aelia from? "He was quite lurid about what he was going to do to me." She set her jaw. "I'll survive it. Then I'll escape. If necessary, I'll kill him first." Her lips tightened. "Even a clay lamp is a weapon, if you use it correctly. Come to think of it, if one of us set the house on fire, we might be able to slip away in the confusion."

Something, some quality of quiet ruthlessness in her tone and her eyes, spoke to Charlie in a way he'd never before experienced. The women he'd known as a teenager had been hard as old leather; they, like he, had known what it was to fight and claw for survival, had known it from early childhood.

He'd have bet money Aelia didn't. There were too many things about her that said, *Nice kid, sheltered from a lot of life's ugliness.* Yet there she stood, on her way to an unspeakable future, having made a decision to survive and grimly outlining one possible plan of attack. Despite her probable protected upbringing, in her determination she reminded Charlie of . . . himself.

He realized quite suddenly Aelia was probably not nearly as young a child he'd first thought. His initial guess of fifteen could be a couple of years short, at least. Charlie narrowed his eyes, recalling the sight of her body when he'd bathed her, that first morning she was ill. He'd thought she was simply a well-developed fifteen-year-old. Hell, he'd *busted* thirteen-year-old whores who'd looked at least twenty. Just how old—or young—*was* Aelia?

He wanted to know a great deal more about her. Who she was, really; where she'd come from. Why everything about her seemed oddly familiar, when he knew he'd never laid eyes on her in his life. In part, that was the cop in him. Wanting to ferret out the facts. But also part of it, Charlie realized, was that her determined attitude (now that it wasn't filtered through the drugs) somehow made him feel less alone.

To not be alone . . . Against his will, Charlie found himself wishing for impossible things—that he could keep her out of Bericus' clutches, that he could have the *time* to solve her mysteries. Then he shook his head, banishing the false mirages. He could deal with only one thing, if he were to survive: what passed for real life in this place.

Quite simply, Aelia's determination must be based on illusion. Charlie could tell Aelia still didn't *understand* what Bericus was capable of doing to her. Charlie knew one thing very well. If she fought him, he'd hurt her. Maybe even kill her.

"I'm starving," she said, breaking off the agony in his mind. She gestured toward the gruel bucket. "I suppose we might as well make do."

He nodded a little distractedly and allowed the cubicle door to bang shut while he fumbled with his crutch. She'd sat down virtually at his feet and had begun dishing up gruel. Light filtering down from the open hatch caught the play of highlights in her dark hair.

Charlie eased carefully past her, taking extreme caution not to touch her at all for fear of frightening her more than she must already be, then sat down on the spare sail again. He poured wine for both of them. Sweating rowers nearby eyed them with cold hatred.

Then Aelia handed him a bowl of gruel and he handed back a cup of unwatered wine. Her hands were trembling just the tiniest bit.

"Rufus?"

It took him a moment to remember his Latin "name." "Yeah?"

He found her peering worriedly at him. "You— Are you ill?"

"Just a little light-headed," he said, truthfully enough. "I haven't eaten since yesterday. At dawn."

A tiny worry frown creased her brow. "You had better eat, then, before Xanthus interrupts us."

Charlie nodded, touched by the kid's concern.

When she lifted the wine to her lips, Charlie said quickly, "Careful, it isn't watered."

She halted in midair, causing the wine in her cup to slosh. A dark frown created vertical lines between her brows. "Watered wine," she said softly. "Watered wine. Where have I heard that?"

The moment passed, too quickly. She scowled and muttered under her breath, then downed most of it in a gulp. "Gah . . ."

A moment later, she held the cup out. "More, please."

He met her gaze. "Are you sure?"

Her stern eyes reflected both her pain and her struggle. "Maybe if I'm drunk enough to deaden those headaches, I'll remember something important."

Wordlessly, Charlie refilled her cup. For her sake, he hoped so. Her amnesia and the crippling attacks of pain whenever she tried to remember still bothered him deeply. If she remained in this condition . . .

Well, her first night with Bericus was going to be brutal, no matter what condition she was in. He wasn't sure whether to admire her bravery or give in to despair. Her innocent ignorance would soon be as dead and gone as the dinosaurs, leaving . . . what? He still remembered, far too vividly, what Bericus had done to *him* for daring to strike the Roman.

Thoughts of Publius Bericus still had the power to turn his stomach. And Charlie Flynn had seen a lot of stomach-churning sights. Even before he'd been dumped here to die.

His helplessness clawed at him.

Charlie downed a cupful of strong wine and refilled it, then poured again for Aelia. Her hair curled softly around her face like a cloud of black silk. Her skin was too pale, although when he'd bathed her that first day he'd noticed tan lines, almost like those left by a bikini. Mysterious kid. She had a wistful, lost look to her face.

He finally placed in his mind who she looked like. He had to smile at his own foolishness.

Aelia reminded him of a dark-haired Shirley Temple. Half grown up, innocent. And since Caelerus claimed she was virgin . . . he wondered if she felt as desperately lonely, as hopelessly lost as he did.

"Rufus? What's wrong?"

Charlie roused himself with difficulty. "I'm sorry. Just a little—never mind. What is it?"

She was biting her lower lip. "You told me . . . what to expect."

He steeled himself.

"I heard Xanthus and Caelerus and *Him* talking, planning to take me to *His villa rustica* by ship. But no one said *where His* house is."

Charlie relaxed. He'd been sure she was going to bring up yet another painful, impossible subject. "You probably won't recognize the name," he said with as reassuring a smile as he could manage. "Not even if you had your memory back. The house is about two hours from a little resort town on the coast, south of Neapolis. Wealthy men retire there for the sun and sailing. I've been there once."

Her brow had furrowed again. "Resort town south of Neapolis . . . What's the name of this town?" She sounded as though it were very important. He wondered why, then shrugged. Who knew?

"Place is called Herculaneum."

Her whole body went rigid. Her eyes widened, then narrowed savagely.

"Herculaneum . . . I *know* that name. I—"

Visible pain hit her like a kick from an angry horse. Her skin turned dirty grey, the color of big-city snow. Then the screams started. He grabbed her around the waist as she toppled. Her arm tangled in his chains as she groped for her temples. Whatever was wrong, it was worse this time. Much, much worse. He didn't know what to do. Aelia felt like iron under his hands. Her cries tore at him, left him panicky in a way he hadn't felt since that snowy afternoon he'd come home from school and found his mother as cold as the unheated apartment, needles and candles and a deep-bowled spoon lying accusingly silent on the nightstand, and hideous white powder spilt everywhere—

Xanthus' fist came out of nowhere. It smashed into the side of his head and sent him reeling backwards. Charlie sprawled against the rough plank hull. His ears rang. His eyes smarted. Blood filled his mouth from cuts in cheek and lip. His angry oath got lost in the salty flood. Charlie coiled instinctively to fight back—then ruthlessly held himself still. He was already chained, already condemned to sale to a human beast. Charlie was aware with a harsh clarity what would happen to him if he dared vent his rage now, if he dared smash his fists into the man's mouth and nose—

"What did you do to her, you crippled *dog*?" Xanthus' fist caught him again. "Answer me!"

Aelia continued to scream and Charlie's heart again lurched in fear. He shook his head slowly. His eye was already swelling shut. "Nothing! Please, Master, nothing, she got sick again . . ."

The unalloyed fear in Charlie (for Aelia) must have allowed, for once, Charlie's submissive attitude to ring true to his master, for, to Charlie's amazement, no further blows followed.

"Conniving trader sold us a lousy epileptic whore—"

Through his one good eye, Charlie could see the near-panic on Xanthus' face. This one sale must be more important to the man than the mere sale of a slave had any right to be. Charlie wondered what political dealings were behind the panic . . . or was it something to do with Aelia herself?

The ship plowed bow-first into a deep wave, catching Charlie off balance. He fell roughly against the planked hull of the ship, scraping bare skin, then lay still, warily watching his master.

"Get up!" Xanthus kicked him.

He couldn't quite suppress a cry of pain. Charlie

hauled himself slowly up off the rough planks. He swayed, then got himself awkwardly up onto his knees and caught his balance with manacled hands against the hull. The ship's motion was such, he couldn't get up the rest of the way.

"Now, Rufus Mancus," Xanthus hissed, twisting a hand through Charlie's hair, "get this girl cleaned up! Then drug her again. I don't want to risk her pitching a falling-down fit in front of Bericus!"

"But, Master, it's the drug that—"

The Lycian Roman slapped him hard. More blood spurted from his split lips. "Defy my orders again and you won't live to see yourself sold! Do you understand me, you crippled cur?"

"Yes, Master," he whispered, hating himself, hating Xanthus more.

Xanthus shoved him backwards. He was unable to catch himself from falling flat on his back because of the manacles. For a moment, all he could do was lie still and try to breathe against pain. Charlie lay very still until Xanthus had climbed back up to the main deck. When he finally let his breath out, it whistled explosively into the silence. He winced. Then lifted chained wrists to touch his mouth and wipe away blood with the back of his hands.

Charlie finally looked over at Aelia. She lay with her back to him, huddled down between the spare sail and the cubicle wall. She'd wrapped both arms around her head. Aelia apparently hadn't moved since he'd dropped her. Charlie cursed Xanthus under his breath and crawled closer.

She was weeping. But Aelia was also muttering softly to herself between shaky, watery breaths, in a language that sounded strange to his ears. He leaned over to listen more closely—

"—just don't get it, my God, how did he *do* it, this is crazy, nobody's got *time travel* . . ."

Charlie forgot about the bruises, forgot about the blood on his face, forgot his swollen eye. He even forgot to breathe.

She was speaking English.

With a Deep South accent he'd heard before, from native "crackers" who called home "North Florida, USA."

"Uh," he said, intelligently.

She rolled quickly and glared up at him.

"Omigod!" She bolted upright. One hand came up, as a horror-stricken expression darkened her eyes. She touched the swelling along the side of his face. He winced back from her fingers.

"What happ—" She broke off abruptly. Then blurted, "Oh, dear God . . ." Something in his eyes must have clued her that she wasn't speaking Latin, because she swallowed and said in that language, "Xanthus beat you because of me. Didn't he?" She touched his bleeding mouth. Fresh tears welled up in anguished green eyes. "I'm so sorry. . . ."

Charlie had to look away. He couldn't talk for a moment. No one, not even his mother, had ever cried over him.

"Yeah," Charlie said heavily, aware that he was taking a gamble he might not be able to afford. He didn't care. English felt as strange on his tongue as it sounded in his ears. The only times he'd used English over the past four years was to curse without being understood— and therefore punished. He used more, gauging her reaction. "The bastard gets a real kick out of it."

For a long moment, she didn't register it. When she did, her eyes widened. Her lips parted over soundless air.

"And my name's not Rufus Mancus," he added bitterly. "It took me a while to figure out what the name Xanthus had given me meant. I . . . had a different name before that one." Red the Cripple. How *appropriate*.

She blinked a couple of times, but still said nothing. The color of her eyes had deepened to the shade of the Emerald City. Charlie suspected from the curious depths in them that her mind was racing well ahead of her expression. When she finally did manage to say something, it wasn't at all what Charlie expected to hear.

"It's not the *theft*, it's the *anachronism*! Of course he

had to get rid of me. One way or another—" Before Charlie could comment on that, she looked directly into his eyes. A steel-hard core had sprung into existence. "Obviously someone thought you were dangerous," she said, with a chill like New Jersey snow. "Or you wouldn't be here. Care to tell me what happened?"

Charlie managed a laugh, a grating, harsh sound. A delicate shudder rippled through her. "That's a good question, lady. They drugged me. Last thing I remember was Carreras' laughing face." He watched narrowly for any hint of recognition, but saw none. He added, harshly, "I woke up . . . here. In chains. You already know the rest."

"Carreras? Who's Carreras?"

Despite the sudden rush of wanting to share everything, Charlie just couldn't risk it. Not yet. Not until he knew exactly who she was and why *she* was here.

Charlie shook his head. "We'll get to Carreras later." He winced and wished for a piece of raw steak, or an ice cube. Or an aspirin. "I, uh, take it your memory came back?"

She shuddered. "Yeah. Nearly threw up, it hurt so bad. It was, uh, hearing the name Herculaneum did it."

"Oh?"

She sat up and rubbed her nose with the back of one hand, like a kid would. "I . . . I spent some highly interesting time there recently. You know, this is beginning to make sense, in a bizarre sort of fashion. I'd only been back in Florida for a week. And after—" She didn't elaborate. Instead, she chewed a thumbnail and said, "I was driving down a dirt road on my way to campus. There was a thunderstorm. Nothing unusual about that, it was late afternoon, summer."

Charlie snorted knowingly. "Yeah."

She looked up, her eyes hooded. "Oh? You've spent time in Florida? You sound more like New York."

The native Floridian's deep-seated distrust of Yankees—particularly "Goddamn Yankees" who came to *stay*—colored that dour observation.

"New Jersey," he corrected unhappily, aware that the distinction probably wouldn't improve his standing in her eyes. "And yeah, you might say I've spent some time in Florida. Go on."

She hesitated. Charlie waited.

"I . . . drove through a hole in the air. Lightning was shooting out of it. I tried to back up, but something went wrong with the car. I lurched forward, instead, right into it. I have really distorted memories of what happened next." Her eyes narrowed as she concentrated. "I remember Bartlett"—her voice took on a vicious edge when she said the name—"and someone else I'd never seen before. I think they must have hypnotized me, maybe under the influence of drugs. I seem to recall needles. . . ."

Christ, which branch of the Carreras family had she gotten mixed up with? And why?

Charlie nodded grudgingly. Her guess made sense with her symptoms. "Drug-enhanced posthypnotic suggestion might account for the memory block and pain."

But again, *why?* He knew only too well why *he'd* been marooned here. Charlie tugged at the chains on his wrists and thought about the relationship he was probably killing with every word he uttered, then said it, anyway. "And? None of what you've said tells me why you were so dangerous they hadda dump you here."

Her expression darkened into a scowl. "Neither have you."

Fair was fair. . . . But he wasn't ready to trust her that completely just yet. An agony of indecision kept him silent.

She glared at him, like a wolverine ready to spit tenpenny nails and rip out chunks of flesh with claws and teeth; then she looked away, a hint of too-bright liquid in her eyes. When she spoke, her voice shook. "Oh, hell. Why not? All we've got's each other."

Great. Make me feel worse than I already do.

But she'd started to talk. "Tony Bartlett tried to frame me for something he did. Something he stole." Her eyes glittered, angry, hard-cut emeralds. "No one suspected him or believed me, not at first. But Professor Clarke convinced the Italian authorities I couldn't possibly have had the connections to fence something like that. Dr. Clarke can be pretty persuasive and he speaks fluent Italian."

"Good thing for you."

She really did resemble a furious wolverine with her back up. "Too right," she growled. "He was the only person who stood up for me. Everybody else just tossed me to the wolves."

Charlie wouldn't have wanted to be the wolf on the receiving end of that wolverine glare. Then she shook her head and the glare faded into an expression slightly less lethal.

"Anyway, there were other inconsistencies in the whole setup, once the police started looking for other suspects. Things like Bartlett's nonexistent background. And that anachronism in the grid sector where Bartlett and I found the stuff he stole. The lowlife creep tried to convince everyone it was *my* mistake, that I'd somehow contaminated the site, cast doubt on the genuine antiquity of what we'd just unearthed."

Slim jaw muscles had clenched. Her eyes flashed again. "Bartlett and I had quite a fight. It was one reason the police were willing to believe I was guilty, at first. I had this supposed motive . . ."

Then she glanced up at him and actually blushed. She looked mortified that she'd had to air such sordid laundry. Did she actually care that much whether or not he believed her? *She's young and scared, idiot. Of course she'd care that much.*

He forced himself to scrutinize her story as dispassionately as he'd once taken apart the testimony of eyewitnesses after a crime.

Either her story was true—it was disjointed and bizarre enough to be—or she was a consummate actress. Charlie was inclined to trust his instincts. God alone knew, he'd had a bellyful of making snap character judgments over the years. She simply did not strike Charlie as the type who would steal. Or lie.

"Anachronism?" Charlie finally asked. "You said something about an anachronism? And what kind of 'grid sector'? What are you talking about?"

She looked blank for a moment. "The grid sector of our dig, of course. What else would it be?"

Well, that was clear as the muddy Tiber.

"Dig?" Charlie prompted.

"Archaeological dig," she said, as if that explained everything.

"Oh. Great." Archaeology had never been one of his interests, not even a minor one. Images of Indiana Jones raiding King Tut's tomb and unearthing glittering golden urns came to mind.

"I'm a grad student," she added helpfully. "Physical Anthropology and Classics, with a specialty in early Imperial Rome. That's why I speak classical Latin. I was," and her voice turned bitter again, "only a semester away from a Ph.D."

He grunted, hardly having heard the last statement. He didn't want to admit the sense of inadequacy her fluency in his "adopted" language had given him. "All right. So this Bartlett was implicated, but not apprehended?"

"He vanished into thin air. And from the looks of things, maybe literally."

Charlie nodded. There had to be a tie-in to Carreras, somewhere. "So, putting aside for a moment the technical how-to's of this, you think he marooned you here because you spotted something which gave him away, or at least something he thought gave him away?"

She leaned against the wall of the cubicle and sighed. "We were in the process of uncovering a sizeable wooden box we found in one of the beachfront grid squares. It was very well preserved. But while we were clearing it, I came across some things that shouldn't have been there. First, there was a problem with the soil. The box was covered with a different kind of soil from the rest of the site."

"Different soil? What are you talking about?"

"It looked like someone had dug a hole and mounded up dirt over the box to protect it, *before* the tufa was laid down. I might not have twigged so sharply to that, though, if I hadn't found the real anachronism." She frowned and squinted, as if looking at something by inadequate light. "It was a coin, a modern coin. He tried to grab it before I could see too clearly what it was. We got into a terrific shouting match. He accused me of trying to contaminate the site and invalidate the find. I yelled right back, said I was a professional, how dare he—"

She halted abruptly.

"It was pretty ugly," she said finally, rubbing the back of her neck. "At the time, I thought maybe the entire grid square had been compromised, but physically the site hadn't been disturbed. You could *tell* it hadn't, just by looking. You've got to chop through that tufa. There's no way anyone could have hidden signs of that kind of digging."

She turned her gaze away and stared at the ship's hull, while kneading her fingers as though they ached. Shafts of slivered light, falling from the barred hatch farther astern, caught the play of tension in her face.

"Anyway, after I was arrested, I decided he'd planted the coin somehow during the excavation, maybe to throw suspicion on me, give him a reason to stage a fight. It was obvious to me who'd stolen the artifacts. He must have planned to use me as a scapegoat all along."

"Probably. Sounds like a setup job from the start."

She nodded, clearly unhappy with herself. Charlie wanted to tell her it wasn't her fault, that obviously she'd tangled with a pro, but he wasn't sure it would do any good.

"At any rate," she sighed, "the artifacts were gone. And shortly after my release, so was Tony Bartlett. No trace, no nothing." She lifted her hands, palms up. "Just . . . *poof*. Gone. It was almost like he'd never existed. The Italians allowed me to come home," her lip curled, "but the university kicked me out of the degree program. Because of the scandal. Then I drove my car through a hole in the air." She shivered. "Obviously, Bartlett thought I knew too much, because of that stupid coin. It wasn't enough he had to ruin my entire career—"

"How was Bartlett connected with your dig, exactly?" He ignored the look of curiosity she gave him.

"He provided the financing." She glanced down into her lap and rubbed her fingers again. "Bartlett endowed the university with a research grant, specified which researchers were to be included, even insisted he accompany us on the dig." She shrugged. "It was a substantial grant. We get money from lots of weird sources. Dr. Clarke didn't imagine Bartlett could do anything to hurt the dig."

Her laughter was as hard as the unyielding wood they sat on. "Isn't that funny? Those manuscripts were priceless, probably worth millions on the black market, absolutely irreplaceable. That hurts almost more than anything else. Lost plays by Euripides, some of Plato's missing work, Julius Caesar's *Oedipus* and some of his poetry. They weren't even charred, the way the scrolls from the Villa of the Papyri were, because they'd already been buried. The most beautifully preserved ancient manuscripts ever found—and I didn't even get to *read* them."

Her eyes had filled with tears again. Charlie shook his head. *Good grief.*

"Sorry," she muttered. She attempted to wipe her cheeks dry. Then held out a hand still wet with tear trails. "I'm Sibyl Johnson, from Newberry, Florida. Well, close enough. Maybe ten miles outside town limits."

Charlie grinned. It must be nice to have such permanence. Apartment living was for the birds. "Charlie Flynn, Ms. Johnson. From Jersey City. Lately from Miami."

The chains at his wrists clanked as they shook hands formally. Hers trembled ever so slightly in his grip. She looked so calm. Charlie knew the stress signs and feared it wouldn't take much more to break her. A brief silence held while Charlie tried to figure out what to say next. She solved his problem.

"Are we really headed for Herculaneum?" That came out sounding little-girl scared. He got the strangest impression she wasn't thinking of Publius Bericus at all.

"Yeah. Should be there in a few hours."

Her face, which had gradually regained some of its former color, paled rapidly, leaving her waxy-pale. "Do you, uh, happen to know . . . What year is this? By our calendar?"

"Are you kidding? What *year* is it? The only thing I knew about Romans before I got dumped here was what I saw on videos of *Ben Hur* and *Spartacus*." He decided to take the risk. "I'm a cop, lady, not a history professor. I got no idea what year it is."

"A cop?" She rocked back and her eyes went round. She actually squeaked when she said it. "You're a *cop*?"

Charlie squirmed. He'd been undercover—*deep* undercover—for months when he'd stumbled onto something Carreras didn't want anyone to know. Not even Carreras knew he'd been a cop. He was two thousand years away from having his cover blown, but was still uncomfortable about admitting it to a stranger. Even one who'd been through everything Sibyl Johnson had been through.

"Yeah," he muttered, trying to ease the fire in his shoulders. "A cop. Miami vice."

"You're kidding?"

When he looked, her green eyes were sparkling. They reminded him of sunlight on the sea. He found himself responding to that look. A grin tugged rustily at the edges of his mouth. "Well, no. I'm not kidding, I mean. I'm no Don Johnson, but I really am an honest-to-god detective in the vice squad, Miami Metro Dade. I can't show you a badge. I don't carry one when I'm that deep undercover—too risky—and even if I had been carrying one, well . . . I didn't exactly get to keep my former wardrobe." He indicated the stained loincloth he wore.

"Carreras—uh, that's Jésus Carreras, head of the Miami branch of the Carreras family—was the key figure in a stolen-arms case I was working on. Crack, smack, horses, dogs, prostitution, numbers, porno films for *lots* of kinky markets, gun running, you name it. They were into it. The trouble was *proving* it. Carreras runs one slick outfit."

The laughter had drained from her face. "I'm sorry. He found out you were a police officer?"

"No . . ."

To gain time while he figured out how much to say, Charlie refilled their wine cups. Sibyl—he had trouble thinking of her as Sibyl, rather than Aelia, even though the name fit her better—drained hers even more quickly than he gulped his.

"No," Charlie muttered after he'd finished the cupful. "And that's the weird thing. Carreras still thought I was a middle-man for a New York buyer. That's my specialty, posing as a buyer down from the City. We were ready to deal, when I stumbled across something he didn't want anyone to know about. Not even a two-million-dollar military arms deal was worth blowing the lid on this particular little secret."

She whistled softly.

He just scowled. "Unfortunately, I didn't have a chance to learn much about it. Whatever the Carreras family has going—and it centers around this time-travel thing—it's important enough to plug any leak at all, fast and neat. And what better place to dump the bodies?" He lifted his hands with a clank of iron and a rattle of chain to indicate the dank hold. "Who'd ever find you?"

She regarded him with a steady gaze. Her lips had pursed slightly. "He slipped up, though, didn't he?"

Charlie whistled in turn. "You're fast. Yeah, he slipped up. For all the good it's likely to do me. Or you. I was supposed to die in that lousy execution his people arranged in the arena. Evidently Carreras' boys didn't stick around long enough to make sure of me."

"Tony Bartlett must be—" Her eyes widened. "My God."

"*What?*" Charlie grasped her arm and felt her tremble under his fingers.

"Caelerus," she whispered, meeting his gaze unsteadily. "*Tony Bartlett is Caelerus!* I didn't realize, I'm still muzzy-headed . . ."

Charlie shook the wrinkles out of that one and didn't like what he ended up with, not by a long shot, although he should have seen it coming. Sibyl wasn't the only one suffering from muzzy-headed thinking. That's what came of four years of protein deprivation.

"All right," Charlie finally said, "if Tony has access to whatever it is that opens those doorways in time, he's clearly part of the 'family.' Question is, in what capacity? He must be pretty high in the organization for Carreras to give him access to the time portals."

Sibyl shivered. "God, what a sight. . . ."

Charlie's skin crawled just watching her remember it. He wondered fleetingly if he should be grateful he'd been out cold when Carreras took him through. It would have been far worse to be fully aware of what was happening, but still powerless to stop it.

Her eyes had taken on a faraway look, the kind of expression he'd always associated with brainless bimbos mooning over stupid romance novels. Charlie got the impression, however, that her mind—far from turning itself off—was actually working at top speed.

Illogically he felt an optimism that should have been completely out of place. There wasn't a snowball's chance in hell that either of their situations was going to improve in the foreseeable future. The thought of both of them in Bericus' hands broke him out into a cold sweat.

She visibly collected herself and looked up at him. Either she didn't notice the strained expression on his face or chose to ignore it. "I'd give a lot to know who made the time-travel breakthrough, not to mention how the mafia got their hands on it, and how *Bartlett's* connected with them; but we don't have time for that right now. There's something more urgent I've got to know." She worried her lower lip with her teeth. It was an endearing habit and made her look more like Shirley Temple than ever. When she finally spoke, her question surprised him. "Charlie, how long have you been here?"

"As near as I can figure, about four years."

She nodded. "Okay, that's what I was guessing. Good. Who was on the Imperial throne when you arrived?"

"I'm not likely to forget *him*. Old guy by the name of Vespasian. I was sorry when I heard he'd died. . . ."

He trailed off. Her face had gone positively chalky.

"And *Titus* is emperor now? How . . . ?" Her voice actually cracked. She stopped, licked her lips, and tried again. "How long has Titus been on the throne? As close as you can figure!"

The intensity in her voice, the white pallor of her skin alarmed Charlie.

"Uh . . ." He thought hard, tried to reconstruct the days. Time had nearly ceased to have meaning for Charlie. "A month, or close to it. I remember the coronation celebrations. They lasted a whole week. Then the week after that Xanthus' favorite gladiator died in the arena and he— Never mind." He looked away from the quick sympathy in her eyes. "Then the week after that, we got in a pair of dancing girls and sold them to Tellus Martonius. Caelerus brought you in maybe six days after that and you were at Xanthus' for a couple of days before we set sail."

She hugged herself tightly. "If the city still exists— That's got to be it. God, what *day* is this? Titus was only emperor for a month or so before— Wait!" She held up an impatient hand when he started to ask a question. "I've got it. The festival was just—" She leaned forward and grasped Charlie's arm, hard enough to raise welts with her fingernails. "Charlie, has Rome celebrated the Festival of Vulcan yet?"

Charlie shook his head. "It's today. Xanthus was angry at having to miss it."

She shut her eyes. Charlie received the impression she was trying to shut out a vision too terrifying to face. He felt a chill creep over him.

"Murdering son-of-a . . ." She drew a quivery breath and opened her eyes. They mirrored a panic that left Charlie feeling positively icy. "Charlie, Tony Bartlett doesn't plan for me to stay alive in this time any longer than Carreras planned for you to survive. Whatever else happens, if you want to live through the next twenty-four hours, you've got to get hell and gone away from Herculaneum. With or without Lucania, you've got to get away."

The chill that had overtaken him crawled its way up his spine to his scalp. "Why?"

The look she gave him reminded him of the looks his teachers had given him all through school. Without warning, he was angry clear through. Then she shook her head and chewed at her lip again. Instant irritation disappeared. She was under tremendous pressure, too, and nowhere near as trained for it as he was. Besides, Sibyl was clearly accustomed to dealing with people who spent their lives reading books, not dragging illiterate slime up out of the sewers.

"I'm not much of an expert on Roman history," he said quietly. "You know the old song, 'Don't know much about history . . .' That's me. I guess I'm thanking Anybody who'll listen that someone who *does* know came along. So why do we need to snatch Lucania and get out of town?"

She reached over and squeezed his hand. It felt like an apology. Her eyes were dark, though, and she had trouble meeting his gaze. Her voice was pitched almost too low to hear.

"Tomorrow night, just about midnight . . . Herculaneum is going to be buried under a lot of very hot mud, ash, and pumice. Between, oh, sixty to a hundred feet of it."

Charlie hissed wordlessly.

"You see," she went on, her voice dull, "most people don't remember that Mt. Vesuvius buried *two* major cities, and a couple of smaller towns, when it erupted and destroyed Pompeii."

Even Charlie had heard of Pompeii. He'd seen the movie.

"Holy shit," Charlie whispered into the silence that followed.

She nodded bleakly. "A lot of people escaped Pompeii before the main eruption—and the fiery avalanches full of poisonous gas and glowing pumice—hit the city. Only the ones who ignored the earthquakes or stayed to wait out the ashfall were trapped. The wealthy resort town of Stabiae—it was famous for its mineral springs, and let me tell you, that place was *loaded* with money, same as Herculaneum—was eventually buried, too. So was the little town of Oplontis. The eruption lasted three days."

She hugged herself, as though chilled by the images she was describing. "The Imperial fleet tried to rescue survivors. Pliny the Elder, he was the fleet admiral stationed at Misenum, took his ships across the Bay of Naples to rescue survivors. But he couldn't get close enough to get anyone out. He was trapped at Stabiae instead, rescuing people there, and was killed. His nephew at Misenum, Pliny the Younger—the famous historian—left a really vivid account. He was afraid *they'd* be killed, once the fiery avalanches started. Took his mother and ran for it. The Bay of Naples isn't all that large. A few miles across, no more. Herculaneum's only about four miles from the volcano's summit."

Charlie whistled softly. "So Herculaneum was wiped out, too. How come nobody ever mentions it, if several cities were buried? And how come anybody was crazy enough to build cities on an active volcano?"

"They didn't *know* it was a volcano. In A.D. 79, Vesuvius hadn't erupted for at least three hundred years. Almost nobody understood what caused the earthquakes all through the Campanian region, like the one that damaged the Temple of Jupiter in Pompeii in A.D. 62. Not even Seneca, who was something of a naturalist, understood it; although Strabo did guess there had been volcanic activity there at one time." She shivered. "*We* used to think everybody got out of Herculaneum. We'd

never found any bodies, not like we did at Pompeii."
She swallowed. "Then we, uh . . . We found the ancient
beach. It's about half a kilometer inland from the modern
waterfront. Most of them made it that far."

She looked like she was about to cry again.

Charlie sympathized. "Holy shit."

He didn't know what else to say.

CHAPTER EIGHT

The guards at the door wore military uniforms, but they weren't Dan's men. They weren't even Uncle Sam's men. They checked his ID suspiciously, even though he was well known to each of them by now. Four months of this treatment had only exacerbated Dan's temper, whipping him with the need to remain submissive at all cost. At one time, this had been Dan's building, Dan's project. At one time, he'd been able to call his life his own. . . .

His face went stiff and cold as he thought of what lay beyond these doors through which he'd once passed so freely. Of what *they* had the potential—and the ruthlessness—to do with it. They'd only begun to grasp what they had hold of. God help the world when they started to figure it out.

And God help him—not to mention Lucille and Danny and the others—when they didn't need him any longer. . . .

Dan had been one of the pivotal engineers on this project from the beginning. Only the physicists understood it better, and while they had the top-security clearances, same as Dan, they didn't have the military connections Dan did. Without Dan to hide behind, the mafioso thugs who'd taken over his life wouldn't have had a prayer of pulling this off.

He drew a ragged breath, hating and blaming himself for that, and clung to the fact that they still needed him, needed what he knew, needed him as a screen to hide behind. As long as he still had access, however limited, to the equipment—

He wondered if Lucille would understand that he had to choose. Soon. Guilt tore at him. Awake or asleep, he remembered Lucy's tears, Danny's quivering attempt at a stiff upper lip. If he ever found out which of his people had originally sold them out. . . . There wasn't a legal punishment on the books that would come close to what he had in mind.

As it was, he was no longer sure which of his people were still *his* people. The entire communications section definitely wasn't. Crighton had rotated out and subsequently vanished. O'Keefe had died in a car wreck on his way to visit his wife in Juneau. . . . The finance officer was definitely in it up to his traitorous little ears. Counterfeit pay vouchers for direct deposit payroll slips for people who weren't even in the army were coming through Tenbroeck's office. Dan wondered how they'd gotten to the man. He'd thought Tenbroeck solidly loyal—until Danny and Lucille had vanished. Someone in Security had to be involved, too; probably Sergeant Manning. Manning was in charge of the duty rosters. Dan wondered how much Carreras had paid him. For all he knew, of course, Kominsky might well be in on it, too. He remembered vividly what First Sergeant Szkolny had said the other day in the mess hall.

"Something strange going on with the MP rosters, sir," Szkolny had muttered in the chow line. "I keep seeing the same dozen or so names pop up for the high-security areas. Come to think of it," he added, glancing at Dan, "that new bodyguard you ordered is always staffed by one of those guys."

"Thank you for bringing that to my attention, Sergeant. I'll take care of it," Dan had answered, trying very hard not to let the man know how very wrong things were on this base. He had not wanted Szkolny's death on his conscience.

Dan thought of Logan McKee and went cold again. McKee definitely wasn't one of his. Nor was Dan certain he was anyone else's. Logan McKee was an anachronism. Ever since McKee's abrupt arrival, Dan had been thinking a whole lot about Dr. Gudekinst's early worries on slippage. And every time he thought about it, Dan began to sweat all over again. If slippage were occurring, severely enough to drop someone through a temporal crack . . .

Christ—what had these goons been up to? What sort of monkeying around with the time stream had they done without consulting *anyone*? There were dangers they didn't begin to comprehend. Dangers which—Dan had to shut his eyes and shoulder the guilt which was his alone to carry—dangers which very carefully had *not* been explained to them.

Explanations would have required revealing aspects of the process which Dan and his physicists had managed so far to keep secret, in the vain hope they could turn this thing into a weapon to fight back. Dan knew the imprisoned scientists were counting on him to stop this madness. He winced a bit. With his wife and son hostages, he couldn't even count on himself.

Dan held fears at bay with less than sterling success and waited for clearance to enter the building. Since Dan was expected this morning, once the scrutiny of his ID was completed, the door guards called for one of their own to escort him inside. The man who arrived was built like a linebacker—or a refrigerator.

Dan hadn't seen this one before. How many of his own people had Carreras brought in by now?

The linebacker confiscated Dan's pistol, then escorted him into an alcove just inside the door. While Dan's bodyguard watched, the man performed a very thorough—and humiliating—body cavity search.

"Satisfied?" he finally snapped.

The linebacker just looked at him. "Get dressed," he said tonelessly.

Dan's fingers shook as he buttoned his shirt and zipped his fly.

He was escorted through a familiar maze of corridors and security devices. An elevator ride dropped them deep into the interior of the mountain which this base skirted. When the doors opened, Dan stepped out into deep pile carpet, as out of place as the man who now inhabited it. Once this had been his situation room. Security monitors were still in place, as were computer linkups to installations across the globe. Inwardly he winced at the thought of the compromised top-secret security installations this room now represented.

The rest of the room had been altered almost beyond recognition. A solid Brazilian rosewood desk at least seven feet long and four feet wide stood opposite the elevator, along one wall of the vast room. Dan recognized some of the paintings. There were ancient marbles, as well, which should have been in a museum, but probably never had been.

Enthroned in a leather chair was the ruling lord of all this. And of Dan's life. Jésus Carreras wasn't yet forty. His body was as sleek and deadly as a rattlesnake's. His eyes were just as cold.

"Colonel Collins," Carreras acknowledged without bothering to rise from his seat. "That will be all, Nelson."

The linebacker retreated silently into the elevator. Dan's personal bodyguard took up a position between Dan and the elevator.

The sweat trickling down his armpits stank. *Don't blow this, don't blow it . . .*

"Four months," Carreras said quietly. "Four very interesting, trouble-free months." He shook his head slowly, then rose almost lazily to his feet and strolled toward Dan.

"Do you know, Colonel," Carreras continued quietly, making Dan feel like a dying fish with the shark circling in for the kill, "in those four months I have almost come to like you?" His black eyes glinted briefly with some inner amusement.

A smashing backhand caught Dan's mouth. The blow sent him staggering back a step. Dan grunted and fought the urge to retaliate. He *knew* better, but his gut didn't. Slowly, to distract the fight-or-flight tension in his belly, Dan wiped blood from his lips.

"How is it, Colonel," Carreras hissed, "that you failed to inform me of this little situation in a timely fashion?"

Dan sounded like a grammar-school truant and knew it. "I wanted to give you as much information as possible on him."

"Ah. I see." Carreras paced a few steps, hands clasped behind his back. "Tell me, Colonel," he asked over one shoulder, "how is your lovely wife these days? And your charming son?"

Dan spat out something profoundly ugly.

Carreras clucked chidingly. "Temper, Colonel. Let me see," he said, tipping his head back in evident reflection, "if we pulled the generators, the temperatures in the shelter would probably drop to fatal levels in, what, six hours? Seven?"

Dan clenched his fists at his sides and didn't dare answer.

"Yes. It would be a pity, wouldn't it? Such a lovely marriage, such a lovely family."

Dan couldn't look at him, couldn't look at the laughter in those reptilian eyes. If he met Carreras' gaze, he'd kill him. And that would be the worst disaster yet.

"Tell me, Colonel," Carreras went on, as though the threats hanging between them didn't exist, "what do you think we should do with this McKee fellow?"

Dan flexed his fingers and risked glancing up. "Lock him in a psych ward. He's crazy. Who'd believe him?"

A brief smile touched the Latin's dark face. "Who, indeed?" Carreras paused for a moment, apparently lost in thought. "No, Colonel," he said at length. "We cannot simply lock the man up." He glanced at Dan. "Do you know what I think, Colonel Collins?"

Dan was sure Carreras would tell him, if it suited Carreras' plans.

"I think our friend McKee isn't crazy at all."

Dan twitched. "What? I questioned him myself, under truth drugs. Carreras, his mind never came home from 'Nam. He's as certifiable as they come."

Carreras smiled. Dan suppressed a shiver.

"I think," Carreras said, leaning easily against the edge of his massive desk, "that our friend is a killer without purpose. Without a job. When he is placed in war, he is like the orca, deadly and efficient in his own element. Take him out of war . . . Tell me, Colonel, have you ever seen a beached whale? The seagulls peck at it, pluck at its eyes, nibble it to death."

"So what do you want me to do with him? Find a nice, bloody little war for him?"

Carreras chuckled. "No, Colonel. I do not want you to find a war for him." Carreras rested his palms against the desktop and glanced into one corner of the vast room. "He knows too much."

"He doesn't know anything—" Dan protested.

"He knows this place!" Carreras struck the desktop with one fist and propelled himself toward Dan. "He knows that he has been . . . displaced. When I get my hands on Tony . . ." Carreras muttered. "I warned that fool. . . ."

Dan didn't want to hear this. Men had died for knowing less. Men, he realized with a sickening lurch, like McKee.

When Carreras straightened, Dan already knew what he was going to say. He wasn't wrong.

"Kill him, Collins."

Dan shook his head in a hopeless bid to save the man's life. "He doesn't know anything, Carreras. Nobody's going to believe a crazy man. And with his record—"

"Need I remind you, Colonel"—Carreras' voice was an icy whiplash—"that you are in no position to defy my orders?"

Dan bit back the rest of his arguments and swallowed. "I know," he managed.

A polished obsidian gaze caught and pinned him in a puddle of stinking sweat. "I could easily arrange an unpleasant transfer for our mutual acquaintances. You do understand that, don't you, Collins? Judea, perhaps, say, 50 B.C.? I'm told leprosy was quite common—"

"You wouldn't—!" Dan halted abruptly. Carreras *would*

dare and there was absolutely nothing Dan could do to stop him. Dan shrank away from Carreras' contemptuous look, from the knowledge that he was a traitor, a coward, a crawling worm. . . .

Jésus Carreras' voice was as cold as the Arctic night wind. "Kill McKee, Collins. See to it personally. I don't care how or where. Pick a time, a place, program the jump. I'll send a couple of my men to help manhandle him through, since he is clearly a dangerous fighter, even unarmed. Once you've taken him through, Collins, kill him. Quickly and neatly. Or I'll start sending you pieces of your family."

Dan stumbled into the waiting elevator. He hid his face in the corner, unable to face his bodyguard or the polished metal of the door. One day, he swore, clenching his fists so tightly his hands hurt, one day . . .

He drove himself home, alone with the hated guard. Dan nearly wrecked the jeep twice and received a jab in the ribs with a gun muzzle for his trouble. Once home, Dan locked himself into his study with a bottle of bourbon. The guard stationed himself, as always, in the hall just outside. He knew from bitter experience there were also guards outside his windows. After three brimming tumblers of straight bourbon, Dan picked up a family portrait and ran his fingertips across the images of his shattered life.

If he'd been any kind of a man, he'd have slid a knife into Carreras' ribs long ago. Hostages never got out alive. Not Carreras' hostages. Dan swore and hurled the picture across the room. It smashed against the wall. The photograph fell with a crash of broken glass and bent metal.

They'd taken him to see Lucille, Danny, and the others, that first week. As long as he lived, Dan would remember the desolation of that place. It wasn't far from the base, actually, a few miles north along the Colleen River, within easy sight of Table Mountain. Not far at all . . .

But 30,000 years in the past.

The cell where they kept his family was crowded, but livable. Well heated, too, with a small diesel plant and several barrels of fuel. They'd stored plenty of food in lockers. Their jailers had even provided army cots. All in one prefabbed package, complete with guards to make sure no one went anywhere. Not that there'd have been anywhere for them to go in the year 28,000 B.C. Not with an ice sheet covering the Endicott Mountains and the Philip Smith range to the west, another strangling the Alaska Range from Fort Yukon south through Fairbanks and on to the sea, and a third that stretched from the Canadian Yukon all the way to the Atlantic Ocean.

Carreras had dropped Dan's family into a neat little ice-free pocket, surrounded by miles and endless miles of nothing. And if they tried to escape anyway, or if someone attempted a rescue . . .

Dan swallowed hard. He would finally have access to the equipment—at least until he'd disposed of McKee—but the guards had orders to kill every last hostage at the first hint of a rescue attempt.

But if he *could* get them out . . .

Dan narrowed his eyes in concentration and tightened down his fingers on the empty bourbon glass. Whether he got them out, or they were killed in the attempt, as long as *he* managed to get away again, there'd be absolutely nothing in the known universe that would save Carreras. Dan would get that bastard, somehow. The question was, could he do it alone?

And what was he supposed to do with McKee? Carreras would demand confirmation on the body and he was sending along some of his bully boys to be certain Dan didn't try a double-cross.

Dan Collins poured another glass and downed the bourbon in one gulp, then hurled the half-full bottle against the far wall. Glass shattered with satisfying violence. Bourbon splattered across the wall and drenched the rug like puddled blood serum. Dan stood up. He felt cold all over. But he knew what had to be done.

❖   ❖   ❖

"Holy shit" was apparently the only thing Charlie Flynn was capable of saying. Sibyl understood at a visceral level, but as a solution to their problem, it wasn't a terribly constructive comment.

"Hey, snap out of it," she muttered.

The numb look left his eyes. "Sorry." He flushed a dull red that left the scar on his throat pale by comparison. "And I'm supposed to be the tough guy." He ran a hand awkwardly through short, matted curls, causing the chains at his wrists to rattle unpleasantly. "So . . . now what? We're headed for trouble, any way you look at it."

"Amen." She shivered slightly. "Where, exactly, is Bericus' villa?"

He frowned, more from memory of something vastly unpleasant, Sibyl suspected, than from contemplation of their short-term future.

"It's completely outside town, maybe, oh, three or four miles around the base of the mountain, but it's on the northwestern slope, fairly high on a ridge." He squinted slightly, as though staring at scenery in his memory. "It's maybe a third of the way up the mountain, over some very rough roads. You can see Herculaneum when you're on that rise, even Neapolis—Naples, I mean—farther off, in the other direction, around the coastline."

"Sounds pretty," Sibyl muttered.

"Yeah. It is a spectacular view, actually. And very pretty country, if you don't know what you built your house on. Lots of vineyards and groves all the way up to the house, some patches of wilder forest above it. Anyway, the main road out of Herculaneum is paved a short way outside town, but to get to Bericus' villa, you have to sidetrack onto some fairly poor dirt lanes. It takes at least an hour, by carriage, to get up there. He's got a big farm, we'd call it a ranch, I guess, pretty much self-sufficient. They say he bought it so his playthings couldn't escape as easily."

Sibyl shuddered. "Wonderful. We can't afford to be taken out there, Charlie, but I don't see any way around it. Do you? I, uh, suppose that's where Lucania is?"

He nodded. "Yeah. Bericus' town house in Herculaneum is pretty much his wife's refuge, poor woman. She won't tolerate his playthings or their offspring. Anyway, Xanthus will take us directly to the *villa rustica*. That won't give us much of a shot at breaking loose. And somehow I don't think Bericus is going to be careless with me. Xanthus has already warned him to keep me chained."

Sibyl thought about the scar on Bericus' chin, studied the look in Charlie's eyes, and decided not to press for details. Some things she didn't need to know that badly.

"Can you ride a horse?" she asked hopefully. "If we set Bericus' house on fire, we could steal horses in the confusion. We wouldn't have to elude capture long—just long enough to get lost in the posteruption confusion."

Charlie was shaking his head mournfully. "I've never been on a horse in my life. Of course, some things I can learn pretty fast. I've fought men on horseback from the ground and won." He attempted a dismal smile.

Before Sibyl could respond, Xanthus bellowed for someone to open the hatch and be quick about it. Sibyl exchanged glances with Charlie. She discovered she'd clenched her fingers in the folds of her cheap *tunica*.

One of the sailors up on deck opened the hatch. Xanthus shouted down, "Rufus! Get your lazy ass over here!"

Charlie paled, then flushed dark red. "Gotta go," he mumbled.

Watching him lose the brief courage he'd gained hurt Sibyl more than she'd thought possible. She bit her lower lip as he struggled toward the ladder and climbed with painful slowness. She heard him say, "Yes, Master?" but couldn't hear Xanthus' low-voiced instructions.

Charlie climbed back down, holding a small ceramic bottle with a stopper. He moved awkwardly toward her.

"Make this look good," he muttered in English.

The next moment, Charlie had thrown her to her back.

Sibyl gasped. Then struggled instinctively. He pinned her with astonishing strength.

"What are you—?"

He pinched shut her nose. Then, in a grating undertone, "Don't just lie there, idiot—fight me!"

She fought. Charlie uncorked the bottle with his teeth. She caught the scent of the drug she'd been given before and fought harder. She smashed an elbow into his lower belly, missing his groin narrowly. Charlie grimaced in genuine pain.

"Shit—"

It came out more gasp than curse.

Running out of air, Sibyl was finally forced to gasp, as well. Charlie tipped the bottle—

—and poured the stuff down her cheek, on the side of her face away from the rowers. A couple of droplets, no more, splashed against the back of her throat. Sibyl coughed and strangled as Charlie pinched shut her nostrils again. He tipped more of the drug down the side of her face. Sibyl continued to struggle until he let her go. Charlie sat back. She spat out a few choice words she'd picked up at church camp and curled onto her side away from him.

"Sorry," he whispered. "I had to make that look good. The stuff should make you drowsy in about, oh, five minutes. For God's sake, make *that* look good, too, or we're both in for it."

"Thanks," Sibyl muttered, aware that Charlie was risking hideous punishment if his ruse were discovered.

"I'll be back," he promised.

Sibyl dragged herself to the edge of the spare sail, using her body to block surreptitious movements. She eased a corner of the woolen sail over to mop up the spilled drug, then collapsed against the folded sail as though dizzy. She lay still while Charlie *scrape-thumped* his awkward way toward the distant ladder, then returned just as slowly.

"We're almost there," he whispered as he eased back down beside her.

Sibyl shivered.

"Remember, you're supposed to be drugged."

She'd flunked drama class. Involuntary shivers deepened. She hoped Charlie didn't notice.

To distract herself from the coming nightmare, Sibyl started cataloging discrepancies from scholarly theory that the reality of an intact Roman merchant ship represented. She'd reached thirty-eight worthy of doctoral dissertations when Xanthus bellowed, "Rufus! Get that slut up here! Now!"

She met Charlie's gaze and swallowed.

"Remember," he whispered fiercely. "Drugged enough to be stupid, not quite enough to be comatose. Pretend you're drunk, if nothing else."

Sibyl had to bite her tongue to keep from giggling a little hysterically. She'd never been drunk enough to simulate the state Charlie was describing.

Later, she told herself. *Survive this now and you can get stinking, roaring, falling-down drunk later, celebrating.*

Sibyl let Charlie guide her to the ladder and pasted on what she hoped passed for a look of moronic imbecility. She felt like a fool, but started climbing. The light was already fading when she reached the deck. Vesuvius slumbered in the bloody light of sunset. Xanthus hauled Sibyl onto the deck and dragged her aside so Charlie could clamber awkwardly up, holding his crutch with one hand.

While Charlie was climbing the last few feet, Xanthus tied her wrists together with stout cord. He tied her expertly, too; no wriggling out of these bonds. Sibyl reminded herself to look comatose and endured it. To distract herself, she began cataloging more discrepancies between scholarly theory and reality. Nobody knew much about Roman maritime construction. Not enough had survived. Too bad Professor Clarke couldn't be here with a good camcorder.

A thick central mast supported the main sail. The rigging fascinated her. *Christ, I could get a dissertation out of the rigging, alone. . . .* The upswept stern made the entire boat look something like a swan ride at an amusement park or a medieval shoe. *Probably where Xanthus' quarters are during long voyages. . . .*

Xanthus. She was supposed to be drugged, not gawking like a New York tourist. She glanced up apprehensively.

Damn.

Xanthus was staring at her. Suspicion flared in his dark eyes. Sibyl managed to recover a properly vacuous look only with tremendous effort. If Xanthus suspected Charlie hadn't drugged her . . . Sibyl cursed the slave-trader silently and held still under his scrutiny until he was satisfied. Xanthus turned his attention to Charlie, who had finally managed to crawl up onto the rolling deck.

The ruddy light of sunset caught the scars on his body, the barely healing welts in his back. Sibyl winced at almost the same instant he did, as scabs pulled and tore visibly. Chains rattled as he dragged himself to his feet with the help of his crutch. His head came up slowly. He towered over Xanthus, taller, even, than the burly sailors. At least six-foot, almost naked, lean and muscled . . .

The scars on his leg reddened in the sunset. His hand tightened around the crutch. Offshore wind ruffled carroty curls that someone had chopped off, probably with a dull knife. She tried to imagine him in a police uniform, then erased that image. He was a detective, an undercover cop. There'd be no uniform. She adjusted the mental image to jeans, a faded t-shirt, maybe a jacket to hide the shoulder holster he'd probably be wearing. . . .

Dying sunlight caught a glint of steely determination in his eyes. He met her glance, then looked away without reacting. Professional training. Sibyl ordered herself not to feel hurt and tried to copy his method.

Xanthus, however, had plans for Charlie to ensure he couldn't so much as attempt escape. Without giving him the slightest benefit of the doubt, he ordered Charlie stripped and chained tighter.

Sibyl couldn't watch. But she couldn't *not* watch, either, risking tiny peeks that jelled her blood. Worse, Charlie yielded to it without a sound. Two years in Xanthus' hands, he'd said. . . . She found it painfully difficult to breathe. Two whole years. And unless they escaped during the next few hours, every minute of his struggle to stay alive would be for nothing.

We can't die this way. We can't . . .

They had come into harbor above the town proper. Sailors were busy dropping anchor beside a utilitarian wooden quay completely unknown in modern times. Xanthus, thank God, turned his attention away from the thoroughly subdued Charlie. He huddled at Xanthus' feet, completely submissive, completely naked now, a tight rope around his throat to throttle any fight out of him.

Xanthus hadn't hurt him, he'd just made certain Charlie was humiliated thoroughly in the process of preventing his escape. Although Xanthus hadn't hurt him *this time*, Charlie was covered, top to bottom, with old, moderately recent, and new scars. Even Charlie's buttocks bore terrible scars that looked as though massive claws had ripped him open.

Leopards . . .

She shut her eyes, then reminded herself forcibly that she, too, had a part to play. *Remember, you're drugged. A zombie. Don't think about what's coming, for either of us. You're a zombie. . . .*

Little frissons of electric terror ran along her nerves every few seconds—every time she thought about Bericus and Tony Bartlett. He'd be waiting at the villa, just to be sure of her. *How're you planning your escape, you bastard?* Maybe she and Charlie could overpower him, somehow, maybe even get back to the twentieth century. . . .

Right, Cinderella. Wake up. The party's over and the prince never found the glass slipper. They had to plan their escape to survive in *this* time. Anything else was tantamount to suicide.

Activity along the shoreline eventually caught Sibyl's

attention. Herculaneum, a city of four or five thousand, rose precipitously from the water, built on a series of terraces in a long, steep hillside that formed a small peninsula. That peninsula jutted out into the Mediterranean, faced by a stone seawall that fronted the whole town. A very narrow strand between the stone wall and the sea was littered with beached fishing boats. Their owners were busy dragging them out of the water for storage in the infamous arched boat chambers.

Sibyl knew this waterfront. Knew it well. Too well.

Near the center of the seawall, opposite the quay where Xanthus had tied up his ship, was the stone staircase she remembered. It led up from the beach, then branched like a capital Y into two other staircases. They led in turn up along another steep wall which formed the second terrace of the town. On the first terrace, just to her right, were the Suburban Baths. Beyond them, on the next level up, would be the House of the Stags, where they'd found the glorious statue of drunken Hercules—the patron deity of the town—and another of hounds bringing down a stag.

A vastly wealthy patrician had owned that villa—not only was it near the sea, on prime real estate, giving a breathtaking view of the Mediterranean from its upper-story windows, but the house hadn't been broken up for apartments, which some of the bigger villas had been. Next door was the House of the Mosaic Atrium, another of the most beautiful villas found in *any* of the buried cities.

Off to the right, back in the heart of town, toward Vesuvius, she could see the rooftops of the palaestra, where athletes trained. To the left, even farther back and marginally away from the mountain, was the 2,500-seat amphitheater. In the distance she spotted a small arena completely unknown in modern times. *Dr. Clarke was right*. It was squarely beneath modern Ercolano. It would probably never be excavated. Like the theater, which had been found in the eighteenth century, it gleamed in the dying light.

Between theater and palaestra was Herculaneum's basilica, the pulse-point of town, along the Decumanus Maximus. Citizens came to seek justice or to do business at the basilica, which was flanked by famous equestrian statues of M. Nonius Balbus. *That* wealthy patrician had restored the city's walls and gates and the basilica itself after the earthquake in A.D. 62. Emperor Vespasian had restored the Temple of the Magna Mater—and there it was in the distance, rooftops gleaming in the sunset. The great Magna Mater, Phrygian Cybele, whose priestesses bore Sibyl's own name. . . .

In her mind's eye, Sibyl recalled the covered portico along the northern section of the Decumanus Maximus, under which were small shops. The other, southern, edge was lined with houses, the monumental entrance to the Forum, the Collegium Augustalium, and the cult center of the Cult of Hercules.

The whole town faced the sunset. Terraces surrounded many villas, especially near the outskirts, open to the cool evening breeze and a spectacular view of the sea. Vesuvius loomed considerably higher than its denuded modern cone. The mountain brooded above the town to the east-southeast, painted by the brilliant dyes of sunset. South along the shoreline, if one followed the road that led through town, one would eventually come to Oplontis and Pompeii, and from there, around the coast to a peninsula that jutted southwestward toward Capri, to wealthy little Stabiae.

The city walls ran along the coastline to gushing, torrential streams on either side of the little jut of land. Water poured down the countryside from Vesuvius and emptied into the Bay of Naples, forming little harbor entrances on either side of the city.

Neither harbor was known in modern times.

Her disseral speculations had been correct, though. The plethora of timbers, half-finished hulls, and stacked planks at the nearest harbor confirmed the theory she was trying to substantiate in her doctoral dissertation. The thriving shipbuilding industry spread out before her must have supported Herculaneum's economy, along with fishing and the vast wealth of patricians tired of the industrial noise and bustle in Pompeii and Neapolis— or Rome, itself. Herculaneum's streets, unlike Pompeii's, were not deeply rutted by the cart wheels of shopkeepers and industrialists producing bread, export-bound fish sauce, or textiles.

Herculaneum's master shipwrights were just finishing work for the day. She could hear shouts and laughter across the intervening stretch of water. It was something, Sibyl supposed, to have one's doctoral thesis borne out so graphically. She'd have traded that confirmation for twentieth-century uncertainty in an instant, despite the awe she felt as the reality of Herculaneum A.D. 79 stretched out before her.

The town was breathtaking, exquisite in every detail . . . and doomed.

Xanthus grasped her arm. Sibyl jumped nearly out of her skin. *Oh, God, you idiot, stop gawking like a fool. . . .* Xanthus stared sharply at her. Sibyl gazed emptily at the sea and let her mouth hang open a little, trying to look doped to the gills. He grunted and dragged her across the deck. They'd run a wooden ramp down to the quay. Charlie, still naked so he'd be conspicuous—and thus more easily recaptured—if he tried to run, was already ashore. Xanthus thumped down the wooden ramp. Sibyl followed, trying desperately to look as though she'd been drugged. She trembled clear through, so badly her knees threatened to buckle. Xanthus' armed escort followed her down, along with most of the sailors. Only a handful of Xanthus' men remained on guard aboard the ship.

The wooden quay was solidly built, although far more utilitarian than the stone quays of the spa-town Stabiae, with their arches and decorative columns. The slap of water against wet wood reminded Sibyl fiercely of home, of summers spent at the beach. Even the smells were mostly the same: salt water, the tang of clean air overlain by the stench of freshly gutted fish. . . . She had to blink rapidly to keep tears from slipping loose.

At the far end of the quay, on *terra firma*, an open, low-slung, unsprung carriage waited on the beach sand, evidently for them. Its wheels were fastened directly to the carriage. Axle shafts hadn't yet been invented. A dull-eyed bay horse stood patiently, one rear leg slack as the animal rested. Leather straps around its throat comprised the harness.

How the poor beast could breathe and pull at the same time was beyond Sibyl. She wished, for the horse's sake anyway, that modern-style harness hadn't been invented so late in history. The driver was dressed as a slave, although more richly than any of Xanthus' men; he was too pretty for his own good. Doubtless that was the reason he'd ended in Bericus' possession. Good-looking as he was, the driver's expression mirrored the horse's.

The tone of his voice when he greeted Xanthus was somewhere between respectful and bored. "My master sent me to meet you, sir."

"Very good." Xanthus turned to his valuable secretary. "Achivus, I want four armed men as escort for the journey. Bericus says there have been bandits raiding north of Vesuvius. Then hire a wagon and bring the cripple in it, with four more guards. I have no intention of putting that bastard in the same carriage with me. We'll return to the ship late tomorrow or early the next day. Set a guard on the ship with the remaining men."

"Yes, Master."

Panic hit Sibyl squarely in the gut. Xanthus was separating them? They had to get out *tonight.* If they were separated and brought up the mountain several hours apart, could *either* of them get away from Vesuvius?

Charlie's face had lost its color, despite the deep red light of sunset. Clearly, the same thought had occurred to him. Charlie glanced at Sibyl, eyes darkened with fear. Sibyl tried to think what to do and drew only a grey, terrified blank. Xanthus couldn't separate them, not now. . . .

"Meanwhile," Xanthus said, fumbling at his belt for a small leather purse, "give me the papers on Aelia I'm holding for Caelerus. I'll have Bericus' secretary scribe me a copy. Here." He counted out coins. "Hire that wagon and follow us as soon as you can. I want that cripple off my hands tonight. Let Bericus worry about him."

Achivus took the coins and handed over the scroll case. "Yes, Master."

Xanthus hauled Sibyl into the carriage and shoved her into the corner, then settled beside her. His hand grazed her inner thigh. She managed to remain motionless, slumped against the side of the carriage and apparently drugged, but she had to fight to stay relaxed under the vulgar caress. The guards jumped in. From his perch at the front of the carriage, the driver lit a lantern with flint and pyrite, then shook out a long whip.

As the carriage lurched into motion, Charlie's voice, thin with distance and fright, reached her: "Hang on!" he called in English. "Just hang on!"

She managed to catch a last glimpse of him as Achivus ordered him put down. Done gently enough, Charlie still hit the ground hard and lay still, just watching her go.

Then they turned off the beach onto a long east–west road that ran from the center of town right out onto the beach itself, bypassing the higher terraces near the Suburban Baths. Once the carriage had rattled around the corner, she slumped down against the jolting side of the carriage and blinked back tears.

Charlie, don't do anything stupid, please or they'll kill you. . . .

Another part of her whispered, *Please get me out of this, Charlie Flynn.*

Despair blanked out awareness of the ancient city, even her ability to think rationally. She had perhaps thirty hours in which to rescue herself and two others from certain death and almost no likelihood of pulling it off. In the last, dying light of day, the black hulk of Vesuvius brooded silently above the town. The cold shadows it cast left Sibyl shivering.

The mountain wouldn't remain silent long. There was

something hideously macabre about winding through sleepy, oblivious streets, knowing what she knew. As they rattled down narrow, stone-paved thoroughfares, shop vendors closed their windows and counters for the night. Poor men and slaves dressed in rags hurried on urgent errands, while fishermen trundled the remnants of the day's catch out of the city market. Wealthy Romans lingered in groups to finish an animated conversation or strolled home for dinner and bed.

None of them suspected how little time they had left.

Sibyl tried to put that out of her mind. She had to distract herself, get her mind focused on what was left of her future. What she needed was a *plan*. Sibyl studied the city with a scholar's intense scrutiny, hoping to learn something—anything—that might give them a slightly improved edge on survival.

She was aware, at some deep level of herself, that part of her would probably be studying the eruption and panicked behavior of the doomed residents with a certain professional curiosity, even as the fiery avalanche swept down across them. Of course, most of her would be screaming right along with the rest of the poor barbecue candidates. . . .

She shivered, overcome by a dreadful, reversed sense of déjà vu. There—she realized it with a shock of recognition—was the moderate, middle-class home known as the Trellis House. Sibyl knew what the interior looked like, what was painted on its frescoed walls. Sibyl knew many of these houses, knew how their garden fountains were shaped, perhaps had even cleaned volcanic mud out of the skulls of those patrician gentlemen engaged in a lively debate on the street corner they were passing. . . .

Quite abruptly, Sibyl realized how Cassandra must have felt on the walls of Troy. And to think she'd begun this twisted, insane adventure by wishing she could have lived up to her namesakes, the *sibyls* of Cumae. . . .

Sibyl blinked. Slowly, her thoughts moving at the speed of a gopher tortoise on a slow day, she grasped at the spark of an idea. Hardly daring to breathe, Sibyl risked a glance at Xanthus. He had settled down, all but oblivious to his surroundings. The guards were more interested in ogling the whores who had begun to show up on the streets than they were in watching her.

It was slim—Christ, it was so slim—but she hadn't thought of anything else half as good.

Which said a lot about her chances.

A great deal rested on how religious—or superstitious—Publius Bericus was. Lots of Romans were extremely devoted to their favorite deities. Others didn't care a fig for the gods: *any* gods. School boys learned classical mythology they didn't believe, because knowing it was considered the mark of a cultured man. Julius Caesar himself, while serving the dying Republic as Pontifex Maximus, had openly admitted his skepticism about the existence of gods he nominally served as the Republic's high priest. And that had been, what, a hundred twenty years previously?

She chewed reflectively at her lip.

Publius Bericus had probably murdered his own father, Charlie had said, but that didn't necessarily reflect his religious convictions. Parricide was a regrettably common social institution because of the *paterfamilias* laws governing male heirs. For all Sibyl knew, Bericus might pray to the household *lares* and *penates* nightly for forgiveness. She probably wouldn't know until she saw the house—or, more probably, until she took the gamble.

Should she take that gamble?

Cumae wasn't that far away. No more than, what, six, six-and-a-half miles up the coast from Misenum? And *that* was just across the Bay of Naples, no more than twelve miles or so from Herculaneum. What if Bericus had *been* to Cumae? He could catch her out in a bald-faced lie.

She chewed her lip and chafed under the restriction of the ropes on her wrists and her impossible lack of the *right bits* of knowledge. How could she formulate a plan when she was operating like a blindfolded bat with cotton in its ears?

At least she'd managed to warn Charlie. Then, as she thought about what she'd said, a gut-wrenching thought struck her. *I didn't tell him everything. Oh, God, I didn't tell him everything and we're already separated. What if he tries to bolt before they bring him up the mountain . . . ?*

Sibyl had told him the truth. Herculaneum *would* be buried just before midnight tomorrow night. But the initial eruption would begin hours sooner—shortly before one o'clock tomorrow afternoon. He might think they had until tomorrow night to actually escape the house, when tonight was really all the time they had.

In the corner of the carriage, Sibyl began to tremble violently. Charlie Flynn had already survived so much. He didn't deserve to die that way, burned and choked by superheated ash. . . .

Sibyl got herself slowly under control. The surges wouldn't begin until tomorrow night. The afternoon's eruption would only blow the caldera open and send debris into the stratosphere. The lethal phase wouldn't begin until the column started to collapse. She clung to that thought, repeating it over and over.

Charlie's a scrapper, she told herself. *If anyone can pull through this, he can.*

The carriage rounded a corner, rattling into deepening shadow from Vesuvius' flank. Sibyl drew a ragged breath and scolded herself roundly for useless panic. She didn't have time for panic. With the diligence of a grad student the night before the oral boards, Sibyl began to study the layout of the streets. She didn't have much of a plan yet, but she wanted to know the shortest route through the city to the waterfront.

Just in case.

Sibyl spared a single, malevolent glance at the brooding mountain. Tony Bartlett had dumped her here to die. Tony Bartlett just might be in for a surprise.

CHAPTER NINE

It didn't take Achivus long to hire a wagon.

"I don't want to be on the road after dark," Achivus muttered, glaring at Charlie, "but Master hasn't given us any choice. Too bad. I don't want to risk being caught by bandits hauling a stubborn fool up a mountainside to a man who'll just kill him."

Charlie, covered with dust, lay on the end of the quay and simply waited. The guard Achivus had sent for the wagon finally returned. The clatter of wheels and the creak of wood was overlain by the sound of horses and the owner's complaints. "You're sure you know how to drive? And your master will reimburse me if you damage my wagon?"

"Yes, yes, of course," Achivus told him. "Here is the gold my master left to pay you. We'll be returning tomorrow night or the next morning. You'll have your wagon back day after tomorrow."

That's what you think, pal. . . .

"Put him in," Achivus instructed.

Charlie was lifted. He fought, but the chains, not to mention the rope around his throat, did their work efficiently. Half-blacked-out from lack of air moving down his windpipe, they were easily able to dump him onto hard wooden slats. Three riding horses moved aside, tethered to the back of the wagon. They rolled white eyes at him and mouthed their bits.

"Ex-gladiator, you say?" the wagon's owner muttered, peering at him in the dying light. "Better chain him to that iron ring, then, before he comes around again."

The guards dragged Charlie across rough-planed wood, regardless of splinters in his bare flesh. The wagon's owner unlocked a chain attached to an iron ring set in the bed of the wagon. They looped it through Charlie's wrist chains and locked it. The wagon's owner gave Achivus the key, which he deposited in a little pouch at his waist.

"Very good. Thank you, sir."

Charlie just shut his eyes. As he had come to be used to over the past four years, he hurt everywhere.

"You three, ride with us as guards. The rest of you, stay with the ship until Master returns. Let's go," he muttered at the chosen guards. "I want to hurry."

They set out only a few minutes behind Xanthus, but the heavy wagon couldn't move as fast as the light carriage Bericus had sent. It was already nearly dark by the time they cleared Herculaneum's town walls and set out on the road. Achivus lit a lamp, which swayed with the motion of the wagon. Charlie watched the rooflines pass overhead and tried desperately not to think of Bericus.

Just get through tonight, we'll be out of here by tomorrow night, just get through tonight . . .

Rooflines gave way to treetops, then to open, dark sky. A night patrol stopped them a quarter hour outside town, demanding their business. Torchlight flickered across the wagon, lighting Achivus' face. Burnished armor gleamed in the darkness. Crested helmets hid the soldiers' faces in shadow. Charlie waited dully as uniformed soldiers searched the wagon and laughed at the scars visible across most of his body.

"Bericus is buying himself gladiator stock, eh?" one of them chuckled. "I always did think he was daft. Very well, slave. Drive on."

The soldiers walked their horses cross-country into the darkness, taking most of the light with them, intent on finishing their patrol route. Achivus shook the reins and clucked to the horses. The wagon creaked into motion again. The outriders assigned as guards peered uneasily into the darkness and nudged their horses into motion, flanking the wagon. Charlie shut his eyes and wished he could sink into sleep. He would need his strength later, when all hell *really* broke loose. But all he could see whenever he closed his eyes was Sibyl in Bericus' hands.

As for Tony Bartlett, aka Antonius Caelerus . . .

What were *his* plans?

If Charlie could just get his hands on Bartlett, they'd have their ticket out of this hellhole. And maybe—just maybe—the information he needed to find Carreras again. Charlie closed his fists, wanting Carreras' neck under his hands. He could all but feel the pulse beat under grinding thumbs, could all but feel the bones snapping under the pressure . . .

Charlie had killed enough men with his bare hands to know the feel of death. And every man he'd been forced to kill in the Circus had—for at least a few critical moments—worn Jésus Carreras' face.

It had kept him alive. Now, the fierce need to make Jésus Carreras pay was almost more than he could bear. Tony Bartlett could give him Jésus Carreras. But first, Charlie had to rescue Sibyl and his child. Only then would he permit himself to think of revenge. So he watched stars appear in the dark sky and made his plans.

The Roman gods, fickle as ever, had other ideas.

Charlie was jolted out of murderous thoughts by an agonized scream. Charlie knew the sound of death, as well as the feel of it. He tried to peer over the edge of the wagon, just as a horse sunfished past the lantern. Charlie could barely see its rider, but the lamplight revealed enough. An arrow had sprouted from the man's throat. Achivus yelled and dove for cover under the wagon's high seat. The other guards turned tail and ran, crying for help as they galloped away.

The horses pulling the wagon broke into a dead run. Charlie yelled and clung to his own chains as the wagon jolted out of control down the road. Whoops and screams of delight floated down from the darkness. *Bandits* . . .

Riders appeared from the starlit night, slung low over running horses. Dark, desperate men, they snatched at the loose reins, cursing at the panic-stricken horses. One of them finally leaped onto the wagon itself and snatched the reins, pulling the horses to a halt. Other riders pulled their mounts up beside the wagon, grinning in the wavering lamplight.

"Oh, ho!" one of them cried. "Look here!"

They dragged Achivus out from beneath the seat. The secretary was trembling and weeping.

"Please . . . don't kill me . . . please . . ."

One of them drew a *gladius*, much nicked from use, and backed him against the wagon. "And who are you, little slave?"

"A-Achivus, please, s-sir, secretary to Xanthus, of— of Rome—"

"You can read and write, then? Ought to fetch a nice price, boy. And what have we in the wagon?"

Charlie found himself looking into the eyes of a short, swarthy man dressed in a coarse linen tunic. His beard and hair were ragged. "Well, well. A naked slave in chains. What exactly are *you*?"

Before Charlie could answer, a shout and the thunder of galloping horses broke into their awareness. Six soldiers roared into the midst of the gloating bandits. Sudden confusion reigned as bandits scattered and soldiers hacked them down. Screams floated in the darkness. The wagon lurched as the horses took flight again. Charlie yelled and hung on. Sounds of fighting receded as the horses flew down the black road, goaded by panic.

How long the horses ran, Charlie wasn't sure. They finally slowed to a jolting trot and then a walk. Then, finally, they stopped, blowing tiredly while the lamp swung on its mounting and finally settled to its original position. Charlie cautiously rose to his knees. The night was utterly silent. He tugged at the chains, then swore. They were solid. And Achivus, the little bastard, had the key that held him chained to the wagon.

He explored the iron ring. Maybe he could gouge it

out of the wagonbed? With what? His fingernails? He explored under the wagon seat, but found nothing that might help him get loose. He swore savagely and studied the chains again. Maybe he could pick the lock? Again, with what?

Then he heard the hoofbeats.

Charlie swung around, lost his balance, and sprawled in the bed of the wagon. The horses shivered, but didn't offer to run again. Several riders were approaching, taking their time. The soldiers, come looking for the lost merchandise? Or the bandits, doing the same? Charlie wasn't certain which would be worse. The soldiers might drag him back to town. The bandits might drag him away to be sold so far from Herculaneum, he'd never have a chance to rescue Sibyl and little Lucania.

Charlie waited in a cold sweat, able to do nothing but listen to their approach. Several dim shapes resolved from the blackness beyond the lamp's reach. Dark, ragged tunics, unshaved chins . . .

Bandits.

They weren't laughing any longer.

The man who'd asked Charlie what he was had survived the fight. He stared down into the wagon, meeting Charlie's gaze steadily for long moments. Then, ignoring Charlie utterly, he started bellowing orders.

"Bring the wagon! It'll be useful to haul the loot."

The bandits returned to the scene of the original attack by the patrol. Four soldiers lay dead in the road. Someone had tied their horses nearby. Of Achivus and the other two soldiers, there was no trace. The bandits pulled the wagon over and began stripping the bodies.

Armor and weapons landed perilously near Charlie's feet. The bandits grunted while they worked, then stripped their own dead and hauled the bodies off into the rocks for the kites and vultures to clean. Charlie watched the proceedings silently and wondered when they'd get around to questioning him.

"Let's go," the leader snapped. "We'll make camp in the usual spot and decide our next move. Now that we've killed soldiers, we'll have to go somewhere else, dammit, or have a detail on our backsides, hunting us out. This was a lucrative area, curse it all. You, drive. You, walk behind and erase those wagon tracks! And put out that Amun-cursed light."

One of the bandits climbed onto the wooden seat and blew out the lamp. Darkness rushed in. Charlie's eyes gradually adjusted. Other bandits untied the captured horses and tied their reins to the wagon. Then they set out, moving down the road for several hundred yards before jolting off cross-country. The wagon tipped and swayed sharply. Charlie slammed into the side. He held back a groan and endured it.

They rattled across an open field, found a winding, rutted lane and followed that for a while, then cut through a large olive grove. The bandits rode for what felt, subjectively, like hours. Charlie noted with growing misgiving that they were taking him farther and farther up the side of the mountain, toward the wild summit.

My God, that mountain'll blow right out from under us. . . . Eventually they entered a tangle of forest. Trees closed in. Brush scraped the sides of the wagon. High boulders loomed in the fitful starlight. They emerged in a tiny clearing which clearly had seen a lot of use as a base camp. Semipermanent fire circles huddled under rock overhangs. Refuse and bundles of loot were strewn about. The bandits turned the wagon and backed it into what was very nearly a cave under one jagged overhang, then set to work preparing an evening meal.

Someone relit the lamp. The light flared and caught the bandit leader's eyes. He was staring down at Charlie.

"Now . . . about you."

"I'm chained to the wagon," Charlie said quietly, lifting his manacled hands.

"So you are. The key?"

"The secretary had it."

The bandit leader spat to one side. "Amun curse him. . . . He got away in the confusion. All that profit, lost. You better be worth enough to make up for it."

The look in his eyes as he swept his gaze across Charlie's ruined leg sent Charlie's blood running cold.

"I'm fairly valuable," he managed to say steadily. "Breeding stock."

"Breeding stock?" The bandit's eyes widened. Then his expression grew speculative. "Well, you're certainly *big* enough for it."

"Two years in the Circus Maximus. I'm school trained, a veteran champion. Publius Bericus wants to breed me."

Interest warred with disbelief at the grandiose claim. "Really? We'll see ... Verecundus! Come here!"

An older, grizzled man whose neck bore the unmistakable scars of a man who had spent years as a collared slave approached the wagon.

"Yes, Pharnaces?"

"Ever see this man?"

Verecundus studied Charlie's face for only a moment.

"Yeah. I seen him, lots of times. Rufus the Murderer. Got close a few times, the night before a bout, when they gave the public gladiator banquets."

Memory slammed down across Charlie: the so-called gladiator feasts, where men with only a few hours to live swilled wine in front of gawking crowds of slaves, freedmen, even thrill-seeking patricians—including wives of the school's owners, who would come and touch him for luck. ...

Verecundus was speaking again. "They used to chain him for the banquets, goad him from the crowd. Should'a seen him fight, though. Never saw a man with so much hatred in him. A champion of the Circus Maximus in Rome, not that pipsqueak little arena down in Herculaneum. What in hell's he doing chained to a wagon out here?"

"Claims Publius Bericus plans to breed him."

"Prob'ly ain't lying. He was worth money. His get ought to be fighters, for sure. I got sold by that bastard owned me before he lost a fight, though. What happened to your leg, Murderer?"

What's it look like, idiot?

He forced his voice to remain low and calm. "I lost a special exhibition bout. Five on one. They hacked my leg out from under me after I killed three. I got the one who did my leg. The last one pinned me with a trident and net when my leg failed. But the crowd was impressed. So was Vespasian."

Charlie was sweating just at the memory of the crowd's roar, the look in the eyes of the man who held his throat pinned to the sand, the agony in his leg and the worse agony of waiting for the signal that would end his life. . . .

"Huh. You're lucky." The former slave spat into the darkness. "He's one mean son of a barbarian, Pharnaces."

Memory faded, leaving Charlie facing a new danger.

"I'm inclined to leave you chained to the wagon," Pharnaces mused. "You sound dangerous."

Charlie laughed bitterly. "Only to the bastards who chained me here. And not really to them. I can barely hobble, Pharnaces." He turned his leg toward the light, showing the scars more clearly.

Even Pharnaces sucked in his breath. "Isis pity you . . ."

Charlie met his gaze again and waited, as he'd waited in the hot sunlight of the Roman arena.

"A man with your experience might be useful," Pharnaces mused. "I lost some good men in that fight tonight. We're not really trained, any of us. You agree to teach us, we'll feed you, carry you with us."

"Do I have a choice?" Charlie asked bluntly.

Pharnaces laughed. "Of course. Join us and we'll take care of you. Otherwise, we'll sell you at the nearest slave market. After we remove your tongue, of course." Pharnaces' eyes glinted humorously. "Either way, we make a profit."

"Huh. I think I like the idea of helping bandits kill Romans. If I can't kill a few myself, I suppose training you is almost as good."

"Thought you'd see it our way. Verecundus, see what you can do about getting those chains off him. Feed him. We'll decide what to do about moving camp tomorrow morning, after a good meal and a good sleep."

Verecundus produced a chisel and maul, which he used to cut through the chains one at a time. First he broke the chain on the wagon itself, which allowed Charlie to crawl down to the ground. Other bandits began unloading their loot while Verecundus helped Charlie limp over to an outcropping of stone.

"Let me see those manacles. Hmm . . . Hold your hands like this. Steady, now. Don't move or I'll slice your hand off."

Charlie ground his teeth together and held still. The chisel struck sparks. But within a few hammer blows, his wrists were free. Verecundus went to work on his ankles.

"You're a mess," he observed quietly. "Somebody beat you bad. Why?"

"I don't like Publius Bericus."

"Can't say I blame you. I killed my last master. There." The ankle shackles broke open.

For the moment, Charlie was as close to freedom as he'd come in four years. *Keep cool, Flynn, play it right, and there's still a chance.*

They gave him a loincloth and fed him—real meat, roasted over a fire. He bolted it down and was given generous seconds. And wine, too. Good red wine from someone's looted stores, not the sour stuff Xanthus had given them aboard ship. Charlie drank enough to ease the fire in his back—the newer scabs had been torn open when the wagon horses bolted—but not enough to completely dull his senses. The rush of a nearby stream was a tantalizing call.

"Anybody mind if I wash off the blood?"

Pharnaces jerked his head in assent. Verecundus escorted him. Charlie leaned more heavily on the former slave than he really needed to and made the most of his hobbling gait. The moon had risen enough to shed light on a rushing stream. Charlie eased down and let his feet slide into the current. To his surprise, the water was not icy cold. It was warm, almost warm as bathwater.

Bad sign.

He washed his whole body, even his hair, and felt like a new man. Verecundus poured water over his back, washing dirt and grit out of the reopened welts. Charlie hissed softly and jerked under the man's touch. Verecundus apologized as though he really meant it. Charlie finally wrapped the loincloth Verecundus handed back around his hips. Amazing, how much less vulnerable one felt with one's genitals covered protectively rather than bouncing around it the open.

Verecundus said, "We'll try to find something else for you to wear at camp."

"Thank you," Charlie said quietly, meaning it.

He hoped he didn't have to kill anyone making his escape from this camp. He hobbled, semi-naked and dripping, back into camp, drawing curious stares from bandits who were busy sorting out the armor they'd taken from the dead soldiers.

"Any of those tunics fit Rufus?" Verecundus asked. "Some of those soldiers were big men."

They found a tunic which proved a reasonable fit. Verecundus wrapped Charlie's back in soft linen strips first, to protect the welts, then Charlie wriggled into the tunic. He felt a thousand percent better already.

"Bed down," Pharnaces told him. "We'll move out at dawn."

Charlie nodded, choosing a spot near a bundle of confiscated armor—the bundle belonging to the man whose tunic Charlie now wore. They'd put everything into a leather bag: helmet, greaves, sandals, cloak, "skirt" of metal-studded leather strips to protect the thighs, leather "jacket" with metal bands to protect chest and back, weapons belts, everything. Charlie lay down a few feet away from it, facing the nearest fire.

Verecundus grunted, then bedded down near him.

The small cookfires were already burning low. Some of the men were still drinking. Charlie pretended to fall asleep. He listened as the camp slowly fell silent. Waited while the bandits began to snore. Watched through slitted eyes while the night watch dozed off. . . .

He forced himself to wait another agonizing half hour, letting sleep deepen its grip on the camp. Then, moving cautiously, Charlie stirred. If caught early in his plans, he'd claim he simply needed to relieve himself. He'd need that bundle of arms from the dead soldier, a horse . . .

The leather sack clanked softly as he picked it up. Charlie grimaced and glanced swiftly around. A couple of men had stirred, but didn't waken. He paused, letting slumber deepen, then hobbled awkwardly toward the stolen horses.

The nearest watched alertly, ears pricked forward. The color of mud, it was the only horse in camp awake. The others dozed, one rear leg slack, heads drooping. *Well-schooled*, Charlie thought, since it made no sound at his approach.

Charlie untied the reins and gingerly led the horse forward. If he were caught now . . . He fished in the bag and drew out the *gladius* with a soft hiss. At least they'd cleaned the blood off it before resheathing it. Forgetting to clean a blade was the fastest way to ruin it. These men might not have the training he did, but they clearly knew their business.

Charlie tied the bundle to the horse's saddle, then— gripping the *gladius* with old skill that made the weapon part of his hand—he led the willing animal toward the narrow exit from camp.

The soft clop of its hooves made Charlie wince.

Gotta get on his back, before we wake up somebody.

Trouble was, the damned saddle had no stirrups. None of the Roman saddles he'd ever seen had them. So he'd need to find some place to crawl up high enough to slither on. Charlie made it to the far side of the camp without raising an alarm. He limped down the brush-lined, narrow entrance still without raising an alarm. He waited until he was outside that narrow corridor to find a boulder, then climbed painfully up. The horse waited patiently.

How hard can this be? he asked himself, eying the

stirrup-less saddle with growing misgiving. *You climb on and sit down all the way there*. John Wayne had made it look easy in film after film. *Yeah, but this ain't no movie*, a small voice warned from the back of Charlie's brain.

Buzz off, Charlie told the voice.

Holding tightly to the reins in case the animal spooked, Charlie dragged himself across the animal's back. A couple of tricky moments broke him out into a cold sweat, but he finally managed to slide into the saddle. The horse snorted and tossed its head a couple of times, then laid its ears back, but thankfully endured it.

God bless the beasts and children . . .

Charlie Flynn knew as much about riding horses as the bandits he'd just escaped knew about riding a Harley Davidson.

Fortunately, the beast seemed mannerly, docile, and well trained. After a moment's reflection, he decided he couldn't very well call the horse "it," even if the poor beast *had* lost the equipment he needed to be a stallion.

"Okay," Charlie muttered, gratified when the horse flicked an ear at the sound, "let's go, Silver. Hi-Ho and away!"

Mud-colored "Silver" set off at a sedate walk. Shortly thereafter Charlie discovered how to fall off. He landed in a bruised heap on the ground and lay groaning for a long moment. Silver danced a step sideways, then bent his head and blew inquiringly at him. The horse pawed twice at the ground and snorted softly. Charlie waited for the alarm to sound from the camp farther up in the trees, but all remained silent. Charlie's pulse dropped back down into the high-normal range. He caught his breath shallowly. Meanwhile, Silver nibbled inquisitively at his hair.

Gingerly, Charlie regained his feet. Silver followed him happily enough to another boulder. Charlie regained his precarious perch in the saddle and set out once more. Balance was the real problem, Charlie decided another nasty fall later. Clearly, there was more to riding without stirrups than met the eye. Without stirrups, sitting on a horse was a lot like sitting on a fat barrel that moved unpredictably forward and sideways. "I'll bet John Wayne never had this problem," he muttered sourly.

Charlie limped along the tangle of wild forest, leading Silver and listening for sounds of pursuit, and wondered what the hell to do now.

"Don't need a genius for that," Charlie growled aloud. "Gotta get me some stirrups."

In the middle of the night? God knew how many centuries before the damned things had been invented. He couldn't very well roust out a blacksmith and show him how to make a set. Charlie halted and thought about it. Silver chewed his bit meditatively and waited.

He had that leather bag. Rig something using strips cut from that? If he cut it up, though, he'd either have to ditch the armor or wear it. He already had the weapon he'd wanted, but the armor could prove useful later.

Charlie dug it out and struggled into it.

The leather jacketlike affair, with metal bands and plates fastened to it, was snug, but it went on and he could still breathe after fastening it. Garrison soldiers were larger than the normal run of peasant. This guy's size made Charlie wonder if he'd come from one of the northern provinces. Northerners tended to run a couple of sizes larger than most garrison soldiers, a fact confirmed by two years spent watching Xanthus' "merchandise" move through the house. Charlie grimaced and tried to adjust the armor. Nope, that was as good a fit as he could get.

Heavy sandals with straps which criss-crossed the leg nearly to the knee were too tight and pinched his toes, but they went on. So did the helmet, although it flattened his ears painfully against his skull and dug into his neck, especially where it met the metal collar locked around his throat. The long cloak, once it was wrapped securely around his neck, ought to hide both his *fugitivus* brand and slave collar. The weight of the sword felt strange after two years in Xanthus' house, but the solidity of it in his hand gave him more confidence than he'd felt in months. He strapped the weapon to his hip.

A smaller dagger hung in another sheath from the sword belt. He tried to snap open the lock on his slave's collar, but the blasted thing would not open. He finally gave up, deeply concerned that someone in camp would wake up. He resheathed the dagger.

That done, Charlie studied the saddle. He cut up the big leather bag, working quietly and quickly, making one long strip of it by cutting in a spiral from the neck. He tied the very center firmly to the saddle and formed a noose for his foot on the near side at what looked like the proper height. He then tossed the end over the saddle. Keeping firm hold of the reins, Charlie ducked under Silver's nose to see how far down it dangled. He used his stolen dagger to cut the leather "rope" to the appropriate length. He tied another noose, then Charlie cut another section and used that to tie the contraption more firmly to the saddle.

"Huh. Maybe it'll work."

Charlie resheathed the dagger and found another boulder to use as a stepladder. Getting into the saddle this time was easier. He used one hand to manually bend his left leg and held it up until he could work his toes into the noose. "Not bad," he muttered.

Charlie gathered up the reins and took firm hold of Silver's mane with both hands. Then he grinned. "How do you like that, Silver? I just invented stirrups."

The horse flicked its ears and snorted.

Charlie thumped Silver's ribs and set out. Staying in the saddle still wasn't a picnic, but it was far easier than before. Charlie learned how to steer and stop. He clung to the mane with a deathlike grip whenever Silver changed direction or speed. Eventually he got the hang of it, though, and his confidence began to grow with each moment that didn't find him sprawled on the stony ground again.

Then, just as he was beginning to feel he and Silver

were old friends, he heard a shout drift down from higher on the mountain. Someone had awakened and discovered him missing. Within seconds, more shouts drifted to his ears. Pharnaces, ordering his men to give chase. . . . Charlie bent low over Silver's neck, said a prayer, and kicked Silver into a gallop.

Charlie clung to the mane, all but helpless in his effort to stay with the panicked horse. He glanced back and saw several mounted men riding in pursuit.

"Aw, nuts . . ."

But he wasn't on foot and he wasn't disarmed and he sure as hell wasn't going to be taken alive. Charlie kicked Silver to greater speed and headed down the mountain at breakneck speed. He gained the bottom of a wild little valley and glanced back again. The horsemen were still with him, gaining ground. Charlie wished for a gun— then was glad his pursuers didn't have one. Silver gained a packed dirt road and pounded toward a sharp bend. The rutted lane snaked around the flank of the mountain. They gained the bend and burst down the other side. Silver's mud-colored mane whipped Charlie's face like cutting wire. He crouched lower and kicked Silver to greater speed.

"Come on, boy, you gotta get me outta this one, they're counting on me, Silver, c'mon, boy. . . ."

The road slithered down toward a little stream overhung by willows and scraggly oaks. Charlie crossed the bridge with a sound of hollow thunder, then pulled Silver around and turned him back toward the water. His only prayer of escape would be to lose himself in the tangle around the stream while the bandits went chasing him down an empty road. Down in the farmland and vineyards, he'd be easy prey.

Silver snorted and tossed his head, then waded down the bank. Charlie steered him back toward the summit and urged him to greater speed. Silver kicked up spray that soaked Charlie from the thighs down. They rounded a wicked bend, which put them out of sight of the road, then Charlie pulled the horse to a shivering stop.

He sat panting and strained to hear. Silver blew softly. The horse lifted one foot, setting it back down with a faint clatter. Back toward the road, Charlie heard the sound of thundering hooves. His pursuers reached the bridge . . .

And kept going. Charlie didn't wait around to see how long it took them to figure out his trick. He set Silver to a cautious walk and went about a hundred yards before he urged the horse up the far bank. He followed the stream for several minutes, criss-crossing it repeatedly, doubling back, riding down the center of the stream again, then finally waded out and headed straight up Vesuvius' hulking shoulder, striking out at an angle from the meandering stream.

In the distance, Charlie heard the muted rumble of running horses. They were coming his way. He groaned softly. Maybe his tactics on the bank would confuse them? Given his luck this past year, he wasn't betting on it. He didn't dare go near the villa, not yet. He had to let things settle down, get quiet, make damned sure he'd eluded those bandits . . .

The drumming of horses' hooves drew closer. They'd figured out his trick and were coming down the stream after him. Charlie urged Silver to a canter and plunged into the wilds above the olive groves. If he stayed ahead of them long enough, they might call off the hunt, fearing to be seen as night faded into dawn. They might start to wonder if grabbing their loot and leaving might be more profitable than hunting down one crippled ex-gladiator. Charlie tried to ease aching thighs and hoped his pursuers started thinking along those lines.

Given the sounds behind him, they hadn't yet. *Blasted tenacious bandits*. Charlie was torn between urging his horse to greater speed and fear that Silver would break a leg among the rocks—or that he'd fall off. Hard on that thought, low-growing willow branches whipped across Charlie's face and nearly scraped him out of the saddle. He'd barely recovered from that when a roaring sound penetrated his awareness.

What—?

The moon sank behind Vesuvius' dark bulk, leaving the patch of willows in sudden, complete blackness. It was so dark, Charlie pulled up on the reins to slow his horse's onrushing speed. The roaring sound was suddenly much louder.

Water . . .

Silver shied and danced sideways, hooves striking stone with a clanking sound. Charlie tried to bring his head around, confused and disoriented. Then the horse bunched his muscles and jumped over something. A fallen log? Charlie clung to the horse's neck—

Silver screamed in sudden panic and lurched forward. Charlie's belly rushed upward, like an express elevator. He bit off a yell as they crashed forward into empty space. They were falling, falling . . . Water smashed across him in a stinging spray. He came loose from the saddle and tumbled sideways, away from his horse. Then he slammed into something incredibly hard.

The world vanished into wet, black pain.

CHAPTER TEN

Francisco didn't like Lieutenant Kominsky. He'd never been sure why, but after five minutes in the man's presence, his skin always crawled, like he'd touched a week-dead snake. Maybe it was the way Kominsky never smiled but always gave the impression that he found everything Francisco did and said triflingly amusing.

Maybe Kominsky just didn't like Hispanics?

"You should have a guard in there with you," Kominsky said before unlocking the stout door. "He's violent. You should've seen what he did to a couple of MPs about an hour ago." Kominsky's eyes glinted. "I bet he remembers you fondly, eh, Major?"

Francisco considered the merit of that, but he didn't want any witnesses. "Just open the door, Lieutenant."

"Yessir."

Kominsky unlocked the cell and swung the heavy steel door open. It looked like something designed to hold a raging dinosaur, rather than one confused man. Francisco stepped inside.

McKee was waiting for him.

One moment, Francisco was in the doorway, stepping through. The next, he was on the floor, seeing stars. He heard Kominsky's voice, barking an order. Francisco shook his head to clear it. McKee was about two feet from the open door, gazing contemplatively into the muzzle of Kominsky's rifle.

"Get back, mister. Now. Major Valdez, please step out of there until I can call additional security."

Francisco rubbed the side of his head, which had connected rather solidly with the concrete floor, then hunted for the medical kit he'd dropped. "No, that's all right, Kominsky. I'm staying."

McKee glanced around curiously. Francisco stumbled to his feet. "You're staying?" McKee echoed. "You think you have a choice? Get the hell out of here, before the nice lunatic breaks your spine or something."

Francisco held McKee's gaze steadily. Despite the threat and the tumble he'd received, Francisco read no hint of real threat in McKee's mad eyes. Just frustration, fear, and stony bitterness.

"McKee," he said quietly, "I'm only here to check your hands and feet. They're probably swollen and hurting like hell."

In a conversational tone, sounding almost cheerful, McKee said, "Up yours, doc. Now be a good boy and get out, huh? Your kind of company I can do without, thank you very much."

Francisco eyed him sourly. "Whatever you think of me, you're my patient. I don't intend to let you stay in pain. Sit down on the bunk, please. I'd rather not have Kominsky's men *tie* you down."

That got a flicker of response. McKee's eyes glinted briefly. "You're all heart, doc. Shut the door, Kominsky. I promise not to kill him too badly."

Francisco's pulse jumped, but he held his ground. "I'll call you when I'm done, Lieutenant."

Kominsky shrugged, as if to say, "Sure. Why not? It's your funeral, Major." He shut the door. The lock snapped shut, trapping Francisco in the cell with his patient.

McKee studied him with frank interest. "Well, you've got a set, doc, I'll give you that. Was the dog and pony show just for appearances, or are you really here to examine my frostbite?"

Francisco couldn't really blame him. "If you'll sit down, McKee," he said, working hard to sound calmer than he felt, "I'll check your feet and toes first."

"Huh." McKee sprawled onto the bunk and tugged

off tennis shoes that were nearly as old as Francisco. He waggled his toes invitingly. "Come and get it."

Francisco ignored the levity. "All right, let's take a look." He set the medical bag aside and hunkered down. "Hmm . . ." Both feet were swollen, although not as severely as he'd feared. "Can you feel this?" He ran a sharp point down the sole of McKee's foot.

McKee came nearly off the bunk. "Watch it, will you?" The growl in his voice didn't quite disguise the lingering wince in his eyes.

Francisco grinned and reached for the other foot. "Be grateful. That just proves there's no nerve damage. Now, let's see if you're as lucky with this one." The examination revealed no permanent damage to hands or feet. "I'll say this for you, McKee. You're lucky. These could've been a lot worse. Multiple-amputee worse. How's the pain?"

McKee muttered something too low for him to hear.

"Thought so. Would you prefer a tablet or an injection?"

McKee narrowed suspicious eyes. "Of . . . ?"

"A codeine derivative, to take the edge off."

McKee didn't answer immediately. Instead, he studied Francisco through eyes about as friendly as a hungry Kodiak bear's. Francisco stood up, trying to appear nonchalant. It was difficult to keep his hands steady as he opened the medical kit and rummaged through it. He'd read McKee's records and had an altogether too graphic idea what kind of pain this man could inflict with his bare hands.

"I can't figure you, doc," McKee finally said. "First you fill me full of babble juice, like I'm some lab rat, and now you're worried I might be hurting? Or do you just want me doped up good for the next unscheduled little visit?"

Francisco frowned. "Next visit?"

"Come off it, Major. I wasn't born yesterday. You know damned well what I mean."

Francisco held his gaze steadily. "No, I don't. Has

someone else been here? Kominsky said you'd injured a couple of MPs."

Francisco received the distinct impression McKee was evaluating risks—or maybe just trying to sort through personal paranoias. At length, McKee rubbed the back of his neck.

"Yeah, well, they got rough first. That colonel of yours was here, with the goon pulling his strings. Real nice fellow. How the hell can you stand working for him?" McKee was still rubbing his neck absently and staring into the corner.

Goon? Someone pulling Dan's strings? "What 'goon'? What are you talking about?"

McKee's glance sharpened. "Don't tell me you haven't met Mr. Silk Suit and Rolex watch?"

Francisco drew a complete blank.

Evidently it convinced McKee, because he said, "Well, I'll be dipped. Just what the hell *is* going on around here, anyway? Your colonel's scared shitless of this guy."

Francisco blinked a couple of times. "I knew something was wrong . . ."

McKee snorted. "You said a fuckin' mouthful. Look, this guy's about, oh, fortyish, Hispanic, I mean *real* Hispanic. You've got a Hispanic name, but you sound, I don't know, California? Nevada?"

Francisco bristled silently, but said nothing. McKee *did* have a reason to hate him. Insults weren't much compared to being forcibly drugged and interrogated.

McKee watched him narrowly through glittering eyes. "Hit a sore spot, huh, doc? You're a lousy spy, Valdez. Maybe you're not one of his, after all. Just following orders, like Lieutenant Calley. Look, all I meant, was, this guy talks and looks like South American drug money. Not a pampered Long Beach medical school graduate. And whoever he is, he's giving the orders on this base. Wherever the hell *that* is. I still don't know where I am."

Francisco thought about telling him, then thought better.

McKee caught Francisco's eye. "Huh. Nobody'll tell

me *anything*. And let me tell you, that puts a real bad cramp in my gut. This civvie didn't even tell me his name, much less where this wonderful accommodation," he gestured at the cell, "happens to be located."

Francisco opened his mouth to ask a question, then shut it again. He wondered with a sudden chill if there were listening devices in this cell.

McKee held his gaze for a moment, then crossed his arms and looked disgusted. "Like I said," he muttered, "nobody tells me jack shit."

"McKee," Francisco finally said, "where *have* you been for the last five years?"

The man shivered and dropped his gaze. "You tell me, doc."

This was going nowhere. Talking to a lunatic probably hadn't been the brightest idea he'd ever formulated. Francisco rummaged for the medication he'd promised. "Let me just give you something to ease the discomfort, then I'll—"

"Doc . . ."

An undercurrent of darkness in McKee's voice caused Francisco to look up. He paused in the act of filling a hypo. McKee's face was utterly impassive, an oaken mask freshly cut from the tree.

"Try to give me that shit," McKee said very softly, "and I'll break your arm."

Francisco couldn't look away from McKee's eyes. *Nothing cold or impassive about those eyes. If I don't put this away, right now, he's going to hurt me. Badly. Kominsky's hell and gone on the other side of a locked steel door. . . .* Francisco realized his fingers were trembling. He wiped them against his pants leg, then put the medication away.

"I'm just trying to help," he said quietly. "A lot of things I don't understand have been happening the last few months. You're just one of them."

"Yeah? Welcome to the club. Tell you what, doc. Go ask your friend the colonel who *his* friend is. Maybe you'll get your answers. Then again," McKee grinned, an evil jack-'o-lantern, "maybe you'll get a bullet in the back of the head, huh? I'll bet your colonel's friends don't play nicely. Not at all."

"Thanks for the warning," Francisco said dryly. "If you change your mind about the medication, get Kominsky to call me."

He closed up his kit and banged on the door. A moment later, Kominsky opened it. As Francisco left the cell, McKee called out, "Hey, doc. Have a nice life, huh? Give my regards to your boss."

Kominsky glanced curiously at Francisco, but said nothing. The security lieutenant locked McKee in again. Francisco left silently, fighting the urge to confront his friend directly. Dan Collins taking orders from a South American drug lord? Ridiculous. But where were Danny and Lucille? If this guy, whoever he was, had hostages . . .

"Mother of God," Francisco whispered to the cold air outside the detention center. His breath steamed on contact, leaving a cloud of ice crystals in front of his face until a gust of wind whipped them away. "Mother of God . . ."

He was beginning to wish he hadn't started digging. He didn't like *any* of the answers he was finding. Too late now. He tightened his grip on the medical kit. He was in up to his freezing California ears. And whoever had come to interrogate McKee earlier would probably figure that out, too. Real soon.

Francisco shivered inside his parka. He couldn't make any phone calls off base, couldn't talk to his commander, had no idea whom he could safely trust. A hundred sixty-eight undocumented personnel. . . . No wonder Dan was losing weight and drinking.

The only bright spot Francisco could see was that Dan was under guard. That meant he wasn't collaborating of his own free will. If he could just get Dan aside for a couple of minutes . . .

"No way," he muttered. He started walking back toward the infirmary. "No way they'll let him near me without a guard eavesdropping."

As he slogged toward his office, Francisco realized he had absolutely no idea what to do next. The feeling left him scared all the way to his frozen California toes.

It was full dark by the time they reached Publius Bericus' villa. During the last half of their journey into the Campanian countryside, Sibyl hadn't been at all sure they *would* reach the villa. The road had been rocked by several earth tremors, a couple of them strong enough to be classed as major earthquakes. Xanthus had expressed doubt about continuing the journey, adding to the innumerable delays created by panicked horses. They even suffered a bruising upset when one jolt rocked the carriage off its wheels, but greed won out in the end. Xanthus kept going.

An hour later than Charlie's one-hour prediction, Bericus' house finally came into sight. The long, low villa which proved to be their destination was, as Charlie had described, situated on a rise overlooking fields, vineyards, and orchards. Rougher forest lay above the villa, creeping silently toward the summit. Bericus' home looked like the last outpost of civilization, huddled on the flank of a slumbering monster. Moonlight silvered whitewashed walls. Far below lay the sleeping town, and beyond that, an endless vista of moon-sparkled sea.

When Sibyl's feet touched the ground, she felt a continuous, subliminal tremor through the soles of her thin sandals. She shivered and unconsciously hunched her shoulders. Deadly harmonics, which heralded the unseen shove and flow of magma in the earth. . . . Xanthus grasped her arm and dragged her toward the darkened villa.

The door was thrown open before they arrived, at the shouted instructions of their driver. A slave stood in the doorway. The elderly man bowed deeply. Xanthus paused to touch an erect, stone phallus which Bericus had set in the entryway for luck—a certain charm to "put out" the evil eye. Beside it were the words, "RUMPERE, INVIDIA!" *To destroy ill-will.* . . .

If only Publius Bericus proved as superstitious as that charm hinted. Xanthus dragged her into her new master's home. Sibyl studied her surroundings through narrowed eyes. Brilliant frescoes adorned the walls. The mosaic floor was a masterpiece, displaying a riot of fauns, satyrs, nymphs, and the figure of a goddess, but there wasn't enough detail visible in the darkness to tell whether or not it was Cybele, Great Goddess of the shrine at Cumae, or one of the other Mediterranean/Middle Eastern goddesses so popular in this early Imperial period.

Still, Bericus *had* put a major goddess figure on his floor, and from the little she could tell, it wasn't Venus, or Venus with Mars, an overwhelmingly popular thematic image in Pompeiian and Herculanean mosaics. She thought she could make out the dim paw of a large beast. A lion? If it were a goddess riding a lion . . .

The pool of water in the atrium reflected starlight through the open roof. A fountain in the shape of Neptune making love to a water nymph lent an elegant, erotic note, with its classical lines and constant murmuring splash of silver water. The entire effect of floor, fountain, and moonlight on water was subtly disturbing, even while she had to admire its artistry.

Music drifted in from the interior of the house. Wherever it originated, it wasn't coming from the *triclinium*. The Roman equivalent of the formal dining room was dark and silent as they passed it, heading deeper into the house. Other rooms, presumably bedrooms, receiving rooms, Bericus' private office, were curtained off with heavy draperies. There was too little light to make out the embroidered patterns.

Given the house's layout, Bericus had built the front part of the house on the classic, native Roman pattern, with a Hellenistic house around a *peristyle* built onto it. She'd seen the pattern again and again in Herculaneum and Pompeii. The result was airy, elegant, uniquely beautiful.

By tomorrow night, the house would be dead, along

with everything and everyone in it. Sibyl's legs threatened to buckle. Xanthus growled under his breath and
dragged her forward. As they neared the central gardens in the *peristyle*, Sibyl heard laughter, singing,
and ... other sounds. Her knees wobbled at every other
step. Bericus was in there and Tony Bartlett. ...

Can I look at him and pretend I don't know him? If
she gave herself away, he might well murder her, just
to be sure. *I can't do this, he'll know the minute he looks
at me, God, I can't do this* ... The elderly slave led
the way through an open archway, emerging onto a
covered portico which surrounded the peristyle on all
four sides. The enclosed garden was surrounded by
gleaming marble columns, which supported a second
floor balcony.

The soft summer air was thick with the scent of flowers and spilled wine. Across the garden, torches blazed
around a group of couches. Musicians played for the
guests. As they approached, Sibyl realized the party had
long since progressed from dinner to the entertainment
stage.

She wanted to look away—and couldn't.

Publius Bericus drank from a heavy lead goblet, which
made her wonder about lead poisoning and madness.
Then he called encouragement to his guest. Dark-haired,
naked in the torchlight, Tony Bartlett was brutally
sodomizing a boy of no more than eleven.

Oh, God, oh, dear Christ ...

Sibyl was aghast. Tony snarled when the boy tried to
lunge away. He grabbed the young slave by the hair and
hauled him back. The boy whimpered, but stopped fighting.

Sibyl tore her gaze away, trying desperately not to be
ill. *Murderous ... perverted* ...

Xanthus motioned for their guide to wait. Sibyl ground
her teeth until her jaws ached. She prayed helplessly—
hopelessly—that Vesuvius would erupt *now* and trap him
here, too. She would have mortgaged her soul for five
seconds with a loaded rifle. ...

Xanthus finally called out a greeting and strode forward. Sibyl glanced up. Slaves had brought towels, a basin of water, a robe for Bartlett. The boy huddled at his feet. Bericus rose with surprising grace to greet his new guest.

"At last! Welcome, Xanthus, to my home. I trust the voyage down from Rome was a pleasant one?"

"Of course, my dear Bericus, what else? And Caelerus, my old friend." Xanthus turned and clasped Bartlett's arm. "I see your taste is exquisite, as always. Lovely lad, isn't he?"

"Best ass I've had in years."

Sibyl choked on bile. And tried to remember that not only was she supposed to be drugged, she was supposed to have no idea who Bartlett really was.

"Aelia is well, I take it?" Bericus asked. Sibyl was trapped, a sparrow caught by a rat snake. She found herself staring into glittering black eyes. He ran an appreciative hand beneath her robe. She steeled herself and permitted it, while forcing her gaze to unfocus. *They mustn't guess I'm not drugged. They mustn't. If Charlie can endure beating after beating . . .*

"The ripeness of womanhood, the firmness of youth," he murmured. "I shall enjoy planting my seed in such fertile ground, my lovely. But not yet. I want you to be . . . fully aware of me. Quintus!" He patted her shoulder absently, then turned away. She managed not to shudder. An enormously powerful man approached from the shadows. His arms and legs were bare, Roman fashion. Sibyl was hard put not to stare. At some point, he must've been a wrestler, a profession which had—over the intervening millennia—lost a great deal of respectability.

"Quintus, see to it she is confined for the evening. Give her a good meal. Make her comfortable. Tomorrow have her bathed and made ready for me. I'll want her by the seventh hour."

Sibyl started involuntarily. The *seventh* hour? Broad *daylight*? She stared at Bericus. He really *was* a libertine.

No wonder he'd moved to the country. In town, his neighbors would've dragged him through the streets and heaped ridicule on his head. The seventh hour. . . . Sibyl felt a chill despite the sultry heat of the August evening. Romans reckoned hours of the day beginning at sunrise and ending at sunset. Winter hours were consequently shorter than summer ones. The seventh hour would put her in Bericus' hands by noon tomorrow, or a little later. The chill on her skin deepened. Vesuvius was due to erupt shortly before one o'clock.

Just enough time to rape me before we all die. . . .

Quintus bowed, acknowledging Bericus' orders. "Yes, Master."

Bericus turned away, clearly dismissing them from his awareness. "Now, Xanthus, do have a cup of wine. As I recall, there was a little Egyptian girl you were particularly fond of—"

Sibyl shut her eyes. Clearly, Bericus didn't give a fig about contemporary sexual mores. It was men like him who'd given Imperial Rome its reputation for debauched orgies. Xanthus, being Lycian, probably had less difficulty accepting Bericus' outlandish behavior. As close as Lycia—modern Turkey—was to Greece, it received far different influences than Rome. Even if he *had* been shocked by it, profit was a strong motivator to look the other way. Tony Bartlett was clearly in hog heaven. Nobody here would arrest him for sexual battery against a child.

Quintus took hold of Sibyl's bound wrists and led her into the shadows. When she glanced up, she found Tony Bartlett's smirking gaze fastened on her. Sibyl held back curses only by biting down hard on her tongue. The sudden sharp pain brought tears to her eyes, but kept her from revealing herself. Quintus dragged Sibyl into the comparative darkness of the villa, toward a side wing which clearly contained bedrooms. Mercifully, the sounds of revelry died away behind them.

She didn't have much hope of overpowering Quintus. Maybe she *would* resort to setting the house on fire.

And where was little Lucania, Charlie's daughter? How on earth could Sibyl find her? And how long before Charlie arrived in the heavier wagon?

Her taciturn guard finally paused before a stout wooden door. A heavy bar lay propped against the wall beside it. He opened the door, paused, and shouted down the hall for someone named Septiva. A young woman carrying an oil lamp appeared hastily from a nearby room. Sibyl eyed the lamp hopefully.

"Yes, Quintus?"

"Bring food," he growled. Quintus confiscated the lamp. He shoved Sibyl inside and shut the door behind him, then drew a wicked-looking knife and cut the bonds at her wrists. A hard wooden bed, covered with a thin mat, stood along one wall. A plain crockery pot had been placed beneath it, for obvious purposes. Sibyl eyed it dubiously and was intensely grateful she wasn't in the middle of her monthly. How on earth had women coped with *that* before the invention of tampons, adhesive napkins, and Midol?

Sibyl eased herself onto the bed.

She wasn't likely to survive long enough to satisfy her scholarly curiosity. Not even long enough to die of some stupid infection. The enormity of Charlie Flynn's will to survive left her awed. She didn't think she'd have been as strong.

Another thought left her trembling harder than before. Even if she escaped, even if she somehow managed to survive the volcano . . . She did not know how long it had actually been since she'd been taken, but this could be an extremely bad time of the month for her to be sexually active. Her throat closed. She curled her fingers into the thin matting of her hard bed. If Bericus raped her tomorrow, she might be carrying his child by tomorrow night.

Come on, Sib, one disaster at a time. Only way to cope. What did Granny always say? Keep your mind on the task at hand?

She eyed Quintus and gloomily concluded that slipping

past him would be impossible. He watched her so narrowly, she began to wonder if he intended standing guard all night. Given Bericus' temper, if she escaped . . .

She could hardly blame Quintus for being cautious. A timid knock announced Septiva's return. Quintus opened the door and took the tray.

"Eat." He shoved a crudely fashioned wooden tray into Sibyl's hands, then stood with arms crossed and waited, his expression utterly shuttered. Only the hint of a watchful glitter in his eyes told Sibyl he still observed her, rather than stared vacantly into space like some prehistoric statue of Arnold Schwarzenegger.

Sibyl gazed down at the plate.

Boiled meat—from what, she couldn't even begin to hazard a guess, although she was grateful there *was* meat, considering the standard slave diet of wheat gruel and figs—lentils, and coarse bread made up her meal. A veritable feast. Bericus obviously wanted his toys well fed. A chipped earthenware mug of wine sat next to the only utensil, a crudely made wooden spoon.

She thought briefly about salmonella, ptomaine, and other equally pleasant subjects, decided if Charlie could survive on worse, she could live on this, and began to eat. The taste was awful. No pepper, no salt, no nothing. The wine was even worse, bitter and sour despite the generous amount of water that had been added to dilute it. Quintus watched through piggish eyes until she had finished everything. Then he took the tray from her, grunted once, and left—taking the lamp with him.

Even before she heard the bar scrape heavily into place across the door, Sibyl knew she'd been drugged again. Probably the wine. . . . She lay down on the hard pallet and wept until the drug in her veins dragged her down into black oblivion.

Larksong reached across the sleeping countryside to herald the coming of the sun. First one, then two or three, then a dozen "birds of the morning" broke into full-throated song. All but invisible in the early darkness, water plunged over a broken lip of stone and foamed down a narrow gorge.

A molten rim of fire appeared along the mountain's crest. The upper edge of the sun cleared Vesuvius' fog-shrouded cone. Burning light shot skyward, spilled down rocky slopes into the narrow gorge. Rumbling water broke and foamed around a stony massif midstream.

Like a broken marionette, a silent figure sprawled across that worn stone. A scarlet cloak huddled in folds around motionless limbs. A battered helmet glinted in the early light. The sun's lower edge cleared Vesuvius' summit and climbed higher into a flawless August sky.

Below, the crumpled figure remained motionless.

The silence in his office was deafening.

Jésus Carreras held the telephone receiver as far from his ear as he could and still hear the caller. He clenched his teeth over the things he wanted to say and listened grimly to the angry words pouring out at him.

He finally made an attempt. "But, Papa . . ."

A few moments later he tried again. "But, Papa . . ."

Then, "No, Papa, Tony's not back yet. He's overdue. I told you sending him back on the same time line might not work."

The invective grew worse. He held the receiver completely away from his ear and waited until his father had calmed down a little.

"Yes, Papa, I know that. Yes, Papa, I know Cara's eight months pregnant. Dammit, Papa, it was your idea—"

He swore beneath his breath and held the receiver away again. Finally muttered, "Look, Papa, you got that crate of manuscripts you wanted from the first trip he made. Why you insisted he take that idiotic graduate student back and dump her *there* of all places . . . Yes, Papa, I know we have to find out what will work and what won't— But, dammit, Cara's your daughter—"

Finally, "Papa, I will call you the minute I get word that Tony's back. Yes, of course the scientists are monitoring everything! That's their job. They'll damned well do it. No, I haven't been back to check on the hostages personally. That's Martin and Bill's job. They have recall boxes . . ."

Santa Maria . . . He held the receiver out from his ear again. "No, dammit, I *don't* have time! Not if you want that Trinity Site job pulled off without any foulups! And you might send John up here to help me out with logistics. At least he's got a brain. Why Cara married that idiot defrocked priest . . . Yes, I said idiot, Papa. You should never have let him into the business! He made a mess of a simple courier job and I'm still getting repercussions on this end! Did I tell you we had an anachronism show up here?

"An anachronism, yes. Some asshole fell in out of nowhere and showed up half frozen to death. When he fell through, he couldn't have been more than fifteen, twenty miles from the door Tony opened to snatch that girl from Florida. I still haven't figured out what Tony did that caused it. —Yes, dammit, we're taking care of the bastard!"

Carreras held onto the shreds of his temper and heard his father out. "Yes. No. I told you already, we'll be set to move on that in two days. The scientists are working up the figures on the jumps now. Papa, I can't make them work faster. That woman doctor is about to drop as it is, and her work is critical to our success. Yes, the one with the daughter. Christ, Papa, get your mind out of your pants— No, I won't risk that. I don't care what— No! Goddammit—"

He was tempted to slam the receiver down. Instead, he said, "Papa, I will not discuss this any further. It is out of the question. If you want my advice, go buy a ten-thousand-dollar whore and work it off. I will not jeopardize our hold on Dr. Firelli for your—"

He counted to ten. Then to twenty. "Papa, I'm out of time. I have fifty things to get done in the next hour. I'll call you when Tony gets in, and I'll call you when we're set for the Trinity Site run. Just be sure things are ready on your end."

This time he did slam the receiver down, so hard the bell on the old-style, government-issue phone jangled in the awesome silence.

Senile old *fool*. . . .

The telephone rang and he snatched it up. *"What?"*

He heard someone gulp. Then Nelson's voice said, "Sir, Martin's back. Trouble, sir. The Hughes kid is sick."

He swore and slammed a fist against the desktop. The framed photo of his wife and sons jumped and fell over with a bang. The photo of his mistress teetered, but remained upright. "How sick?"

"He thinks it's the kid's appendix."

He treated Nelson to his favorite curses and threats. Nelson was a stolid sort, though, and heard him out. Carreras finally muttered, "Get a doctor and send Martin back through! I'm busy, Nelson!"

"Sir, which doctor?"

A very good point. He considered. That fellow Valdez had been snooping around, had seen McKee, had even talked to him, alone. The tape from McKee's cell had Carreras worried—McKee had said too much. And clearly Valdez was already suspicious. Collins had asked the man to sit in on the initial interrogation, too. He knew too much.

"Use Valdez. Take Joey over to the clinic and pick him up. Have Martin fill up a medical bag with a bunch of junk, then hustle him through. Don't bother bringing him back. He's been poking around, asking questions, trying to make phone calls off base. And he talked to McKee. Send Martin back when you're through; I need him for another job."

"Yessir."

The line went dead.

Carreras cradled the receiver and pondered what Valdez' official army death certificate would say. Death by exposure? Avalanche? Accidental poisoning?

He shook his head. He had too much to worry about. His father had damned well better send John up here.

With Tony gone, he had too much to keep track of to worry about details like death certificates.

He thought of the well-endowed Firelli girl and snorted. He certainly had better things to worry about than pandering to his father's increasingly weird sexual appetites. Christ, didn't that old *macho cabrio* ever get tired of screwing girls a third his age?

Jésus Carreras thrust the thought from his mind and returned to his interrupted computer session. He pulled up the file he'd been working on and got busy again.

Somebody had to keep the family business going.

Awareness returned slowly. Charlie stirred and gradually registered a hard surface under him, the heat of sunlight on his face, a sound that beat at his whole body. Eventually he realized the roar was water cascading over the lip of a waterfall somewhere nearby.

He blinked his eyes clear and tried to get his bearings. When he moved his head, the first sensation to wash across him was overpowering nausea. He swallowed it down with difficulty and gradually took in more information.

He lay crumpled on one side, atop a slab of native stone that jutted out of the stream bed. He squinted against a bright glare. Out of the hot light, water shot over the lip of a waterfall fifteen feet above his head. Charlie had been thrown considerably farther than the reach of the waterfall. High and dry on his rock slab, Charlie was stranded several yards from the nearest bank.

He spent a couple of unbelieving minutes staring up the long expanse of roaring water. *How the hell did I live through that?* Then, as memory reasserted itself, *What happened to my horse?* There was no sign of Silver.

Judging from the angle of the sun, he'd been out cold for several hours. Breathing hurt. A whole new series of aches and sharper pains had been added to old ones, but the pain in his back, from Xanthus' last beating, had sunk to a dull, bearable ache. He'd have cheerfully killed for a painkiller—any painkiller—but old bruises felt merely stiff.

"About time the breaks came my way," he muttered aloud.

His optimism was short-lived. When he tried to sit up, a white-hot knife stabbed his chest along the side, down low. He recognized the feel of a broken rib from his violent childhood. He lay back down again hastily. The hurt thumping through his head and side left him light-headed and nauseated.

"Aw, man, this just tears it. . . ."

Charlie fumbled with the catches on his armor, then thought better. If he took the armor off now, he'd never get it on again over the swelling. Besides, the constriction of metal bands was closest he could come to wrapping his chest in adhesive and bandages. He did, however, flounder around with the straps on his helmet until it came loose. He pulled it off and poked gingerly at a swelling the breadth of a chicken egg above his ear.

"Ow . . ."

He rolled cautiously to lie on his back and covered his eyes with one arm. The movement pulled at his side, but the pain was bearable. Slowly, it occurred to him that his pursuers must have called off their hunt. He tried again to sit up and made it this time, although the waterfall and the walls of the gorge swung crazily for a couple of minutes afterward.

"Wha' time's it?" he muttered, groping stupidly for the watch he hadn't worn in nearly four years. "Oh, yeah . . ."

Things have just gotta start looking up, for once. Just this once . . .

Not with Vesuvius set to blow, they wouldn't.

The unnerving heat of what should've been an icy mountain stream added to his growing sense of disaster.

Charlie lay motionless in the sunlight for several minutes, gradually recovering his strength. At length, when he thought he might actually make it without blacking out, Charlie pushed himself up again. He recovered his helmet and jammed it back on over the swelling, then eyed the distance from his rock slab to the nearest bank.

"Huh. Good thing Mom paid for those swimming lessons at the Y."

Swimming proved very nearly fatal.

After four years on very little more than gruel and lean rat meat, Charlie's body was literally nothing but bone and muscle. Any fat he'd ever carried, he'd long since burned for desperately needed fuel. Stark naked, his buoyancy would have matched that of a two-hundred-pound lead weight. In a heavy leather jacket covered with metal, Charlie sank straight to the bottom.

He held his breath and clawed his way over the streambed with fingertips, grabbing at any rock or weed that offered a handhold. As the vacuum in his lungs deepened, Charlie kicked and pulled himself toward shallower water.

Gotta breathe . . . shit . . . I've gotta breathe NOW . . .

Charlie gulped reflexively and swallowed water. He strangled and lunged forward, dragging himself closer to shore. The roar of the waterfall, traveling underwater as a thundering rumble, mingled with a roaring of blood in his ears. Charlie's vision began to go dim. He fought to keep from snorting down another mouthful of water.

Christ, I'm gonna die down here . . . I'm really drowning—

Panic sent him thrashing toward the surface. Charlie gulped and got a glorious faceful of air. Then he slithered forward across sharp rocks. He landed with his cheek against rough, wet stone—but his nose and mouth were above water. Charlie coughed and cried tears of raw agony, but he didn't slither back into deep water.

Charlie clung to the boulder he'd landed against. He lay still, just breathing, mostly submerged in the heated water.

God, it feels good to hurt this bad. Didn't know pain could be so damned wonderful. Swirling, heated water breaking and bubbling around him reminded Charlie of the spa at Angie's health club. The heat soothed aches and bruises and multiple pains. As he lay quietly in the stream, trying to work up the courage to stand, Charlie discovered an intense desire to simply stay where he was for however long it took to stop hurting. It would be so easy to just close his eyes, let the heated water work its magic, fall asleep. . . .

Hey, asshole. Why do you think this stuff's hot? You're lying on a time bomb, moron.

Charlie blinked slowly and looked up. Two yards of shallow water separated him from the bank. Charlie gathered his strength one strand at a time, until he could force his body up and into motion.

He slid and slithered his way ashore like a drunken moose, then collapsed on a sunny patch of grass. He groaned aloud, then lay panting. The breeze on his heated skin brought a chill.

Some rescue this is turning out to be, huh? City-slicker cop versus the volcano. Hate to break the news, buddy, but so far, the volcano's kicking butt.

Charlie pulled off his cloak and spread it out to dry, but he couldn't get the wet tunic off without removing the armor. So he lay in the sun, drying out as best he could, and tried to figure what came next.

He'd lost his horse. That left him on foot, alone, without even his crutch. Odds of survival were slim to slimmer. Even if he could've walked all the way back to Herculaneum, he'd never be able to steal a boat in broad daylight. By now, Achivus, the little prick, had probably reported his disappearance. Even if Xanthus hadn't gotten word yet, the garrison in town would be looking for him and the rest of those bandits. Besides, he still hadn't given up on Sibyl and Lucania. He couldn't. He'd just have to figure another way to bust them out of there.

Charlie groaned softly. "Yeah, right, Flynn. You and what army? You can't even stand up without hurting. I got about as much chance as that beetle over there does."

The blue-black beetle, oblivious to Charlie's despair, crawled on past and vanished out of sight. Charlie shut his eyes. He was so tired, so hungry and sore . . . An odd sound insinuated itself gradually into his awareness. *Scrunch, clop, crunch, crunch . . .* Charlie lifted his head curiously. Then gulped and held still, abruptly afraid to move.

Silver . . .

Charlie's pulse shivered and beat a rhumba rhythm. *His horse . . .* Saddle askew but still attached, Silver wandered toward him, munching on thick, sweet grass. The gelding scrunched another mouthful, tugging it upward with a tearing sound, then began to chew while hunting for another bite.

In movies, horses always ran away.

Charlie wet his lips and risked a whisper. "Hey, Silver . . ."

The horse flicked an ear and looked up briefly. Then he blew contentedly and returned to his grazing. Charlie hunted behind him for the cloak and fastened it around his throat. He didn't dare risk standing up. He was afraid if he fell—which he was more than likely to do—he'd startle the horse into bolting.

So he crawled.

On hands and knees, dragging his bad leg and the end of the sword sheath, Charlie crawled toward the gelding. Slowly, agonizingly, Charlie eased his way closer. Silver didn't pay him the slightest attention. He neared the animal's head. Found the reins trailing in the grass. Closing his hand around the leather felt like closing his grip around a life preserver. He shut his eyes for a moment, then started whispering to the gelding.

"Good fella, yeah, good boy, let's see how you are, old boy . . ."

Charlie clambered painfully to his feet, still hanging onto the reins, and leaned against Silver's shoulder. The horse was warm, solid, and utterly unconcerned about his presence. Charlie looked for signs of injury and found a bad scrape along one flank, but when he pulled ten-tatively on the reins, Silver moved without limping.

The horse shook his head and tugged on the reins, trying to reach the grass again. Charlie laughed shakily and stroked a velvet-soft nose. He hadn't realized a horse's muzzle was so tender, so silky. The gelding blew softly into his hand and lipped the cupped palm inquisitively.

"You're okay, Silver," he whispered. "Christ, you're okay. There's still a chance. . . ."

He hadn't realized how completely he'd lost hope, until it was restored. Charlie dragged the back of one wrist across his cheeks and sniffled sheepishly, then cleared his throat. Enough dawdling.

He limped along the edge of the stream, leading his placid horse, until he found a fallen tree he could climb up on. He eyed the saddle with a jaundiced eye and managed to straighten it out and recinch the belly band; then considered. His worst trouble was proving to be his bad leg. Any time he had to walk—and after a plunge over a waterfall, he wasn't holding onto any more illusions—he needed a way to brace his leg.

Charlie tied Silver's reins securely to a jutting branch. Then he used his sword to cut a new crutch, which he padded with some grass tucked into a strip cut from his loincloth. Then he started hunting for deadwood. He found some branches about the right size and dragged his stolen dagger out of its sheath.

If he could just keep the knee stiff, that would let him move faster. Xanthus had never permitted him to try a brace. The bastard had wanted Charlie as helpless as possible. Charlie felt a savage satisfaction as he began fashioning a leg brace out of thick branches and the cut ends of his sandal laces.

It took him considerably longer than he anticipated, but eventually he had something that vaguely resembled a leg brace. It was crude. Very crude. But then, Long John Silver had made do with a peg, and all Charlie needed was something to keep his knee stiff. Charlie used his stolen dagger to scrape the inside surfaces a little smoother. Then he carefully cleaned off the dagger, resheathed it, and used strips cut from the remnants of his cut-up leather satchel to strap the thing to his leg. The fit wasn't bad.

He was showing fair promise as a woodworker.

He grinned briefly. If he got Sibyl and his kid out of the villa, and they got away from the eruption—and thus found themselves merely stranded together in time . . . Maybe he could set himself up as a carpenter somewhere.

The smile slipped away from his face.

First they had to survive.

He used the crutch to lever himself upright, then to provide extra balance. The first step wasn't as bad as he'd expected. The brace did help. With his leg braced as solidly as a peg leg, and his person literally bristling with bladed weapons, all he needed was an eye patch and a parrot to complete his persona as Charlie the Mediterranean Pirate on his next raiding mission.

"Arr, listen well, me matey," he growled. Silver snorted, lifted his great brown head, and flicked one ear toward him. "Arr, this be Cap'n Flynn, matey, Red Charlie Flynn, an' don't ye ferget it!"

The horse whickered, rolled one liquid brown eye and tugged, trying to return to his interrupted grazing. Charlie laughed quietly, winced as the forgotten rib reminded him by grating broken ends together, then steeled himself to practice with the weapon he'd used for two long years in the gladiatorial contests. He tried practicing short, experimental swings with his *gladius*, but not only was the Roman shortsword designed for stabbing rather than hacking, he was so sore and clumsy he could barely stay on his feet.

He kept at it, though, the drills coming back to him, albeit much less efficiently than the last time he'd performed them. So Charlie practiced stabbing nearby bushes, visualizing Carreras' face on each leaf, and sweated profusely from sharp, tearing pain in his chest.

He missed nearly every leaf he cut at or stabbed, leaving him depressed as well as in pain. Each movement hurt, grating that broken rib, but Charlie was out of practice and previous experience with Bericus told him that breaking Sibyl and little Lucania out of that villa was likely to get violent.

Finally, Charlie decided he was as ready as he was likely to get—and that his body was threatening mutiny. He adjusted the leather-strap stirrups for his now-straightened leg, then clambered awkwardly onto the fallen tree trunk. He untied the reins and clutched them in one hand, then turned cautiously and urged Silver a little closer. He wasn't sure he'd have been able to drag himself up without the aid of leg brace and stirrups. He slithered into the saddle and immediately felt about a thousand percent better.

Charlie peered around, trying to get his bearings from the mountain and the sun. He'd need to work his way back downstream. Judging from the angle of the sun, he'd been unconscious not only the whole night, but most of the morning. The sun was rising rapidly toward its zenith. Midday, or close to it. How much time was left? He bitterly regretted not getting as many details from Sibyl as possible, but Xanthus' timing had prevented it.

All he knew for sure was, Vesuvius was supposed to blow sometime between now and about eleven o'clock or midnight tonight. Either he had enough time to break Sibyl and his daughter out of Bericus' villa and get them both to safety or he did not. Charlie chose the likeliest direction that would take him toward the villa and set out.

Sibyl woke in darkness. Her body was sluggish, her mind lethargic. Her mouth tasted like live bait. From the far corners of her cell, blackness crept toward her, touched her with slimy tendrils of panic. Half-suffocated, Sibyl struggled to push herself up off the hard bed. When the bar rattled loudly on the far side of the door, she gasped, an airless shriek in the darkness.

The door creaked open. Weak sunlight streamed across the floor and came to rest on her skin.

Morning? Or evening? She couldn't hear anything resembling the preliminary stages of eruption. . . .

She blinked away the blurry aftereffects of the drug and focused on Quintus' surly face. He was flanked by two women.

"Get up."

So much for a cheery "good morning."

She could barely stand. The women hurried forward to support her buckling weight. They escorted her through a long, open, airy corridor. Sunlight poured warmly through the open portico. She squinted and stared into the light. Flawless blue sky, pale golden light . . . Shadows streamed out long and distorted toward the west, where sunlight poured in through the open *peristyle* roof. Morning, then. Early morning, at that.

She allowed panic-born tension to drain from her muscles. Sibyl would have fallen without the support of the women holding her arms. The preliminary steam explosions which would herald the main eruption—due to begin at approximately one-o'clock this afternoon—hadn't occurred yet. But she didn't see any way to escape, either.

She didn't dare think about where Charlie might be, or what might have happened to him. The wagon he'd have been in must have arrived while she was unconscious. What had Bericus done to him during the intervening hours? What if he were too injured to be moved? Or already dead?

If he'd tried to rescue her while she was drugged . . .

At least she hadn't *seen* any evidence so far to think he had, and Sibyl had a feeling Bericus, at the very least, would have dragged Charlie in front of her, just to see her horrified reaction.

They finally entered a thick-walled room which served as a bath. Murals painted on the walls depicted a garden with nymphs at play. The air was steamy and moist.

Light came from dozens of oil lamps set about the room. A marble basin the size of a child's wading pool, set into a beautifully tiled floor, was filled with heated water.

"Come, Aelia," one of the women urged, "sit down."

She let them guide her to a backless chair. They removed her rough, travel-stained tunic. When she glanced up, she discovered Quintus' gaze fastened on her body. There wasn't much she could do about that, but she felt her cheeks redden.

The shorter of the two women murmured, "I am Livia, dear. This is Alcesta. Master has ordered us to ready you for him." Alcesta was an inch or two taller than Livia and very pale. She looked like a rabbit run to ground by a dog—a rabbit that's lost the strength to run any farther.

Sibyl shivered.

"You are cold, Aelia," Livia murmured. "The water will warm you. Master keeps the fires lit beneath the pool day and night."

Sibyl couldn't quite disguise momentary surprise. *That* was an expensive luxury. No wonder he'd needed the old man's money, if all his habits were that decadent.

The water steamed. She sank down cautiously, then sighed. It felt heavenly, a balm from the gods on her roughened skin and knotted muscles. But she hadn't been bathed by someone else since her fifth birthday. Sibyl was deeply embarrassed to have someone else performing the chore for her. Livia and Alcesta were experts. Sibyl was washed and shampooed—with a horrible mixture of sand and mud that took forever to rinse out. Then she was oiled, scraped, oiled again (more lightly, with a scented sweet oil), and finally perfumed in places she'd never used perfume.

Once she was clean to their satisfaction, another woman arrived to begin work on her hair. Long, pale blond hair had been pulled back with combs and simple ribbons to create a stunning effect. *She must have been brought here from Gaul, with that coloring.* An angelic child with strawberry blond hair, its gender hidden by extreme youth and a shapeless tunic, toddled behind her. The child stared up at Sibyl through wide green eyes. Sibyl smiled, delighted when the little cherub smiled back.

The child's mother, barely out of her teens, also smiled shyly and set to work, carefully combing and toweling Sibyl's wet hair. "Here, let's bring her out of this damp room. Her hair must dry in the sunlight."

"Yes, Benigna," Alcesta murmured.

Sibyl started violently. *"Benigna?"*

The young woman glanced into her eyes. "I am. Do you know me? I don't know you."

Sibyl dragged her gaze down to the child, the little *strawberry blond child*. . . . "Dear God. Lucania?"

Benigna cast a frightened glance at Quintus, who ignored them. "Please," she whispered frantically, "how do you know me and my child?"

Sibyl swallowed hard. "I—I know Rufus."

Benigna's eyes widened. "Rufus? How can you know Rufus?"

"He's—he's not here?"

"No. Should he be?"

"Yes. They should have brought him last night. By wagon. We came on the ship together from Rome."

"But—*why?*"

Then realization struck the young girl. She fell to her knees and threw protective arms around her child. "No! Please tell me Master won't sell her to that horrible Xanthus, please . . ."

Lucania clung to her mother's *tunica*, eyes suddenly dark with fear. Sibyl touched the little girl's bright hair. "Shh . . . No one's sold anyone yet. And they won't. I swear to you."

Benigna's glance was frightened, hopeful, skeptical in rapid succession. "You, a slave, swear to me?"

Sibyl drew a steadying breath. *No time like the present to start the ball rolling.* "Yes. I swear it. As I am *sibyl*, I swear it."

All three women started violently.

Sibyl plunged on. "The mountain on which this house is built will roar with fire and thunder before Bericus does such an evil thing."

All three women turned frightened gazes toward the unseen summit of the volcano. Everyone had felt the earthquakes all through the night, for miles around.

Sibyl whispered, "And if the mountain *does* roar, Benigna, try to get into a doorway. The house may fall. And if it does, a doorway is the only safe place."

"Yes," Benigna whispered, face white with terror. "As doorways represent the gateway between this world and the next, such a gateway *could* be the only safe place. I thank you for the warning, *sibyl*. But how can you be here? Enslaved to Bericus?"

"By a mistake he shall regret," Sibyl said tightly. "Soon."

Again, all three women blanched.

"I— Please forgive me, but Master will beat me if you are not prepared as ordered," Benigna whispered miserably, still clinging to her child. "I am only a poor slave, far from my home. Please do not blame me or mine."

Sibyl shut her eyes. *So much for asking help to escape the house.* She just nodded. They wrapped her in a soft robe and escorted her out to the *peristyle* garden, where they sat her down in a chair placed on the sunny portico. Quintus, surly and silent as ever, followed and took up a watchful stance. While the sunlight did its work drying her hair, the women rubbed perfumed salves into her hands and feet. Once her hair was dry—and an unruly mass of curls it proved to be, Sibyl noted wryly as they struggled with it—she was allowed to eat a light breakfast of bread and cheese. Once they had tamed her hair, the slave women applied cosmetics. Sibyl grimaced and endured the ritual.

Lucania played on the soft grass at her mother's feet, making cooing noises and occasionally smiling up at Sibyl. Sunlight turned her hair red-gold, her eyes the same sunny amber-green as Charlie's when he smiled. Tears prickled behind Sibyl's eyelids. Lucania was a beautiful little girl. She had her mother's face, her father's eyes and smile and hair. Terrible images of the skulls she'd dug out of volcanic mud tortured her, superimposed over Lucania's face. A few of the skeletons they'd found had been children younger than Lucania. Much younger . . .

We'll get her out. We have to.

The women preparing her finally finished. When Livia held up a polished bronze mirror, Sibyl hardly recognized herself. The women had pulled her hair back with gold combs. Benigna had woven a strand of tiny pearls into it. The makeup was garish by modern standards. Heavy black kohl outlined her eyes, Egyptian style, making her eyes appear twice as dark—more nearly pine than emerald. Rouge reddened her cheeks and lips. She looked—and felt—like a cheap whore. Sibyl endured in silence when Alcesta rouged her nipples and genitalia.

She couldn't bring herself to see if Quintus still watched.

The linen gown they wrapped her in could have been made only in Egypt. She'd studied tomb paintings of these pleated, transparent sheathes. She'd wondered even then how many hours a slave woman had labored to sew down and press all those tiny pleats into the cloth. The material was even more transparent than the paintings had indicated. When sunlight fell across her, Sibyl felt she might as well have been dressed in sunbeams.

She wondered if Bericus enjoyed Egyptian fantasies in general or if this were just one of many passing whims. She closed her eyes and tried to think about Charlie, about her battered old VW, about classical Latin verb conjugations, about solving complex integral equations. . . .

If only she'd said yes to that kid in her calculus class, the one whose interest had scared her spitless. Sibyl stiffened her spine and stared at the far portico wall. She would endure *anything* in order to survive long enough to escape.

Livia made a clucking noise and fussed with her earlobes. Sibyl winced as the woman struggled to unfasten the little silver posts she'd picked up in the Naples airport. Pierced earring posts and backs were a modern development in the history of pierced-earring wear.

Livia finally mastered the secret and removed the earrings, then replaced them with massive gold hoops. The wires were almost too thick for the holes in her ears. The earrings were extremely heavy. Within minutes her earlobes ached from the weight. Benigna slipped gold armbands onto her upper arms, added bangles to her wrists and ankles, and produced soft house sandals of kid leather for her feet. As a finishing touch, they hung a heavy, Egyptian-style collar of gold and lapis over her neck and shoulders.

Sibyl thought wildly that when they found her skeleton, they'd think she was an upper-class Egyptian lady visiting Herculaneum at just the wrong time. She couldn't restrain a semihysterical hiccough of laughter.

"What is it, *sibyl*?" Benigna asked fearfully.

"Nothing," she choked.

The woman murmured something intended to be soothing, but Sibyl paid little attention. The sun had moved ominously closer to the zenith. Underfoot the floor vibrated to a never-ending rumble.

God, how can they be so blind?

"She is ready for the master's pleasure, Quintus," Livia said. Sibyl's flesh crawled like cold lizard skin. She clenched her fingers tightly to keep her hands from trembling. Benigna bent near and whispered, "Be brave. Do whatever he bids you at once, no matter what, and he may not beat you. I will try to help you afterwards, *sibyl*."

She drew a shuddering gulp of air. God . . .

Bericus arrived at the far end of the garden. She followed Quintus on trembling legs. She had very little attention to spare for the fountains which splashed quietly all through the sunlit space. The flowers were a blur of color, too confused even to notice types. Golden sunlight fell in a blaze of summer heat across her skin.

The hot light turned the linen dress to a wisp of nothing.

Bericus' eyes ravished her well before he laid so much as a finger on her body.

"Master," Quintus bowed, "your new slave, Aelia."

"You may go," Bericus said curtly.

She noted the tell-tale bulge his excitement made in the front of his tunic. She had to gulp back panic. The balding, sallow-faced Roman stalked in a complete circle around her, smelling of sex and cruelty. She thrust back memory of his mere "examination" and steeled herself.

"They tell me," he said softly, his gaze fastened hungrily between her thighs, "that you have no memory of yourself, Aelia."

She willed her voice not to waver. Now or never . . . "They lied."

He halted and lifted his gaze to hers. His brow rose slowly. "Is that so?" Bericus pursed his lips, then resumed his pacing. Without warning, he seized her arm from behind. Bericus twisted it savagely, nearly to breaking. Sibyl cried out, panting against the agony.

"They lied, *Master*," he hissed.

"They—lied—Master," she whimpered.

He twisted her arm an inch further, then released her. A sob escaped her as she cradled her throbbing arm.

"Very good," he purred. Bericus caressed her jawline with one fingertip. "Very good." He strolled to a small table and poured himself a goblet of wine. Sibyl noticed he did not water it, as custom dictated.

"You have fire inside you, Aelia," he said. "It burns in your eyes. It makes you even more desirable than when I first saw you in Bericus' shop, still dazed from the long sea journey." A chuckle escaped him, sending a chill down Sibyl's back. "I shall enjoy every moment I spend extinguishing that fire."

God, oh, God . . .

"You should not have fought me, little Aelia," he purred, glancing over the rim of his goblet. "Tell me, why would Antonius Caelerus lie to me about such a thing as your memory?" He sipped his wine.

Sibyl risked a look at the sun. Past noon. She was running out of time, whichever disaster she chose to consider. Sibyl took a deep, steadying breath and sent a tiny prayer skyward.

"Because Antonius knows he has committed great sacrilege in stealing me. Master," she added, putting as much disdain as she could muster into the title.

He paused with the winecup halfway to his lips. "Sacrilege?" he echoed, clearly surprised.

She plunged ahead, forcing her voice to remain steady. She strove for a tone of angry warning. "When Ulysses ransacked the great temple of Troy and stole the Palladium from it, he insulted the great goddess as Minerva. She allowed Neptune to hound his steps like a dog trails a bitch in heat. Ten years of rage were vented on his head. All because he dared desecrate the temple and insult the gods."

"You speak nonsense! Old women's tales to amuse the young!" There was, however, a detectable shadow of puzzlement in his eyes. "What has Ulysses to do with you?"

"With me?" she asked softly. "Why, nothing at all, Publius Bericus. It is *you* I speak of when I mention Ulysses. You, and a slave trader who seeks to hide his villainy, to stain you with a guilt as great as his own."

Bericus slammed his goblet onto the table. Wine splashed unheeded onto his expensively embroidered tunic. "You speak in riddles, woman! Out with it!"

Sibyl forced a predatory smile. "Riddles, indeed, Publius Bericus!" She stooped slightly, feigning a nonchalance she was far from feeling, and plucked a blood-red flower from the bed beside the marbled path. "Beautiful, isn't it?" She held it up. Then deliberately crushed it and hurled the mangled petals at his feet. "Yet my hand crushes it without effort, as the Magna Mater crushes those who despoil her holy places!"

A hint of worry appeared in Bericus' face. She pushed

her slight advantage. "Of course I speak in riddles! Tell me"—she advanced on him and felt a savage delight when he gave way a step—"what women speak in riddles, Publius Bericus? What women see the fears behind a man's eyes when he comes to them for guidance?"

Bericus' face began to lose what little color it normally possessed.

"You begin to wonder, do you not? A sale made in haste. The slave too unusual to offer on the open market. Where did Caelerus steal me, Bericus? Why did he advise you to keep me drugged? Why does he fear my tongue, my *wrath* so deeply?"

"Who are you?" His voice came out hoarse and strangled.

She drew herself to her full height, standing so tall she matched him in height. The breath she drew was as much for courage as for dramatic projection.

"I am called *sibyl*, you little fool!"

"You lie!" The denial ripped from him. His face had taken on a waxy pallor.

"Mother Cybele as my witness, Bericus, I am Sibyl. If you dare to violate what is sacred to the Magna Mater of all Rome, the Great Goddess Cybele herself, the very earth will roar and cover your abomination with fire and death!"

Bericus clutched at the table.

Behind her, a single set of handclaps broke the silence. Sibyl whirled, badly startled.

Tony Bartlett stood in the shadows.

Oh, God, no . . .

"Very entertaining, my dear Aelia," he called out. "Bericus, my good friend, her performance seems to have moved even you." Bartlett strolled out into the sunny garden.

Son-of-a—

Sibyl clenched her fists, knotted with rage and terror.

"I told you she was talented, Bericus. When I first captured her off that godsforsaken island where her tribe lives, she told me her father was a wizard. Said he would

change me into a turtle if I did not return her at once."
Bartlett chuckled and held his arms out to either side.
"I seem to have suffered no lasting harm."

"You filthy snake!" she hissed in English, too angry
to care any longer.

His eyes widened, then narrowed savagely.

"Furthermore," he continued darkly, "she needs to be
taught a few civilized manners."

Bericus passed a shaking hand across his eyes and
pushed himself away from the support of the table.

"Then this prophecy—"

Bartlett threw back his head and laughed. Sibyl wanted
to smash her fists into his teeth. She wondered how far
she'd get if she made a break for it. *Probably about as
far as Quintus. . . .*

"Bericus," Tony Bartlett was saying smoothly, "how
often does the earth shake here? It's been shaking now
and again all week. Of course she felt the tremors. And
some slave probably told her about the shock that damaged the Temple of Jupiter in Pompeii a few years ago."

Bartlett brushed the nape of her neck with his knuckles. Sibyl jerked away from the caress. "Don't touch me!"

His smile promised pain and terror.

"She is very clever. And very convincing. And an incurable liar." He shrugged. "Perhaps you will be able to
discipline her sufficiently to break her of the habit."

Bericus' eyes began to glint. He licked his lips and
eyed her with greater interest.

Bartlett shrugged again. "If the earth does roar, it will
be far more likely the Goddess Herself is outraged at
such a contemptible deception. And from a mere barbarian slave chit, at that."

*Where'd you learn Latin, Bartlett? Your accent's good.
Who the hell are you?*

Bericus still wasn't convinced. "But if she is telling
the truth—"

"You've been up the coast to Cumae, Bericus, to con-
sult the *sibyls*. Ask her the name of the current high
priestess. Ask her simply to *describe* the woman."

She was trapped. Bartlett knew it and smirked.

"Out with it, girl!" Bericus snapped.

Tears stung Sibyl's eyes. She had to look away from Tony Bartlett's gloating expression.

"Go ahead, little *sibyl*," Bartlett urged. "Tell your master what he wants to know."

Now would be a very good time for Vesuvius to erupt.... "Her name is Flavia," Sibyl said steadily, giving it a wild shot in the dark.

Bericus narrowed his eyes. "And her appearance?"

"Small, slender," Sibyl answered carefully, giving a general description of the Mediterranean type, "dark ... "

Bericus hit her. Sibyl landed in a flower bed. She'd never been slugged in her whole life. Her entire head rang. Dread of another blow made her cringe. Above her, Bericus snapped, "The high priestess of Cumae is a horse-faced crone, taller than you are, and uglier than my wife. As you say," he told Bartlett, "an incurable liar."

When she dared look, Bericus' eyes were glittering. Sibyl held back a whimper. Running now would only make him angrier. Tony Bartlett gave his host a brief bow.

"I will return to my rooms now, my good friend, and prepare for my journey. Enjoy your new pet."

She listened to his footsteps die away into silence. Listened to Bericus' breath quicken. Listened to the sound of her heartbeat banging at her eardrums....

Then Bericus closed his hands brutally around her arms.

Chapter Eleven

Close to an hour after he set out, Charlie found a good spot to lie up and scout out Bericus' villa. A stand of wild oak trees crouched on an outcropping above a quiet grove of olives just above Bericus' villa. Jupiter's sacred trees gave Charlie plenty of cover and a good, unrestricted view of the whole valley.

Bericus' villa lay a couple of miles from Vesuvius' summit and at least another two miles line-of-sight from Herculaneum. By road, town was much farther; the road snaked around the flank of the volcano, taking the easiest route. Part of the way, the rutted lane actually headed for the interior of the Italian peninsula. Given his druthers, Charlie would've headed that way—fast.

Instead, he scouted out the villa and tried to come up with a sound plan of attack. Behind him, Silver grazed contentedly under the trees, tearing audibly at the deep, rich grass with strong teeth. Charlie envied the horse his easy meal. As a precaution, he'd tied the long reins to a stout branch.

He observed activity around the villa for several minutes, getting a feel for normal "traffic" and waiting for inspiration to strike. Unfortunately, it didn't seem to be striking anywhere near him. High above his hiding place, Vesuvius loomed like somebody's bad idea of a gothic novel cover. Charlie could feel constant tremors in the earth through his belly.

A feeling of extreme caution prompted Charlie to drag himself up and limp over to the horse. Earlier, he'd found long leather straps attached to the back of the

229

saddle and finally figured out what they were for: hobbles. Charlie carefully fastened them to Silver's legs. The horse snorted, but offered no further protest. Feeling marginally better, Charlie returned to his observation post.

All quiet down there, not much activity near the house, except for a carriage which rattled away toward the distant town. There were three occupants. Charlie wished bitterly for a good pair of field glasses. He'd like to have known who was leaving. Tony Bartlett, making his escape? Probably. The bastard . . . With Tony went Charlie's hope of getting hands on Jésus Carreras in this—or probably any other—lifetime.

He turned his attention back to the silent villa. Unfortunately, there were plenty of people out in the fields, working the harvest. It was August. Scores of slaves had been dispatched into fields and orchards to gather the bounty. Goatherds and sheep tenders had driven their flocks out to the rich pasturelands, aided by wiry, alert little dogs. Charlie grumbled into the stubble of his beard. Dogs could be a serious problem.

The dogs weren't his only problem, however. Those slaves could be marshaled as a hunting expedition at a second's notice. Charlie hunkered down, belly flat under the ancient oaks, and made plans for—then discarded again—several approaches. After a moment, a wry smile tugged at his lips. Despite a healthy dose of fear, he had to admit one thing. Of all the stakeouts he'd manned during his career, this definitely qualified as the weirdest. He'd have felt a lot better if he could have called for backup. As it was, Charlie probably didn't have a chance in a million of rescuing them.

But he had to try.

As midday heat built up despite the shade, Charlie began to wonder if it were his imagination, or if the ground really did feel hotter under his belly. He tried to remember everything he'd ever heard or seen about volcanoes. Didn't they sometimes split down the sides and vent gas and lava and suchlike?

He cursed his own ignorance. He knew how to drive a fast car as skillfully as A. J. Foyt. He could draw either a revolver or a semiauto pistol from concealment and dump six rounds into a playing card at fifteen feet in under three seconds. He had the shuck and jive down so well, he could have convinced a New York gang banger to don a set of concrete Nike's—and the punk would probably think he'd gotten the better part of the deal when they were done.

Unfortunately, none of the things he really *knew* were going to help him one bit. All the crap Charlie had survived while growing up had given him a great background to work as a vice cop. But he'd never been a hero.

And right now he needed Superman to come sweeping in and save the day.

Charlie had never really believed in Superman.

The sun climbed higher. He laid his forehead on his arm and waited. Sibyl had said they had until nearly midnight tonight. Once the volcano blew . . .

She'd also said the Imperial Navy, stationed across the Bay of Naples, had tried to reach the doomed towns to pick up refugees. And that the navy hadn't been able to get close. Once the volcano blew, there was no hope of rescue from outside. Maybe after dark he could try to force his way into the villa, find her and Lucania, and toss them onto his horse?

He grimaced. "Some plan, Flynn." He didn't like cutting it that close. He wanted them out of there *now*. But if he tried to force his way in now, the chances of *his* getting out of the villa with them were about as great as the chance he'd ever see the dark side of the moon in person.

Well, there were worse ways to die. He'd seen slaves who'd gone on eating and breathing and shitting years after they'd died inside. Charlie knew he'd rather take his chances with Bericus and Vesuvius and a fiery death—

Wait a second . . .

What was it Sibyl had said about fire? Charlie sucked in his breath. Then banged the side of his helmeted head. *Of course* ... "Charlie Flynn, you addle-brained *idiot*. *Set the house on fire!*" He could grab her during the confusion, find his little girl, make a clean getaway—

Charlie was moving before he even finished forming the plan. He didn't need to wait for dark to set Bericus' filthy little sex retreat ablaze. All he needed was an amphora of olive oil and a torch. And Bericus' own groves ensured a liberal supply of sweet, burnable oil.

Charlie grinned nastily. "Bericus, you pissed off the wrong damned slave." Homeowners insurance wouldn't be invented for several centuries. And even if it had, Bericus wouldn't live long enough to collect the settlement check. Charlie laughed and hobbled toward his horse, already planning his secondary diversion and main plan of attack. He felt savagely good. The shortsword at his hip swung in its sheath like a promise of vengeance.

Bericus would never know what hit him—

A deafening concussion blasted through air and ground alike. Silver screamed and reared. Charlie fell sideways. The landing jarred his broken rib. He gasped and scraped an elbow on rough ground, trying to curl around the pain. Silver tried again to rear and was brought up short by tied reins and hobbles. Another explosion shook the earth. Charlie cursed—and couldn't hear his own voice. He scrambled into the open, out from under the oaks.

"Aw, shit . . ."

Billowing white clouds of steam poured from the summit of Vesuvius. "Midnight, dammit! She said the town would die near midnight! So how come it's blowing *now*? *Think*, dammit!"

The only suggestion his numbed brain made was *RUN!*

He cursed again, agreeing wholeheartedly, and gained his feet. Another steam explosion knocked him flat. The ground rocked like a rowboat in the mid-Atlantic. That cursed broken rib ached fiercely, a belt tightened down to the last notch around his lungs. Even *thinking* about moving hurt. Sprawled on his back, scarcely able to breathe, never mind move, Charlie watched in morbid, fatal fascination. The volcano hurled grey rock debris aloft, along with spewing steam and gasses. Prevailing winds caught the cloud, blew it southeast, toward Pompeii.

The top of the mountain had merely blown open, not blown up. Two miles down the flank, Charlie swallowed down a throat gone painfully dry. *Maybe there's a chance, if the stuff keeps blowing that direction. . . .*

His ears hurt like they were bleeding. Silver was screaming mindlessly and fighting the hobbles.

"Hell and damnation—"

If the stupid nag broke a leg . . .

He managed to crawl to his knees. Charlie found his new crutch and staggered over to the horse. He caught Silver's bridle and hauled the horse's head around. For a moment, the horse fought him in mindless panic. Charlie stroked the animal's sweating neck. "Easy, fella," he soothed, the language making no difference to the horse. The animal gradually stopped fighting and flicked his ears toward the sound of Charlie's voice. "Easy, boy, I know it's scary, easy, now . . ."

He craned around for a look at the villa, while continuing to soothe his spooked mount. A few slaves scurried toward the main house. Others ran for the hills. He didn't blame them for taking advantage of the confusion. Beyond the villa, down toward the sea, Herculaneum paused in the summer sunshine and held its breath.

Steam continued to blast free of the volcano, but no more explosions rocked the earth. Charlie remembered Mt. St. Helens. Hadn't there been a series of smaller explosions and earthquakes before she finally blew apart? Maybe he had a little time yet. . . .

Charlie started to breathe again and only then realized that he, too, had been holding his breath. A whiff of sulfurous fumes with his first deep gulp of air left him deeply anxious.

"Hey, Silver, how's about you and me blow this joint, huh, before the joint blows us?"

Charlie unsheathed his dagger, not wanting to take the time to untie the hobbles. Silver pawed nervously and tested the air with distended nostrils. Then neighed uneasily. Charlie glanced up, not wanting Silver to step on him while he was trying to cut the hobbles. Silver trembled and sweat into his shaggy brown coat.

Steam continued to rise from the peak, turning the mountain into a gigantic whistling teakettle. The ground felt like one of those old-fashioned twenty-five-cent hotel vibrating beds. Charlie sliced through the hobbles and resheathed the dagger. A quick glance over his shoulder revealed disturbed-anthill activity down at the villa. What would he be doing, Charlie wondered as he hauled his good foot up into the stirrup, if he were a scared, rich man living in that villa?

Getting the hell out of Dodge.

Charlie nodded sharply. Right. And a soldier on a horse would look mighty welcome to a rich man in panic. He didn't need to torch the place, after all. Vesuvius had provided his diversion. With the helmet to disguise his features, he might not even run afoul of Xanthus. If that sadistic slime hadn't already hightailed it for town. Whoever'd left in that carriage hadn't looked fat enough to be Xanthus, though.

Charlie hauled himself painfully upward. He was halfway into the saddle when Silver shied away. Charlie lost his balance. His foot slipped out of the improvised stirrup. Charlie slithered unceremoniously to the ground, jarring his side painfully.

"C'mon, Silver," he wheezed, "lemme on, fella..."

He reached again for the stirrup. The horse's eerie groan arrested his attention. Silver had lowered his head as far as the still-tied reins would allow. Charlie widened his eyes. Silver had braced his legs, wide apart.

"What the—"

The world blew up in his face.

Fluorescent lab lights were not kind to Sue Firelli. Dan halted in the doorway, momentarily stunned. His "shadow" stopped in the corridor behind him and waited. Dark circles and etched lines beneath Sue's eyes had aged her thirty years. She'd lost an appalling amount of weight, leaving her lab coat to hang on skeletal shoulders. When she looked up and saw him, a momentary flicker of hope lit Sue's pale eyes.

"Dan." She tried to smile. "It's . . . been a while, hasn't it?"

He accepted her outstretched hand and squeezed it briefly. Her fingers trembled, like winter-bare twigs in his hand. Both were aware, Dan knew, not only of his bodyguard, but of the electronic ears secreted about the lab.

"You know how it is," Dan replied with forced nonchalance. "How's the work going?"

She compressed dry lips and shook her head. "Not well. My latest readings . . ." She shrugged helplessly. "I haven't been sleeping much."

She shoved a lab notebook at him, then abruptly sat down on a lab stool and leaned against the counter, eyes closed. For a moment, Sue Firelli looked closer to ninety than forty-six.

Dan was only partway through the page when the significance of her notations hit him.

"Holy—"

He bit back the rest of what he'd been about to say. Sue's face was—if possible—even more pinched and waxen than before.

She couldn't take much more of this. He set the notebook aside and rested a hand on her thin shoulder. "Sue, you've been working 'round the clock, haven't you?"

She nodded.

"When was the last time you fell asleep?"

She shrugged. "Last week?" she suggested helplessly. Her eyes reminded Dan of men he'd seen coming out of the jungles in Cambodia and Laos.

"I'm calling Frank."

"No!"

She jerked to her feet, then swayed and toppled toward him. Dan caught and steadied her. Naked panic was building in her eyes. "I have to keep monitoring—"

"Sue."

He tried to convey with his eyes what he couldn't say aloud. If Sue collapsed, Carreras' bloody work would continue, but their last chance to stop him might well collapse with her.

She opened her mouth, then closed it. Her shoulders slumped. "Okay," she whispered. "You're right. I'm no good to anybody this way." She tried to give him a wan smile. It was a heroic effort.

"Okay." Dan steered her toward a chair. "I'll call Frank. Meanwhile . . ." He glanced significantly toward the guard, then toward one of the known bugs. She followed his gaze and nodded. Dan said lightly, "I've got an assignment. From Upstairs."

She seemed to brace herself, reaching unsteadily for the nearest counter. Her fingers tightened down on the edge. "Yes?"

"We have a small problem in, uh, logistics and security. Something of a Gudekinstian problem."

Her eyes widened. She glanced toward the discarded notebook, with its clear evidence of slippage in the fabric of the time stream. Well, clear to a physicist, anyway. Thank God Carreras didn't really understand what was in Sue Firelli's notebooks.

It was very nearly his only weakness.

Sue licked her lips. "What, um, did you have in mind?"

"Firellian Transfer."

She started badly. Dan had to brace her in the chair. Sue looked like she desperately wanted to protest. Dan closed his hand over hers and gripped hard. She met his gaze.

"Trust me," he tried to say silently.

"Yes-s-s," she finally muttered, as though contemplating a physics problem, "that would be the logical solution to a Gudekinstian problem. I'll have to work out the math, program the variables."

"How long will you need?"

She managed a weak smile. "I may be dead on my feet, Dan Collins, but I'll be doing physics problems in my grave. When and where?"

He snagged an atlas from the pile of reference materials that had spilled over from her bookshelves. He flipped a couple of pages and opened it to the Pacific Basin. "Here." His fingertip rested on a tiny dot. Her eyes widened. "And here." He returned to Alaska, to the area where their base sat. He traced a number with his fingertip. She swayed. Squeezed shut her eyes. Then nodded. He said in as normal a tone as possible, "Set the primary for no less than a one-day margin. The timing ought to be obvious."

She nodded. Then said, "The Firellian Transfer is going to be dangerous. Really dangerous."

Their gazes met, held.

"Good luck." She looked like she was about to faint. She added hoarsely, "Go call Frank."

She sat down at her computer and called up esoteric files only she and Zac Hughes genuinely understood. Dan moved across the lab to the phone. It, too, was bugged. Probably every phone on base was bugged by now.

The line clicked as someone picked up in the infirmary.

"Valdez."

"Frank, I'm over at the lab, in Building Z. Dr. Firelli is ill. She hasn't slept since last week. When I came in, she was literally weaving on her feet. I'm worried."

Across the room, Nobel Laureate Susan Firelli glanced up. Her glare dared him to add just how seriously out on her feet she was. Dan had to admire her spunk. She was tough. He just hoped she was tough enough to get through this.

Then he hoped they *would* get through this. Those notations in her lab book still had him sweating. Much more slippage and the whole time stream would start to unravel, leaving them smack in the middle of anywhen, anywhere, and maybe even *nowhere*. Given those notations, Dan wasn't sure *any* further jumps would work properly, much less a triple-leg Firellian Transfer. The thought of Lucille and Danny, and the other hostages, trapped forever in a howling Pleistocene Ice Age . . .

Francisco Valdez' response was dry. "Order yourself a checkup while you're at it, Dan. You need one."

"Later."

"Yeah, sure. With you it's always later. But it better not be *much* later. I'll need security clearance to get in there. I've never been inside Building Z, Dan."

The phone line went dead. Frank's observation felt like an accusation. Well, maybe it was. Frank had to be damned suspicious by now. *God, what am I getting him into, bringing him in here? And they know he's unsettled about McKee.* . . . But Sue Firelli needed the best available and that was Frank. Dan dialed security and arranged for Frank to be admitted to the building. He then cradled the receiver and leaned his shoulder against the wall to watch Dr. Firelli. She was completely self-absorbed now that Dan had given her something concrete to do besides sit and watch the fabric of the universe unravel around their ears.

He'd felt so fortunate, securing Sue for his research team. If things had gone differently, he might have added her daughter, Janet, to the team in a few years. Janet was every bit as brilliant as her mother, although the daughter had chosen engineering instead of physics.

Dan had always wondered who Sue Firelli had chosen as the unsuspecting father of her child. Her method had been unorthodox, to say the least. Someone he didn't recall, now, had told him Sue's bishop had threatened excommunication when she told him it was none of his business who, how, *or* why. She was tough, all right. But Dan had to admit that it had worked out well for both mother and daughter. Janet Firelli was a senior at MIT this year, due to graduate with highest honors. Rumor had it she'd already been scouted by no less than Lawrence-Livermore Defense Labs and she hadn't even entered grad school yet.

Except she'd taken an indefinite leave from classes, due to a serious "illness in the family" which had begun four months ago. The only consolation Dan could find was that Janet and Lucille had adored one another the first time they'd met, last Labor Day Weekend, when Janet had flown up to spend the holiday with her mother and Dan's little family. If they had to be trapped together in hell . . . He wondered bleakly how Lucille and Danny, Jr., and the other hostages *were* coping. Then he prayed this wild chance he was taking would pay off.

If it didn't . . .

He didn't dare fail.

"Okay," Sue said. She shoved back her chair.

Dan was impressed with her talents all over again.

"This ought to solve your little problem." Her eyes seemed to add, "I hope." She held out three high-density floppies and a printout. "Have Zac program the jump like this. You'll need special equipment to handle the Gudekinstian problem."

She opened a locked cabinet and removed their prototype recall box. "This ought to do it."

He scanned the printout.

She had understood.

Her hands were unsteady as Dan took the heavy oblong from her. Fortunately, their prototype hadn't resembled the later field-use boxes at all. That was the only reason they'd been able to convince Carreras it was simply part of the monitoring equipment. This was the first time since Carreras' takeover that either of them had been given the chance to program a jump without direct supervision.

It might well be their only chance.

When Dan left the lab, Sue Firelli's prototype was tucked safely away in his briefcase and Sue Firelli was tucked safely away in bed under Francisco Valdez' watchful eye. Dan headed through familiar corridors for the main control lab. He carefully schooled his features as he approached the "MPs" planted at the doorway.

"Good evening, gentlemen."

The nearest eyed him suspiciously. "You got clearance?"

Dan went on the offensive. "Dammit, didn't Carreras call? He tells me to dump some excess baggage someplace safe and doesn't even clear it. . . ."

The other guard muttered, "Yeah, he called while you were in the can, Al."

"Oh. Where they sending this one?"

Christ. How many people had Carreras done away with? No wonder the time stream was a mess. . . .

"Someplace very cold." Dan forced a grin. "Care to join him?"

The guard shivered. "Man, I ain't warm yet."

They stepped aside. Dan walked past. The skin on his back crawled. His bodyguard, of course, walked through security without a single question asked.

More of Carreras' men were inside the control complex. Overseeing the operation was a tall, gaunt man with a face like carved ebony and an astonishing shock of thick white hair.

"Evening, Zac," Dan called.

Dr. Zachariah Hughes turned a startled glance in his direction. For an instant the furrowed strain eased from his face. "You old son-of-a-gun! I thought you were dead or something. Why don't you visit me more often?"

Dan grasped the proffered hand. He was acutely aware of the listening ears. From the look in his eyes, so was Zac.

Dan produced a grin. "Hell, I have to run this whole show. This *is* an operational army base, you know."

"Right." Hughes grimaced. "So what's the occasion?"

"Need a transfer programmed and locked in." He set his briefcase down on a countertop and retrieved Sue's printout and disks. "Special run for the boss."

Zac's eyes darkened dangerously. "Right." The sound was vicious. He glanced at the notes. Then looked more closely. Then stared at Dan.

Dan said evenly, "Pretty much a standard run, except for the Gudekinstian problem. I've got equipment with me to compensate and Sue's done some creative programming to counteract the effect."

Zac Hughes followed Dan's glance and saw the prototype in Dan's briefcase. Zac swallowed exactly once. Then a ghostly smile flickered across his face, gone instantly. His expression settled into the professional, calm mask he presented to Carreras' people. "Right."

Dan never ceased to be amazed at the wide range of shaded meanings which Zachariah Hughes could inflect into that one word.

"Right," Dan echoed with a smile. "So let's get cracking. How long?"

Zac studied the notations again and pulled thoughtfully at his lower lip. "Five, ten minutes to load Sue's programs into the main jump-system databases, another thirty to double-check everything. Then an hour till aperture. I can handle this end of it if your team needs prep time. And let me get you a recall box."

It took fifteen minutes for Hughes to get permission to turn over one of the priceless devices to Dan. He didn't really need it, but appearances had to be maintained to divert suspicion. And if anything went wrong . . .

"Thanks. Aperture at—" Dan consulted his watch "—0845?"

"Right." Zac gave him a genuine smile this time. "Have a good trip. I look forward to each data set you guys give us. And Dan . . ."

He glanced up from closing and locking his briefcase.

"Be careful." Zac's brown eyes were nearly as dark and worried as the rest of his face.

Dan forced a grin. "You know me, Zac. I'm always careful."

Zac snorted. Dan grinned wider at the inevitable, "Right." Then Zac muttered, "Get out of here and let me get some work done."

Their parting handshake revealed a tremor new to Zac's steady hand. Dan wondered how much of it was due to Sue's notes and how much was due to thoughts of twelve-year-old Zachariah Hughes III, missing child?

CHAPTER TWELVE

Francisco returned from Dr. Firelli's lab determined to find a way of placing a phone call off base. *Someone* had to be told what was going on up here. Surely he could find a satellite phone somewhere on a base as high-tech as this one was. What was that sergeant's name, the one who'd said something about a way to call home to his wife to be sure her labor went okay?

He had just sat down at his desk and was reaching for the base's phone directory when loud footsteps echoed through the nearly empty clinic. He frowned and glanced up just as the door to his office was thrust open. Two MPs he didn't recognize invaded the cramped space.

"Major Valdez, come with us, please." Despite the polite phrasing, the man's tone was curt, virtually insubordinate. Francisco leaned back in his chair. An involuntary chill trickled down his spine. *Oh-oh.*

"Why? There are two other doctors on duty in the wards."

The man's shrug was insolent. "Orders, Major."

"From?"

A flicker ran through the man's eyes. "Colonel Collins."

Francisco's chill deepened. The MP was lying.

"If you don't mind, I'm awfully busy right now, soldier. I'll just call Dan and see what this is all—"

He was reaching for the telephone when the first MP crossed the room with rapid strides and forcibly held down the receiver.

"You don't need to do that," the man said softly.

"Now, look here—"

With his other hand, the MP opened his parka and slipped out an obviously well-used Colt Woodsman pistol. But instead of a slender barrel and high-bladed sight, Francisco saw a long, cylindrical metal tube the thickness of a fluorescent lightbulb, at least seven inches long. He froze midsentence, afraid even to breathe.

They're going to kill me. Mother of God, they're going to kill me....

"Now, Major," the MP was saying quietly, "we both know how quietly you want to come along. Just about as quietly as this little friend of mine would sing for you. Why, five shots from this wouldn't even attract their attention." He nodded toward the ward, where Francisco's medical staff worked in sweet oblivion. "They might look in, of course, and think you'd had a heart attack. And, naturally, they'd come in to check on you. It'd be a shame if we had to kill everyone in this building, wouldn't it?"

The man actually smiled at him.

Mother of God ...

The spokesman said softly, "Put your hands flat on the desk, Major. Do it *now.*"

Francisco complied. He sat motionless, palms slick against the cluttered desktop, and waited. The MP who hadn't spoken yet came around the desk and frisked him. Then pulled the chair—with Francisco still in it—out into the middle of the room. He didn't protest.

"Very good. Get up."

Francisco eased to his feet.

The MPs shoved him into a heavy parka. Briefly, he shut his eyes. Where were they taking him? A body could lie in those mountains for years ... hundreds of 'em.

"Very good, Major. Now, we're going to go out there very quietly and watch you put together a field surgical kit. For an appendectomy."

"*What?*"

"I would advise you, Major, not to argue."

Francisco swallowed once and stared at the silenced pistol barely concealed by the other man's parka.

"Right. Sure. No problem. Field surgical kit." He licked his lips. "Anything else?"

"Your complete cooperation," the MP smiled. "I would hate to have to persuade one of your colleagues, instead."

Francisco found what he needed. When Dr. Allen and Dr. Kowalski asked what he was doing, he told them shortly that the base commander had summoned him for a medical emergency.

"What kind of emergency, sir?" Kowalski asked. "Anything we can do to—"

"Stop chattering when you're both three hours behind on your paperwork! Have you seen the mess that office is in?"

Allen and Kowalski exchanged puzzled glances and made themselves scarce. Francisco started breathing again once they'd gone.

"Excellent, Major," the MP murmured. "Let's go."

They shoved him into the back of a waiting troop truck and climbed in with him. The MPs took seats on opposite benches. The spokesman said, "On the floor."

He sat.

"And not another word from you, please."

They manacled his wrists with heavy bar cuffs.

Francisco was cold with more than the Arctic air as a third MP shoved the tailgate closed with a clang and disappeared around the side. Moments later the truck lurched into motion. The ride left him battered. From the little he could see out the back of the truck, they had climbed right across one of the nearby lower mountain ridges and descended the other side.

Where on earth were they taking him? If they were just going to shoot him, they wouldn't have forced him to assemble a surgical kit, but there was absolutely nothing out here but snow and ice and rock. Francisco eyed the silenced Colt Woodsman with a growing sense of foreboding. When the truck finally idled to a halt, nobody moved. Francisco tried to ease a cramp in his thigh. The nearest MP snapped, "Sit still!"

"Look, mister—"

Francisco had never been pistol whipped in his life. It *hurt*.

He spat blood and groaned, then lay very still where he'd fallen. He did not want to be hit again.

The incongruous sound of thunder rumbled in his ears. Flashes of lightning blazed outside the truck. The thunder grew louder as false night descended over them. Then the MPs lowered the tailgate, jumped down, and dragged him out by the arms. The third MP grabbed the medical bag. Francisco stumbled and tried to regain his feet. As they hauled him bodily forward, he looked up.

And tried to stop.

"Mary, Mother of God—"

The men holding his arms ran him straight toward it. A glowing rip in the fabric of reality filled the air ahead. Blinding white light poured out of nowhere at all. Lightning blasted into the ground all around them. Francisco yelled—

Then they were inside it.

He fell . . . or thought he fell . . .

Frigid air that made Alaska feel like a balmy spring day hit him with a body slam. The shock robbed him of breath. He blinked and tried to see where he was. They had emerged onto a snowfield. The mountains looked vaguely like the Davidson Mountains north of the base, and that mountain off to the west looked like Table Mountain, in the Philip Smith range, but it *couldn't* be Table Mountain. Not far to the west stretched a sheet of ice that towered toward the sky, glittering a painful blue-white in the harsh sunlight. He tried to look around. To the east he found another massive ice sheet, farther away and much, much higher. *That ice must be a mile thick. . . . Where in the name of Christ are we?*

Between that ice sheet and the hole in reality they'd just dragged him through, Francisco focused on something dark brown and massive, moving slowly in the distance, but couldn't make his numbed mind identify it. Closer at hand was a prefabbed concrete building, similar to what the army used in Antarctica.

They dragged him toward that.

The MP holding the surgical kit pounded on what seemed to be the only door in an apparently windowless building. The door opened a crack.

"Special delivery from the boss." The man grinned.

"Joey! About bloody time!"

The door was thrown open by a man in blue jeans and a loud Hawaiian shirt with purple parrots on it. "Get him *in* here!"

The second MP of his escort turned and jogged back toward the lightning-filled crack in reality, disappearing into it. Francisco's mind reeled. Joey and the remaining MP—the same guard who'd pistol whipped him—shoved Francisco bodily inside. It was warm in the bunker, although very cramped. There were only four small rooms and no doors, only open doorways. One of the four rooms was a bathroom. The air stank of stale cigarette smoke, urine, sweat, and fear.

"Frank!"

He started. And swung around to see Lucille Collins' white face.

"What—?"

They shoved him in the opposite direction. In one of the corner rooms, they'd stacked up a collection of army cots. Janet Firelli sat crouched next to one of them, holding a young black boy's hand. The child was grey with pain. His eyes were shut. At their footsteps, the slim girl turned, a snarl on her lips. At sight of Francisco, she halted. Her eyes widened fractionally.

"Major Valdez! Hurry!"

They unfastened his wrists and shoved him forward. He put aside the questions crowding into his mind and knelt beside Janet.

"I think it's his appendix," she gulped. "This is Zac Hughes. The Third."

Hostages. The abrupt chill in his blood had not a solitary thing to do with the temperature: inside the bunker *or* outside in the frozen air.

Francisco checked Zac's pulse and pupils, then pressed

lightly on his abdomen. When he let go, the boy screamed. Then fainted. Francisco swore. If it hadn't burst already—which would mean massive infection, peritonitis (and the probable death of Zac Hughes III, no matter *what* Francisco tried under these conditions)— it was very close to bursting, might well go at any moment. *Madre Maria, please don't let it have burst yet, he's just a boy—a prisoner. Help me, so this child doesn't die like this, in this terrible place.*

Taking a deep breath for courage, he growled, "Give me the medical bag." Someone complied. He tore Zac's shirt open, exposed the child's belly. He rummaged quickly through his woefully meager supplies. This was a helluva place for emergency surgery.

Better than a battlefield, of course. . . .

He administered anesthesia, then swabbed Zac's stomach and groin with alcohol and used more to wipe his hands. "Janet, tie that mask around my face, then put one on yourself and scrub your hands with those swabs."

She did so efficiently.

He motioned with his head to the gauze sponges and clamps he'd laid aside. "I hope you don't faint at the sight of blood, Janet. When I say 'sponge' reach in and swab up for me."

She gulped and nodded, then obeyed as Francisco made the incision.

She didn't faint. Didn't even make a sound after an initial whimper. She did make a fine nurse, everything considered. Mostly she did exactly as she was told and kept out of his way.

He finished suturing the incision closed, reached for a fresh alcohol wipe, and cleaned the area in and around the stitches. Then he reached for gauze and tape. Janet watched wordlessly and handed him a clean towel from somewhere for him to wipe his hands.

Then she burst into sobs. "I'm sorry—I'm sorry—" He reached out and hugged her.

"You did just fine, Janet. Your mother would be very proud."

That only brought fresh sobs.

"How touching."

Francisco turned to glare at the man in the Hawaiian shirt. He lolled in the doorway. Francisco noticed a pistol stuck casually in the waistband of his jeans. *Stupid way to carry a firearm. . . .*

"Who are you?"

The man grinned and touched fingertips to brow in a mock salute. "Your jailor, doc. Welcome to cell block Alaska."

"His name is Bill," Janet said in a dull voice. "He works for somebody named Carreras. We're hostages, Major Valdez."

Bill gave him another jaunty mock salute.

"I figured that out," Francisco muttered, "but what *for?*"

She shook her head. "It has something to do with my mother's work. I'm not sure what. She's very close-mouthed when it comes to classified research. But I do know the general thrust of her work before she began this project. Before she was *approached* for this project," she added significantly.

"And?"

Janet glared at Bill, who was still grinning down at them.

"We're still in Alaska," she said dully. "But I wouldn't advise trying to escape. It wouldn't do a whole lot of good."

"Why not?" he asked irritably.

"Because we're about thirty-thousand years in the past."

She was serious. Francisco felt strangely disconnected and quite suddenly very, very afraid. *Those ice sheets. And brown shapes that had looked vaguely elephantine . . .* Bill began to chuckle.

Janet added, "Not only is there nowhere to go, we're stranded in the middle of the Pleistocene Ice Age. It's twenty below out there, without windchill. Last week, the wooly mammoth herds started migrating south for the winter, through the ice-free corridor. I figure the nearest *people* live somewhere in the middle of Russia, if Russia *had* any Cro-Magnons. Or would it be Paleo-Indians? Uh, I'm afraid anthropology isn't my thing."

Her eyes were bleak.

Francisco didn't want to believe her. But he'd seen the . . . *thing* . . . they'd taken him through. And that brown, moving mass he'd seen in the distance . . . It really *had* looked like a herd of elephants. Brown ones. With lots and lots of hair. And enough ivory on each beast to put a modern elephant to shame.

"We're treated pretty well, everything considered," Janet said in a low, scared voice. "They need us."

It occurred to Francisco Valdez in that cramped, foul little room, that he had no family to hold hostage. He was entirely superfluous now that Zac Hughes' life was out of danger. And he knew far, far too much about these people—whoever they were—for them to risk letting him get back alive.

Something dull and scared in Janet Firelli's eyes told him she knew it, too. Bill's laughter echoed in his ears.

CHAPTER THIRTEEN

Sibyl roused to sounds of panic. Screams, crashes, running footsteps ... Above those sounds was an awesome, earthshaking *noise*. *Vesuvius*. She tried to move, then groaned, instead. Nothing seemed to be working properly and she was mortally certain she did not want to try moving again.

Sibyl tried to move, anyway. She had to get out of the house before the *real* eruption started. The steam explosions had already begun. Which meant the main eruption couldn't be more than minutes away. Sibyl rolled over and tried to gain her knees. Pain stabbed through her belly, her groin, her back. She sobbed aloud. She wouldn't have to wait for the volcano to kill her. She felt as though she were bleeding to death where she lay.

She heard Bericus shouting orders to bring out the spare carriage and heavy wagon. Then he vanished from her awareness. She was alone in the *peristyle* garden under a hot, sunlit sky, with the ground shaking so violently she knew it might be only seconds before the walls started to go.

Sibyl tried again to gain her knees. She cast a frantic glance upward. The sky was still a flawless, burning blue. She twisted to peer at the volcano. Her eyes widened. Vesuvius *steamed*. Billowing clouds of white vapor, mixed with grey ash and rock, rose majestically from the crater. The sight brought a chill to her spine.

The mountain had barely begun to blow open, after so many years of somnolence. Some poor shepherd or two had probably just died a violent death, along with the flocks which had routinely been driven up there to graze in the old caldera. *First to die. But not the last, by a long, long shot.*

Judging from the position of the sun, there wasn't much time before the famous one-o'clock explosion tore the entire top of the mountain off. *That* explosion would send rock and poisonous gas belching twelve miles into the atmosphere.

Gotta get out of here, now. . . .

"Sibyl!"

The incongruous sound of her name startled her. She swung around, dazed and shaken. "Wha—"

Benigna. Clutching her child. Lucania wasn't crying. She clung to her mother's neck with a fierceness Sibyl had seen so often in Charlie.

"Please, *sibyl*, help us! You warned us, please, have pity—"

"Help me up . . ."

Benigna lifted Sibyl to her feet. Her clothing, torn in places, bloody in others, fell around her seminakedness. She hardly noticed, except to wince in pain at each step. Benigna put an arm around her, guiding her toward the nearest doorway.

"We have to get out of the house," Sibyl mumbled.

"There is no time! We must take shelter in the nearest gateway!"

Gateway?

Still dazed and uncertain, Sibyl stumbled across the garden toward the nearest doorway, guided by the trembling slave woman. The ground lurched sharply under their feet. Benigna screamed. Her daughter whimpered and clung more tightly to her neck. "Hurry, *sibyl!*"

Xanthus ran into the garden, making for the doorway that led to the front of the house, and literally ran them down. Sibyl sprawled, jarring her lower body painfully. The slave trader roared and kicked at her, then swore at Benigna, who had fallen at his feet.

"You!" He snatched Lucania from her mother's arms. "I'll just take what Bericus promised and cut my losses!"

"*No!*" Benigna tried to grapple him.

Xanthus slapped her to the shaking ground.

Lucania began to scream for her mother.

Sibyl searched for a weapon—any weapon—and found the broken remains of a fountain almost under her hand. She snatched up a heavy section of lead piping and lunged forward. Xanthus had already begun running for the far end of the garden again, with Lucania struggling over one shoulder.

Sibyl panted and ran after him, gaining ground fast. "Stop!"

When he kept going, Sibyl swung the heavy water pipe in a vicious arc. It connected with the backs of his knees. Xanthus screamed and went down. Lucania was flung to the ground. The little girl wailed and rolled to a stop in a flower bed. Sibyl hit Xanthus again, across the small of the back, then felt the warning rumble in the ground.

Oh, God—

"*Sibyl!*"

Benigna's scream of terror distracted her. The woman was pointing to the mountain. Sibyl craned her neck around to see Vesuvius more clearly—

—and the whole sky exploded.

The top of the mountain blew apart. Vesuvius hurled itself toward the stratosphere. Almost simultaneously the sound smashed down across them. Benigna lost her footing and fell. Sibyl couldn't hear any screams, not even her own. The ground heaved like hurricane-maddened surf. Blackness the shape of an evil umbrella pine blotted out the sun, engulfing them in choking nightfall in an instant. Sibyl held her breath, terrified that hot ash and poisonous gas would envelop them. Rocks from what had been the top of the mountain smashed down within a few feet. Then the house wall above them cracked, began to go . . .

Someone shoved her violently forward, pushing the small of her back. Sibyl sprawled forward under a doorway. Little Lucania landed beside her, as though thrown by a supreme effort. Sibyl snatched the child close, looked back for Benigna—

The slave woman had fallen to all fours a few feet short of the doorway. Then masonry and wood crashed down. Benigna vanished under it. Sibyl screamed. Lucania clung to her, weeping hysterically now. Sibyl huddled over the toddler, trying to protect her with her own body. More masonry crashed down, burying them deeper. Something massive grazed her shoulder. Sibyl sobbed in pain. Lucania was screaming.

"Shh . . . Shh . . ." *Oh, God, we're going to die. . . .*

An eternity later, the house stopped falling on them. The ground still shook and Vesuvius still roared, but they were alive. It took Sibyl a long, long time to stop shaking as violently as the ground. Even more slowly, she risked a look. All she saw was brick and splintered wood.

"Oh, my God . . ."

She touched debris with a trembling hand, just to confirm the worst. Solid as stone, it didn't budge. They were alive. But utterly trapped under rubble.

And no one—*no one*—was going to stop long enough to dig them out again.

"Nnnhh . . ."

With painful slowness, Charlie moved his head. He swallowed, tasted dirt, spat. Charlie licked his lips and spat again. *Hey, I'm still alive. . . .*

The ground lurched sickeningly. Then dropped three feet out from underneath him. He gave a startled yell and grabbed wildly at thin air, then landed heavily on his side.

"Nhh—"

Renewed pain from the broken rib sent a jolt through him. His arm felt bruised from wrist to shoulder. He couldn't hear his own groans. Couldn't hear anything, in fact, except a skull-splitting roar which smashed down from above and beat up through the very ground. There was nothing in his varied and colorful life with which he could even remotely compare this—"sound" seemed far too mild a word—this awesome noise.

He thought about rolling himself into a fetal ball and hugging both arms over his ears. Instead, Charlie dragged himself painfully to elbows and knees. Bit by bit, he hauled himself over to a section of ground that had remained at its old height and peered up over the lip of the fault. It was hard to see, as though night had fallen hours too early. Whistling impacts nearby raised the hair on the back of his neck. Charlie squinted. *Red-hot stones, falling out of a black sky....* The oak tree to which he'd tied his horse was down, its shattered roots jutting obscenely toward the maddened sky.

Above the shoulder of Vesuvius, the heavens were black as hell for miles. Wild discharges of flame shot through that hellish darkness. Streaks and meteoric flashes marked the passage of rocky, half-molten missiles. Far too many were landing in his vicinity. *Gotta get the hell outta here.* Charlie groped across the trembling earth. He discovered his crutch lying miraculously near his hand. But relief was a bit premature. *One step at a time.*

He grabbed the crutch, got his bad leg under him, and hauled himself up over the edge of the thrust fault. Then Charlie rolled over to sit up. Through the volcanic murk, he caught a glimpse of motion and crawled closer to investigate. Silver was down, flat on his side, struggling to rise. The horse was covered with lather. Charlie found the reins, still tied securely to the fallen tree. Thank God the violent crack hadn't broken the animal's neck. At least, he didn't think it had. He'd better check for broken bones in Silver's legs, too.

Charlie couldn't make his shouts heard even to himself, so he just rubbed the animal's sweating neck and held on. The gelding surged once. Charlie felt, rather than heard, the rumble of a groan in the animal's throat beneath his hand. Then the poor horse lay back, eyes rolling white. Silver's whole body shivered. Charlie crawled around the fallen horse and ran exploratory hands across its legs. Nothing felt broken. Nor did Silver make any sudden protests.

Charlie crawled back to the horse's head. The animal whickered softly into his palm when he stroked the velvety nose. He groped for his crutch and, taking a calculated risk, tied it securely to the saddle. Then Charlie pulled himself awkwardly across Silver's side and positioned himself as best he could.

Then he cut the reins, close to the branch, and snatched them up. Charlie grabbed double handfuls of coarse mane hair, blessed whatever gods had prompted the Romans not to shave their horses' manes, and urged the animal up with legs, hands, and voice.

Silver rolled heavily, dragging Charlie with him, then heaved and got all four legs under him. Charlie slid precariously sideways. Pain stabbed through his chest. He gritted his teeth and pulled himself up until the muscles in neck, shoulders and arms strained nearly to breaking. He hooked his good leg over the animal's back just as the horse surged drunkenly. The momentum lifted Charlie into the saddle—and almost off the other side.

He slid facefirst toward the ground, bashed his chin on the horse's bony withers, and struggled madly for balance. He tried to grip with his hamstrung leg, his elbows, even his ribs. Charlie nearly blacked out, but he hung on. He pulled at mane hair until he was convinced entire tufts would come loose in his grasp. Silver stood stock still, head hung low and legs trembling. Without that tiny miracle, Charlie would never have halted his slide toward the ground or gotten himself back up into the saddle.

For long, shivering moments, Charlie sat as still as his horse and simply gulped air that stank of only God knew what. Then, trembling with haste, Charlie slid his feet into the homemade stirrups and thumped the horse's sides with his heels. Silver didn't need any further encouragement. The gelding put his head down and *ran*. Charlie tried to guide him, with almost no success.

His heart leaped into his throat every time the animal slipped or jumped across a nearly invisible fault in the earth. Finally Charlie gave up and let the horse have his head. If Silver stepped into a hole and broke a leg, there wasn't much Charlie could do about it. Not only was he too poor a horseman, Silver could probably see where he was going better than Charlie. What he wouldn't give for a lousy trail bike. . . .

Ash had begun to fall along with the heavy stones, and with it, lighter, stinging missiles of pumice. Charlie winced as he was pelted with showers of smoking debris. He was glad for the helmet and the metal armor. *Just don't let any of that big, glowing stuff land on us. . . .* By the time Charlie had worked through the worst of the fight-or-flight panic, he found it was nearly impossible to get Silver turned toward the villa, since that was marginally "toward" the erupting mountain.

He fought the horse's head and hauled desperately on the reins, kicking with his good leg as hard as he could. Silver screamed and fought the pressure, then bucked hard enough to send him sailing out of the saddle toward the horse's ears. He dropped the reins, grabbed the mane with both hands, and jarred himself hard when he slid back into the saddle.

"Unnhgh . . ."

If he hadn't had stirrups, he'd have been on the ground.

Charlie caught his breath, unable to hear his own cries in the black noise that surrounded them. Then he stubbornly tried again. He finally convinced the horse that he *meant* what he meant. Although the animal refused to move faster than a walk toward the mountain, he did at least walk in that general direction. Charlie just hoped he could *find* the villa in the thick ashfall.

Clear daylight had turned into a grotesque parody of a severe winter blizzard. He wrapped a corner of the cloak around his face to keep thick, hot ash out of his nose and mouth, then worried about Silver's respiratory system. Just about the time he was convinced he'd missed the villa in the thick, pelting debris, the walls loomed through the murk.

He found utter chaos. Several walls had fallen. Part

of the roof had caved in. Most of the slaves had hauled makeshift packs onto their backs and were running, singly or in groups of two and three, toward the sea. One heavily laden wagon had already lurched on its way toward town, crammed mostly with people. Charlie pulled Silver to a sweating stop near the villa's main doors. A bear of a man with an armload of foodstuffs and a torch stopped as Charlie reined around to block his path.

Quintus.

The man scowled up at him. "Get out of the way!"

Charlie read his lips almost more than he heard the furious bellow. "Where is your master?" Charlie bellowed right back, breathing between his teeth through the pain.

"Gone, asshole!"

Son-of-a—

"Where is Aelia? The new slave woman?"

The man spat something vile and started to grab at the reins. Charlie moved instinctively, his hand shooting toward his hip for the holster. . . . His fingers closed over the sword hilt, instead. He had it free of the scabbard before he could even think about it, moving with the ease and speed of two years' deadly combat training in the arena. The horse screamed a warning and came off the ground, biting suddenly and savagely at the man's arm.

Charlie grabbed mane hair with his free hand and fought pain in his ribcage. *Bloody war horse. . . .* But Quintus' eyes had widened. Charlie shoved the tip of the *gladius* right up against his windpipe and drew a droplet of blood.

"Where is she?" Charlie snarled. "I don't give a damn about you! All I want is the woman, Aelia!"

"I don't know! In the house! Try the *peristyle* garden—"

Charlie urged Silver through sagging doors into the damaged house, snatching the slave's torch as he shouldered past. Silver's hooves clattered and slid on broken mosaic. The horse snorted and shied. Charlie stayed with him. "Easy . . . Come on, boy . . ."

The horse surged ahead again, fighting Charlie's grip on the reins and the urge to panic and run again. Charlie could literally *feel* that urge in the bunch and play of muscles under his legs. Heart in his throat, Charlie held him to a walk and urged him steadily forward. The gelding danced through the shattered villa, where nothing stirred but dust and volcanic ash.

He held the lighted torch aloft and tried to peer through the darkness. "Sibyl! Sibyl, where are you?"

Nothing . . .

The entrance to the *peristyle* garden had partially collapsed. Charlie hugged Silver's neck and urged the gelding through the tight opening. Silver snorted and tried to rear, then moved obediently forward. Fallen beams scraped armor along his back. Then they were through. The garden he recalled so cruelly was wrecked. The fountains were down, twisted into ruin. Part of the upper floor had collapsed into the side of the garden, burying half of it.

If Sibyl had been over there . . .

"SIBYL!"

"Help!" a faint voice cried out, from somewhere to Charlie's right, toward the collapsed rubble from the upper floor. "Help me!"

Charlie couldn't tell who it was, but they were calling out in Latin. He started to ignore the plea, then thought better. Whoever it was might know how he could find Sibyl. Or Lucania. Charlie eased Silver closer and held the torch down to light the face.

Xanthus.

Charlie's master lay at Silver's feet, his lower body pinned by debris. Blood snaked down the slave trader's face. He peered up at Charlie, lifted a trembling hand. "Please, help me . . ."

He thinks I'm a soldier come to rescue him. . . .

"Are there other survivors here?"

Xanthus blinked. "I—I don't know— Bericus ran when the walls began to fall. There was a slave woman—I don't know—"

"WHERE WAS SHE?"

Xanthus' hand shook. "Please, my legs are pinned, broken . . . Please, help me . . ."

Charlie stared down at the man who had tormented him, had tortured him for nearly two full years, and felt hatred turn to disgust somewhere down in the pit of his belly. Xanthus was a dead man, whatever Charlie did or didn't do to him. Or for him. And in just a few hours, he would be paid back a million-fold for every minute of Charlie's suffering. Lying there trapped while Vesuvius burned him to death. . . .

Charlie didn't feel very proud of himself for reaching that conclusion, but his own survival came first. He still had others to find, far more important in his world than Xanthus ever could be.

Besides, Xanthus wasn't the one ultimately responsible for the hell Charlie had been living. He was only a Roman doing what a Roman thought was proper and right; the real villain still lay far beyond Charlie's revenge. Charlie couldn't quite bring himself to end Xanthus' suffering with a quick dagger thrust—the risk of dismounting now from Silver's back might be never getting into the saddle again—but he couldn't hate Xanthus quite so deeply, either. He, at least, would pay for his crimes.

Too goddamn bad it wasn't Carreras lying there with his legs crushed. . . .

Charlie turned his back and left his "master" screaming for help. He had to find Sibyl and his daughter. If they were still alive.

Sibyl rocked Charlie's little girl in the cramped space of their prison, murmuring softly to her until hysterical sobs quieted. Chubby little fingers clutched at her neck, her hair. Soft arms and a trembling little body pressed close in the darkness.

"Shh . . . Shh . . . It's all right, Lucania, it's all right, shh, it's all right . . ."

Maybe if I say it often enough, it'll be true.

"Mama?"

"Shh, no, your mama isn't here, Lucania. Shh . . ."

How to explain to a toddler who could scarcely speak that her mother had just died?

Very faintly, Sibyl heard voices. She tried to hear above the noise from Vesuvius. "Hello!" she called, as loudly as she could. "HELP!" She tried pushing at the rubble and felt more than heard the ominous shift of weight. "HELP US!"

So faint, the voice might have been transmitted from orbit, "Where are you?"

Hope—so sudden and unexpected it *hurt*—stabbed through her. "*Under the doorway! Please, there are two of us! We're not hurt, we're just trapped!*"

Again, so faint she could barely hear it, the voice came to her. "I'm looking for someone. I'm sorry . . ."

"NO! PLEASE!" Sibyl shoved at rubble with her bare hands.

When she didn't hear anything further, Sibyl sagged back against the wall of rubble trapping them and hugged Lucania tight. *Don't cry, don't break down and terrify her all over again. . . .*

But she couldn't stop the tears leaking silently down her face, any more than she could stop the murderous pillar of debris belching out of Vesuvius from collapsing a few hours hence into fiery avalanches that would burn them alive.

Out of hope, Sibyl huddled with her arms around Lucania Flynn and wept.

He was about to give up the search of the garden and start picking through the surviving rooms when he heard the faint, faint cry for help. Charlie almost left them.

Almost.

But the voice had sounded like a woman's.

He didn't dare hope, but he couldn't just walk away, either, and never know. Charlie slithered awkwardly to the ground and risked tying Silver's reins to a broken fountain. Water poured across the splintered garden from a dozen twisted pipes. The horse lipped at it eagerly. Charlie ignored Xanthus' screams, pleas, *demands* for help, and eyed the pile of rubble with deep misgiving, then thrust his torch into the wet earth and started clearing rubble away, brick by brick.

It was murderous work. Especially with a broken rib. But he kept doggedly at it, pausing now and again simply because his flagging body gave him no choice. Ashfall and debris rained down steadily, pelting his arms and back and zinging painfully off his helmet. He kept digging. The whole pile shifted ominously. Charlie looked for something to brace it and found a shattered beam.

Using Silver's superior strength to drag it over, Charlie wedged it into place and shored up the mass as best he could, then started digging again. When he uncovered a slim, shapely hand covered in blood and dust, he paused sharply. *Her* hand? He kept digging, cold and afraid now inside his sweat and pain. It was a woman. The face was beyond recognition. But that long, beautiful sweep of ash-blond hair wasn't.

Not Sibyl. *Benigna.*

His gorge rose. Frantic, sick, Charlie dug through the rubble, knowing at any moment he would find another, smaller body near her mother. *Please, God, please . . .* He found only rubble. Bricks and broken plaster and splintered wood. And then, finally, a dark hole low to the ground, where a fallen beam had wedged in at a forty-five-degree angle across a doorway.

Something moved inside that hole.

"Give me your hand!" Charlie shouted above the terrible noise from Vesuvius.

A trembling hand grasped his. He hauled her out, bent over and awkward, holding herself. She collapsed at his feet, shaking almost as violently as the ground. Torn Egyptian linen, a king's ransom in jewelry . . .

She looked up. Charlie's gut sucked in, almost as hard as his breath. Despite the makeup, the scrapes and the dirt—

"Sibyl!"

Her eyes widened. Then she was in his arms, just clinging to him, sobbing. He held her close, thanking God she was still alive, *alive*. . . .

"Charlie, I found her, she's all right, she was so lucky, oh, God, you don't know . . ."

Sibyl was pulling loose, reaching for something pale on the ground.

Then he had a child in his arms, a wide-eyed, white-faced little girl with red-gold hair and a smear of blood down her brow. Charlie touched his daughter's face with fingertips that shook, then he started to cry, silently, helplessly. His daughter wriggled and tried to reach Sibyl. "Mama!"

"Shh . . ." Sibyl stroked her hair. "This is your father, Lucania. Your father . . ."

Lucania, face smeared with tear trails and blood, stuffed an uncertain fist into her mouth. Then peered into Charlie's eyes. "Pater?"

"Yes," Charlie choked out, remembering to speak to her in Latin, "I'm your father. I've been looking and looking for you. Ever since you were born. . . ."

A tiny, chubby hand tugged at the cheek-piece of his battered helmet. "Miles!"

Soldier . . .

He let her believe the lie. She was too young to understand, anyway. Charlie felt the delicate little slave's collar at her throat and snarled something incoherent, then used his dagger to snap open the tiny lock. He hurled the collar away into volcanic darkness.

"Sibyl," Charlie said raggedly, "we have to get the hell out of here. Now, before the rest of the house comes down. Here . . . take her."

Handing his only child over to Sibyl so soon after holding Lucania for the first time was one of the hardest things he'd ever done. Before she could protest, Charlie picked Sibyl up. He grunted in sudden, agonizing pain, then hoisted her to Silver's back.

When the world had more or less steadied under his feet, he wrapped Silver's reins several times around his arm and grabbed his crutch. Then he found the torch and led the horse back through the ruined garden. Charlie ducked under the broken doorway into the house proper, then steadied the gelding through and led him past the shattered atrium. Before he led them into the open again, Charlie yanked off his helmet.

"Put this on!"

Sibyl didn't argue with him. She jammed the helmet over her own head and bent more protectively over Lucania.

Like Joseph fleeing the wrath of Herod, Charlie led Silver out of the villa and fled on foot before the wrath of Vesuvius. Everything in the world he cared about followed mutely in the darkness, tethered to his arm by one slim leather band.

CHAPTER FOURTEEN

Feeble light from the torch Charlie carried barely pierced the volcanic gloom. Sibyl could see hardly anything beyond Charlie's outstretched arm—not even the width of the road. Their slow-motion flight, with Charlie limping ahead, felt like waking nightmare. Scores of terrified slaves, small landowners, and rich men like Bericus fled hovels and rich country villas alike, passing them on the road.

A few, Charlie had to fight for their horse.

Sibyl had never seen a man disembowelled before. She hid Lucania's face in the folds of her own ruined garments and swallowed down horror. Arm bloodied, sword bloodied, face and armor spattered with gore, Charlie gasped out, "Can you hold the torch?"

Sibyl simply nodded and held out one hand. "Hold tight, little Lucky," she whispered to Lucania. "Hold real tight." Sibyl clung to the horse's mane with one hand, drawing Lucania close in the crook of her arm and trying to tuck her dress around to form a pocket, then took the torch in her other hand and held it aloft for Charlie. She ignored the pain in her lower body. Ignored the fatigue which shook through her arm in almost no time.

Keep it high enough to do some good, she told herself fiercely again and again, fighting the pain of burning muscles in her arm. *What you're going through is nothing. He's got to* walk *the whole way. On a ruined leg*. Sibyl received fleeting, ghostly glimpses of running figures, panic-stricken faces. Heard cries for help, cries for lost loved ones in the darkness. Refugees carried their valuables and their families tucked into anything that would roll, or ran on foot if they had no other transportation. Helter-skelter, they all fled for the false security of the seaside town.

Sibyl shut her eyes and tried to close her mind to the images her memory insisted on producing: whole-body burns, blackened skin slipping off, blistered lungs and throats. . . . And two thousand years later, infants discovered abandoned in their cradles, women's bones found clutching those of their children, slaves and soldiers and bejeweled patrician ladies, hapless skeletons huddled together for safety which, ultimately, none had found.

How many more had died out in the farmland, slaves and peasants whose skeletons would never be unearthed?

For an aching passage of time, all Sibyl could do was hold back tears and the terror that their own skeletons would be among them. The one thought she clung to was that Charlie had found them. They were together. Whatever happened, they were together.

It was slim consolation, at best, but it was all she had.

Herculaneum, when they finally arrived—hours later, battered, bruised, exhausted—was in a state of panic. There was actually daylight, of sorts, over the town. The ashfall was blowing southeast, with very little falling on Herculaneum. Roof tiles and partially collapsed walls littered the streets. Sibyl craned around for a glance at Vesuvius and shuddered.

The umbrella-pine cloud hovered above the city, rent with flashes of red, yellow, even bluish fire. Glowing stones hurled aloft by the volcano shot upward, then arced outward and fell onto Vesuvius' upper slopes. They looked like insane bottle-rockets plummeting down out of the blackness.

Frantic householders hauled cartloads of possessions from some of the damaged houses. In front of others, men openly jeered at those who fled, scoffing at the danger. Arguments she overheard as they passed reminded Sibyl of hurricane watchers too foolish to leave the coast for shelter. Nothing would happen to *them*, so why miss all the fun?

"Look at it, the whole cloud's blowing toward Pompeii. . . ."

Others, panic-stricken, implored the gods to save them and ran for the sea. Sibyl's head throbbed, with a headache born of too little water, too much pain, and far too much fear. Her throat was raw from swallowed smoke and ash, too raw to call out warnings which wouldn't have been heeded, anyway. She shut her eyes to blot out images too stark to bear.

When the ground shook again, so violently the street cracked underfoot, Sibyl screamed. Charlie's horse screamed, too, and reared so sharply he dragged Charlie completely off the ground. Sibyl felt her tenuous grip on the mane slip, slide away—

The landing jarred everything in her. Charlie's helmet clattered away across the paving stones. Lucania fell on top of her, wailing in terror. Charlie battled the panicked horse. Someone nearby helped Sibyl to her feet, braced her while Charlie fought the horse down again and held him.

"Get back in the saddle!" Charlie yelled.

"Hold Lucania! I can't climb up while I'm holding her!"

She handed Lucania over to her father and started to haul herself up. Another earthquake hit. The street cracked farther open. A nearby wall crashed down. Charlie's horse screamed, a high, piercing sound—

Then dragged Charlie into the crowd, beyond Sibyl's view.

"CHARLIE!"

She ran after them.

Another wall collapsed, pouring rubble into the street between her and the fleeting horse.

"Oh, God, no, please . . ."

She climbed *over* the rubble.

In the distance, blocks away already, she could just see the panicked horse and—flopping awkwardly beside

it, trying to keep up—Charlie. He clung to Lucania with
one hand while the horse dragged him by the reins
wound around his arm. Then the rubble shifted and
more of the wall started to topple. Sibyl flung herself
sideways, down, *away*.

By the time she was able to scramble after them,
Charlie had utterly vanished into the crowd.

Numb with shock and horror, Sibyl ran—limping—
in the direction Charlie had gone.

"Have you seen a soldier with a runaway horse?" she
gasped out to people she passed.

A few pointed out a direction; others just shoved her
aside. Sibyl kept running. Always, he was just a little
farther ahead or down a twisting, rubble-choked side
street. She couldn't catch up. Pain in her lower body
reminded her with every jolting step that she'd been
violently raped and beaten just hours previously. The
bruises were beginning to stiffen.

"Charlie!" she sobbed uselessly, knowing he couldn't
possibly hear her this time.

She had to pause for breath. Sibyl leaned drunkenly
against a none-too-steady wall and sucked down filthy
air through the filter of a torn piece of her gauze dress
tied around her lower face like a bandanna. Her whole
body shuddered. The streets were far more crowded than
Sibyl had anticipated. Roman towns—including Rome
itself—went to sleep virtually with the chickens. This
evening, in doomed Herculaneum, a party atmosphere
like a mad Mardi Gras had seized the city.

Citizens and slaves, like the revellers in a story by Poe,
drank and laughed and chased one another in lunatic
circles while red death loomed above their heads. She
wanted to shout warnings and understood with a wrenching pain something she'd never guessed about time
travel: people never changed.

How much time was left?

She set out again, asking about the runaway horse,
the soldier carrying a baby, and was told, "That way,

several minutes ago." Charlie and his runaway horse
were headed toward the Decumanus Maximus.
Wineshops did brisk business as patricians and plebe-
ians gathered on street corners and beside fountains
to talk about the volcano and debate the dangers. As
she half ran, half stumbled past, Sibyl overheard snatches
of conversation.

". . . lots of times the ground's rumbled. And look at
that quake we had twelve years ago, when the Magna
Mater was damaged. I tell you, nothing will come of
it . . ."

". . . Tillerus and his family have already gone, slaves
and all, spent a hundred-thousand sesterces for a *fishing
boat*, I tell you, can you believe that stupid fool . . . ?"

". . . wife's been screaming at me so long, I came out
here to get drunk . . ."

". . . never saw anything like it in my life, let me tell
you, and I didn't get these white hairs overnight. Of
course it's beautiful, never saw anything so awesome in
my whole life. I'm going to sit right here all night and
watch it, so pretty against the night sky, probably never
see a thing like this again before I die . . ."

Sibyl wanted to cover her ears.

The Decumanus Maximus was a solid throng of
people. Along the porticoed side of the street, vats of
hot oil in the sausage vendors' stalls sizzled and spread
the scent of frying meat into the night air, disguising
the brimstone stench lingering like rotten eggs.

"Please, have you seen a soldier and a baby, a brown
horse . . ."

The man whose arm she'd grasp shook his head. Sibyl
kept asking. "That way," somebody finally said, "several
minutes ago. Shouting for a priestess of the Magna
Mater."

Sibyl swayed. "Thank you . . ."

As she ran, she tried to listen for her name above
the babble of night noises in Herculaneum's streets.
Staked out in the entrances to dark little alleyways and
slouched beside the winestalls, painted whores did a

trade nearly as brisk as the winesellers and sausage vendors. Some of the men looked nearly as scared as the prostitutes. These disappeared into dimly seen doorways to make frantic love, which sometimes could be heard above the street sounds as Sibyl passed hurriedly by. Other men lounged on the streets beside the women and caressed them beneath their short *tunicas* and joked and teased and plied them with wine until the prices went lower.

Sibyl barely heard music that drifted down from rooftop gardens to mingle with the roar in the streets. She concentrated on watching the shadows and the men in them and tried to ignore the crawling sensation between her shoulderblades. Somewhere just ahead, surely. She risked a call.

"Charlie! CHARLIE!"

Nothing.

Sibyl gained the basilica and paused again to catch her breath in the political heart and soul of Herculaneum. The basilica was where justice was dispensed, from the tribunal seat. Sibyl doubted that either Charlie or herself could find justice from that tribunal seat tonight, not even if the magistrates had kept the court open. If either of them were captured with slave collars locked around their throats, they wouldn't live to tell their story.

An archway next to the basilica led, as had been surmised, into the Forum, which was completely unexcavated in her own time. So much of the city lay in that direction. "Please," she caught the arm of a man coming from that direction, "have you seen a soldier carrying a small child? He has a brown horse and—"

"No. Let go of me, girl!"

He swung the lantern he carried at her. She ducked and ran the other direction, straining to see through the crowd for a tall, red-haired figure with a bad limp. Equestrian statues towered overhead at the entrance to the basilica. A bronze chariot and bronze horses loomed out of the near-darkness. The basilica was closed for the night and would not be reopened for nearly two thousand years.

Sibyl ran past the temple of the priests of the deified Augustus and the Forum Baths, across a narrow street from the House of the Wooden Partition. She asked a group of men standing on the corner and one of them pointed toward the sea. She cut down a side street past the House of the Mosaic Atrium, which overlooked the Mediterranean next to the House of the Stags, with its soaring sun terrace which overlooked the rooftop of the Suburban Bath and the Mediterranean beyond.

And ran slam into a tall man emerging from a narrow alleyway. "Hold," the man cried, steadying her. "You've nearly fallen, there, girl."

Sibyl dragged air into her lungs and glanced up—

Into Tony Bartlett's wide, shocked eyes.

"You!"

Sibyl twisted against his grip.

He hit her.

She landed in a heap at his feet, cringing from another blow. Her traitorous body remembered the beating Bericus had given it, didn't want another . . .

Tony laughed and dragged her to her feet.

"Well, well. Such a resourceful little *sibyl*, aren't we? Bericus will be so pleased to have his new pet back."

"Let me go! My God, Tony, isn't it enough to maroon me two thousand years in the past?"

He tightened a hand through her hair. He smiled slowly, the kind of smile a corporate shark wore when announcing a hostile takeover. "Oh, no," he whispered savagely. "Not nearly enough."

"But I can't possibly threaten you—"

He hit her again. Sibyl went to her knees, ears ringing, mouth bleeding.

"I didn't think you'd get rid of that memory block, but you did. Either those Army drugs aren't as good as Jésus thought, or you're a lot tougher than you look. Not

that having your memory will do you any good. Not now."
He smiled down at her. Sibyl whimpered.

His gaze lingered on the torn, transparent linen which
revealed far more than it hid. Tony smiled directly into
her eyes. "I'm in no great rush, Sibyl, dear. We have
all evening." He dragged her up, pulled her against him.
Tony's hand against her breast was almost worse than
Bericus' brutal treatment. She thrashed against his iron-
hard grip, then flinched involuntarily when he raised the
back of his hand. Tony laughed softly and leaned closer,
lips all but brushing her earlobe.

"I know how much you wanted me, when we were
here before," he breathed. "I used to watch you work,
Sibyl, in those tight little shorts, digging up all those
lovely manuscripts for the old man." His smile sent chills
down her back. She strained away as far as his grip would
permit. His hand caressed her again, leaving her shaking. "I couldn't possibly leave without giving you what
you want, Sibyl."

She gave a strangled sound that was part laugh, part
choked disgust. "Me—want *you*—"

He slapped her, hard enough to bring tears to her
eyes. She bit his hand in reflex, hard enough to draw
blood. Tony backhanded her, sending her sprawling to
the street. Sibyl lay where she'd fallen, deeply dazed by
the blow. Her whole face ached. Not even Bericus had
hit her that hard. Tony cradled his hand, then narrowed
his eyes into dangerous slits. Very softly, he said, "You
will pay for that before you die."

"Better not waste any time, then," she said thickly.
"I'd sure hate to see you trapped here with me." The
taste of his blood—and her own—was bitter on the back
of her tongue.

Astoundingly, he chuckled. "Waste time? I have all
the time in the world, Sibyl. Do you?"

She did not share his humor. Sibyl turned her face
away and huddled miserably on the street. She didn't
have the strength to stand up again and he clearly knew
it. Bartlett, still chuckling, hauled her up and dragged

her, stumbling, into the two-story villa owned by Publius Bericus.

She halted abruptly, just across the threshold. Her cheeks went cold. A tiny shiver crawled up her spine. She had been here before. *Two thousand years from now—and three weeks ago.*

The House of the Stags. . . .

She knew without looking that beyond the atrium would be one of two dining rooms. She knew the size and shape of the central garden that ran from the "front" of the house toward the sea, where wide windows had been placed on both stories to catch the spectacular view. She knew the outline and dimensions of the second dining room at the seaward end of the house, overlooking an arbor right on the primary terrace wall, almost overlooking the Suburban Baths.

Bericus undoubtedly spent many an enjoyable evening on that terrace or out in the arbor, watching the spectacular sunset over the Mediterranean and fondling whatever pet he'd brought into town with him. She even knew the number of rooms off the hallways that surrounded the garden, both downstairs and on the second floor.

In the entrance room where she now stood, hot air and occasional drifts of ash fell through the *compluvium,* a square hole in the ceiling. The frescoes on the walls were vivid, unscorched. Tony watched, smirking, as she touched painted, lifelike forms. And there were the statues, the famous one of the dogs bringing down the stag, for which the house was named, and the drunken Hercules, reeling backwards in wine-befuddled clumsiness, holding his naked genitalia in one hand in the classic moment of weakness so beloved by pagans, who were delighted by portrayals of virtuous, civilizing power momentarily falling into a state of ordinary humanity. . . .

"Enjoy it while you can," Bartlett murmured in her ear. His hand cupped her breast through soiled, torn linen.

Sibyl rammed an elbow into his gut. He grunted and dropped his hand. Sibyl whirled, trying to escape him, but lurched off balance and caught herself with one hand against the wall.

"*Don't touch me!*"

"Baby," he grabbed her shoulders, "before I split this hellhole, I'm gonna do a lot more than touch you." Tony backed her against the wall. His physical strength terrified her, left her trembling with rage and helpless hatred. He must have felt the tremors, because he smiled coldly.

"I owe you, bitch. For plans you screwed up. I had to make two trips, one to set up the deal in the first place and the second to ditch *you*. Did you think I planned to pay for that stuff with just you?" His tone was scornful.

"It was all set. Then you slithered out of the frameup. Jésus said we had to get rid of you. Says, 'See if you can go back and change it, Tony. Don't worry about a thing, Tony. I'll tell your wife you died brave if you screw it up, Tony, I'll even cry at your funeral.' My own brother-in-law . . ."

Sibyl wanted to shrink away, but was jammed solidly against the painted wall. *He's mad. Genuinely mad. My God* . . . When she tried to push free, he tightened a fist through her hair. "Forget it, bitch! You're going nowhere. I'll take my grief out of your hide, then be on my way."

His kiss was brutal. He drew blood with his teeth. Sibyl fought for a handhold in his hair, against his throat, anywhere. He pinned her wrists. His breath stank in her mouth. Sibyl squirmed, thought about a knee to the groin, decided she didn't dare. She couldn't risk any further injury. When he came up for air, she fought the impulse to gag.

"Not bad, little Sibyl," he grinned. He licked blood off his lower lip with the tip of his tongue. "I thought you'd fight harder. Guess you wanted me after all, huh?"

He ground his hips lewdly against her.

Sibyl snarled in his face. He just laughed and forced another brutal kiss. Sibyl came up spitting.

"So help me God, Tony, you'll pay for this!"

He just laughed. And kept laughing. The sound echoed off the walls and blended with the continuous roar of Vesuvius' wrath to form an insane harmony. Bericus—for better or worse—chose that moment to walk distractedly into the room. Tony immediately released her. Sibyl lurched away from him. She didn't care *where* she was going, just so long as she was just *going*. A moment later, Bericus collided with her. He swore and slapped her to the floor. Sibyl, too dazed to struggle against anything any longer, lay where she'd fallen. *Please, don't hurt me any more, please . . .*

Bericus dragged her up. "You! How did you get here?"

She simply hung in his grip, unable to answer. He snarled something she didn't understand, then dragged her toward the nominal front of the house, away from the sea and toward the kitchen. He locked her into a tiny, dark hole of a room and left her there, giving her neither food nor water.

Sibyl sat in near darkness for a long time, nursing her injuries as best she could and just listening to the distant sounds that reached through the thick-walled house. Voices . . . Traffic in the street . . . And beyond that, the endless, ominous roar of Vesuvius. The heat was stifling. Sweat trickled into numerous abrasions in the most sensitive parts of her anatomy. Every one of them stung like fire-ant bites.

Gradually, shock wore off, leaving her in the grip of mere pain and terror. Sibyl held herself and wept. She would cheerfully have killed any number of people to obtain a Tylenol-3 and a bucket of lukewarm water. She sobbed curses at Publius Bericus, at Tony Bartlett, at the man she had never seen, the man who had ordered this done to her: Jésus Carreras.

Occasional earthquakes, sharp, violent, rocked floor and walls. The villa groaned and trembled on its foundations. Each time the earth shook, Sibyl covered her head with both arms and waited for the roof to fall in on her. Eventually, fear of being buried alive—again—drove Sibyl to explore her prison. There *had* to be a way out!

But there wasn't.

There were no windows and the bar on the door was too strong. She discovered this only after bruising one shoulder. Sibyl concluded that either movie heroes were a lot stronger than she was, or they bashed open specially constructed doors. There wasn't a single piece of furniture in the empty room she could use as a battering ram, either.

So she sat on the floor in one corner and wondered how far Charlie would get before she died. Her mind moved in aimless circles. Part of her wondered *why*, exactly, people were being dumped back in time to die. The energy cost alone must be staggering. Surely there were cheaper, easier ways to dispose of witnesses? Of course, God knew where Jimmy Hoffa had ended up; probably in a sausage grinder somewhere. Or the foundation of a building. Organized crime had a way of disposing of folks where no one would think of looking.

Charlie's guess had been that all of this was to protect the secret of time travel itself. In the hands of the mafia . . . If you refused to dicker, you simply ceased to exist. Or maybe your family did. *Talk about a big stick.* But they didn't seem to be using it that way. Of course, neither she nor Charlie had been in on the palavers of the high muckety-mucks.

Who knew what they were really up to or how many poor souls had been disposed of already. Had they possessed the thing long enough to *be* up to anything substantial? Or were they still just feeling their way around, playing with it, seeing what could be done? Tony's comments about *his* trips suggested the latter, but she couldn't be sure and she *needed* to be.

And just who was the "old man" for whom Tony had secured the manuscripts, anyway? Not Carreras, Tony's brother-in-law—that much, at least, had been easy to see—but someone else, someone more powerful than Jésus Carreras. Someone Charlie evidently hadn't known about. She groaned and thumped her forehead with folded hands. She just didn't have enough information.

"So what else is new?" *Not knowing* was the story of her life. Why should this be an exception?

Sibyl straightened her back cautiously and leaned her head against the wall. "All right, Sib, try to think this one through. We're not getting anywhere at this rate." She took a deep breath and calmed her thoughts.

The cost ratio still bothered her. If the only thing Carreras was using time travel for was witness disposition and artifact acquisition, he was a fool. Either he didn't understand what he had and how it worked, or simply didn't care.

She shivered despite the heat.

Somehow, she didn't buy that.

How in the world had he gotten hold of it in the first place? Who had developed it? Government research? A private corporation? University researchers? Tony had said something about Army drugs. The military, then? She sighed. It didn't matter nearly as much *where* he'd gotten it, as what he was *doing* with it now that he had it. If she were a mafia crime boss, what would she do with the ability to travel in time?

Sibyl didn't like any of the answers she came up with.

A slave finally came for her. When she emerged from her stuffy little prison, Sibyl gratefully breathed in cooler air, then coughed. Ash stung her nostrils and throat. When they passed the open doorway to the garden, the lack of daylight alarmed her. Darkness had settled deceptively soft violet wings across Herculaneum. Vesuvius still roared ominously in the distance.

"What hour is it?" she asked the slave, still peering into the dark skies visible above the open garden.

"It is past the eleventh hour," the woman replied, with a touch of surprise, "and nears the twelfth."

Sibyl gulped. Nearly the twelfth hour of daylight? The time was well past dinner, then, somewhere between 6:00 and 7:00 P.M. Sibyl's lips trembled so badly she bit down on them. Blood oozed from cuts Tony had left behind.

Nearly 7:00 P.M. . . . That left maybe four hours before Herculaneum died.

The slave woman who had unlocked Sibyl's door peered uneasily toward the sky. The evening wind was brisk. It ruffled Sibyl's hair even under the shelter of the portico, but it wasn't strong enough to carry away the entire ashfall. Like hot snow, volcanic debris whipped around in eddies and evil little dust devils, then settled silently onto the garden and the baked clay roof tiles. The air smelled like one of Dante's Circles.

When a stray gust blew ash into their faces, Sibyl coughed and wiped streaming tears.

"It has been dark like this for hours," the slave woman whispered fearfully. She glanced toward Sibyl. "You were at the *villa rustica* when the mountain blew up?"

"Yes." The answer came out a little thickly.

"Then you and Master are very lucky. The wagon he ordered to follow his carriage has not arrived."

That probably had more to do with the slaves bolting rather than the volcano. Talk about a golden chance to run for it. . . .

"I am to help you bathe, Aelia," the slave said, forcibly tearing her gaze away from the black skies. Her voice trembled nearly as violently as the floor. "The Master wishes to see you again tonight."

Sibyl stumbled and braced herself against the wall. *No . . .* She couldn't endure another rape. She just couldn't. And if she complied with Bericus' orders tonight, she was lost.

"Please, tell me," she whispered, "has a soldier come to this house, looking for me?"

"A soldier? No, girl. Why would a soldier be looking for you?"

Rather than answer, Sibyl asked another question. "Has . . . has Master found his other new slave? Has Rufus the Gladiator been brought to this house today?"

The woman stared at her as though she'd taken complete leave of her senses. "No. There's been no one brought in today except you."

Thank God. . . .

Sibyl drew a quick breath for courage, then slugged the woman as hard as she could. The woman staggered back with a dazed cry of pain. Sibyl shoved her into the dark little room and dropped the bar in place. For long moments, Sibyl leaned against the closed door, shocked—horrified—at what she'd just done. Her hand ached, the knuckles abraded and swollen. *I'm sorry, really, I'm sorry, but there was nothing else I could have done.* The poor slave woman would die anyway, in just a few hours.

Sibyl shoved off and ran down the portico, heading for the "front" of the house where she knew of a way out through the kitchens. *I know this house, its layout. I can get out of here. . . .*

Voices sent her trembling into the shadows.

Bericus . . .

He was arguing violently with a shrill-voiced woman.

"I tell you, Lucretia, I will hear no more of this nonsense! Either shut up and go to bed, or by Attis, I will cut that tongue out of your head!"

"Try it and my brother will *make* an Attis of you! Mother Cybele curse the day I agreed to marry you!"

They were between her and the kitchens. Bericus' wife was tiny, barely five feet tall, thin and frazzled as a dinette waitress. Her hair stuck out in all directions from a disastrous coif. She was not a pretty woman, although, once, she might have been.

"*Get to your room!*" Bericus roared.

Instead, his wife seized a heavy goblet made of lead and flung it violently. Publius Bericus ducked, almost too late. It clanged against the wall like a battered Christmas bell and crashed to the floor.

The Roman lady's face flushed deep red. The heavy platter that followed the goblet narrowly missed Bericus' head—

His temper snapped. With a soundless snarl, he crossed the room in one leap. Bericus seized the woman by the wrists and shook her once, hard enough to jar her teeth together with an audible crack. Lucretia

screeched and reached into her coif. Then jabbed
Bericus with a long, sharp pin. "Murdering parricide!
Boy lover! Maid chaser!"

Sibyl watched, helpless in the shadows, while Publius
Bericus beat his wife to the floor. He panted for breath
when she hung limp in his grasp, then tossed her aside
and bellowed for slaves.

"Take that bitch to her rooms! Lock her in!"

He stalked away. Trembling slaves bent to Lucretia,
who hadn't moved.

"She's dead!" a terrified woman sobbed. "She's
dead . . ."

The slaves ran, scattering into the house.

Alone with a dead woman, Sibyl skittered across the
open room and plunged down a corridor. She found the
kitchen, right where she knew it would be. "Mistress
is dead!" Sibyl cried.

Slaves at the hearth stared, then broke and ran past
her to verify what she'd said. Sibyl found water in a basin
and gulped a dipperful, then snatched up a loaf of bread,
some cheeses, a bit of fruit, and dropped them into fold
of her torn Egyptian gown. She spotted a long knife—
nearly as long as a *gladius*, with a wide, heavy blade—
which had been left on a table from the butchering of
a carcass.

She grabbed it and ran. Sibyl tucked the knife into
a fold of her long dress and held the cloth closed around
it. She would have given almost anything to rinse her
stinging, bruised body with some of that clean water from
the kitchen. But she couldn't reach the whip marks in
her back, and anyway, there was no time. Bericus *or* Tony
Bartlett might discover her at any second.

She dodged past the house wall into a dark, narrow
street.

Where should I search?

When last seen, Charlie had been headed toward the
waterfront. Trying to secure a boat? Fortunately, the
House of the Stags was very close to the waterfront. Sibyl
crept through the darkness toward the Y-shaped staircase

that gave the nearest access to the beach. As she approached the dark opening that marked the entrance to the southeastern stair, a drunken man of nearly fifty lurched abruptly toward her. He seized Sibyl's arm.

"C'mere," he growled, trying to drag her into the dark, filthy space behind him. Sibyl snarled and whipped her knife into the open, dropping her food and not caring. She shoved hard against the shorter man and knocked him off balance. He let go and fell against one wall, then swung awkwardly with his free fist. Sibyl ducked and whipped the long blade against his throat.

"Go hunt other game!"

"Please," he gasped, "don't kill me, girl. . . ."

Spittle sprayed from wet lips. Sibyl brought her knee up sharply between the man's legs. He went down with a strangled scream. She hit him over the back of the neck with her balled fist, then ran for the stairs while her attacker lay retching on the street. Her legs shook so badly she could hardly keep her feet. She slid to a sitting position on cold stone and swore viciously in English. Then dragged the back of one wrist across her eyes. Dammit, she couldn't afford to go soft now. It was her *life* on the line. Civilized niceties were out the window.

So she regained her feet and plunged down the black maw of the stairs, which tunneled down through the first terrace and out into the open, where it turned to descend the face of the wall, meeting its northwestern counterpart at the bottom of the "Y." Wind caught her hair and gown, whipping them back from her face and body. Sibyl kept one hand on the cold stone of the terrace wall until she gained the wider steps at the bottom, which ran straight down to the beach.

She knew where she had to go. Sibyl figured it was the same place Charlie would try to go. She'd told him about unearthing the manuscripts on the beachfront. It was the one place they both knew about. He would go there to try to find her—or to find Tony Bartlett.

Tony . . .

If *he* knew of her escape, that was the most dangerous place she could go. Maybe he'd already left Bericus' house? While she'd been locked into that dark little room off the kitchen? Tony was certainly their only prayer of getting home again. Charlie would know that as well as she did. And Charlie was the kind of man to wait for him, ambush him, get hold of whatever it was he used to get back.

Tony Bartlett had to get back *somehow.*

I'll find Charlie again there, surely I will, and everything will be all right. . . .

She reviewed every scrap of information she knew about the waterfront's layout, trying frantically to remember where she might discover a safe hiding place from which she could scout out the territory, find out if Tony were burying his box of loot alone or if he had a score or so of "friends."

She didn't know the first thing about skulking in the darkness, or scouting the enemy, or laying out ambushes. What she needed was some good military training—

Yeah, right.

What she *needed* was a machine gun, about a million spare rounds of ammo, and a working time machine.

And Charlie Flynn with a sword in his fist, even better if he had one of those ban-list, high-capacity semiautomatics the press had such a field day with (she'd learned a lot in the few years since her grandmother's death).

The stairs emerged abruptly from between buildings. The sea was a maddened beast. Waves lashed up by violent undersea shocks pounded against the narrow beachfront. Every few seconds, wild surf foamed into the arched mouths of gaping black boat chambers. The next moment, the sea would retreat a dozen yards or more, sucked back by violent submarine turbulence, stranding helpless fish on the shore.

Then it would rush back and smash into the seawall again, completely submerging the little wooden quay. Wild spray fountained up against the seawall. Every time the sea smashed forward, the entire lower story of the Suburban Baths was inundated.

Xanthus' ship was missing. His sailors had probably been paid by somebody hours ago to take them to safety. A lantern out on the water marked someone's getaway by sea. The prevailing wind would blow them straight toward Pompeii and Stabiae and further danger.

But escape by sea was the only way out of Herculaneum now. At least the people in Stabiae had had time to get away from the ashfall and fiery surges. Many of the *people* in Stabiae would survive, even if the town was doomed.

Sibyl finished descending the long stairs to the stone chambers that lined the sea wall. Once she reached the beach, violent surf threatened to drag her down. Maddened breakers smashed across her body, foaming right over her head before sucking debris back toward the sea. She clung to the seawall every few seconds, waiting out the water before dashing another few feet forward while the sea retreated.

Given the hour, Pliny the Elder was probably somewhere offshore of Pompeii just about now, hampered by falling debris and the heavy, hot ashfall from landing. The fleet would come ashore at Stabiae, instead, where Pliny would take refuge with his friend Pomponianus. Impossible seas and contrary winds would trap and kill him on that beach sometime during the night. Sibyl shut her eyes, terrified that impossible seas and contrary winds would trap and kill *her*, as well.

Sibyl kept flush against the wall and gripped with both hands as she made her way through boiling water. Sand and salt water poured into her shoes. The breakers soaked her floor-length garments until their heavy weight tugged at her legs like diving weights, impeding her progress. She didn't dare let go of either the knife or the wall to hitch the dress to her knees.

The chamber she sought was well down the beach from the stairs. Sibyl endured several terror-filled minutes, creeping along past gaping boat chambers. She was nearly sucked out to sea when a breaker caught her in one of the broad openings and knocked her down. Sibyl clung to the beach with toes and fingernails and held her breath until the water receded, then scrambled back to her feet and lunged for the wall on the far side of the opening. She shuddered for breath and gulped down terror, but kept going.

Almost there . . . Just another few yards.

She finally made it and pressed back against the crumbling stone edge, then peered cautiously around the corner. Sibyl caught her breath.

Silhouetted against golden lantern light, his back turned toward her, stood Tony Bartlett. He was watching two slaves dig a deep hole near the back of the chamber, just where she remembered it. At his feet rested the heavy wooden box she had helped unearth less than a month previously. . . .

He was whistling the song she had grown to hate from their days on the dig, about the only man who'd ever been to hell and come back alive. There was no sign of Charlie Flynn or anyone else who could help her.

Okay, Sib, you've caught him, all right. Red-handed.

Just what, she wondered wildly, was she supposed to do now?

CHAPTER FIFTEEN

Silver nearly killed them both.

Charlie couldn't really blame the horse. But the panic-stricken gelding very nearly killed Charlie and Lucania before he managed to wrestle the animal under some semblance of control—with the help of several men who jumped to his aid.

"Thank you!" Charlie gasped.

One of them held the horse for him while another asked, "Are you hurt, sir? You're limping."

"I'll be fine," Charlie managed. "Thank you again. . . ."

He led the horse farther down the street and rounded a corner before sagging against the nearest wall and giving vent to tears of agony. His daughter clung to his neck, trembling.

"Pater . . ." She was touching his face. "Pater. Wet." Her baby giggle was one of the most beautiful sounds he'd ever heard. *She's not afraid. . . .*

"Papa," Charlie said softly in English. "Papa."

"Pa-pa." He closed his eyes. He had one *bright* little girl to raise. He kissed her forehead, afraid she might break in his grasp. Then, very carefully, checked his little girl for injuries. *If I'd dropped her . . .* But he hadn't. "We're okay, little Lucky, we're okay. Let's find Sibyl, now. . . ."

It was harder than ever, climbing into the saddle while trying to balance a baby over one shoulder, but Charlie managed it. He settled her onto his lap, chubby little legs on either side of Silver's bony withers. She squealed and played with the horse's mane.

The men who'd witnessed their initial upset handed Charlie back his helmet, which he jammed on before any of them could notice the brand on the side of his throat or the collar half hidden by his cloak.

"And my slave woman?" he asked hopefully.

"She ran that way, calling for you."

Charlie headed back the way he'd come, cursing fate and the foul luck that had separated them. He set Silver at a brisk trot, which elicited squeals of alarm from Lucania—squeals which turned to delighted gurgles once she realized "Papa" wasn't going to let her fall off. Charlie marveled, felt something hard and brutal inside him soften. *She trusts me.*

Nothing—*nothing*—was ever going to threaten this child the way it had threatened him. The *gladius*, secure for the moment in its sheath, hugged his hip reassuringly. He was armed, mounted . . .

More than a match for anything.

Except Vesuvius.

He started calling Sibyl's name every few minutes, not caring how many passersby stared in his wake. Charlie searched for hours. Lucania fell asleep in the crook of his arm, a limp little bundle of damp red-gold curls and dirty linen. He asked people if they had seen a woman wearing an Egyptian gown and collar, gave them Sibyl's description. A few had seen her. But every time Charlie set out in the direction they pointed, he came up empty.

Everywhere he looked, Charlie found earthquake rubble and wavering torches and lanterns. Citizens and slaves were busily shoring up roofs, repairing walls, or simply gossiping. Charlie couldn't believe anyone with two brain cells to rub together was still here, but the streets were crowded. Many houses appeared to be occupied, judging from the number of rooftop parties in progress.

He tracked Sibyl in circles for at least three hours, shouting her name until he was hoarse. Then people simply stopped reporting having seen her. As he sat beneath the massive equestrian statues of the basilica, trying to figure out why, a terrible thought occurred to him. What if Bericus had somehow laid hands on her again? She could be imprisoned at the townhouse.

How much time had passed since the eruption's first explosion at midday? He tried to gauge it, failed utterly. The false twilight had deepened into the genuine darkness of night. All he knew for certain was, the town would die near midnight.

He was running out of time.

He had no trouble recalling which house was Bericus'. The main door stood wide open, spilling torchlight carelessly into the street. Agitated slaves milled uncertainly in the entrance. Charlie halted a safe distance away and called out to them.

"You there, is your master home?"

"Sir?" The slaves turned. One stepped forward. "No, sir. He is gone, and the mistress is dead, and we are afraid." The man was actually wringing his hands.

Charlie frowned. Another slave pushed his way to the front of the group and glared up at Charlie. A nasty bruise swelled one side of his face. "The crazy fool went running into the streets with a sword. Swore he was going to kill the bitch."

"Kill who?" Charlie asked sharply.

"His new plaything. He's already killed his wife, beat her to death, then he went to look for the slut. She was gone."

"What was this slave's name?"

The man spat. "Who cares?"

The sword was in his hand before he could even pause to think about it. He kicked Silver around. Lucania woke up and squealed in surprise. The slaves scattered, all except for his target. Charlie pinned the insolent cretin to the wall with Silver's massive shoulder. Charlie pricked the man's throat with his sword tip.

Very softly, he repeated his question.

"Please—sir—mercy—" The man's eyes had widened. His lips quivered.

Another voice broke into Charlie's awareness. "Sir—

I beg of you— Marcus does not know. Her name is Aelia, noble sir—"

Charlie stared down into a terrified woman's face.

"And no one knows where either of them have gone?"

General murmurs of denial reached his ears. Charlie swore.

"Get me a lantern!" he snapped.

The woman fled and returned so fast Charlie wondered if they'd had it waiting, already lit, for a planned search party. He took it on the point of his sword and backed Silver away. Lucania wriggled and said distinctly, "Sibyl!"

The unfortunate Marcus said something irreverent and fainted. Charlie reined Silver away from the slaves and left them standing in the street.

Damn, damn, damn . . .

The sea was terrifically rough, smashing into the sea-wall with foaming whitecaps. There was no sign of anyone along the visible stretch of beach in either direction—and no sign of a boat anywhere in the harbor.

Charlie balled his fist under Lucania's arm and spat something vile into the wind, which whipped the cloak back off his shoulders with a snap of heavy cloth. Somewhere in this shrouded, doomed city, Sibyl Johnson was fighting for her life.

He had to find her.

Sibyl huddled at the entrance to the boat chamber while Tony Bartlett's slaves covered his precious manuscript box with earth they'd dug from the hole. They didn't put it *into* the hole, just covered it with a heaping mound of solidly packed earth. She waited impatiently while Bartlett growled something under his breath. He set his lantern down to shovel dirt over it with his bare hands and pack it down tighter.

Almost done. You're clever, Tony—most people might not have noticed the difference in the soil types and you knew better than to put it into *the hole, 'cause it would've been in the wrong stratum. Where are you going next, Tony? Home?*

He certainly wouldn't be taking those slaves with him. Sibyl didn't dare let any of them see her. She couldn't fight three at once. She probably couldn't even fight Tony Bartlett. She remembered with a shiver the feel of his fist on her aching face. But could she follow him without being seen? Sibyl chewed her lip, agonized by the impossibility of the choices facing her. If he caught her now, he'd murder her, quietly and ruthlessly.

Part of her wanted to cut and run now, to escape Herculaneum by any means available and get as far away from Tony Bartlett as time and space would allow. Another part of her knew if she did, she would hate herself for the rest of her life. Yet another part wanted, impossibly, to find Charlie and hide in his arms, have him stroke her hair and whisper that everything would be okay. . . .

Sibyl blinked fiercely. Cora Johnson had not raised her only grandchild to indulge in useless fantasies. She hadn't found Charlie in the one place she'd expected to find him. She could spend hours searching those crowded streets and never find him. She already *had*. It was like one of those impossible searches through a crowded department store: should she wander around hoping to run across him, or find a strategic crossroad and scan the crowd passing by? Whichever, Bericus would be out there somewhere, stalking those same streets, searching for her.

Bartlett dismissed his slaves. Sibyl flattened herself against the sea wall. They waded out past her and went the other direction, toward the street Xanthus' carriage had taken earlier, without seeing her shadowy form. In fact, they kept their gazes on their feet and tried to negotiate the hazardous footing without being swept against the stone wall or out to sea.

She held her breath and peered into the boat chamber again. Tony Bartlett had picked up the lantern. He was gazing down at the freshly tamped earthen mound.

His low chuckle reached her, then he fumbled beneath his tunic and drew out a modern pack of cigarettes and a book of matches. Something glinted in the light as it fell to the ground. A coin from his pocket. He moved without seeing it and ground it into the softer earth with his foot.

She gripped her knife handle more tightly. *That stinking coin. . . .* He'd dropped his own anachronism and hadn't even realized it. He turned and stalked toward the opening of the boat chamber. Sibyl ducked back, heart pounding against her ribcage. The glow of his cigarette appeared in the darkness at the entrance. He paused, evidently gazing at the maddened sea, then took a long drag on his cigarette and chuckled again.

"Not a bad week's work," he said laughing, not bothering to use Latin. "Not bad, at all." The cigarette glowed brighter as he drew smoke into his lungs. "Well, old boy," he muttered, flipping the cigarette into the foaming breakers, "time to go." He chuckled, then held the lantern out in front of him, stepped into the surf—

And saw her.

For an instant he froze. His jaw went slack. His eyes widened. Then a snarl transformed his face.

"You—!"

For just an instant, Sibyl cringed. Tony's snarl turned to laughter. She drove the knife straight at his belly from below. He yelled and twisted aside as steel grazed his ribs.

"Bitch!"

A crashing wave against his ankles knocked him off balance. The lantern flew out of his hand and fell with a clatter into the boat chamber. Shadows tilted crazily as it arced downward and rolled to a stop. Somehow it didn't go out. Bartlett came up coughing seawater. Sibyl hurled herself at him, stabbing grimly at his shoulderblades. He screamed as the knife grazed his back, then kicked her feet out from under her. The sodden dress caught at her legs.

A smashing wave caught her with smothering force.

Water battered her. Scouring sand and stinging salt abraded her whole body. She felt a fist strike her chest. Instinctively, she lashed upwards with the knife. A hand closed around her wrist. Agony shot through her arm. Granite fingers dug into the tendons.

Sibyl twisted frantically, half-drowned as another wave smashed into her from behind. His grip loosened. He fell sideways, dragged by the water. She managed to wrench free. She crawled toward the boat chamber, coughing violently, nearly paralyzed by the wet cloth around her legs.

His weight slammed into her from behind. She sprawled forward into sand. Bartlett's fingers closed on her neck. He forced her head back and sideways. She lunged upward, kicked madly with both feet. *No good* . . .

Pain mushroomed through her neck. Sibyl stabbed blindly backwards with the knife. He howled and let go. Sibyl rolled heavily onto her side.

Bartlett was on his knees above her. His face had twisted into a grimace, his flesh waxy white. He clutched at his side. Blood dripped from between his fingers.

"You—*bitch*—"

He lunged awkwardly. Sibyl came to her knees as he dove forward, off balance. Sluggish, staggering drunkenly, Sibyl brought the knife up between them. The shock of his weight slammed her to the ground. The impact jarred her from wrists to shoulders. They toppled over backwards. He landed heavily on her chest. An agonized cry ripped loose. He tried to right himself, managed to push himself up with one arm.

The knife was buried to the hilt in his chest.

Two inches below the right collarbone.

Sibyl shoved hard. He windmilled and crashed backward. Tony fell heavily into the entrance of the boat chamber. For a moment, the only thing she could do was huddle on the sand and let the waves crash over her. Then, slowly, she forced her knees to function. She managed to crawl into the chamber beside him.

His breathing was shallow, hoarse. In the light from

the fallen lantern his skin was grey. His lips were drawn back in a rictus grimace.

"Sibyl—" One hand groped. She avoided it like a water moccasin. She heard a dreadful sound and looked up. Bartlett had wrapped both hands around the hilt. He was trying to wrench it loose. A moment later, he collapsed, keening in agony. He'd failed to budge it. "Sibyl—" His lips barely moved. "For the—love of—God—"

Lamplight flickered crazily across his face. His eyes were ghastly burned holes in a cadaver's face. She felt detached, apart from his pain, as though he were a flickering image in a silent movie. Like thunder in her brain, words rumbled unbidden into her thoughts. "For the love of God, Montresor. . . ."

Sibyl crouched above him. She didn't even recognize her own harsh voice. "How do you get back, Tony?"

She waited while his lips worked. "Recall—device—"

"Where?"

His fingers clawed at the knife embedded in his flesh. "Where?" She leaned a fraction of her weight on the handle.

He screamed. She clenched her teeth over bile.

"Ahh—p-p-pocket—"

She searched under his tunic. Beneath it he wore khaki military-style shorts, with deep, button-down pockets. She found a set of keys and a variety of coins, which she impatiently shoved back. In a second pocket she found a dense metallic oblong he'd wrapped in several layers of plastic and metal foil. It was an inch thick, six inches long, three inches wide. A latch-type cover opened to reveal a miniaturized, color-coded keypad of no obvious pattern. Number keys and blank, colored keys ran in rows beneath a series of glowing LED numbers. Time coordinates? Or geographic? Or both? Something else entirely?

"How does it work, Tony?"

Bartlett's lips moved again. "Take—me—too—"

She smiled coldly. "Sure, Tony. I'd be glad to turn you

over to Interpol. Just tell me how to work this little gadget."

"Red—button—preset—mash it—takes ten—fifteen minutes to—open time hole—"

She closed the lid. Carefully rewrapped it. Then relieved him of the money pouch at his outer tunic belt. She dumped out the Roman coins and slid the recall device snugly inside it, then ripped off the lower half of Bartlett's tunic. Sibyl used the strip to fashion a belt and tied the pouch securely to her waist. When she glanced up, Tony was watching her. Pain had dulled the characteristic glitter of his eyes.

Blood-sucking leech . . .

"I'm going to need this, Tony." She took hold of the knife with both hands. She straddled him and braced both feet, then thought better and placed one foot on his chest. Sibyl yanked up, hard.

He jerked. Screamed. Then fell back, panting hoarsely, eyes squeezed shut. Blood soaked the front of his tunic, welling up in a terrible flood. He reeked of fear, dirt, and the coppery stench of blood. She searched him more thoroughly and relieved him of a short, wicked-looking dirk. There were a lot of people out and about on the streets. Granny Johnson had always told her, "Sibyl, never overlook options."

She stuck the dirk through her belt. Smart old Granny. . . .

He opened pain-dulled eyes as she rose to her feet. He blinked and slowly focused on her. It took him several moments to assimilate the stony expression that seemed to have frozen her face. She imagined the headsman must have looked much the way she did before he relieved Anne Boleyn of her lovely head. . . .

"Sibyl?" he whispered. "Sibyl—please—"

She held his gaze for a long moment. Thought about forcing him to quote Poe for her.

Settled for: "Burn in hell, Tony."

He screamed her name until she was so far away, the noise from volcano and earthquake-tossed surf drowned

out the sound. She gripped the blood-slippery handle
of the knife until her hand ached. Sibyl gritted her teeth
as she waded through angry, frothing water.

She'd vomit later.

Right now, she just didn't have time.

Charlie began his search with the shipyard. Any boats
that might have been in the harbor earlier in the day
were gone now. Xanthus' ship was conspicuously absent.
At least he wouldn't have to worry about search parties
looking for *him*. He scowled, then urged the horse down
into the pounding surf. Silver protested once, tossed his
head, then waded doggedly forward. Breakers slammed
into the horse's side and drenched Charlie within seconds.

"Hold tight, Lucky!" he called, tightening his own grip
on the little girl. Small fingers closed over his arm. He
checked dark boat chambers, holding his lantern out on
the end of his sword to light the dark, wet spaces. There
were a few dinghies left, far back in the chambers, and
a couple of masted fishing boats with the masts
unstepped, but nothing which looked capable of han-
dling that seismically ravaged sea.

There was no trace of Sibyl, either.

He worked his way down past the main part of town
and shivered under the ghostly outline of the Suburban
Baths above him. Its wide, glassed-in main windows
overlooked the sea like monstrous black eyes. Charlie
hunched his shoulders unconsciously, aware that Bericus'
villa was just above that terrace wall. He kept searching.

When he saw a faint glow coming from one of the
chambers ahead, his heart shuddered to a halt. Then
his pulse kicked in at triple time. He urged Silver forward and gained the entrance. Charlie reined the horse
around to find a huddled figure lying far enough back
that the breakers didn't swamp across it. He started to
dismount—

—and the man he knew as Antonius Caelerus lifted
his head. *Tony!* The man stared dully up at Charlie.

Bartlett had bled into a crude bandage he'd pressed to his shoulder. The thug wet his lips and tried to focus his vision. Charlie debated whether to address him in Latin or English.

"Help . . . me," the man croaked in Latin. "Slave escaped . . . attacked me . . . got to find . . ."

Charlie had to know.

"How were you planning to get home, Tony?" he asked in English.

The grey pallor of Tony Bartlett's skin washed white in the lantern light. "What—? Who—?"

"I *was* Big Joe's middleman."

Tony blinked. Licked his lips. "Mr. . . ." he seemed to search for the name Charlie had used when dealing with Carreras ". . . Mr. *Ireland?*" His voice wavered badly. "Listen—I know you've got to be furious, Mr. Ireland, I don't blame you." He tried, and failed, to manage a disarming grin. "But you got to know, you *have* to understand—I wasn't part of that deal, I had nothing to do with that decision—"

Charlie reined Silver closer and stared down at the fallen thug. "Tell me how you get back."

He shook his head. Frustrated rage transformed his dying face into a ghoul's mask. "*Can't* get back. Bitch stole the device. Got to *find* that—"

"*Sibyl?*"

Tony started badly. "You know her?"

Charlie's instantaneous, visceral reaction was, *Thank God, thank you, dear, sweet Lord, she got away.* His next thought shamed him to his bones: *She didn't take me with her.* He knew Sibyl would have had no way of finding him, but the overpowering loss of coming *that* close, and failing to make it home, made breathing difficult. He tightened his grip around his child and hated the man at his feet.

Tony glared up at him. "Mr. Ireland, you've got to find this bitch, I'm telling you! She's got the recall device."

"Get real, Tony. She's long gone."

Tony shook his head, his face a sculptor's study in pain

and desperation. "No, she can't be gone yet. Hasn't been a storm."

"What?" Hope and fear blossomed simultaneously. "What are you talking about?"

"A storm. No thunderstorm out there. When she pushes that button, gonna be one Holy Mother of a thunderstorm. It's a side effect, like. Takes time to build up. Maybe quarter of an hour. You see the storm brewing, you got maybe ten minutes. No storm, then nobody's pushed the button."

Charlie frowned. If this slimeball weren't lying . . .

"Strip."

"*Huh?*"

"Down to the skin. Move it!"

"But—my shoulder—"

Charlie shifted his sword. "I could always drop this lantern off my sword tip and kill you first. Searching corpses doesn't bother me much, Tony. Thanks to your boss, I spent two *years* killing men in the arena. *Lots* of tough men, Tony. Now *strip!*"

Tony undressed. He was slow and he whimpered like a baby, but he undressed. Charlie made him dump everything from his clothing onto the ground. There was nothing larger or more sinister-looking than a pack of cigarettes. Charlie made him rip open the pack and shred each one.

He was telling the truth about the device, at any rate. Charlie didn't think he'd ever seen anyone more genuinely terrified.

"Huh. So you want my help finding the broad? What's it worth?"

"Anything—God, you name it—"

Charlie parted his lips in what might have been a grin. Naked, bleeding down his chest, Tony swallowed hard. Very softly, Charlie said, "Tell me about Jésus Carreras, Tony, and the family's new business. . . ."

Twenty minutes later, Charlie was at the end of the seawall, where a torrential stream cascaded into another small harbor. He'd run across several surly fishermen guarding their beached boats from thieves and had seen some hastily negotiated transactions between a rich patrician family and one particularly seedy-looking lout with a good-sized, masted fishing sloop. There was, however, no sign of Sibyl. Tony hadn't possessed a clue as to which direction she might have gone.

Charlie grimaced. He would hear Bartlett's curses in his dreams, but he wasn't in the business of rescuing cold-blooded killers caught in their own traps. He *was* a cop, sworn to uphold the law—but this was A.D. 79, and Charlie'd been a tough street hood *long* before he'd taken a badge. Tony "Bartlett" Bartelli would get his own ass out, or die in Sibyl's place. Charlie peered up at the sky, but saw no hint of a storm brewing. Where had she gone? Looking for *him*? Charlie spat an oath into the teeth of the wind and reined Silver around toward town again.

She was a scientist. He'd never been able to figure *those* birds. Was she planning on staying to watch the disaster unfold, just to satisfy some stupid scholarly itch? If he did find her, he was going to shake her so hard . . .

Charlie headed Silver up off the beach and began to search streets and alleys near the northwestern harbor. Where would she have gone to activate the device? Tony'd said there would be a lot of lightning discharged right around the portal. Sibyl probably wouldn't want to activate it in town, then. He turned Silver and set the horse at a brisk trot for the city's outskirts. He rode from the waterfront inland, calling Sibyl's name every few feet.

Nothing answered but the ominous roar of the volcano.

By the time he'd ridden around the entire city and returned to the beachfront on the opposite side of town, the night had progressed so far he didn't dare waste any more time. Lucania was asleep again, nestled inside a fold of his cloak. He could feel her breaths against his bare arm. Charlie stopped his horse. He glared impotently at the volcano, then squeezed shut his eyes. He was out of time. If he didn't escape *now* . . .

He swore and turned Silver back toward town. He had to search one last place. If Bericus had recaptured her before she'd had a chance to use the device . . . Bericus' villa was still in chaos. He watched from the shadows as Bericus himself strode about in the street, shouting at his slaves and exhorting his neighbors to help search for his missing slave.

Charlie breathed a faint sigh of relief.

Then reluctantly turned his mount back toward the waterfront. Sibyl hadn't been recaptured. Wherever she was hiding . . . Bitterness filled his throat. She'd probably searched and searched for him, while he searched for her, playing a stupid, fatal game of cat and mouse and missing one another by minutes. The weight of his daughter against his arm made Charlie want to cry.

Charlie wished Sibyl the best of luck getting home. He closed his mind to the crushing loss of hope. He couldn't afford the risk of waiting for the lightning storm to begin brewing in an attempt to return with her. Not only might he never pinpoint the actual location of the portal . . . he had a gut feeling they were all nearly out of time. If it had just been his own life to throw away, he might have stayed.

But with Lucania's life at stake, too . . .

He couldn't see any stars through the pall of ash drifting down from the volcano, but he knew the night was well advanced. It had taken a damnably long time to ride all the way around the city. Charlie was betting it was already past eleven. The eerie, hair-raising sheets and gouts of flame shooting through the blackness overhead frightened him more deeply every time he looked up.

Charlie tried to ignore the ache in his chest and throat when he thought of sunlight dancing on Biscayne Bay. Of skilled surgical reconstruction. Of someone else touching her hair, watching her green eyes light up with laughter . . .

Charlie kicked his horse into a fast canter. The lantern on his sword danced and swung, casting plunging shadows across the dark walls of houses and public buildings. Silver plunged through thinning crowds, hooves rattling on stone. Charlie ignored curses flung after him. He guided the horse back down to the beach and set out to find the fishermen he'd seen earlier. *Please, God*, he prayed, *let them still be there. Let at least one of them be willing to leave now.* Or if unwilling, then able to see reason at the point of a sword.

Most were gone, along with their boats. A few beggars dressed in rags had fallen asleep in the boat chambers. They'd wake up, soon enough; then, of course, they'd sleep forever. One poor fellow was working on an overturned boat, caulking its bottom and casting fearful glances over his shoulder.

He'll never finish that job in time, not even with help.

Charlie rode past him and kept searching.

Desperation was beginning to overtake him when he found, near the end of the seawall, a young man and woman trying to drag one of the heavy fishing boats out of a deep boat chamber. They'd put the mast up, but were making progress across the breaker-washed sand by inches only. Deep breakers smashing into the seawall lifted the boat and tossed it backwards; then, when the sea retreated again, left the boat high on wet sand. The woman—a tiny thing, barely four feet tall—could scarcely keep her footing in the rough surf. They paused, gasping for air, when Charlie thundered through the breakers toward them.

"I am not a thief!" the man began defensively. "This is my boat. The longer I watched that mountain, the more it frightened me. I'm not a thief!"

"Did I say you were?" He pointed to the heavy boat. "You'll never get that thing into deep water by yourselves."

The man's voice was bitter. "My friends laughed at me when I asked for help."

"Then tie a rope to my saddle. I'll have my horse drag

it down for you. If"—he paused significantly, and watched a wary, frightened look come into their eyes—"if you take me with you. Me and my child."

The man blinked in open surprise. His wife whispered into his ear, her face a mask of terror.

"Why does a Roman soldier wish to sneak out of the city by night?" The question came out with transparently false bravado. In the light from Charlie's lantern he could see the man's knees knocking together.

Charlie didn't know spit about the administration of Roman legions or what their rules of conduct were. It was entirely possible citizens were given rewards for turning in an AWOL trooper.

He felt instinctively this was not the time to play it tough.

"You're not the only one, my friend," he said quietly, "who's been watching that mountain. You must know from my accent I'm a provincial recruit. I've seen mountains blow up before, just like that one. Sometimes they'll spit fire and ash like this for hours, even days, harmlessly. Then, without warning, they'll destroy everything for stadia and stadia around. Cover it with fire and death. I owe the Empire my best service, to keep her strong and safe from danger, but I can't serve Rome if I'm dead and burned on the beach at Herculaneum. And there will be a great many dead on this beach."

As one, the three of them turned to look at the baleful glow of the mountain. Eerie lightning discharges played through the ash cloud and shot down the upper slopes of the mountain. The glow from the volcano's mouth lit the underbelly of the boiling black cloud. It visibly churned and seethed like something alive and infinitely malevolent.

Charlie held in a shiver and added, "Think about this, as well. When you make harbor, you will undoubtedly find chaos and much fear. Will you not be better off in the company of a soldier of the Empire than alone?"

They went into a fearful huddle. After a moment, the man straightened. "I am Decius Martis. Phillipa and

I would welcome your presence on our boat, Centurion."

Huh. That's a decent rank. He'd wondered what kind of soldier those bandits had killed and robbed. Charlie just nodded. "Get me a stout rope."

Decius strung a rope from the prow of the boat around Silver's chest and secured it to the saddle. Charlie, holding tight to Lucania, clucked and kneed the animal forward. The stout horse dug in and pulled. Charlie kept Silver guided into the swells, while Decius and little Phillipa pushed and guided the prow over the beach.

Knee-deep, belly-deep, chest-deep, Silver plowed forward into heavy surf, dragging the fifteen-foot boat, lunging forward as Charlie shouted encouragement. Abruptly the pressure let off and the rope went slack. Silver began to swim straight out to sea. Charlie fought to bring his head around toward land. The boat floated free behind them, rocking violently up and down as the sea surged, retreated, surged again. The two Romans were already aboard, working to get the sail up.

"There is not space for your horse," Decius called as the tired animal waded toward the little craft. "He has saved us. I am sorry."

For a moment, Charlie sat frozen on Silver's back. Not take Silver? Charlie turned his head away to hide a sudden rush of grief. He would have died—many times over—without this animal. He couldn't simply turn Silver loose on the beach to be roasted alive. Not and continue to look himself in the eye. What was it they said a man had to be able to do? Shoot his own dog?

I'm sorry, dammit, I'm sorry.

"Take Lucania!"

Decius manhandled the toddler aboard.

Charlie drew his sword and cut the rope between his saddle and the prow of the fishing boat, then handed over his crutch to the waiting Decius. The fisherman dropped it into the little boat without so much as glancing at it. Charlie's lantern, he secured to the rigging, near the mast. Carefully, Charlie slid out of the saddle into rough water.

He wallowed, half-floating, waist-deep in the troughs, nearly chin-deep in the swells and foamy whitecaps. He gripped the sword, then pulled Silver's head down. Charlie stroked his ears, murmured softly to him.

"Hey, fella, you did real good, Silver, you did real damned good . . ." He shut his eyes, trying not to think about what he had to do. "I'm gonna miss you, you big, faithful lummox . . ."

I can't . . .

He'd killed untold numbers of men. But one, stupid horse . . . Ruthlessly, Charlie brought to mind the image of Silver screaming, burning to death, trying to run into the sea, his mane crisping in the lethal, burning air—

With a quick thrust, he cut the great jugular vein.

The horse screamed. Charlie's insides flinched from the sound. Silver tried to rear. Blood sprayed horribly. Charlie grabbed the edge of the boat and pulled himself clear of Silver's thrashing legs. Decius and Phillipa grasped his arms and hauled him aboard.

They'd lit more storm lanterns, which swung wildly from ropes running from mast to stern and prow. Charlie slithered over the gunwale like a gaffed fish and landed with a pain-racked thump in the bottom of the boat. He dropped the sword and lay still for a moment, fighting waves of pain and weakness, then struggled to sit up. He was half blinded by salt water, only partly from the Mediterranean.

When he could see, he found Silver in the water, still struggling. But the light slowly went out of the horse's eyes. His front legs buckled and the frightened sounds faded. Silver finally rolled over onto his side, wet hooves glinting in the lantern light. The horse went under once, then finally bobbed quietly in the churning black water. Charlie squeezed shut his eyes, then groped for his daughter and cradled the sleepy little girl close. He would not think about Sibyl.

"Get the hell out of here!" He didn't care that his voice broke raggedly.

As the Roman fisherman set his prow seaward, Charlie didn't know whether he wept for the horse, for Sibyl, or for himself.

CHAPTER SIXTEEN

"Don't I even get a last meal?" Francisco asked quietly.

Lucille sobbed in one corner and pleaded with a man named Nelson. "Don't kill him—please, Nelson—"

"Shut up!" Nelson backhanded her.

Francisco swung before he could think better. He ended up on the floor, doubled over and retching.

Janet Firelli ran to him, kneeling at his side to see how badly they'd injured him. She glared at Nelson while Francisco fought for sufficient breath to hush her.

"*Why* kill him?" The young woman's voice shattered on a sob. "He's no danger, not here . . ."

"Janet . . ." Francisco wheezed around the pain in his middle. "Don't . . ."

"Get him into that parka," Nelson snapped. "I'm not taking any chances. He might poison us all just for the fun of it."

Francisco didn't think he could gain his feet. Not without assistance. So he just glared up at Nelson from the floor and said around the blood in his mouth, "At least . . . let me make sure the others are healthy. Unless you want to risk losing someone else? Conditions here are bad. Real bad. I'm surprised they aren't all sick."

Nelson locked gazes with him, then grunted. "Sure, why not, doc? But make it fast."

Francisco nodded and tried to sit up. Janet helped him. He leaned heavily on her shoulder, feigning more pain and grogginess than he actually felt. *Anything to gain time.* . . . Not that he expected the cavalry to save him. Francisco doubted anything could save him.

Both Janet and Lucille were crying. Danny, Jr. met his gaze bravely. "They're going to kill my dad too, aren't they?"

Francisco pushed himself awkwardly to his knees and tried to ease the pain in his gut. *Stall 'em, long as you can.* "Not for a while, Danny. They still need him. Janet, can you give me a hand?" With her help, he tottered to his feet and wobbled across to the nearest army cot. "Let me take a look at you, okay?"

He took his time despite pointless threats from Nelson and performed very thorough physicals on each of the hostages. Lucille winced when he bathed her bruised cheek and dabbed alcohol and antibiotic cream on her split lip.

"How's Dan?" she quavered. Her eyes were far too bright. The circles under her eyes were far too dark. How long, subjectively, had they been here?

"He's holding on, Lucy. I wondered what was wrong. He told everyone you and Danny were spending the winter in Juneau."

"They haven't hurt him?"

He held her gaze. "No. He's lost some weight and I doubt he's been sleeping much, but he's fine. They need him, obviously. He's smart, Lucy. Hang on a little longer, okay?"

She nodded. "I'll be fine, really."

He managed a smile around the sudden lump in his throat.

Then he returned to Janet. As he put her through the exam, he murmured, "About Zac . . . Do what I told you, okay? Keep the incision clean and keep him quiet. Zac should heal quickly. Kids that age do."

"I'm scared," she whispered, eyes brimming. "I don't have any medical background at all. I'm a *physics* major, not a med student."

"You did fine in surgery. This will be easy potatoes, compared. And remember, if there are any complications"—he allowed his gaze to slide briefly toward Nelson—"you'll still have the surgical kit."

She caught her breath, then nodded. Hope flared for a moment in her eyes, then grief blotted it out. "I can't bear this! They can't just murder you!"

They not only could, they would. All too soon. And both of them knew it. He squeezed her hand. "Thanks, Janet," he said a little unsteadily.

He couldn't delay any longer. He'd already repeated a couple of things as it was. His hands shook as he stood up. Francisco drew a quick breath and turned to face Nelson—by far the hardest thing he'd ever done. Nelson's eyes were glacial.

"All right," Francisco snarled, "let's get this over with!"

Nelson and the man called Joey had already shrugged into parkas. Joey handed Francisco another, which he donned with fingers that shook so badly, he couldn't work the zipper. Danny muttered, "Here, let me."

"Sit down!"

He got the damned zipper closed. Danny flushed dark red and sat down, but he shoved his lower lip out and glared at Nelson with murder in his young eyes. For just an instant, he looked exactly like his father. Francisco drew a ragged breath and turned his back on the others. Bill held the door and flipped him an arrogant salute.

"So long, Major," he grinned. "Have a nice trip. I hear the skiing is great this time of year."

Francisco stumbled out onto icy ground. Nelson and Joey followed silently. The door slammed shut behind them. The cold was dry and bitter in his lungs. They marched him out across the snow field, away from the building. How far would they walk him? Out of range of the gunshot, maybe. Then again, maybe not. If the hostages heard him die, they'd be less likely to cause trouble in the future.

What was left of their future.

Francisco walked stiffly between his executioners. He wondered if dying would hurt much. He stumbled and was dragged upright again. Francisco shut his eyes, helpless in their grasp, and tried to focus his mind, tried to think of something—anything—he could do besides quake in his boots.

Maybe he could take one of his killers with him? Nelson was a hopeless bet, unless Francisco had a gun. Like many Latins, Francisco was a slim man and proud of it, especially at forty. Nelson must've been three times his mass. Tackling him would have been tantamount to tackling a city bus.

Joey, on the other hand . . .

Joey was taller than he was, but not by much. And he wasn't all that much heavier than Francisco. And Joey had a gun that ought to drop even Nelson in his tracks, if Francisco could just get his hands on it. He narrowed his eyes against the cold and slowed his pace slightly. Nelson didn't notice. Joey closed the distance and grabbed his arm to hurry him along.

Francisco drew a quick breath, muttered a heartfelt, "Hail Mary . . ."

And spun around. He planted a foot in Joey's stomach and an elbow in his face. Joey yelled and staggered off balance. Francisco lunged for the pistol at his waist. He got gloved hands on it, yanked it loose, managed to work the action—

Nelson hit him from behind. He crashed into Joey. Everybody went down in a tangle of arms and legs. Somebody punched his ribs hard, but the heavy parka absorbed most of the damage. He tried to roll free of an octopuslike embrace and actually managed to squeeze off three wild shots. Then Joey got an arm around his windpipe. Nelson came in from the side. Someone let fly a kick that paralyzed Francisco's whole left arm. While he was gasping, Joey wrestled the pistol away from nerveless fingers.

Nelson snatched him up by the front of the parka and jerked back the hood. Freezing air hit him in the face, shocking him out of stupor. He groaned, struggled feebly. Nelson seized a fistful of Francisco's hair, then shoved his head down until his chin was jammed against his breastbone. Joey grabbed his arms from behind and held him pinioned.

No . . .

An icy gun muzzle jabbed the base of his skull. Francisco squeezed shut his eyes—and waited for the bullet to rip through his brain.

What on earth do I do about Charlie and Lucania?
Finding them was imperative. But *how?* The image of the department-store conundrum flashed into her mind again. Herculaneum was one *big* "department store." And Charlie and his little girl were awfully small targets.

In fact, there was only one logical place Sibyl could think to look. She shivered, despite the sticky, close heat of the rumbling night. He might stake out Bericus' townhouse, looking for *her*. If either of them were caught . . .

Sibyl headed resolutely for the House of the Stags. She was several blocks southeast of it, which took her through streets unexcavated in her own time. Sibyl was so preoccupied with pain, exhaustion, and fear, she scarcely noticed details that once would have consumed her entire attention. *Gotta find Charlie and Lucania,* was the only thing running through her mind. *Gotta find them.*

The adrenaline rush of the fight with Tony gradually wore off. Pain began to catch up. She *hurt*. As her energy seeped away and pain crept more and more crushingly into her movements, visions of ripping out Bericus' guts out with bare nails and teeth, of gouging Tony's eyes with her thumbs, of shooting both of them multiple times—with nonfatal shots for the first fourteen or fifteen rounds she dumped into them—plagued her.

Those visions frightened Sibyl at one level.

At another level entirely, she felt something soft and liberal and naïve die within her. And found she didn't mourn its passing.

Nobody raped Sibyl Johnson and got away with it.

It was a hard, bitter lesson, but she understood at last

why Granny Johnson had proudly displayed a needle-point sampler which read, "A woman with a gun is nobody's victim."

Sibyl took a deep breath and let it out silently.

Hating Bericus and Tony Bartlett wouldn't help her find Charlie and Lucania. Sibyl kept doggedly on toward the House of the Stags and pressed flat against buildings or recessed doorways any time she saw groups of men with torches or lanterns. Terror of recapture left her trembling in the darkness long after such groups passed by. Her progress was excruciatingly slow. Once Bericus himself stormed past her hiding place, several of his slaves trailing behind him like the wind-tossed tail of a kite caught in a storm.

She huddled in the recessed niche where she'd taken refuge for long minutes, until her heart stopped its triphammer lurching. Eventually, she found the courage to set out again. Sibyl finally gained a vantage point that let her observe the entrance to Bericus' townhouse. *Looks clear and quiet. . . .*

She carefully searched each of the streets adjacent to the house—there were only two, since one side abutted the House of the Mosaic Atrium and the fourth side was an open sun terrace—but found no trace of Charlie, his daughter, or his horse. She returned to a vantage point from which she could watch the entrance and prayed Bericus didn't spot her.

At least an hour later, the door opened. Several of Bericus' slaves emerged furtively. Their low voices carried above the rumble of the volcano.

"I still say this is madness!"

"That mountain isn't? I'll risk Bericus, but not that fiery mountain!"

"Well, even if the mountain don't get him, maybe the Emperor will! I tell you, they're on to him! Why else would a soldier be after him? Him *and* that *sibyl* he bought? You heard what his carriage driver said. She warned him this morning and he took her anyway and now Vesuvius is on fire and the Imperial Army's sent a *centurion* after him! Just watch and see if I stick around another night!"

Sibyl watched them leave and chewed her thumbnail ragged. Charlie had come and gone. Had discovered she was missing and ridden on, searching elsewhere. But *where*? Again, logic dictated only one possible destination: the beach. He would know they had to get away—and that the sea offered the only real escape left them. She groaned and clenched her hands together.

She couldn't think of a likelier destination. With or without her, he *had* to get out of the city. And they were running out of time. It had taken what felt like hours to maneuver her way from the waterfront through town to this vantage point.

And now she had to go back. Had to face those appalling breakers again. So tired she could scarcely make her legs hold her weight, Sibyl hauled herself back to her feet. Did she dare the sea stairs? They looked dark, safe.... She decided to risk it a second time, since that was the closest way to the beach. Sibyl found the entrance and groped her way downward in utter blackness.

By the time she fled down the steps into the breakers, the night was well advanced. A quick glance at Vesuvius left her chilled. Gouts of flame tore upwards. Funnel-shaped coils of fire and glowing ash which cooled into darkness on their way up were eventually lost in the stratosphere-climbing blackness. Up to twelve miles above Vesuvius' crater, sheets and curtains of fire tore through the sky, caught by cross winds at various elevations. That fire shivered and licked southeastward with every gust of high-altitude wind, toward Pompeii and Stabiae.

Sibyl couldn't be certain, but felt at a primal level she might have only minutes left in which to activate the recall gadget. *Tony warned me I'd need fifteen minutes. Do I have fifteen minutes left?* She found shelter in the dark lip of a boat chamber. Far out toward the horizon, nearly invisible between wave crests, Sibyl saw the winking light of lanterns as someone made a last-minute dash for safety. She didn't have the courage to hope that someone might include Charlie Flynn and his beautiful little girl.

She turned away from the crashing stretch of earthquake-ravaged breakers and swore softly. Then, tears stinging her eyes, she dug into the pouch at her waist. The reassuring glow of the LED display startled her for a moment. She'd half forgotten modern niceties during the past few days. Sibyl paused briefly. Was that all it had been? A little less than a week, subjectively? She shook her head. A week in the life of a time traveler. . . .

She wasn't entirely certain of the wisdom of activating the recall button this close to town, but a sense of extreme urgency had crept across her. That urgency prevented her from seeking a quieter spot outside town. The hole in time was undoubtedly going to be spectacular, if what she'd seen on a back road in Florida were anything to judge by. There were still far too many people up and about for her to feel comfortable about opening the portal here. But when the column of ash and gas belching out of Vesuvius began to collapse, it would race down the slopes as a fiery avalanche and separate into two equally lethal phases.

Not as though there would be witnesses to the *second* phase. No one living in Herculaneum would need to worry about the slow-moving pyroclastic flow of molten pumice and mud which would eventually engulf the city and bury it beneath sixty feet of solid rock. They'd be long dead from the fiery surge of two-hundred-degree gas, ash, and pumice which would rip through the city at speeds of anywhere from one hundred sixty to four hundred eighty miles per hour.

Even at its slowest speed, the surge that killed Herculaneum would reach them in a fraction more than four minutes after it blasted its way clear of Vesuvius' crater.

And I need fifteen *minutes. . . .*

Sibyl stepped out of her shelter and waded cautiously

into the wild breakers. She cast a final look at the virulent red glow of Vesuvius' eye—

The shape of the eruption cloud had changed. Its color shifted wildly, shot through with whitish-yellow masses, punctuated by tornado shapes and flaring sheets of withering orange and red.

"Forgive me, Charlie."

She mashed the recall button.

Nothing happened.

Not that she was certain what to expect.

The glow from the LED display remained unchanged. Uneasily she looked again toward Vesuvius, then back at the display screen. Then blinked. And held her breath.

The numbers were changing.

Sibyl watched, transfixed. What, exactly, did those numbers mean? Absently, she rubbed the hairs on her arm, then paused to frown. Every hair stood erect, like winter-dry fur on a cat, shedding static electric sparks every time it's petted.

The air smelled like lightning.

Deeply uneasy, Sibyl backed farther into the arched boat chamber. From that refuge she watched in silent awe as a time storm brewed above the narrow beach at Herculaneum. Seemingly nothing more untoward than an extension of the black hell boiling out of the volcano, thick black clouds formed out of nowhere and clustered low above the furious sea. Lightning flashed from cloud to cloud.

The lightning was pink.

Despite possible dangers, Sibyl felt herself drawn out into the open to watch the display. She stood her ground against the sea and stared. Massive, cloud-splitting bolts stabbed from the time storm into the roaring volcanic eruption. The air began to tremble as violently as the ground.

A cracking bolt blasted into wave-churned sand not five feet from Sibyl. She jumped backwards even before she screamed. Slowly, through the numbing aftershock of thunder, it occurred to Sibyl that in order to get through the time doorway, she would have to run a gauntlet of that lightning. Sibyl slid to her haunches in the boat shelter. *Oh, God, I have to go* through *that*....

Lingering terror of thunderstorms, of lightning and murderous wind, held her immobile inside the boat chamber. She hunched her shoulders and watched, shell-shocked, as the night grew wilder. Memory—traitorous and cruel—returned her to the black night of her childhood when the tornado had ripped through their house, spewing lightning and death in its path.

Screams from very close by roused her from near-stupor. *Vesuvius* ... New terror, more shockingly immediate, drove her to her feet. Sibyl stumbled out onto the beach, cringing from the lightning which now crashed all around.

Vesuvius had gone mad.

Fire crawled down its slopes. Great, surging waves of flame blasted upward and outward, not in a ground-hugging lava flow, but in a boiling, seething mass a half-mile high. She was unable to tear her gaze from it. It split into distinct waves as lighter elements separated from heavier components, gas from ash, ash from pumice, pumice from the ground-hugging pyroclastic flow ...

All of it spilled down the mountainside. The first rolling wave blasted halfway down. Then the leading edge dissipated on the wind. But the weight and mass of the next surge was right behind it. Sibyl caught her breath in a sob that hurt her whole body. The second wave roared closer still, headed on a crash course for Herculaneum.

First surge at midnight, fourth an hour after that—it'll kill Pompeii—fifth surge 7:00 A.M., last surge 8:30, and it'll blast all the way to Misenum....

Sibyl wouldn't have to worry about surges two through seven. Number one was going to kill her. Terror-stricken people fled right at her. The first refugees to reach her were the members of a wealthy family. They carried lanterns which swung insanely as they ran. The woman screamed, *demanded* to be taken away. Children cried or—worse—clung to their parents' hands and clothes, wrapped in terror too deep for expression. More refugees arrived. Some led hard-to-manage horses. People spread out along the seawall, sobbing frantically for boats.

Someone actually managed to launch one. A riot ensued as people swamped it, trying to get aboard.

Four minutes. How much time's gone? How much is left? WHERE'S THE DAMNED TIME PORTAL?

A heavy man slammed into, then past her. Sibyl stumbled badly. Curses scalded her ears. *No boat in the chamber.* More people crowded onto the beach. Lightning blazed. White faces lit with a hellish pink glow. The panicked crowd shoved into the boat chamber. Sibyl was pressed toward the rear by a throng that would soon be too thick to push past.

Oh, shit. . . .

Sibyl kicked and shoved. When people refused to give ground and let her past, she stabbed blindly with her dirk. Cries of pain sickened her. "Let me out! Let me through!"

Sibyl shoved until she stumbled onto open beach again. The sea sucked back from the seawall, crashed forward. She staggered into the wall, half dazed by the weight of water. How many minutes had passed? She glanced up at the mountain—and froze.

The surge was enormous. It was halfway to the city already. She whirled around to stare wildly, but the blinding white doorway in time was nowhere to be seen. For one agonizing moment, Sibyl was paralyzed by fear more intense than anything she had ever felt.

Then, surrounded by mad lightning and screaming people, an eerie calm settled over her. Panic-stricken cries, crashing thunder, the roar of the volcanic surge . . . All of it faded into near silence. It was hopeless. The blast alone would knock her off her feet, scour the skin from her body with blistering heat. But it was all she could do. And it beat running in frantic circles waiting to die.

Sibyl began to hyperventilate.

Who knew? Maybe she could hold her breath long enough to crawl through and spend a year or so in a burn unit somewhere, growing new skin. . . .

Then, shockingly, hands closed around her throat. She moved blindly, slashed out at her attacker. Too tall for a Roman . . . Lightning blazed. She found herself staring into Tony Bartlett's mad eyes. His face was waxy white, his features contorted. He was shouting at her, but she couldn't hear him. Sibyl broke his <u>hold</u> and windmilled backwards. She sucked down air. He lunged again. Sibyl stumbled away and was knocked down by a crashing wave.

She coughed salt water. Tried to get away from crushing hands. *Why hadn't he died?* Then an immense black shape reared up out of the night. A horse . . .

"CHARLIE!"

No familiar voice answered that primal scream. The horse stood on its hind legs, fighting a grip on its trailing lead rope. The man holding that rope wasn't Charlie Flynn. Then Tony Bartlett slammed into whoever it was and seized the rope himself. The horse's hooves smashed into the surf within inches of Sibyl's head. She lost sight of Tony as she scrambled to her feet. Another glare of lightning showed Tony astride the horse, clutching his shoulder and the horse's mane.

Then it happened.

Between them, a brilliant crack of white light opened out of thin air. *Oh, God, please, it's too late, it won't open fast enough* . . . Peripheral vision showed her a looming wall of fire bearing down on them. She could hear the roar as the fiery avalanche swept through the dying town. Could smell the brimstone stench as death blasted closer . . .

With agonizing slowness the sliver of white light widened. Became a bar. A window. Screams and sobs for divine help rose in a shriek behind her. A frantic look over her shoulder revealed a half-mile high *tsunami* of fire crashing down on her. Glowing white streaks and seething balls of incandescence flashed through it.

The cresting mass swirled orange and red where it

was cooler. In places it was shot through with black smoke and pumice. It engulfed buildings, whole city blocks, sweeping down through the town at tornado speeds. Where the white streaks and glowing masses touched buildings, they ignited. People ran screaming toward the seawall in front of it, were swallowed alive. . . .

The leading edge was less than a block away and coming like a derailed freight train. The time portal wasn't quite as wide as a closet doorway. Just wide enough if she didn't misjudge.

Sibyl drew a frantic breath of air—

—and launched herself straight into the still-widening glare. Three feet away, Tony Bartlett kicked the horse after her. As she fell forward into the portal, Sibyl twisted, disoriented and lost. She caught a final, horrifying glimpse of Herculaneum. That glimpse burned into her mind with the force of nightmare: a woman with hideous buck teeth, dressed as a whore in a short *tunica*, stood frozen atop the seawall. The prostitute was pointing directly at the portal, transfixed, her form lit insanely by the light pouring out of the time doorway. Her mouth worked, shaping words . . .

Venus and Mars, help us—

The fiery avalanche caught her up and flung her to the beach.

I've seen her bones, the buck-toothed woman thrown from the seawall, I've seen her bones. . . .

Then brilliant white light blotted out everything.

Time crawled to a meaningless standstill. Sibyl twisted helplessly without reference points. She was spinning into nowhere. . . . Some unknown distance after her initial fall into the light, she felt a concussion along the length of her body. Something heavy had crashed through with her.

Tony and the horse.

She couldn't see them, couldn't hear anything. The surge was right behind her, but she couldn't see it, either. *When I drop out the other side, it'll be right on top of me.* If she crawled straight forward, it would blast through and kill her. *Gotta get off to the side or maybe get behind it . . .*

Could she get behind it?

The force of landing jarred her so deeply she couldn't breathe. Sibyl lurched to her knees anyway, flung herself sideways on a perpendicular line away from the open portal. A gagging stench and lethal heat blasted loose behind her. The volcanic surge blew out through the time hole. The portal widened like a dilating camera shutter. Sibyl lunged forward, rolled away from the heat, toward the back side of the rip in reality—

She landed in clear, sweet air the temperature of an industrial-grade freezer. Sibyl gulped reflexively. For an awful moment, she couldn't distinguish the burning of knife-cold air in her lungs from the burning of superheated volcanic gasses.

Then she collapsed, simply breathing in and out.

She was barely cognizant that she lay belly down on a hard-packed surface of snow and ice.

CHAPTER SEVENTEEN

A couple of sunny Saturday afternoons on the glassy waters of Biscayne Bay had not prepared Charlie for the maddened seas off Herculaneum. Decius Martis thrust him toward the tiller, shouting, "Hold her on course—got to get the sail down in this storm! My wife will watch your child!"

So Charlie hung grimly to the tiller, manfully not screaming when the broken rib grated. *I'm gonna die, it's gonna puncture a lung and I'm gonna drown in my own blood....* He whimpered and clamped his lips and struggled to hold the tiny vessel stern-first to the ravaged swells. Charlie was convinced if punctured lungs didn't kill him, he'd traded death by burning for death by drowning in the Mediterranean. Every time a wave crested above their tiny boat, terror for Lucania's life choked him a little tighter. He was amazed the boat hadn't capsized already. Seas were running at least twelve feet. The ceaseless plunging and tilting was like riding Space Mountain while half submerged on the biggest log flume in the universe—blindfolded.

The lanterns the fisherman had hung earlier had swung so violently on their mounts, they'd gone out. Insane lightning flickered through the black night, strobing across a lightless abyss where the boat hung poised on a wave crest. In the next instant Charlie's stomach would roll over as they plunged straight down into darkness, swallowed by the trough. Then another lightning bolt would reveal more mountains of water towering above them. Salt water surged across the gunwales, all but swamping them with each crashing wave.

Charlie was so scared, he wasn't even seasick.

The fisherman emerged finally from the gloom and caught Charlie's shoulder. "Get forward!" He had to shout in Charlie's ear to be heard. "Don't need you for now! And hang on! Don't fall overboard!"

Decius Martis took the tiller from Charlie's aching grasp. Charlie crouched on his belly in the bottom of the boat grabbing at anything that looked grabable, then inched his way past the footings for the mast. A lightning bolt cracking through nearby clouds revealed Phillipa huddled in the bow. She cradled another child he hadn't noticed before, hiding it protectively under her tunic. Lucania clung to her. The little girl's wide eyes found his in another mad flicker of lightning.

"Papa!"

Charlie hugged her close, wedging himself in as best he could facing the stern. Every time thunder crashed, Lucania's little body flinched in terror. Charlie wrapped his cloak around her and kissed her hair. "Shh . . . It's okay now, Lucky, Papa's got you safe and sound. . . ."

The bloody red glow that marked Vesuvius swung violently in a fifty-degree arc as the waves tossed them about like dried leaves in a tornado. His daughter, drenched as a drowned rat, trembled under his cloak. He wrapped it more tightly around her, trying to protect her from the maddened night. *If she wasn't afraid of the dark before, she will be now.*

The sky was as crazed as the sea. As the little boat gained distance and perspective, the storm seemed somehow to center itself on the tiny, doomed town behind them. Could the eerie display be the time storm effect? Lightning, clouds, and wind all seemed to fit with the descriptions. Something like that would be visible for miles.

Sibyl, where are you?

Had she'd gotten safely away? Did that storm mean she was getting out? *Please God, let it be Sibyl. . . .* He was just beginning to appreciate the lesson Marcus the gladiator had learned in the old movie *The Last Days of Pompeii*: threaten a man's child and he'll do anything.

Anything.

That didn't mean he had to be proud of it.

Charlie managed another look at Vesuvius, then sucked in his breath. The fiery glow surrounding the volcano was bigger. And getting bigger by the second.

A seething cloud of brilliant, glowing gas—orange, baleful yellow, incandescent white in mad, churning patterns—enveloped the mountain. The fiery avalanche ran shrieking down the mountainside, miles wide. It lit up the whole night. The lethal glow split into waves of different speeds, illuminating the doomed town. Herculaneum huddled against the sea like a child's abandoned playset.

Except it wasn't abandoned.

The end had begun.

Charlie discovered he couldn't breathe. Couldn't even move. Fear held him, fear that ran to the core of his genes, like the leftover fears of some cave-dwelling ancestor, echoing down time to take up residence in Charlie's nerve endings. Sibyl had warned him, but not even her dire warning had come close to the reality of that . . . that . . .

God . . .

It smashed down the mountain. Vesuvius throbbed against the blackness. The surge spread over the countryside, churning and discharging lightning through the whole mass. Farms and groves Charlie had passed earlier in the day vanished under it.

Get out, Sibyl, get out of there. . . .

A third wave overtook the slower-moving second. Charlie shut his eyes. *No way that's gonna miss town.* He couldn't watch, couldn't *not* watch. The surge raced down the mountain, on a baleful course for the time storm brewing above the beach at Herculaneum.

Whoever had summoned the time portal . . . *could* they get out before it struck? *Was this ship far enough away not to get caught in the blast?* Numb, battered, Charlie hugged his child close and watched the fiery surge roll down the flanks of Vesuvius. It smashed across the town. Phillipa's hoarse cry reached his ears. She pointed wordlessly. An odd darkness had split the surge, widening even as they watched.

A time hole, draining it off? My God, whoever went through, that surge blasted right through with *them.* Charlie felt sick, more helpless than he had the night they'd gunned down his grandfather right in front of him, more helpless than when Bericus had held him down. . . .

Sibyl was dying, he was watching her death, and *there was nothing he could do.* Grief choked him, but the volcanic surge didn't let him grieve long. The rest of the seething, glowing gas belched out across the sea, right toward their fleeing boat.

Charlie clutched the gunwale, sucked in air against the constricting pain in his chest. *It's going to catch us. . . .* Charlie dragged frantically at fishing nets nearby. The darkness around the fishing boat glowed brighter and brighter as the surge raced across wild waves. Gagging fumes set them all coughing. Charlie dragged the nets over himself, dragged Phillipa and her baby down into the lowest part of the boat with him, shoved Lucania under his own body. She was crying, struggling against him. He huddled down right on top of her.

"Don't breathe! Whatever you do, don't breathe! Cover your child's mouth and nose!" He covered his daughter's whole face tightly with his own hands. Then heat and a blast of ash poured over them. The boat rocked madly, lifted stern-first. They slithered sideways into a trough. Water poured over the side. Stinging, cold seawater engulfed them. Charlie held his breath under the flood. The boat threatened to swamp. His lungs ached. Burned. He needed to breathe, *had* to breathe. . . .

Lucania was struggling against him. *I'm suffocating her, dear God, I'm suffocating her to death—* Then the boat righted itself. The puny craft rocked again as another wave poured over the side. But the next time the fishing vessel righted itself, the heat had dissipated, replaced by a rain of ash and rocks. Charlie gulped air reflexively. He coughed and choked, coughed again, while burning pain in his ribcage sent a stab of terror through him. For a split second, Charlie was convinced he'd inhaled air the temperature of a steel furnace. . . .

But the worst of the surge had passed, leaving them in a cloud of grit and ash. The pain in his chest was the pain of a broken rib, nothing more. He uncovered Lucania's face. She screamed and breathed against him. *She's alive. . . .*

He spent precious moments weeping.

Then, cautiously, Charlie poked his head out from under the fishing nets. They were hot to the touch, but the boat had held together. A flare of lightning showed him the mast, smoking and charred. Water pouring over the rest of the boat had saved them from death. At first he couldn't see Decius Martis. Then another flare of lightning revealed fitful movement in the stern. Under the strobe of multiple lightning flashes, the spare sail shifted, moved. Decius Martis finally emerged and gulped air.

"Phillipa?" Fear trembled in the man's voice.

She managed to poke her head into clear air. "I am all right, husband. And our son, too. The centurion pushed us under the nets. He saved us from burning to death!"

The fisherman shouted shaky thanks, then went back to fighting the tiller. The little fishing boat came about, stern-first to the waves again. Slowly Charlie uncurled his death grip on the coarse nets. He eased Lucania out from under him and made sure she'd taken no other injury. Then he wiped her tears and hushed her, rocked her in his arms and crooned a lullaby his mother had sung to *him* until she finally quieted. *Were* there mockingbirds in Europe now? He didn't think so. . . .

A measureless sweep of time flowed over them. Another fiery surge burst down across the town. This

one barrelled farther across the heaving sea than the
last. Once again, they all dove for cover under spare nets
and sails. Again, water pouring into the little boat cooled
them just enough to survive. By the time it was safe to
emerge again, the mast was little more than a charred
stump, two-thirds of it snapped off. The gunwales were
a smoking ruin. But—once again—the little fishing boat
had held together, saved from burning by the rough seas.

Charlie held his terrified daughter, rocking her once
more into silence. While he sang of mockingbirds and
looking glasses and pony carts, he eyed the ruined mast.
*So much for using wind power to get us out of this
nightmare.* Back toward shore, the time storm was breaking up. The anguish that came with just *looking* at the
diminished lightning flashes was nearly unbearable. *Sibyl,
I'm sorry. . . .*

Then baseball-sized rocks and glowing volcanic debris
hit the ship. "Get down!" He dragged the heavy nets
over Phillipa and her child again. "Hold Lucania! I'll be
back!"

The little girl screamed in terror when he left her.
Charlie struggled toward the stern. Salt water poured
over the charred gunwale and he was suddenly breathing
the Mediterranean. Charlie coughed and spat, then a
rocky missile impacted against his armor. He yelled.
Another spreading bruise for already-battered ribs. . . .
He finally fought his way back to Decius. Charlie yanked
off his helmet and jammed it onto the fisherman's unpro-
tected head.

"Get under cover!" Decius yelled. "Thanks—but don't
be a fool!"

Charlie didn't argue. He rescued his daughter from
Phillipa and crawled under the spare sail with her, giving Phillipa the privacy of the fishing nets. Lucania
wrapped both arms tightly around his neck, in a baby
version of the universal panic-stricken stranglehold.
Charlie huddled beneath the sodden sail, leaving the
sailing to the professional sailor, and whispered to his
little girl. "Shh . . . Papa's got you now, honey, shh . . ."

Lucania quieted almost at once. He kissed her brow in the darkness and told her how wonderful she was, how brave and beautiful and fine she was, how proud of her he was. Charlie was still talking when he realized she'd fallen asleep under the protective curl of his body.

Oh, my sweet baby, that's it, just sleep the nightmares away. . . . He grunted when another rock smashed its way down onto him. *Oww* . . . He had no idea where Decius was heading. At this point, they were probably just running *away*. They could figure out a port of call later.

Couldn't they?

He wondered with sudden apprehension if Romans— and this fisherman in particular—knew anything about navigation on the open sea. Hadn't his sailing instructor in Miami said something about ancient sailors never getting out of sight of land because they didn't have the faintest idea how to navigate without landmarks?

Oh, great. Adrift at sea.

And quite apart from every other terror, Sibyl's face floated into his mind, the way she'd looked when she'd first learned he was a cop. All sparkle and laughter and delighted surprise. If he hadn't been so acutely embarrassed, he might have kissed her, then.

The sunlight and sparkle faded into hissing blackness. Another pebble struck painfully across one thigh. He yowled and tried to rub the spot, then gave it up as pointless. Sibyl was dead. Burned alive, horribly. And Tony Bartelli? Carreras' brother-in-law . . . Thinking about Carreras made him crazy. How far did the whole thing stretch? The time travel, the snatchings, the murders?

Tony Bartelli had not told him everything, not by a long shot. Tony himself probably hadn't been told everything. If he'd been Jésus Carreras, Charlie wouldn't have told him much, either—just enough to carry out his mission of the moment. What Tony *had* known, he'd spilled. Freely. Charlie wondered just how a defrocked

Jesuit Latin instructor had ended up married to Carreras'
sister?

The thought that Sibyl was dead over a box of mouldy,
crumbling *manuscripts*, made him even crazier than
thoughts of Carreras. He didn't give a damn about a
bunch of Greek and Roman writers who'd been dead
and buried for twenty, twenty-five *centuries* before
Charlie's birth. He would gladly have set fire to the
manuscripts himself, box and all, if doing so would have
saved Sibyl's life.

Of course, *she* might never have forgiven him. . . .

His snort of almost-laughter was a strangled sound
under the wet sail. Lucania stirred, brushed a tiny fist
across his mouth. He kissed the fingers until she went
back to sleep. Then Charlie Flynn took a deep, deep
breath and let it out slowly. *Okay. I'm the hot-shot Miami
detective. It's about time I start acting like one.*

Sibyl had been right on a number of points; but
Charlie didn't put much credit in her idea—or Tony's
claim—that museum-quality artifacts were what the family was after. A sideline, maybe, but not the whole story.
Not even close. There had to be more. A *lot* more. The
Carreras family, with its ties in Miami, New York, Chi-
cago, LA, South America, the Continent, Asia . . .

If his sources were correct, the Carreras family was
one of the most powerful organizations in America.
They'd bought out or eliminated nearly every major
competitor—

Charlie blinked.

Power. Of course.

Financial. Political. Even military . . .

Especially military. Change the course of wars, elec-
tions, anything. It would be just the thing to interest old
man Carreras, too, Jésus' father—something to entice him
back into an active role in family affairs. Charlie narrowed
his eyes. Come to think of it, that retirement story had
rung a little hollow all along. Carreras men retired when
someone dumped dirt over them. The more Charlie
thought about it, the more he knew was he was right.

Julio Carreras had always been more subtle, more given to complex setups than Jésus, although Jésus was *good*. This whole setup was so convoluted and carefully hidden, it fairly screamed of Julio Carreras' touch. Charlie wasn't certain Jésus would have been able to pull it off single-handedly. Why the devil hadn't he considered any of this earlier?

Charlie called himself several kinds of fool. He refused to accept any excuses, even the fact he'd been trying to stay alive in a world as alien as anything he'd ever seen on *Star Trek*. For four entire years, he hadn't been *thinking*, let alone thinking like a cop.

It had taken Sibyl to jar him back on track.

Sibyl . . .

Charlie closed his eyes. He wished for just the tiniest, selfish moment he could cradle *her* close and hold onto her until the aching emptiness in him disappeared. How long he lay on his side, curled up in a ball around his daughter and trying not to cry, Charlie had no idea. Eventually, the combined stresses and physical abuse he'd endured took their toll. While arguing with himself about whether or not he ought to confront Decius Martis with a request to know where they were headed, Charlie fell asleep.

He woke slowly. His first response was surprise. He hadn't slept so soundly—or, he suspected, so long at one stretch—in four years. He started to sit up—

"Nnngh—"

Moving involved a whole series of agonies. They began in his neck and ended in the soles of his feet. Breathing hurt. Saddle-galled thighs burned so badly he hissed between clenched teeth. Welts in his back had glued themselves to his stolen tunic. His back felt as stiff as his armor. Dull pain in his ribcage shuddered and stabbed like bright lightning when he shifted position. Above it all, he was so hungry, he could've gnawed on the woolen sail which draped across him in wet sags and folds. And when he tried to move again, he discovered he'd been efficiently tied up.

The sea still heaved and bucked, reminding him of the ground the previous day. The boat tilted sharply every few moments, giving him an unobstructed view of Herculaneum. Vesuvius still belched destruction. The whole coastline looked like a madman's vision of hell. The crazed movement of the fishing boat as it slid and tossed across the wave crests caused the whole landscape to shift crazily. What little he could see was a glowing sea of lava and gas stretching right down the mountainside into the sea itself.

Of beautiful, idyllic Herculaneum, there was no trace.

The air was thick and heavy. It smelled of rotten eggs. Rocks and ash continued to pelt them. A lamp hung forlornly from the charred stump of the mast, casting dim light into the volcanic gloom. Everything was coated with a dull grey film. Blurred movement in the bow showed him Phillipa, her breasts bare as she nursed her child.

Lucania, fast asleep, lay across her lap. Charlie sagged in relief. *She's all right.* Whether or not she stayed that way very likely depended on *him*. Again, he thought of old movies he'd watched. Hollywood had certainly got *that* part right. Nobody pitied the child of a disobedient slave.

The fisherman still manned the tiller, drooping visibly in exhaustion. Sometime while Charlie slept, Decius Martis had dragged him closer to the stern. *Probably after tying me up, to keep me away from his wife and kid.* Predictably, he had confiscated Charlie's sword belt.

The fisherman had, by his own standards, shown astonishing leniency. Nonetheless, Charlie felt nothing but utter defeat. It was worse, almost, than the day he'd lost the use of his leg in the arena. Then, he'd had only himself to think of, only his own freedom to somehow win. The ropes Decius Martis had tightened around his wrists and ankles were more than symbols of imprisonment. They represented loss of all hope. The *best* that could happen now was a return to slavery—not only for him, but for little Lucania.

He said in a low, hard voice, "You hold our lives in your hands. Denounce me . . . they'll kill me without pity. Then they'll take my daughter and sell her to some stinking brothel to be raised a whore. . . ."

Decius' brow furrowed thoughtfully. "You have courage. I will grant that. And a good mind. I would have you know, slave, I see a great difference between quietly killing a man in his sleep and turning him over to an Imperial garrison to be tortured to death."

Charlie shivered. Graphic images of the executions he'd been forced to witness still haunted him.

"It is little enough to offer, but when we reach the port of Stabiae, we will tell no one in authority of this." He gestured to Charlie's stolen armor.

Charlie remained silent. Decius seemed to understand. The fisherman wiped ash and grit off his face. Lantern light revealed burns on his hand and lower arm. He must have kept hold of the tiller, or tried to, during one of the surges.

The fisherman lifted his gaze from the sea and met Charlie's eyes. "You must realize you cannot simply go free? Not with that brand on you?"

Charlie nodded, hardly daring to hope this man might show his child, at least, some pity. He winced when a pebble at terminal velocity stung his shoulder and wished he could wipe ash and grit off his own wet face.

"I know."

Decius' voice was a little less harsh this time. "We are not wealthy, Phillipa and I, but a fisherman can always earn a living and seldom starves."

It didn't take ESP to know the fisherman was afraid of him—and in his shoes, Charlie supposed he'd have been afraid, too—but equally clearly, the man was trying to be fair.

"Yeah, well, I guess that's true enough," Charlie agreed. "I'm not much good on a boat."

"No . . ." Decius pursed his lips slightly. Exhaustion made the man's eyes water and brought a tremble to his burned hand. How many hours since he had slept?

"But there are other things a man who is slow of foot can do. I never have enough hands to keep nets mended. And the rigging and sails must be repaired constantly.

"Then there is the job of cleaning and sorting the catch, hauling it to market. And I will need a new mast, which you can help shape with wood-working tools, and the boat needs recaulking. And the gunwales are damaged. And once you learn woodworking skills . . . even a crippled man can work wood and earn himself and his master a living."

Too true.

"Or buy his child's freedom," Decius added softly.

Charlie's glance was sharp. But he said nothing. Not yet. He wouldn't risk Lucania's future on his temper.

"There is plenty of opportunity to do this—and more. You begin to see?"

Charlie's forced laugh came out badly strained. "Yes. I begin to see. Master," he added bitterly.

Decius grunted softly. "I have never been a slave. But I am not a citizen, either. And when you cannot claim citizenship, you suffer abuse from *all* Romans, rich and poor." He held Charlie's eyes steadily. "That cannot have been easy for you to say."

Charlie was surprised by even that small measure of understanding. He hadn't expected to find *any*. If he were doomed to live out his life a slave . . . There were worse men he could call "master."

Charlie wondered how one mended fishing nets.

"I have no choice," Charlie answered slowly. "You could have me killed when we reach port. You could throw me overboard *now*. You could throw my *child* overboard. As you say, with this brand, who would believe I was a freedman? I have no manumission papers. No freedman's cap. And I certainly can't pass myself off as a citizen. They might believe *you* had lost my ownership papers in the disaster, but never that *I* had lost my manumission."

Decius relaxed marginally.

"I'll work for you, Decius Martis, because I have no

choice, but I hope you won't expect me to be cheerful about it."

Decius' rusty laugh surprised him. "No, I won't expect that. In your place, I think I would hate me very much."

"Huh. If I don't work out to your satisfaction, I suppose you could always sell me. Provided you can find someone stupid enough to give you gold for a cripple and his baby."

"I would not sell the man who saved my family, whatever you may think of me. I would free you first, myself."

Charlie stared. Trust came hard, but something in Decius' eyes told him he could believe that. "Very well. Master." It came out sounding a little less bitter than before. Then, because the question burned his insides and Decius Martis had not made his intentions clear, "What will you do with Lucania?"

Decius tightened his lips. "I don't know, exactly. Somehow I don't think I'd live long if I tried selling her. And after what I've seen, I wouldn't do that, in any case. We'll decide later what's to be done about the child. After we're safe." He nodded toward the volcano. "And we are not safe yet. The wind and current are carrying us toward the blackest part of that ash cloud."

"I know," Charlie agreed darkly. *More than you, pal.* He knew exactly what they'd find when they reached shore: more death. Maybe even their own. Somewhere in the blackness they were heading into, the whole Imperial Navy from Misenum was stranded. Its commander—according to Sibyl—would be dead already.

Decius merely nodded to himself and shoved the naked sword under his seat in the stern, out of reach. Charlie let his head drop to the bottom of the boat and shut his eyes. He ached everywhere. Even in his soul. At least Lucania was safe for now. He'd held his temper, held his tongue. He couldn't do much for his daughter as a slave, but he'd secured his child's safety. For now, anyway.

Decius leaned forward from the stern. "Slave. You have never told me what name you are called by."

Charlie considered. Nothing short of torture would force him to reveal the name the roaring crowds—or Xanthus—had given him. How to Latinize his real name?

"Carolus Flineus," he finally said, "is how you would say my name in Latin."

"Flineus," his new master repeated. "An odd name, but it suits you, somehow. Your old master treated you ill." He did not phrase it as a question.

Charlie started to answer, then paused. "Yes. He beat me, sometimes for the pleasure of it. Often. But," he added candidly, "I did not adapt well to slavery. I was born a free man, a citizen, in my own country."

He wondered how to explain the concept of police officers to someone who possessed no inkling of a similar organization. "I held a position of authority. Something like the Praetorian guard or the provincial garrisons. When I was captured and sold, I fought—as any proud and free man would—and tried to escape."

"So your master branded you and maimed you to keep you from running again?"

Charlie's bark of bitter laughter clearly startled the fisherman. "Branded me? Oh, yes. He enjoyed that, too. But my leg was already ruined. I was crippled after two years of fighting in the Circus Maximus. When I was struck down, the crowd spared me. Emperor Vespasian himself ordered me to be tended by a surgeon. Alas, he did not instruct that if I lived, I was to be freed. So I was sold."

"You fought in the great circus at *Rome*? When you said you'd fought, I thought— What does it look like? What champions did you fight? What weapons did they use? Which did *you* use?"

Charlie couldn't believe it. He'd found a sports fan. The *last* thing he wanted to do was remember the years in the arena. But talking about it would please his new master. And there was Lucania to consider. . . .

So he talked of Rome, which the poverty-stricken

fisherman had never seen. He talked of the arena, of the Emperor and the great Flavian Amphitheater (which in Charlie's time was known as the Colosseum, or so said his textbook captions), which was still under construction. He answered a thousand other questions Decius Martis had for him as best he could. And wondered the whole while when Lucania would wake up—and if Decius Martis would let him hold her when she did.

At length the fisherman changed the subject. "We must be getting close to land. If I'm right, the current and winds are carrying us toward Stabiae. I would come ashore elsewhere, given a chance, but I don't think we can make the straits off Capri." The fisherman's glance fell on Charlie's battered armor. "And the first thing you must do, Flineus, is get rid of everything from that soldier. Dump it overboard."

"I don't have any other clothes," Charlie pointed out.

"Then wear a loincloth and go barefooted. If you're caught wearing a soldier's uniform, or with a soldier's personal possessions, nothing I say will save your life. Or very possibly mine."

Charlie stripped to the skin. The moment he unfastened the armor, the ache in his ribs thundered to life, leaving him pale and sweating. Very awkwardly, Charlie pulled off the armor. He had to pause when ribs grated.

He managed to pull the armor off, then dropped it overboard. When Charlie tried to pull off the tunic, he discovered he couldn't raise his arms above his head. A single attempt left him whimpering in the back of his throat. A sheen of cold sweat broke out over his entire body. Muscles trembled uncontrollably in his arms and chest, even his legs.

"Master?" he said, through clenched teeth. Almost worse than the pain, Charlie was embarrassed, *humiliated*, at having to ask . . .

Decius looked up in surprise. "Yes?"

"I cannot get the tunic off. I cannot lift my arms high enough."

The fisherman's eyes narrowed, but he said nothing. "Hold still." Decius recovered the sword belt from beneath the tiller seat and retrieved the dagger.

"I cannot leave the tiller. Come here and turn around."

Charlie suspected leaving the tiller had less to do with it than distrust, but he did as he was told. Charlie scooted across the intervening space and presented his back. Decius cut the tunic from neck to hem and pulled.

Charlie yelled ...

Dimly, he felt his face connect solidly with something hard. Gradually he returned to full awareness with his face pressed against wet wood. Phillipa had knelt over him. She was rinsing his back with fresh water—not salty seawater, but precious drinking water. Charlie tightened his fingers on the wet sail and ground his teeth and fought blackness that roared in his ears.

From somewhere above him, Decius' voice said, "Flineus ... ?"

Then Phillipa's voice trickled into his awareness. "He can't hear you, husband. He's fainted. And it's little wonder. He's been shockingly abused."

She sounded angry.

Charlie wished to God he *had* fainted. Phillipa's ministrations brought another whimper to the back of his throat. When she prodded his ribcage with strong fingers, bone grated on bone, hideously. He closed his hands convulsively in the wet sail. Charlie finally got his wish. Blackness crashed down on the heels of a strangled cry.

He roused all too soon, to find Phillipa wrapping his ribs in her own stola. They'd propped him against the gunwale to give her room to wind the cloth around his torso. When Charlie's eyes fluttered open, Decius Martis met his gaze. The fisherman rested a calloused hand gently on his shoulder.

"Flineus ... I'm sorry. I didn't realize."

That was all the fisherman said, but it was enough.

CHAPTER EIGHTEEN

Logan had passed through several successive stages of cell-pacing and bunk-slouching and was well into another bout of pacing when his cell door swung silently outward. He halted and found his gaze locked with that of Colonel Dan Collins.

A muscle jumped once in Collins' jaw, but his grip on the 9mm pistol in his hand was as steady as his gaze. Two anonymous MPs stood behind the colonel, armed with loaded and cocked M16A2s. Something about the way they wore their uniforms, the way they gripped their weapons, the way they held their eyes, told Logan those two weren't military personnel at all. They must belong to Mr. Silk Suit.

Logan's adrenal glands lurched once and kicked in full-tilt. *He can't afford to let me live.* And since Collins appeared to be his chief flunkie . . . The MPs didn't much look like they'd come for tea and crumpets, either. Feigning a nonchalance he was far from feeling, Logan drawled, "Evenin', Colonel. Or is it mornin'?"

To his astonishment, Collins gave him a strained smile. "Good evening, Captain," he allowed. "If you'll cooperate . . . ?" He gestured with his head to the waiting MPs.

Logan snorted. "Cuffs and hobbles, or a bullet in the brain?"

Something flickered deep in Collins' eyes, but Logan couldn't decide how to interpret that moment of intense emotion. Uneasily he waited for a response.

Collins replied softly, "Just cuffs," as though he were

trying to convey something more than the simple meaning of those two words. A moment after that, the colonel added in a more normal tone, "Give him that parka."

Logan's brows rose. One MP carefully tossed him a thick, regulation parka.

"Goin' out, hunh?" he asked conversationally.

Nobody answered the obvious. Logan shrugged into the heavy jacket, zipped it up, and eyed Collins.

"Hood, too, I presume?"

"Unless you want frozen ears again."

Logan snorted. "You're all heart."

He fastened the hood, then—under the unwavering threat of Collins' Beretta Model 92-F and the first MP's rifle—he allowed the second MP to cuff him. The bar steel felt cold against his skin. The MP slid mittens over Logan's hands, then stepped out of the cell and retrieved his rifle.

Collins moved back. "Okay, McKee. Let's go."

"What? No last meal?" He spoke only half in jest. He was ravenous.

"Out." Collins' gaze remained perfectly steady this time. Logan felt a sinking sensation in the pit of his belly. *Damn. Looks like I'll die in the snow after all.*

He walked out of the cell, flanked by the MPs. Collins followed several paces behind. The colonel wasn't taking any chances. They took Logan to a truck which sat at idle in front of the stockade and shoved him toward the back end. Logan barely had time to take in a smallish military base, ablaze with electric lights under a frozen night sky, then he found himself locked into a lightless, cold compartment. Logan swore under his breath. They'd locked him in alone. Collins had seen him drop two guards in about four seconds and knew all too well what he could have managed in a dark truck, even cuffed, against armed men.

At least they'd given him a parka. Making him freeze on the way to his execution would just have added insult to injury. The truck lurched into motion. Logan slid off balance. He caught himself painfully on one elbow, then banged a shoulder against the wall when the axle dropped into a pothole that must have been the size of a 55-gallon steel drum. He swore into his scraggly beard and propped himself upright again, then scooted into one corner and braced himself with both feet.

It was hard to gauge time, but by the end of the tortuous ride, Logan was convinced they'd left behind any semblance of road and had climbed straight up one side of a mountain and plunged down the other. He'd have bruises on bruises, if they let him live long enough for bruises to form.

When the truck finally stopped, Logan drew a quick breath, then gained his feet and sank into a defensive crouch. He waited as footsteps crunched around toward the back. The doors creaked open. A halogen flashlight beam struck him square in the eyes.

"Nnh—" Reflexively he turned his face away from the painful glare.

"Get out." That was one of the MPs.

Logan couldn't make out how many of them were standing in the opening.

"You want me out?" He braced himself for the hot pain of gunshot wounds. "Come in and get me." Maybe they'd be stupid enough to try it, instead of just shooting him and hauling out the body. . . .

Another set of footsteps came around the side of the truck. Then, instead of the expected rifle shots, Collins' voice issued from the electric glare. An odd timbre colored the tone.

"Gentlemen, get him out please. Alive."

Logan blinked once. Collins wasn't that stupid . . . was he? The MPs—rifles carefully clutched in one hand—handed over the flashlight to Collins. Then, like obedient little puppies, they clambered up into the back of the truck. They'd taken only three steps toward him when, unbelievably, Collins switched off the light.

Utter blackness crashed across them.

What the—?

One of the MPs echoed him aloud.

Logan didn't even stop to think. He got the first one with a boot to the jaw. The man crumpled with an audible grunt. His inert body fell against the second man, who lurched off balance. Logan swung manacled arms in tandem and connected with someone's crotch. The man retched and folded up. Logan dropped him with a snap of the manacle bar across the back of his neck.

For a moment, Logan stood breathing softly in the darkness. Neither MP moved. He used his teeth to tug off mittens while he listened. Collins was unbelievably silent out there, but one helluva thunderstorm seemed to be brewing.

Logan blinked, distracted for a moment from the business at hand.

Thunderstorm?

In the middle of winter?

Collins' voice came from the side of the truck. Apparently, he hadn't moved so much as a toe during the brief fight.

"McKee? I know you took out those two fools."

Logan stooped cautiously, felt for and retrieved both rifles. They were loaded and ready to fire, with a round in each chamber. The soft snick of the magazines snapping back into place broke the brief silence.

Collins continued, still without moving. "That means you've got two rifles to my pistol. Think about it a minute, McKee. If I'd wanted you dead, I'd have shot you from out here and had those two toss your body into a ravine."

"What game are you playing, Collins?" Logan yelled. Then he stepped softly and swiftly three feet to one side, while bringing up the muzzle of the rifle to ready position, but Collins didn't shoot through the thin wall of the truck. Didn't, in fact, move at all.

"No games, McKee." The colonel's voice suddenly sounded weary beyond belief. "It's not your fault you stumbled into this mess. I'm risking lives that aren't mine to risk just to try and get you out of it again in one piece. And—maybe you can help."

Huh? "Oh, really? Is that why you and your doctor pal went through that little Mengele charade back on base? Piss off, Collins."

"Dammit, McKee! I'm trying to save your life! I know you aren't stupid! If I'd shown up the way you did on a top-secret post you were in charge of, what would you have done?"

He had a point there.

"We don't have much time, McKee. If you make a break for it from here, alone, Carreras will hunt you down and butcher you. But if you work with me, I'll do everything in my power to help you get safely clear. No more hospitals, no more lockups—and no Carreras."

Footsteps slowly approached the open tailgate, crunching softly in the snow. Logan stepped into an attack posture just inside the opening, ready to fire. A glow of light sprang up, revealing the resurrection of the flashlight. Collins stepped cautiously around the corner, pistol held harmlessly overhead. He'd pointed the flashlight at the sky, too. Collins' face inside the parka trim was waxy pale, full of stark blue shadows.

"Truce?" Collins offered.

For a moment they stared at one another. Lightning flared, insanely. A beauty of an electrical storm raged overhead. Deeply etched strain in Collins' face told Logan he hadn't told the whole truth yet.

Logan asked softly, "You got the keys to these things?"

Collins' glance traveled to the manacles locked around Logan's wrists. "The manacles? Yes—"

Logan kicked him in the temple. The colonel crumpled. Collins slid soundlessly into a dirty snowdrift. Logan landed beside him and glanced hastily under the truck to be sure no others were lurking out of sight. *All clear.* Rising swiftly from a crouch, Logan retrieved the colonel's Beretta and the other rifle. He then searched Collins' pockets for the manacle keys.

Ahh . . . Freedom felt wonderful. Even better than he'd expected, considering his grim thoughts on the way out here. Logan rubbed his wrists and blew on his fingers to warm them, then confiscated Collins' leather gloves and locked Collins' arms behind him. Once his aching hands had unfrozen, Logan relieved the unconscious MPs of assorted knives and small-caliber handguns, then locked his erstwhile guards into the back of the truck.

By the time he'd appropriated the colonel's holster and belt, fastened them around his own hips, and distributed the confiscated weapons into various pockets and pouches, the colonel was beginning to stir. The man groaned and tried to move. For a moment, as realization sank in, Collins went rigid in the snow. He tested the manacles. Then groaned again and lay still.

Logan squatted comfortably and rolled the colonel onto his back. Collins blinked groggily. A thin trickle of blood had frozen to the side of his face. His lips worked to form a question. "Going to . . . shoot me now?"

Logan held silent for a moment and studied Collins' face. He saw no overt fear, but a crushing weight of despair had settled over the man's features.

"I want to know what's going on."

"It's a long story—"

"I've got time."

The colonel's eyes were haunted by an inexplicable terror. "No, you don't! Not on this side, anyway. And Carreras is waiting, damn him. . . ." His voice shook. Logan began to wonder if that kick to the head hadn't addled the man's brains. Collins added desperately, "He's got hostages, McKee. If I blow this, they die, too."

The other lives he had mentioned? "Whoa, Collins. Slow down. Start over."

The colonel squeezed shut his eyes, then drew a long, unsteady breath and released it slowly. "You're never going to believe this. Never."

"Try me."

Collins met his gaze squarely. "I'm the military liaison for a research project involving some very funky physics, Captain. I have a team of physicists here on base, mostly civilian. We're out here because this place is isolated. Some of the side effects of our research are

pretty disruptive." He gestured with his nose toward
the sky. Logan glanced up at the underbelly of a massive thunderstorm. Thick black clouds had come boiling down the mountainside. Phenomenal bolts and
columns of lightning crawled out of the clouds in every
direction.

The lightning was pink.

Logan's scalp crawled.

"It's effin' time travel. Isn't it?" he muttered.

"Yes. It is." The uninflected response sent a shiver
down his spine.

He remembered vividly the disorienting drop through
endless mist. . . .

Collins' voice reached through Logan's momentary
disorientation. "It's still experimental. And it's dangerous, in unconventional ways. I mean ways other than
the old question of paradox—can you change the future
by altering the past. The very physics involved is
potentially—" He stopped in the middle of the sentence.
He closed his eyes and whispered, "We don't know yet
the full range of side effects, but one of them is the
backlash. Slippage." Collins finally opened his eyes again.
"That's what you got caught in, McKee. When someone opened a portal near you, it caused . . . cracks. You
fell through one." He shivered and added hoarsely,
"You're the only one we know about."

"You mean there might be more? Christ, Collins, why
are you running full-scale operations with this thing?"

Collins' face looked ghastly in a glare of hellish pink
lightning, all taut lines and purple-blue hollows. "*We're*
not."

A chill which had nothing to do with the air temperature gripped Logan. The pieces began form more coher-
ent patterns. "The Hispanic . . ."

"Carreras. Miami mafia."

"*What?* Whoa, fella, you gotta be kidding."

"*Do I look like I'm kidding?*"

He didn't. Logan had rarely seen a grown man in the
grip of such profound terror. The hollows under—and

behind—his eyes deepened. "Someone on my staff is into debt with them. Big time debt. I haven't found out who, not yet. Somebody's relative, maybe, or lover, or simply a customer without enough cash. *Somebody* leaked it, showed them enough proof from our first trial runs to convince them. They've got Sue Firelli's daughter, Janet. She's twenty, brilliant career ahead of her. Zachariah Hughes' grandson is only twelve. And . . ." His voice faltered. "They've got my wife and son, too, McKee. Neat, clean, quick. And quiet. Not even my best friends have figured out what's wrong."

Logan frowned. "Where are they being kept?"

Collins shook his head. "Not where. *When.*"

"Christ . . ."

"I've seen them, once. A show of power, to keep me in line while they need me. It's near here, a mile or so that way." He nodded toward a distant ridgeline. "Before they dragged me into the block house, I saw a herd of wooly mammoths on the horizon."

Collins didn't look mad. His eyes were as sane as anyone's. Anyone whose family is held hostage by terrorists, anyway. But *wooly mammoths*?

Abruptly Logan stood up and stalked a few steps away. This whole business was nuts. But he was undeniably *here* and yesterday—five years ago—he'd been in Florida. Collins hadn't lied about that time span. Logan's presence had jarred him badly.

And if he were telling the truth about everything else, Collins would've been genuinely desperate to find out who—and what—Logan was, before Carreras did. The thunderstorm lowered ominously. Lightning struck a tree not twenty feet away. The crash of thunder deafened him.

If Collins were lying . . .

He turned on his heel and stood above the colonel, rifle levelled casually at Collins' head.

"What were you planning on doing with me, Collins?"

To give Collins his due, the man didn't flinch.

"Take you with me through the portal. Dump my

so-called bodyguards someplace they wouldn't come back from." *His* guards? Logan narrowed his eyes. He hadn't considered that.

"And?"

"Make another jump and hope I could persuade you to help rescue the hostages."

Collins *was* desperate.

"I've read your service records, McKee. And I've seen you fight. You're good. If we got the hostages clear, I'd be free to stop Carreras. I could just sort of lose track of you. You could go anywhere. Anywhen, for all I care. Just help me stop Carreras. Otherwise, he'll track you down wherever you go. You knew almost nothing before and he ordered us to kill you, anyway. He bloody well won't let you live now."

Logan spat something profoundly obscene.

Before the colonel could respond, a brilliant beam of white light distracted Logan. He paused to stare. Out in the clearing, a blinding crack of light had begun to open out of thin air.

"That's the doorway opening, McKee!" Collins' voice was tinged with desperation. "We're out of time, dammit! Once that closes again, if we're still on this side of it, not only will you die, I'll never get a chance to open another one. They'll probably kill Lucille or Danny just to punish me."

"Where does it lead?"

He wanted to keep his gaze riveted on the widening crack, but glanced at Collins just as the other man's answer reached his ears.

"To the year 1883. The island of Krakatoa."

Charlie realized just how accurate Sibyl's knowledge had been when they approached the wave-battered harbor at Stabiae. The Imperial Navy rode at anchor well beyond the outermost pier, all but blocking the harbor's entrance. Decius Martis cursed and fought the tiller, but they swung inexorably toward the main harbor and the looming warships.

"Shall I try and rig the spare sail to what's left of the mast?" Charlie offered.

"No, it was too late for that five minutes ago, before we could even *see* the harbor. We'll just have to ride it out and pray the gods are smiling on us!"

Charlie nodded and strained to see past the pitching bow. Long, narrow, and low-slung, deadly warships rose out of the volcanic gloom like misshapen, breaching whales on some insane National Geographic Special. Massive bronze battering rams, normally hidden beneath the waterline, reared up out of the swells with each wild pitch of the triremes. The rams looked for all the world like oversized beaks on the biggest swordfish ever hooked by a Sunday afternoon sportsman. Charlie's best guess put each ram's weight at something over a couple of tons. If one of those things so much as brushed against the little fishing boat's hull . . .

Decius made his crippled way toward open beachfront near the edge of town. The little boat slid past the warships, crept between them. Charlie held his breath and prayed.

Almost through, almost . . .

A seismic jolt rocked a pier which Charlie could just make out through the gloom. The sea shook and sloshed against the beach, then sucked back again. The nearest trireme broke loose from her anchor line and swung around—

"Look out!"

Charlie yelled, stupidly, in English. The warning was too late, in any case. The trireme rose out of the swells right above their boat. Charlie heard Phillipa's high, ragged scream—

The immense bronze ram smashed downward. The rolling swells pitched them to port. The ram missed their starboard gunwale by inches. The monstrous splash all but swamped them. They rolled back to starboard, even as the trireme began its return, upward swing. Phillipa was frantically tying her son to her breast. Lucania, bewildered and crying in terror, sat in the bottom of the fishing boat. Charlie dove toward her.

The ram impaled them. For an instant, they were lifted clear of the water. Wood splintered. Charlie was hurled violently against the starboard gunwale. Pain exploded through his torso. Lucania tumbled like a doll. Charlie managed to grab the back of her *tunica* just as she arced out over the gunwale. He held on. Decius yelled and toppled completely out of the boat, vanishing over the stern.

Then they were plunging down again, toward the sea and death. Phillipa was thrown clear of the boat. Charlie gripped Lucania's *tunica* tighter and tried to jump overboard. His bad leg twisted under him. Then the boat was splintering all around him, breaking up and falling away from the ram. He fell . . . Tons of water closed over his head. Charlie held his breath and thrashed for the surface. He reached it, sucked down air, thrust Lucania's face above water. She coughed, choked, coughed again. Then wailed like a half-drowned kitten.

Charlie gripped the back of her *tunica*, keeping her head above water, and struck out for the nearby shore. He tried to find Phillipa or Decius Martis in the darkness, but saw no trace of them. "Decius! Decius Martis! Phillipa!"

No answering cry reached him.

Grief caught him. Most Romans couldn't swim. They'd come through so much, had come so close to safety. . . . Then heavy surf caught and hurled him forward. For a moment, all he knew was blackness and stars before his eyes and excruciating pain through his ribcage. Foaming seawater smashed across them. Charlie clung to his daughter. Pain caught his ribs again. He floundered in the surf, rolled beneath another wave and felt a treacherous undertow pull at his legs. Another breaker lifted and flung him forward. Charlie lost his grip. Lucania slid away.

"Lucania!"

Charlie smashed forward into the beach like a basketball slamdunked against concrete.

He didn't bounce nearly as well.

Charlie clung to abrasive sand with his fingers. Undertow sucked greedily at his legs. Laboriously, inch by tiny inch, he crawled forward, clear of the surf. Charlie collapsed, scarcely able to breathe against pain in his chest.

When he craned his neck around to look, he saw Lucania in the breakers. She bobbed awkwardly on a wave crest and was thrown forward. Charlie dove toward her. Undertow sucked her out of reach. She went under.

"Lucania!"

Charlie's leg brace splintered and dumped him headlong into the receding undertow. He peered through the blackness, but couldn't see anything of her.

Then . . .

There!

A breaker sent her tumbling toward him.

He lunged forward on hands and knees and grabbed her hair. Then he dug in, leaned backwards, and held on. The backwash sucked sand out from beneath his knees and feet. Charlie toppled backwards, dragged toward the sea on his back. Pain tore through the welts, but he held his grip on his daughter. The moment the undertow released its deadly grip, he scrambled backwards like a crab stranded at high tide.

Lucania wasn't breathing.

For one gut-wrenching moment, Charlie didn't know what to do. *Rescue breathing*, his training whispered, when his brain couldn't formulate a plan of action.

He bent over her, got the baby onto her back. Charlie pressed sharply upward on her abdomen. Seawater trickled from her mouth. He tilted her head back, checked for obstructions in her throat, found none. He picked her up by the ankles and pounded her back hard enough she threw up seawater.

Breathe . . . Breathe, dammit! Please, Lucky, breathe . . . She stirred, then, under the pounding of his hand against her back; she coughed and threw up more seawater. Charlie pressed up under her ribcage, forcing the tiny diaphragm up against her lungs. The little girl coughed violently, then vomited yet more seawater. Then she drew in a shuddering gasp . . . and another. . . .

Charlie sank down beside her. He discovered his hands were shaking. Her eyelids fluttered open and she mewled, a baby sound without sense. Charlie snatched her to his aching chest and held her close. She stirred against him, hiccoughing a little, then put baby arms around his neck. *Oh, honey.* . . .

He touched Lucania's ash-streaked hair, just sitting on the beach, not even thinking yet about what would happen when he was discovered with a damaged collar, a fugitive brand, and no master to speak for him. Bad as slavery to Decius would have been . . . there had been practical aspects to it.

He stared emptily at the sea. Three more deaths. Decius Martis had been a fair man. Charlie was sorry he and his little family had died so close to safety. Sorrier than he'd believed possible. Eventually he realized he couldn't just sit on the open beach all night. Volcanic bombs were dropping from black skies with frightening regularity. He needed to find shelter, some food for his child. Maybe, if Decius' body were recovered, the authorities would believe Charlie's story and spare his life. . . .

Charlie struggled down the beach toward town, dragging his bad leg awkwardly and straining to maintain his balance. Lucania gradually stopped crying against his scarred neck. Her head drooped. She stuffed a fist into her mouth and grew quiet. It was only then, as the adrenaline surge died away and left him almost too weary to move, that Charlie made a startling discovery.

Part of the numbing roar in the air was the ominous rumble of *thunder*. Charlie slowed his footsteps, tilted his head to stare up at the black sky. Ash and grit rained down onto his upturned face. Without conscious thought, he guarded Lucania's little head with one hand. Overhead the blackness which choked the air seemed to boil. Pink lightning flashed . . .

Pink lightning?

An abrupt, wild stab of hope tore at him, left his pulse shuddering as raggedly as it did after sex.

A time storm?

Lightning slammed into the beach eight feet away. Thunder stunned them. Lucania sobbed in new terror. Charlie turned in circles, looking for it. Surely he wasn't wrong? The descriptions were so similar—

A sliver of white light opened out of thin air.

It was at least twenty feet away. Lightning blasted out of it, struck the sand and the waves, arced upward and outward into the clouds. Charlie stood immobilized and watched the white light grow larger. The unearthly blaze bathed Lucania's face with its unnatural glow.

Charlie's heart pounded so hard he couldn't hear anything else. His whole awareness shrank and centered on that crack through time itself. Wherever it led, it *had* to be better than a volcanic eruption in ancient Stabiae. Could he force his flagging body and crippled leg twenty feet across the sand before the portal disappeared again?

He cupped one hand behind Lucania's head, narrowed down his eyes against the hurtful brightness, and *ran*—

A familiar snarling sound roared out of the brilliance. Charlie yelled. A flash of metallic grill and glass impacted on his awareness.

Truck!

They were right in its path.

"What's that?" Joey asked.

Francisco stopped breathing. The cold gun muzzle remained locked against the back of his neck. Nelson's fingers stayed twisted through his hair, but Nelson didn't squeeze the trigger.

Rough ice underfoot had cut through Francisco's parka and uniform pants. Packed snow was red where his knees and his nose had bled into it. He knelt in the snow and shook while his executioners stared off into the distance. *Don't let them shoot me first and go look later. Please, God, don't let them shoot first. . . .*

A rumble of thunder allowed him to guess what they stared at.

"Nobody's due to come though, are they?" Nelson muttered. "You didn't mash the recall too soon, did you?" he asked Joey suspiciously.

"I haven't touched it! Jeez, Nelson, I'm not that stupid!"

"We better find out what's going on over there. I don't like this."

They seemed momentarily to have forgotten Francisco. He prayed with all his strength, hardly daring to hope. Nelson let go of his hair. Then pulled the gun barrel away from his neck. Francisco's breath shuddered out reflexively. *Please . . .*

Nelson paused a moment longer. "Bring the doc along, Joey. We'd better find out what this is before we do him. If it's trouble, we might need him again."

The bitter air seemed momentarily sweeter as Francisco drew it into his lungs. Tears froze against his eyelashes. Then Joey yanked him to his feet. He followed wordlessly on rubberized legs. The imprint of the steel gun muzzle lingered along the back of his neck. He had to scrub at his eyelids to wipe away the crust of ice that had formed.

I'm not out of this yet; it's just a reprieve. . . .

But he was still alive.

They set off across the ice field toward a lowering thunderstorm. Nelson led. Joey followed suspiciously behind Francisco. They were still two hundred yards away when the air split open with a deafening roar. A surge of glowing gas belched out of the rumbling sky. Incandescent gas and ash—the whole mass glowing brilliant yellow, even white—scalded at least a mile along the snow field, melting everything in its path.

All three of them dropped flat to the ice. Francisco shielded his face. He coughed as a stench of sulfur and other noxious fumes reached them. Joey began to swear monotonously. Nelson's vocabulary was more creative.

The explosion of hot gasses cut off abruptly as the now visible time portal shrank and closed. Nelson coughed and cautiously regained his feet. Joey followed, dragging Francisco. The snow was black a hundred yards away from the path of destruction. Francisco stooped curiously and gathered up a mittenful. It *was* ash. And pumice.

"What is it?" Joey asked suspiciously.

"Volcanic debris," Francisco said slowly. "Somebody punched open one of these crazy holes in time during a volcanic eruption."

Nelson began to swear. He ran forward.

What—?

"Bring the doc!" he yelled over his shoulder.

They ran after him, slipping and sliding across slushy black ice, until they hit steaming mud. Francisco saw movement out in the middle of the mess. Nelson had bent down across something alive. *Dear God, something lived through that?* Francisco caught a glimpse of something else moving, farther away, clear of the mud. A lone figure struggled to crawl farther away still.

He moved instinctively toward that person. The person who'd been caught squarely in the center of that blast might be alive, but not for long. Even the best medical care couldn't do much for a victim of *that*. Joey, however, hauled him back. Nelson was yelling for him.

They waded out into steaming muck. Nelson had crouched beside a dead horse and a horribly burned man. Nelson was practically gibbering.

"Keep him alive! It's Tony—oh, Christ, Carreras will have our *heads* if he dies—"

Francisco knelt beside the dying man. There was absolutely nothing he could do to keep this person alive. Tony's skin was black and crusted. If Francisco even tried to move him, that skin would slough off, probably in one piece. His mouth and nostrils were choked with ash. There were at least two stab wounds visible in his torso.

"Even if we had the best burn unit in the world, I couldn't do anything," Francisco protested.

As he spoke, the man died.

Nelson went nuts. First he kicked the corpse and screamed at it, not noticing how skin slid off and the abdomen burst like a fried melon. Then Nelson hit Joey and turned toward Francisco, belting him across the mouth. "You didn't even try!" He pulled the pistol from his belt and pointed it unsteadily at Francisco's head.

"What was I supposed to do? He died before I could even do a tracheotomy! Look at those burns! My God, half his skin slid off when you kicked him! And somebody stabbed him before the volcano blew!"

"What? Who?" Nelson demanded unreasonably.

Mother of God . . .

"I don't know who! Why don't you ask the other person who came through with him?"

Nelson stared around wildly. He spotted the sprawled figure lying inert on mushy ice just clear of the mud and stared uncomprehendingly at it. Without warning, Nelson grabbed Francisco by the lapels. His pistol caught Francisco's jaw. The big man shook him, hard. "You'd better keep this one alive, doc! Or so help me, I'll take a whole *week* killing you!"

Francisco didn't bother to reply, grateful for *any* reason they had to keep him alive. He already dreaded finding the type of injuries he expected. Francisco led the way, half running through slippery, melted muck, then knelt above the other survivor. She was dressed in what appeared to be a genuine ancient Egyptian gown. Whoever she was, she wore a fortune in gold jewelry that could only have been made deep in antiquity. Hair streamed wildly across her face, obscuring bruised features. But he didn't see any burns.

Francisco shucked out of his parka and wrapped her in his coat. He shuddered violently and steeled himself to ignore the fatal cold for as long as he could. Francisco checked rapidly for her vitals, for broken bones. She was relatively unscathed, having crawled sideways from the volcanic blast when she came through. They couldn't keep her out in this cold, though. Francisco was already numb.

"Get us back to shelter!" His teeth chattered so violently he could barely make himself understood.

"Joey, give the doc your parka!"

Joey protested only once, then gave Francisco his parka. The thug began a miserable dance to keep warm.

"I'll carry her," Nelson growled. He bundled her up. Francisco pulled the parka hood down across her face to protect her as best he could from the bitter temperatures.

"Move," Francisco muttered. "Get her inside!"

She stirred, struggled briefly, then sank back into a stupor. They set off for the shelter at a run.

Bill opened the door and gaped. Then stumbled back as Nelson shoved his way through. Francisco followed. Joey moaned for blankets and coffee. Janet and Lucille gave twin shrieks. Francisco managed a weak smile. "Unexpected arrival. They, uh, needed me again. Bring some hot water, Janet, and several blankets."

He followed Nelson into the room where Zac Hughes still slept. Janet rummaged in the next room. Bill said, "Siddown, Collins. You, too, brat."

"Put her onto one of the cots," Francisco instructed. He reached for the medical bag he'd left beside Zac Hughes' cot and pulled out a stethoscope. Her heartbeat was strong and steady. Miraculously, her lungs sounded clear. He didn't see much debris in her nostrils or throat. She was one very lucky lady. He wondered who she was.

He stripped off torn, bloody clothing—and paused fractionally. He glanced up as Janet arrived. "Thanks. Bring some clean towels, please. And I want Lucille's help on this one. When this lady comes around, she's not going to be very trusting of anyone male. Nelson, get out of my way."

He examined the unconscious woman minutely. She hadn't been out in the weather long enough to sustain frostbite. Her pupils reacted well and her reflexes were normal. Her face and body bore ugly bruises and her back was badly marred from what looked like a rope whip. Somebody had very recently raped her.

She moaned and began to stir.

"Janet! Lucille! I may need you in here real fast! She's going to be scared to death. . . ."

Both women skidded in and hunkered down anxiously. "Why?" Lucille asked breathlessly. "What's wrong?" She saw the bruises, the ugly abrasions. "Dear God."

Janet swallowed hard.

"My God. Poor, poor girl . . ."

Francisco dragged a blanket up just as her eyelids fluttered open. She moaned softly and tried, without much success, to focus on his face. She seemed deeply confused, her dazed, searching gaze touching Francisco's face, then Lucille's, finally Janet's.

Then she saw Nelson in one corner. Her gaze sharpened from confusion to certainty—and hatred the likes of which Francisco had never witnessed. She half lunged, half fell out of bed, fingers curved to strike, and banged straight into Nelson, which saved her from falling. She didn't seem to notice. It wasn't much of an attack, but she did manage to scratch his face pretty badly and just missed gouging an eye.

Nelson yelled, then struck with a fist the size of a baseball glove. It connected brutally. She sprawled back against the army cot, which collapsed under the force of her landing.

She didn't try to get up again, just hissed out, "You stinking *murderer*! I'll kill you, I swear it!"

Nelson's eyes darkened as he reached for his gun.

Nelson'll kill her! Francisco jumped forward, managed to put himself between her and the enraged guard. Francisco heard Janet yelling . . .

Confused shouts and crashes reached his awareness as he stared down the enormous hole in the end of the .357 Magnum's barrel.

"Get away from her," Nelson snarled.

"Why? So you can shoot her? Forget it."

A thick finger tightened down ever so slightly on the trigger. Nelson's expression was beyond description; his eyes were alight with something so unholy it made Francisco's skin crawl.

An enormous crash and shouts from the outer room distracted both men. Nelson and Francisco glanced as one to focus on a struggle out in the main room. Bill had grappled Danny, Jr. and discovered he'd grabbed more than he'd bargained for. Lucille picked up a chair and hit Bill across the back of the head with it. Danny, Jr. launched himself at Joey's back. The boy clung like a leech while tearing at the man's eyes and face with clawed fingers.

Nelson strode into the thick of it and fired a series of gunshots. They blasted deafeningly in the confined space. Everybody froze. Nelson stood in the center of the room, holding a machine gun. Holes pierced the ceiling. Freezing air seeped through. Nelson glared impartially at everyone, then pointed his rage at the newcomer. He took two steps back into their room, snatched Francisco aside, and backhanded the half-crouched girl savagely. She sprawled across the upturned army cot and slid to a stop against Lucille.

Lucy dropped to her knees to cradled the woman protectively. "You stinking *animal*!"

"Shut up, Collins!"

Joey managed to dump Danny onto the floor. Bill was still out cold.

"That"—Nelson pointed at the groggy girl in Lucille's arms—"is the woman we sent back in time to die! Tony was supposed to kill her. Little whore got him killed instead!"

He raised the machine gun muzzle and pointed the weapon at her. "I don't need *two* Collins hostages, lady. Move away, or I'll shoot both of you."

"Nelson—" Francisco tried to intervene.

The bastard didn't even turn around.

"Dammit, Nelson, listen to me!" He lurched forward,

dared to grab Nelson's gun arm. "Answer this: Was Tony supposed to come here? After he killed this girl?"

That got his attention. "What? No."

"Then why did they come through *here*? Into *this* time?"

Nelson paused. Frown lines jumped into existence across his thick face.

"If you don't know, then Carreras will want to talk to her. Obviously something went wrong. Something your boss will want lots of answers about. Answers *you* can't give him."

Nelson glanced at him. "And you figure she's in bad enough shape, we'll need you to keep her alive?" He laughed nastily. "Nice try, doc." The machine gun barrel now pointed solidly at Francisco's midsection.

Francisco shrugged with a profound air of nonchalance he didn't feel at all. He hoped Nelson couldn't see how badly his knees wobbled. "Okay, Nelson. Don't say I didn't warn you." He held Nelson's gaze steadily. "You said yourself heads would roll if Tony died." He gestured toward the sprawled woman. "Go ahead. Kill the only witness who can tell Carreras what happened." He managed a nasty grin of his own. "I hope you like it here, Nelson. My guess is, you won't be leaving. Ever."

Nelson just scowled. He finally spat at Joey, "Fix that stupid roof. You"—he fixed Lucille with an icy stare—"get that bitch back in bed. Tie her down if you have to, doc. Next time, I *will* shoot her. And you with her."

Francisco began breathing again. He became aware of Janet's shoulder just behind his, grazing him in the slightest of contacts.

"Are you okay?" she whispered.

"Yeah. You?"

"Peed on myself," she whispered shakily, "but I'm okay."

Francisco took a deep breath. "Why don't you go clean up a little, change into dry clothes if you've got spares, then come back here."

She nodded, scooped up a gym bag from one corner, and headed for the open-doored bathroom.

"Let's see if I can get one of these cots turned back over," he muttered, righting the one the unknown girl had sprawled across.

Lucille was struggling to lift the semiconscious woman. He helped haul the girl to her feet, then together they lowered her into the bed. Janet reappeared in record time, now wearing black cords instead of jeans.

Out in the main room, Bill groaned. Hammering reached them distantly from the roof. Nelson yelled, "Doc, come look at Bill's head. *Now.*"

"Lucille, would you help Janet bathe this young lady while I take care of my other patient, please?" He paused long enough to add, "By the way, good shot with that chair, Lucy."

"Dan always did say I swung a mean baseball bat." She almost managed a smile as she said it.

Francisco reluctantly stepped out to the main room and squatted beside Bill. That worthy was swearing nonstop. A lump had grown to amazing proportions on the back of his head. "How many fingers do you see?" Francisco asked, holding up two.

"Effin' four of 'em," Bill snarled.

Francisco prodded cautiously.

"Ow—dammit—effin' head's killin' me—gonna break that bitch's neck—"

Francisco prodded a little harder than was called for. Bill yowled and squeezed shut his eyes over involuntary tears.

"He's suffered a concussion," Francisco told Nelson shortly. Then lied. "I think I can also feel a skull fracture, although without an X-ray, it's hard to tell for sure. There could be multiple hairline cracks I can't detect in addition to the crack I *can* feel."

Nelson swore. Bill fell unnaturally quiet.

"How serious is it?" Nelson wasn't so inhumanly cold this time. He sounded worried.

"He should be kept flat on his back for at least two

days. Otherwise, he'll end up vomiting all over himself and the rest of us. If there's a serious hematoma on the brain itself, he may be bleeding internally. Again, I can't tell without an X-ray.

"He's got a foul headache right now because of the bruising. If it's serious enough that the brain swells too much against the skull cavity, he may lose consciousness. Or motor function, speech and sight . . . he might even die. It all depends what area of the brain is affected most seriously. Blood can leak from one area and put pressure elsewhere."

Bill had gone positively chalky. Francisco worked hard to keep the corners of his lips from twitching. *Bastards. Serves 'em right.*

Nelson was very quiet, as well. "I want you to keep a close watch on him, doc. You understand me? If he gets bad, we'll take him back to the base."

Francisco shrugged. "If you can. Looks to me like Tony didn't plan to end up here, either, but here's where he ended."

Nelson thinned his lips, narrowed his eyes to mere slits. "I don't like this. Not one damn bit," Nelson muttered, eying Francisco suspiciously.

"It doesn't matter whether you enjoy it or not. I'm the only doctor you've got. If you want this asshole to pull through, you'd better make *damned* certain nothing happens to me."

Francisco didn't have time to dodge the blow. Nelson's fist connected with the pit of his belly. Francisco landed in a crumpled heap on the floor, retching.

"Sure, doc," Nelson drawled. "Just so long as you remember who's in charge. Now get busy."

Francisco caught his breath over a groan, then dragged himself back into the improvised sickroom. Nelson followed, manhandling Bill carefully onto one of the cots. A moment later, the unfortunate Bill began vomiting over the side of his bed. Nelson appeared to be coping, so Francisco yanked another of the cots over and sat down on it.

The young woman who'd fallen through the open time portal had regained consciousness. Her face was pale beneath bruises. Green eyes had narrowed, mirroring deep suspicion. Francisco received the distinct impression her thoughts were moving so fast, her brain was probably smoking. Lucille had dressed her in someone's nightgown and pulled a couple of blankets over her.

"How are you feeling?" he asked quietly.

"Rotten, thank you."

"I don't doubt it. Janet, hand me that stuff, would you?" He gestured toward the open medical bag. She hoisted it across and set it down beside him. He rummaged for a moment. "This is going to sting like the blazes for a couple of minutes."

He wiped her split lip with an alcohol swab and was surprised when she controlled a flinch. She blinked a little rapidly and watched like a tigress as he applied antibiotic cream. The look in her eyes was impossible to interpret. "If you'll turn over, I'll do your back."

She studied him through slitted eyes, then turned over without a word. Francisco eased back the blanket and nightgown. Lucille's breath caught.

"My God . . ."

"This," Francisco warned softly, "is going to hurt like a bitch."

She just nodded. A tiny sound escaped her; other than that, the only reaction was a tightened grip on the cot frame. Francisco had seen hardened troopers blubber over less serious injuries. He dealt quietly with the appalling welts and carefully bandaged them, then gave her an injection for pain.

"That ought to help in a couple of minutes." He paused. "I'll need to check you internally for injury. I don't have an evidence kit with me."

An odd sound escaped her. Francisco was horrified when he identified it as choked laughter.

"No problem." Her voice was as hard as the icy ground outside. "Bastard's dead."

Tony Bartlett?

Francisco didn't have a speculum, either, which made his examination more difficult and considerably more painful, but they got through it. Again, she didn't make a sound.

"Sorry," he murmured.

She didn't answer. Francisco finished as gently as possible. Lucille, on the other side of the bed, was pale as wax. Janet was biting her lips.

"There. All done. I don't think you've suffered any internal hemorrhaging, thank God." He eased the gown over her hips and checked her pulse. It had dropped back down into the normal range. *Good.* They carefully turned her over again and pulled up the blankets.

When they'd done what they could, Francisco noticed that her face had closed in a dark, shuttered look that hurt to witness. "Who are you?" Her voice was low, hard.

"Francisco Valdez. Major in the U.S. Army Surgeons' Corps. And currently, a prisoner scared half out of my wits."

Her eyes widened just slightly, then her glance darted over to Nelson. Then rested briefly on Lucille and Janet in turn before returning to him.

Francisco said as steadily as he could, "I owe you my life, by the way. They were in the process of shooting me when you came sprawling through that portal so abruptly."

She studied him. He held her gaze. She seemed to notice for the first time the bruises and cuts on his own face.

"I'm sorry. I thought . . ." She shook her head. "Never mind what I thought. I can see I was wrong. Where am I?"

"Alaska."

She eyed him warily. "When?"

Janet drew in a sharp breath. Whoever she was, this lady was quick.

"Um, about 28,000 B.C., I think. I haven't been here very long, either."

She didn't even blink. "Wonderful. That puts us, what, right in the middle of the last Pleistocene glacial?"

Janet whistled appreciatively. "More or less. You, um, do this sort of thing often?"

She gave Janet a sharp stare. Then laughed harshly. "No." She tried to sit up, then groaned, instead, and sagged back again. "Dammit . . ."

"Take it easy," Francisco cautioned. But he was careful *not* to restrain her with even a touch of his hand. "You'll be sore for a while, even with the Demerol I just gave you. If you move around too much, you'll break open those weals again."

She shot a venomous glare at Nelson's back. "If I live so long."

Lucille murmured, "Frank bought you some time. He convinced our guards Carreras will want to talk to you about Tony's death."

The young woman stared at Lucille, then shuddered and squeezed shut her eyes. "Great. Just peachy. Thanks a whole bunch. I think I'd rather have been shot."

"You've met Carreras?" Francisco asked.

She shook her head. "No. But somebody . . . really nice . . ." Tears squeezed out from beneath her closed lashes.

Francisco wondered what kind of horror it would take to reduce this very tough little lady to tears.

Lucille squeezed her shoulder gently. "Go ahead and cry, hon, it's all right to cry now. . . ."

Francisco felt helpless as the girl turned and sobbed in Lucille's arms. She clung to the older woman's blouse like a child and hid her face. Janet turned away, her own cheeks wet. Francisco rummaged through the contents of his bag, but found nothing remotely resembling a sedative. It was Demerol, surgical anesthetic, or nothing.

Francisco didn't want to waste the surgical supplies unless it were a dire emergency—like drugging the guards and finding out where they kept their recall device. Gradually the young woman's sobs quieted. She lay still in Lucille's arms for a while longer, then slowly pulled herself together again.

"I'm sorry," she whispered. "I hate snively women . . ."

Lucille dried the girl's face with a corner of the blanket and smiled warmly. "Somehow I don't think this qualifies as snivelling."

The uncertain look she gave Lucille tore at Francisco's heart.

"Who are all you people?" she asked, still sniffling. "And what are you doing in Alaska in 28,000 B.C.? Besides being hostages, I mean."

Lucy's eyes widened. "Good Lord, girl, you're quick for somebody in as much pain as you are."

The young woman shrugged it off, winced and found a more comfortable position. "You didn't answer my question."

"My name is Lucille Collins. You've met Frank. This is Janet Firelli. My son Danny is out in the kitchen getting some dinner together for us. That little boy over there is Zac Hughes. His appendix was almost ready to burst this morning. That's why they brought Frank through in the first place. When they thought they didn't need him anymore . . ." Her voice faltered.

Janet said harshly, "They took him outside to shoot him. Next thing we know, they're back with you. Then all hell sort of broke loose." She scowled at the guards. "*That* creep is Nelson. One of Carreras' men. They keep switching off our guards so none of 'em start sympathizing too much with us."

Nelson just grunted. Then stalked out of the room, bellowing for Joey. The slim girl watched him go through slitted eyes. "Yes. I've met *him* before, although I didn't know his name. He and Tony drugged me. They dropped me into a place and time I shouldn't have lived through." She shivered. "I got lucky."

Janet closed her hand over the girl's. "Our other guard, there, the one with the lump on his head, is Bill. We never know their last names. Anyway, Lucille hit him over the head with a chair during the confusion."

The girl stared at Lucille. Then grinned. Her whole face lit up. For just a moment, her eyes sparkled and Francisco realized she was *beautiful*. "Way to go!" she said happily. "*Anything* we do to 'em, they deserve. And then some."

"Anyway," Lucille added, "Joey's up on the roof plugging the holes Nelson shot into it. Joey's our other guard."

"Well, that tells me who all of you are," she said, "but it doesn't answer why you're hostages. Unless, of course, idiot, it's got to do with the time travel thing Carreras is into, doesn't it? Why you people, specifically?"

Everybody hesitated.

Lucille finally said, "Yes, we're hostages. My husband is the chief military officer and engineer on a classified project. Carreras runs it now. Janet's mother and Zac's grandfather are the head physicists."

"I wondered about that," she mused. "So did . . ." She paled. "Never mind."

Francisco wondered who had died. And why she seemed to want to keep that person's identity secret.

"My name's Sibyl," she said at length. "Sibyl Johnson. Tony Bartlett . . . Well, I'm not sure if that was his real last name or not, since Interpol couldn't trace it. He used me as a scapegoat to steal some antiquities from a dig at Herculaneum, one of the cities Vesuvius buried in A.D. 79."

Francisco's blood chilled. "*That's* what blasted through the portal?"

She nodded grimly. "I was a graduate student in anthropology. Tony used me as a front to locate the stuff in the present, then kidnapped me and used me as payment to buy the stuff in the past. Then left me to die."

"So you're the one who stabbed him?" Francisco asked quietly.

She stared.

"He came through with you, on a horse. You crawled off to the side and got clear. He went down right in the middle of it. He didn't live long."

Unholy joy lit her green eyes.

Francisco looked away. "It wasn't a pretty sight."

Her voice was icy. "I hope he died hard. *Real* hard."

"He did. He was still alive when we got to him."

She turned her face away. "Sorry if it shocks you," she muttered.

Unexpectedly, Lucille said, "Don't apologize. And it doesn't shock me."

Sibyl groped for and squeezed her hand. Janet reached out and squeezed her shoulder in silent support.

Francisco decided the time was right to go check on Danny. His background had not quite prepared him for what he'd just witnessed in these women. Francisco realized Sibyl Johnson wasn't the only one who had recently lost a certain innocence. He wondered whether it was a loss worth mourning.

God help Carreras if those three ever got hold of him. Given his own near brush with death, that was something he'd give a great deal to see.

CHAPTER NINETEEN

For one, awful moment, Dan Collins thought McKee would shoot him out of hand. He didn't go crazy wild. He just went very still, with the silent deadliness of a viper poised to strike. He stared down at Dan, eyes narrowed. His fingers tightened slightly on the M16 he'd been holding casually trained on Dan's belly. . . .

Then he was moving, almost faster than Dan could follow. He grabbed Dan by the front of his parka and hauled him to his feet, then grunted and heaved him up into a fireman's carry. Dan's breath whistled out sharply. His aching head spun. He landed in a heap sideways on the passenger's seat of the truck and lay still. At least McKee hadn't left him to freeze to death in the snow. . . .

McKee climbed behind the wheel and slammed the door shut, then propped the M16s between himself and the door. Dan grimaced. Did McKee think he could take the stupid things away from him and use them? With his hands manacled behind him?

The knowledge he'd failed at his one pitiful chance threatened to crush him. Lucille and Danny and the others would die because this madman had gotten the drop on him—or, rather, the drop-kick. Dan didn't feel much like splitting hairs at the moment. The truck lurched into motion. Lightning sprayed madly all around. McKee gunned the engine and sent the truck plunging forward.

Without warning, Dan felt as though he were falling. He clenched his teeth. *I've been through this before, it lasts only a moment.* A long *moment.* . . . Invasive white light he couldn't escape, even with his eyes squeezed tightly shut, blinded him. He couldn't hear the truck. Having his hands manacled helplessly behind him only worsened the gut-wrenching sensations.

Then solid ground reached up and slammed against the wheels. Dan yelled. He was thrown violently forward. He landed against the dash with rib-cracking force and slid helplessly onto the floor, jammed in sideways. He groaned, then bashed his head again as McKee stood on the brakes. The lunatic sent the truck fishtailing across a shifting, unsteady surface. Heartfelt oaths reached him as McKee fought the wheel. . . .

Then, blessedly, the truck skidded to a halt and stopped bashing Dan around like a pea in a pinball machine. McKee swore again, then the big maniac threw open the door and jumped out. Something hard slammed into the steel roof. Muggy air blasted in through the open door. Muggy, hot, and foul beyond belief. Hellish, unidentifiable noise bombarded his ears. Dan coughed and tried to squirm around into a sitting position. He could barely move.

Then McKee was back, yanking open the passenger door. The look on his face sent Dan's blood pressure into the stratosphere. McKee seized him and bodily hauled him clear of the truck, with no regard whatsoever for Dan's head, knees, or feet. He grunted, then he was stumbling in sand. He blinked and tried to focus. McKee swore monotonously in his ear. Something which was neither rain nor hail nor snow pelted down steadily from utterly black skies: *pebbles*, some of them glowing. . . .

McKee dragged him around the fender of the truck and pointed wordlessly across maddened surf. The truck's headlights cut a swath through the murk, revealing a harbor crowded with stone jetties, piers built over arches, tall, graceful columns. . . .

Beyond, riding at anchor on an endless stretch of black water, was an entire flotilla of Roman triremes.

"Where the goddamned hell are we, Collins?" McKee shouted. "You lying son-of-a—"

"I don't know! This was supposed to be Krakatoa the day before the big eruption! The Firellian Transfer didn't work!" He heard the panic in his own voice and didn't bother to disguise it. "I don't know where *or* when we are!"

McKee outdid his previous vocabulary. Some of it didn't even sound like English. He ended with, "What do we do now?"

"I don't know. We can try the second jump—"

"And end up on the backside of the moon?" McKee interrupted caustically.

"—but since the first one went wrong, we could very *well* end up on the backside of the moon. Firellian Jumps are damned dangerous. And with the time stream slipping already . . ."

McKee's jaw worked. Then he spat. "Great. Just great, Collins. Marooned God knows where and we don't even dare try to get home—"

He grunted sharply.

Then slid to the ground.

Dan stared, slack-jawed, at a nearly naked man. He'd managed to creep up silently behind McKee, without either of them noticing. He held a fist-sized rock in one hand.

"You okay?" the astonishing apparition asked.

In English.

Dan blinked. He'd spoken *English*. New Jersey English. Twentieth-century New Jersey American English. Involuntarily Dan glanced again at the triremes, then back. He focused on the man's horribly bruised face. Noted with some shock the misshapen burn scar on his neck, the thick metal collar which half obscured that scar, then noticed a welter of other bruises and older scars. The man wore nothing but a loincloth and improvised bandages around his ribcage.

"Uh—yeah," Dan said, intelligently. "I'm fine . . ." He blinked and managed to add, "Who the hell are you?"

Whoever he was, he'd stooped over McKee. He was busily rifling the man's pockets. He came up holding the manacle key. "Somebody else who got marooned, obviously," he answered unhelpfully. He unlocked Dan's wrists, then began stripping McKee of weapons. "Who are you?"

"Dan Collins." Dan was shucking off his arctic-weather parka as fast as he could. Sweat had pooled under his shirt. What looked and felt like ash rained down steadily. An occasional large rock fell from the sky and impacted hotly on the sand. Lightning from the time storm still blasted through the air, although the doorway itself had already closed.

The stranger glanced up briefly from looting McKee's pockets. Dan saw a quick gleam of white teeth. "Nice to meet you, Dan Collins. What'd you do to merit execution?"

Dan sucked in air between his teeth. Who *was* this guy? "I take it somebody sent you here to die?"

He snorted. "Something like that."

"Carreras?"

The man went utterly still. Then finished his search and straightened up. He seemed perfectly at home with the rifle in his hand as he checked the chamber and magazine. "And if it was Carreras?"

Dan managed a wan grin. "Then you're one lucky son." He didn't elaborate. This guy would figure it out once McKee woke up, but in the interim, Dan had an ally. And he *needed* allies.

"How so?"

"There's a tremendous chance we won't live through it, but we're going after Jésus Carreras. At least I am. Two members of his goon squad are locked up in the back of the truck."

That earned him a sharp glance. "*What?* Show me."

He moved ahead of Dan, dragging one nearly useless leg behind him. A clearly handmade brace should have stiffened it, but one side had broken and hung in splinters. Dan bit off an exclamation. The scars on that leg . . . The man's spine went rigid. When Dan kept his mouth shut, he seemed to relax again.

Christ—what had this man been through?

The stranger limped awkwardly to the rear of the truck. Dan opened the doors with a cautious, "They might be awake."

They weren't. Dan retrieved his flashlight and played the light across them.

"I don't know that one," the stranger mused. "Him, I recognize. Richie or Ricky, something like that. He was one of the ones who brought me through."

The stranger shot Ricky through the temple. Dan jumped nearly out of his skin. He shot the other one while Dan was still reeling, then turned and offered Dan the other rifle.

"Two down."

Dan's ears still rang from the concussion of the shots. The stench of gunpowder, blood, and human brain overpowered even the stink in the sulfurous air. His hands shook when he accepted the weapon. He'd never actually seen anyone die before. . . .

The stranger began to limp toward McKee, who still lay sprawled in the sand.

Oh, shit—

Dan sprang forward as the man raised his rifle to fire. At the same moment, McKee shook his head groggily and opened his eyes. The fallen lunatic stared up at the rifle trained on his forehead. Dan slammed desperately into the man holding that rifle. The blow knocked off his aim—

The shot ripped into the sand two inches to the right of McKee's head. Whoever he was, the stranger snarled and came up fighting.

He fought *dirty*.

Dan grunted, got in a punch to the solar plexus—

McKee's boot connected with Dan's ribs. Another kick caught the stranger on the point of the shoulder. A third sent his rifle spinning away across the sand.

"*Halt!*" McKee thundered. He'd retrieved Dan's

9mm semiauto. The unwinking muzzle refused compromise.

They rolled apart. Dan blinked grit and ash out of his eyes and wondered a little hysterically what came next.

McKee spoke first. "Collins," he grunted reluctantly, with a darting glance in Dan's direction, "I owe you my life. And that surprises the living shit out of me. I really didn't believe you."

"Great. You're welcome."

McKee turned a glare on the man who'd just tried to shoot him. Dan noted with grim satisfaction that McKee had the pistol trained on someone else for a change.

"Now just who are you?" McKee demanded.

Instead of answering, the battered, nearly naked man stared from McKee to Dan and back. "Will somebody please tell me what hell is going on?"

"Logan Pfeiffer McKee," Dan said drily, glancing at the escaped madman who held that 9mm steadily in his direction, "meet another one of Carreras' victims." He gestured toward the nearly naked man crouched nearby. "He hasn't bothered to tell me his name. Not that I blame him. If I were in his shoes, that is, if he had any, I wouldn't be too trusting, either."

The men studied one another. The stranger said to McKee, "If you're supposed to be Carreras' victim, how come you had this guy cuffed?"

McKee gave him a bark of laughter. "What would you do if you got the drop on one of Carreras' hired killers?"

"Shoot him."

The calm answer clearly startled McKee.

"He shot both guards through the head, McKee," Dan offered. "Didn't even wake them up first."

McKee's glance at the stranger was piercing. "Did you, now? And logically thought I was one of them. Thanks for saving me till last." He nodded toward Dan. "Carreras ordered this guy to kill me."

The scarred stranger shook his head. "You just lost me again, pal. If he's one of Carreras' men, why didn't he just shoot both of us? I gave him a rifle," he added brusquely, with a dark glance toward Dan.

"Yeah, well, it isn't real clear to me, either," McKee muttered. McKee rubbed grit out of his hair. "Look, buddy, I don't know much about what's going on, so there isn't much I can tell you. My name's Logan McKee, like the colonel, here, said. I'm nobody special, just an escaped lunatic who found out too much about Carreras by accident. This guy is Colonel Dan Collins, in charge of this whole mixed up time-travel mess."

The stranger shot Dan an intent stare.

McKee was still talking. "He claims his family and a bunch of other people are being held hostage. I didn't believe him. Now I'm not so sure. He did keep you from shooting me. Like you say, I don't figure he'd have done that if he was one of Carreras' men."

"*Hostages?*" the stranger repeated. "Jesus H— No wonder . . ." He focused on Dan's face. Then glanced at McKee. "I don't know what he told you, McKee, but I'd be inclined to believe him. Carreras *does* have hostages. I've seen the list of names. Somebody called Firelli"— both McKee and Dan started—"and some kid named Zac Hughes, and a woman and her son." He swung on Dan. "Collins. Their names were Collins. Lucille and Danny."

Dan asked very quietly, "How do you know that?"

The stranger hesitated. Then his face closed into something completely unreadable. "I've had a few business dealings with Carreras. Snooped into some things I didn't expect to find."

Dan began to sweat again. "Mister, what you know about us is not only one of the most classified military secrets in history, it's also enough to get a whole lot of innocent people killed. And we don't know jack shit about you."

The stranger just grinned, a red-haired imp in the light from the truck's headlamps. "Good. I think I like it that way. You can," he added, "call me Charlie."

"Well, Charlie," McKee said dryly, still holding the rifle, "would you mind at least telling us where we are? We weren't supposed to end up here at all."

Charlie's brows dove together. "That's very interesting, gentlemen. Very interesting, indeed. No wonder you were arguing so intently."

McKee grimaced and muttered under his breath.

Charlie laughed aloud. "You don't know how good that makes me feel, McKee. I haven't exactly had a good year—"

"A *year?*" Dan gasped.

Charlie darted him a surprised glance. "Well, actually, it's been four. But the past year was, in some ways, the worst. *You're* the hotshot engineer, Collins. Can't you see it? Time on *this end* is completely irrelevant. For all I know, back home it's the same day Carreras' crew dumped me here to die. Or maybe that was twenty years ago. Or fifty years from now. Time on this end doesn't mean a thing."

Dan shook his head. "No, it can't have been more than four months. They haven't had access to the equipment longer than that."

Charlie's glance was keen. "That so? Good. Then they're still learning."

Dan shuddered. "Yes."

"Well." He seemed to shake off some impenetrable thought process, then glanced at McKee. "To answer your question, you're standing on the beachfront near the spa town of Stabiae, on the southeastern edge of the Bay of Naples, sometime on the morning after Vesuvius blew up. The year's, uh, A.D. 79, the way *we* count years. That"—he pointed off inland, into the heart of the black ashfall—"is Vesuvius. That"—he pointed across the bay at the triremes—"is the Roman Navy, which tried to get to Herculaneum and Pompeii last night to rescue survivors." His voice darkened. "They didn't make it. *We* almost didn't. We got out of Herculaneum harbor right ahead of the eruption." Something in his voice made Dan's skin crawl.

McKee's keen insight startled Dan. "Who *didn't* make it out, Charlie?"

Charlie turned away from them. He stared across the dark water. Ash settled blackly across his shoulders and hair and scarred back. "Another of Carreras' victims." After a moment, he added, "She's the only reason I'm alive now. She knew the eruption was coming and warned me. . . ."

Dan shut his eyes.

Charlie added with a growl, "Look, let me get my kid. Then let's get the hell *out* of here. If that's all right with you?"

Dan turned his head to see a child huddled on the beach sand. He hadn't even noticed. Evidently, neither had McKee, from the surprise in his eyes. Charlie picked up a little girl who couldn't have been a year old and carried her back toward the truck. Her hair, in the glow of the headlights, was a bright red-gold. Her eyes were wide and scared. Charlie hugged her close.

"If it hadn't been for Lucky, here, I'd have stayed and kept looking," Charlie said quietly.

Dan didn't know what to say. McKee holstered the pistol. "Letting yourself be killed never stops the enemy, Charlie. They just keep on killing as long as civilized pansies let them."

The look Charlie shot McKee was dark and deadly. "Watch your mouth, McKee."

The lunatic held his gaze. "You know I'm right."

"So how *do* we find Carreras?" Charlie asked. His voice was anything but civilized.

The naked brutality in Charlie's eyes shook Dan to the core. Clearly, there were several forms of hell worse than the one he'd been living.

"Get into the truck," Dan said quietly. "This'll take about ten, fifteen minutes."

Another time storm was already beginning to rumble when Collins suggested quietly, "Why don't you go around back, Charlie, and salvage some clothes? Boots,

socks, parka, and all. It's going to be colder than a—"
Collins glanced at the wide-eyed little girl watching him
and said, instead, "It's going to cold if we get where we're
trying to go. Bundle up the kid, too."

Charlie nodded. He was grateful neither man followed
him. Lucania drooped across his shoulder, watching
Collins and McKee and even the truck with curiosity.

Modern clothing felt unbelievably alien. The combat
boots were a little snug, but not bad. The trousers felt
oddest of all. He twisted his lips in a wry grimace. It'd
taken *months* to get used to going without them. Now
they felt weird. He shook his head and finished getting
dressed, then snagged both parkas. He bundled up
Lucania in one of them, tying the sleeves shut around
her. Then he swung the truck tailgate shut. Collins and
McKee were staring out at the triremes.

"It's still hard to believe," McKee was saying. "A.D.
79 . . ."

"Be thankful you didn't wake up here in chains,"
Charlie growled. "It's not an experience I'd recommend."

"Where did you injure that leg?" McKee asked quietly.

"In the arena," he answered shortly. His whole manner
said, "Topic is *off limits*."

Collins shivered and looked ill.

Collins, Charlie pegged as a bureaucrat. Good at his
job, probably, or Carreras wouldn't have bothered to keep
him. But not exactly a line officer. McKee . . . McKee
looked like he might possibly understand some of what
Charlie had been through. More than time was etched
into that craggy face.

Neither man pressed him for details. They divvied up
the weapons between them, then stood beside the truck
and watched the time storm brew. The short hairs on
the back of Charlie's neck prickled. He understood, now,
why Sibyl had been so unnerved by sight of the time
storm. He squeezed shut his eyes. *Sibyl* . . .

At least his daughter was safe. As safe as he could
make her. Was he doing the right thing, risking her life

going after Carreras? *Stupid question. Would you rather
keep her here, to grow up as a slave?* When lightning
began crackling down into the beach sand, Collins said,
"Let's be ready for it, shall we?"

They piled into the truck. McKee drove by unspo-
ken consent. The engine, left at idle, had died. McKee
pumped the accelerator and restarted it. Charlie held
his breath until it actually fired up, McKee nursed it
on idle while they waited. Charlie watched ahead while
McKee kept watch inland. Collins watched the big side
mirror. About three minutes later, Collins said, "It's
behind us."

McKee gave the big truck some gas and turned it
around on the narrow beach. The doorway slid eerily
open ahead of them.

"Well," Charlie muttered, "here goes nothing. Pray,
if you believe in anything." He clutched Lucania and
swallowed hard.

The truck roared ahead into the light.

Logan felt like he might possibly be getting used to
this. The disorienting drop through nothingness still
turned his belly inside out, but at least he knew what to
expect. He gripped the steering wheel hard enough to
leave his knuckles white.

The truck jounced.

We're through—

They skidded madly across a slick surface.

"Shit!"

Logan fought the skid and tried to straighten out the
wheels, only to have the truck spin in crazy circles. Charlie
yelled. Collins swore. Logan fought the wheel. He managed to counteract the spin, then *Collins* yelled.

"Look out—!"

They lurched sideways off a low dropoff. The truck
skidded backwards at least five yards, spun around sideways, then slammed into a solid wall of ice. Collins
grunted as he bashed against the door. Charlie fell sideways, ending up in Collins' lap, with a serious threat of

falling all the way to the floorboards. His kid wailed in terror. As Logan threw in the clutch and kept the engine going, Collins managed to rescue Charlie from his dangerous slide and righted him in the seat. A miniature avalanche of brittle snow and ice chunks cascaded across hood and windshield.

The silence that followed was deeply ominous. The only sound outside the truck's engine and the little girl's sobs was a howling wind that rattled through the big truck's frame and shrieked past the doors.

"Well," Collins muttered. "So far so good."

"Oh, really?" Logan sat forward and glared at him past Charlie's shoulder.

Collins shrugged. "We're not on the backside of the moon."

"Yeah," Logan agreed dourly. "I'll give you that, Colonel. At least we've got oxygen to breathe. But where the hell *are* we? There's nothing *out* there. Or hadn't you noticed?"

He punched the windshield wipers to underscore his sour observation. The wipers scraped and groaned across the glass, shoving snow and ice chunks aside. Beyond, Logan saw more snow and ice and a towering mountain off to their right. In the distance, beyond its flank, was another range of mountains and a solid wall of ice at least a mile high.

Where'n hell are we? The heat inside the passenger compartment had vanished as though sucked out through a soda straw. Logan was already shivering. Charlie reached wordlessly for the heater controls and turned up the fan full blast. His little girl sniffled a few more times, then quieted.

"Well," Collins leaned forward, "if this jump worked, then we're back in Alaska. Way back."

Logan tightened his grip on the steering wheel. "Like, say, thirty thousand years back? Where the hostages are?"

Charlie whipped his head around to stare. "Thirty *thousand* years?"

Whoever he was, Charlie could be rattled. Logan

began to feel better. Their mysterious guest unsettled him, and not just because he'd succeeded in bashing Logan over the head.

Collins' jaw came up defensively. "That's how the jump was programmed. I can't change that once it's been set. *If* it even worked right. The last one didn't. We ended up on the other side of the planet and about two thousand years off. Probably because Carreras is screwing around with the time stream so much, slippage is worsening. Was there another time doorway opened anywhere near you recently?"

For some reason, that question drained the blood from Charlie's face. He shut his eyes. "Yeah." It came out raspy, like the wind outside. "At Herculaneum. A few hours ago."

Logan wondered just what had happened on the beach at Herculaneum. Charlie's face was pinched, the cheeks and brow so pale his face looked more like parchment over bone than sun-darkened skin.

Collins saw it, too. He glanced out the window and said quietly, "That's it, then. Slippage opens cracks in the time–space continuum all around a doorway, letting things fall through. Things like McKee. That's how he got mixed up in this. My guess is, the more we use the portals, the more cracks we open, and the more cracks there are, the likelier we are to punch sideways through one of them and end up in the wrong place. Dr. Gudekinst worried about that, early on." He swore softly. "What I wouldn't give to have Sue Firelli along, or Zac Hughes. Maybe one of them could figure out a solution."

"You can't?" Logan asked.

"Me? Hell, no. I'm just an engineer. They're the brains on this project."

"Huh," Charlie said. Collins had given him the time he needed to pull himself together. "Well, I guess I'd rather freeze a free man. . . ." But he tightened his arms around his little girl. "It's possible more than one time doorway was opened near Herculaneum. Tony Bartelli," the name came out knife-edged, "has been there more than once. Probably setting up the scam to get the manuscripts in the first place, then again to kill—"

He clamped his lips shut and said nothing further.

Time to get us out of here, Logan decided. *Get his mind off it and onto this crazy rescue scheme.*

Logan put the truck in gear and eased cautiously away from the ice wall they'd hit. The truck groaned and slid, then settled down to a slow forward crawl. "Which way, Collins?"

"We programmed it to come in from the south, so drive north."

He handed Logan a compass. Logan glanced at it, nodded, and corrected direction.

Collins was studying the terrain. "Looks like we came through on a chunk of detached glacier west of Shoulder Mountain. That should be the mountain directly east." He nodded toward the massif off to their right. "We ought to see the Colleen River pretty soon, frozen solid, of course, but that'll be our guide. We'll follow the Colleen north, toward Table Mountain. If we don't find Table Mountain, or the Colleen, then we didn't make it to the right place."

Logan muttered something appropriate and pressed the gas. They bounced across the rough surface of the glacier. Logan checked the fuel gauge and muttered again. Under half a tank. This place had better not be far. Troop-transport trucks got lousy gas mileage and that terrain didn't look like it'd be much fun to hike across.

He set course by Collins' compass and the sun and picked his way cautiously north. The terrain forced them to backtrack frequently to circumnavigate crevasses and icy hillocks. Their tires didn't have enough traction to climb over, so they had to go around. Fortunately, there *was* a mountain off to the north that Collins said looked a lot like Table Mountain. Logan hoped that boded well. Collins seemed to relax a little, once he'd seen it.

Charlie just sat grimly silent between them and rode

it out. Odd bird, that one. . . . But who was to say he didn't have the right, after what he'd clearly been through? Besides, Logan was legally nuts. Compared to an escaped lunatic, Charlie was probably a normal Joe. Too bad about his leg. And the person who hadn't made it out. Logan felt sorry for this Carreras character already. He grinned. He just hoped he was around for the fireworks when Charlie got his hands on the bastard.

Ought to be fun.

Provided they survived.

It was nearing nightfall and Logan had accumulated a whole battalion of cricks and aches in his back by the time they were close enough for Collins to pick out landmarks. They'd eventually slid off the edge of the glacier, bouncing across a wide gravel moraine before they slipped down onto a snow field that was less densely packed than the ice sheet they'd just left behind. The truck's tires gained more traction, which let them pick up speed.

When they found the Colleen, Dan Collins relaxed another notch and started looking for other landmarks. They followed the frozen river for several crawling hours. Fortunately, her tributaries were frozen so solid, they had no trouble crossing. By now, however, the truck was dangerously low on fuel. Despite the heater, all four of them were stiff and numb from the paralyzing cold. By common assent, they let the little girl hog most of the heat coming out of the truck's vents, which at least helped Charlie a little, because he'd tucked her under his parka, using body heat to help warm her and leaning forward so the vents blew directly across her—and thereby, into his parka.

Dan Collins pointed. "That ridge over there, McKee. Steer for that. I recognize that outcropping. We're not far from the concrete bunker. Five minutes, maybe."

Logan nodded and turned the truck. They skirted a hillock of ice which rose squarely between them and the ridge. *Probably a piece of glacier that broke off. Got left behind when the ice wall retreated.* Logan steered around it, glancing upwards at the landbound iceberg. The thing was the size of a tramp steamer. He caught a glimpse of something moving, just as Charlie yelled.

"Jesus—"

Logan hit the brakes, which sent them skidding again.

"—Christ—"

They slid sideways and slammed into the side of a shaggy animal twice the height of the truck. A bellow of mingled pain and rage shook the whole windshield. Others echoed it. The truck was abruptly engulfed by a whole herd of angry, trumpeting animals.

"*Elephants!*" Logan snarled. "Goddamned elephants!"

Something huge slammed into the back of the truck. The impact threw Logan into the steering column.

"Wrong," Collins gritted. "Get us out of here, McKee. There's a bull mammoth ramming us—"

The truck jarred again. Charlie's kid screamed. Another bull charged from the side and smashed the truck solidly on the right-hand fender. Metal shrieked and crumpled. Logan glimpsed of about twelve feet of curved ivory as yet another bull trumpeted angrily. . . .

The driver's side window shattered. The impact slammed Logan against the steering wheel again. The horn jammed. Its strident noise blared out into the growing darkness. Squeals and trumpetings broke loose. Then the herd moved away, picking up speed as it went.

"They're running!" Charlie gasped. "McKee, they're stampeding right for the ridge. Follow them!"

Logan grinned, ignoring bruises across his sternum. "Roger that!"

Collins just stared.

Logan threw the truck into gear and stomped the gas. They raced after the fleeing mammoths, horn still screaming. The immense beasts broke into a shambling run. Logan glanced once at Charlie. He'd pulled his lips back into a feral grin that matched the hideous scar on his neck.

"Been in this kind of thing before, haven't you?"

"Not exactly," he chuckled. "But closer than Collins, I'll bet."

"I can figure out a diversion when you wave one in front of my nose," Collins muttered. He clung grimly to both dashboard and door to avoid being jounced off the seat or into Charlie. His kid—now that the terrifying crashes had ended and the adults were laughing—squealed and laughed, too.

Cute kid. . . . Collins grinned and tickled her under the chin.

Logan laughed. "You're okay, Collins. I just hope you can shoot as well as you can put together time machines."

"I qualified expert."

"Good. How about you, Charlie?"

"Won't be much good in a running battle, but I can lay a mean covering fire."

"Then keep one of the rifles in the truck and do just that. You'll fight better from here, anyway, with your kid in the truck. Keep her on the floor, under the dash. More metal for any stray bullets to go through. Collins, you and I go in. I'll take the rifle, you take the Beretta and those handguns we took off Carreras' goons. With any luck, that stampede will confuse 'em long enough to get us through the door. Hopefully, we'll do that before they realize we're hitting 'em. Describe this place. In detail."

"I've only been there once," Collins began. He drew a deep breath. "Okay. Four rooms. One main and three small ones off it. The whole thing's laid out in a square about twenty feet on a side. There's one door on the northern exposure, no windows. When you go in, you're in the common room, where the diesel heater is. Straight ahead is the sleeping room, full of army cots. The kitchen is on the right, in back, and there's a small bathroom beside it. None of the doorways have doors on them. I have no idea how many men they'll have posted. I saw four last time."

Logan was impressed. Collins couldn't have been in very good shape during his one visit to this place. Between jump disorientation, the shock of being kidnapped, worry for his family . . . For a desk jockey with no combat experience, Collins had a good eye for detail. Of course, he'd probably been mapping out this rescue attempt for months.

Logan said only, "How many hostages?"

"Four that I know of."

Logan nodded. "Okay. They may have somebody outside to investigate this stampede or to keep watch. In this weather, I doubt it, but Carreras seems like a thorough sort."

Charlie snorted. "You said a mouthful."

"Let's hope the stampede drives 'em all inside. If it does, we shouldn't have to worry about snipers. Charlie, if there are any, they're your responsibility."

"Right."

"Collins, I'm more experienced at this than you are. Cover my back and shoot anything that shoots back."

"Got it."

"Good. If anybody screws up," he added cheerfully, "then probably we all die. Including the hostages."

Nobody said anything.

Logan sent the truck full tilt after the stampeding mammoth herd. He grinned. Then bellowed out the theme from *Rawhide*. "Movin', movin', movin', keep them mammoths movin'—"

Charlie gave one snort of laughter. "Lunatic."

"That's what they tell me."

Collins just grunted.

Up ahead, the shaggy brown wall parted. The stampede flowed around a low, squat obstacle. The glare of headlights picked out a dingy concrete-slab structure. Logan laughed out loud, earning dour glances from Charlie and from Collins. He waggled his eyebrows and laughed again. He hadn't felt this good since the early days in Ethiopia.

"Hold onto your butts, gentlemen. Here goes nothing."

CHAPTER TWENTY

Francisco was just about to call the others for dinner when Danny cocked his head to one side.

"Major Valdez? What's that sound? I can feel it right through the floor."

He listened. "I don't know. I can't hear any—" Francisco paused. There *was* a sound. Low, rumbling, like ... thunder? Somebody else coming through?

The outer door slammed open with a blast of icy air. Joey yelled, "Stampede!"

Nelson roared to his feet. *"What?"*

"Mammoths! Crazy, stupid elephants are headed right for us!"

Nelson swore. "What spooked *them?* Doc, you and the kid, get into the back. *Now.*"

"Come on, Danny. Let's go."

Nelson herded them into the makeshift sickroom. "Bill," Nelson growled, "you're in no shape, but Joey and I are gonna be busy for a while. Keep these people covered."

Nelson dragged him into a sitting position against the wall. Bill groaned. The pistol Nelson gave him shook in his hands.

Mother of— Nelson's a fool. Bill can't even see us without double images. He'll blow a hole through one of us by accident.

Francisco edged his way between the concussed guard and the women. Danny glanced curiously at him, then tightened his lips and manfully followed suit. Francisco had to swallow hard.

"Don't nobody move," Bill groaned. "Sit."

Francisco said quietly, "Lucille, I want you and Janet and Sibyl to sit in that corner over there. Janet, take Zac with you."

They moved. Bill squinted at them, evidently trying to decide which of the double images he was seeing was the ghost and which was real.

"Danny," Francisco said, when he was satisfied with the women's position, "drag that cot over here and sit down behind it, on the floor."

He obeyed. That got the women, Zac, and Danny out of the direct line of fire from the open doorway—just in case Bill decided to start shooting at ghosts. Or mammoths. There wasn't much he could do about Bill and his pistol.

"Siddown," Bill muttered.

He sat. On the floor between Bill and the others.

Then he just waited and listened. The rumble grew into a thundering wall of sound. Occasional blasts from trumpeting mammoths reminded him of old Tarzan movies. The floor shook. His medical bag vibrated on one of the cots.

The stampede swamped across them. Francisco braced. He realized he was waiting for something to crash right into the building. The door slammed open, causing him to jump. Bill fumbled the pistol on his lap, then regained control of it. Nelson and Joey retreated into the shelter in white-faced terror. Francisco caught a glimpse of massive shapes moving in the near-darkness outside.

Then the rumbling stampede was past.

For an instant, Francisco's ears registered another, incongruously loud sound in the darkness.

Nelson blinked—

A low, black shape hurtled in through the partially open doorway. It opened fire. Bill yelled and started shooting wildly. Somebody screamed. Francisco launched toward Bill and his gun. Hot pain flashed through his ribs. A brutal kick caught his side. Then he was grappling with Bill. Gunshots ripped through the main room.

Lucille screamed, "Janet!"

Bill's fingers tightened down across the trigger. Five shots blasted out of the muzzle. A shrill scream cut off behind him. Francisco twisted. He rammed an elbow into the guard's face. Bone crunched with a shocking sound. Francisco smashed his elbow into Bill's nose again and again. The bastard finally went limp.

It's over. . . . Relief swept through him, followed instantly by intense, gut-churning nausea. Francisco retched, then tried unadvisedly to get up. He retched again, bringing up clear fluid. *C'mon, doctor, someone was hit, got to find out what's happened. . . .* He sagged forward, instead, and fought the topsy-turvy rebellion in his gut. Wet, sticky pain clogged his side. Dimly, he saw Danny, Jr. huddled over his mother.

"Danny . . ." he tried to say.

Something dark loomed above him.

"Don't move!"

The voice was male, angry, scared . . .

Francisco couldn't have moved, even if he'd wanted. So he didn't. Whoever it was, they rolled him onto his back. An involuntary cry broke from his lips. Then he blinked groggily up at Dan Collins.

"Dan . . ."

"Frank?"

From across the room came a single, explosive syllable.

"DAD!"

Dan vanished from view.

Francisco tried to lever himself onto one elbow. Vertigo seized him, but the room steadied down after a moment. The sight that greeted him left Francisco cold. Janet Firelli lay sprawled against the base of the wall. Lucille was down, too, dead or unconscious. Danny, Jr. was crying. Dan had huddled down beside his wife. He was searching for a pulse.

Francisco grunted against pain and dragged himself up. "Dan—give me a hand—"

Dan Collins' face was ashen. His friend hauled him

bodily across the room, without regard for his cry of pain.

"She's alive, Frank, she's still alive. . . ." Tears clogged his voice.

"Gimme the kit." His hands were badly unsteady. "Janet?"

Her voice, whispery soft, said, "I'm okay. Just winged me, is all, nothing but a scratch. Lucille's hurt bad."

A bullet had struck Lucille high in the chest. The exit wound had missed her spine by an inch. The bullet had dislocated her shoulder blade two inches outward. *Massive tissue damage in there. Clean it out, Francisco. You've got to pull your shit together, right now, or you'll lose her.*

Francisco's hands were so unsteady he couldn't even hold a swab. Pain rushed through him, receded like the waves at Malibu, crashed back stronger than before. His own pulse was racing, unsteady. *Shock*, he self-diagnosed, *blood loss . . .*

From out of the grey fog surrounding him, Sibyl Johnson said steadily, "Let me." She pulled the swab out of nerveless fingers, then swore under her breath. The next moment, she'd wrapped something tight around his torso to control bleeding down his side. "Dammit, don't faint on us! Tell me what to do."

Francisco shut his eyes, fighting darkness. "Dan, get the hell out of here. Sibyl, get an alcohol prep . . ."

Under Francisco's guidance, Sibyl cleaned around both wounds, then taped down plastic to create an airtight seal in case she'd punctured a lung. Without X-ray equipment or ultrasound it was impossible to determine the full extent of damage and cracking her open under these conditions would kill her.

"Turn her onto her side, no, so the gunshot wounds are down," Francisco instructed, trying awkwardly to help. "If she's bleeding into a lung, she'll fill up *both* lungs with blood if you turn the other way. Can't do a damn thing about that dislocated bone. . . . Going to hurt like a mother. Don't want to hit her with a painkiller yet, not while she's unconscious." Sibyl dragged a blanket up across her. "Good, that's the best we can do." He clutched the edge of the cot, fighting the need to faint. "Now start an IV; she's in shock, her electrolytes will be messed up something terrible."

Sibyl found the vein on the fourth try, and taped the IV needle down, then started a saline solution running. Francisco showed her how to add medications, how to deal with infection and shock. Francisco's vision kept greying out as he talked her through it. When it was done, Francisco felt himself slipping.

"Will she live?" Sibyl asked, from an incredible distance.

"Hope so . . ." he mumbled.

She tore loose his shirt. "You did a good job, doctor. Now let me see how badly you're hit." She swabbed at his side. "It doesn't look too bad. Not nearly as bad as Lucille."

For an endless moment, all he could do was yell. Sibyl Johnson had a sadistic bent. When his vision began to clear again, she was taping gauze into place. Dan Collins had reappeared from somewhere. His friend's face was waxy white.

"Frank?"

Sibyl answered for him. "The bullet grazed his ribs. He's lucky. I take it Lucille's your wife? She's pretty bad, but we did our best. Right now she's sleeping quietly. Help me get him onto a cot, would you?"

Tough girl, Sibyl Johnson.

They lifted him cautiously and deposited him on one of the cots.

"How much of this should I give you?" Sibyl asked matter-of-factly.

He managed to focus on the small vial of remaining Demerol and a clean hypodermic.

"No, Lucille's going to need that—"

She shrugged, stuck the needle into the rubber seal, and began filling the hypo herself. "If you slip into shock from pain and die on us, what are *her* chances?"

Footsteps in the other room heralded somebody's arrival.

"Hey, Collins," somebody called, "where are you?"

"Infirmary."

Francisco roused himself with a supreme effort. "No, that's too much! Half that . . ."

She arched one brow in his direction. "That's better." She complied, using the plunger to squirt the medication back through the rubber seal so none of it was wasted, then neatly injected him before he could protest.

Francisco yelped. Sibyl packed the Demerol carefully away and went to look at Janet's injuries. Dan clasped his hand as though Francisco were made of blown glass. Dan's hand shook. He'd been crying.

"Frank, what are you *doing* here?"

"The Hughes boy's appendix was about to burst," he gritted. "They figured . . . I was expendable."

"And who's—who's this young lady?"

Dan's voice control was shattering. His gaze kept straying from Sibyl back to the cot where Lucille lay, bandaged and silent.

Francisco discovered deep gratitude for the spreading bliss of Demerol. "Sibyl Johnson. Anybody going to relieve my curiosity? Can't believe you showed up like that, didn't think the cavalry showed up anymore . . ." He was babbling in the grip of the drug and didn't care.

Before Dan could answer, Logan McKee strolled into the room. Francisco groaned. McKee, the lunatic, loose and armed with a rifle. . . .

"Frank, I think you'll remember Captain McKee," Dan said quietly.

McKee strolled over and leaned down from an incredible distance. "Major," he saluted sloppily. "Didn't expect to find you here. We got 'em, Colonel."

Dan stood up and rubbed a hand across his face. "My wife's hit pretty bad." His voice shook. "Frank's hit, but he's not critical, thank God. Janet Firelli was grazed. Janet? How bad is it?"

Sibyl Johnson answered. "She'll smart for a few days, but it's not serious."

Janet made a strangled sound under her ministrations.

He heard Sibyl talking quietly to someone, but her voice and face grew incredibly muzzy as the Demerol took deeper hold. He tried to get Dan's attention, then forgot why.

Then he slipped quietly into darkness.

Charlie finished loading the last of Carreras' men into the back of the truck. He swung the door shut with a savage bang. Two at Stabiae . . . Three here. Five down. A veritable army to go. To get them all, they would have to declare war on global organized crime.

Charlie snorted. They were already *at* war with global organized crime. The bad guys just didn't know it, yet. He shivered in the intense cold and rescued Lucania from the floor of the truck. Thank God, none of the bullets had punched through anywhere near her. Wrapped up in her miles-too-big parka, she was fast asleep. Charlie headed slowly toward the bunker, holding her close as he could without waking her.

Logan McKee met him partway to the door. "Got to wondering if you were going to come inside."

"Just taking care of the meat."

McKee nodded. "They'll freeze solid out here. Thank God. Figure we'll just dump 'em before we go and let the vultures at 'em next spring.

"How'd it go in there?"

"Collins' wife was hit, real bad. Collins is taking it pretty hard. The doctor was hit, too, but not as seriously. If he makes it, maybe Collins' wife has a chance."

Charlie glanced up curiously. "Doctor?"

"Yeah. They had a couple of other hostages Collins didn't know about. One of 'em's a doctor. I'd met him a couple of times."

Charlie rubbed the side of his face. "Great. Two walking wounded."

"Four, actually. That Firelli girl was grazed by a stray

round and the doctor's here in the first place because one of the hostages damn near busted an appendix."

"Great. Oh, that's just fine. With that many wounded, we're going to be stuck here for a while." Charlie drew in a lungful of biting air and glanced at his sleeping daughter. "Okay, maybe that's not so bad. We could use a little time to catch our breath, make some plans."

"Yeah, well, I'm freezin' my butt off. See you."

McKee headed back inside.

Charlie followed more slowly. He hunched his shoulders and pulled open the door. It creaked against the pressure of the wind. Charlie latched it behind him, then surveyed the shambles of the main room. It was hard to believe, but that biggest guard, Nelson, had actually made it out past McKee and Collins. The place was riddled with bullet holes. Charlie remembered Nelson. Shooting that bastard had given him more intense satisfaction than his very first orgasm with a girl, when he was all of fifteen.

Shooting Nelson would never return Sibyl's life, but killing another of her murderers helped, just a little.

Past an open doorway, Collins had huddled down beside a cot. The place smelled like blood and death. He didn't see any sign of Collins kid. He must be in there, too. It looked crowded, in fact, jammed with cots and injured bodies.

Four wounded . . .

Charlie gently set Lucania down and eased open her parka, so she wouldn't overheat, then shrugged out of his own. He draped it across a chair with a bullet hole through the back. He wondered emptily whether or not the food he could smell was still hot. It had been hours since he'd eaten *anything*.

He shrugged. He ought to go say hello, first, at least. He found to his surprise he dreaded having anyone else see him. He dreaded, more than he'd believed possible, the shock and pity he'd see in their eyes.

Christ, what was wrong with him? He and Lucania were safe—safer than his daughter had ever been in

Bericus' house, safer than Charlie had been in four years. He squared his shoulders against burning welts and limped slowly across the room. It was too bad the doctor'd been hit. He could have used some medical attention for his back. The room was knee-deep in people and cots.

Charlie found McKee peering at an injured man dressed as an Army officer. Which, considering Charlie's stolen MP uniform, meant nothing at all. He must be the doctor. A dark-haired woman with her back to him had bent over a boy of about eleven or twelve. She was busy adjusting bandages along his abdomen. That had to be Zac Hughes. He wondered who the woman was and why Carreras had considered her a necessary hostage.

Charlie leaned tiredly against the doorframe. A kid of about fifteen, looking exactly like Dan Collins, glanced up. The boy noted his presence through fear-bruised eyes, then turned his attention back to his mother. McKee crouched down beside Collins and murmured something which Collins clearly didn't hear. McKee shrugged and stood up again. The woman kneeling beside the injured boy glanced up at McKee . . .

Charlie felt as though somebody had slugged him. With a baseball bat. He actually staggered.

Sibyl . . .

He must have made some sound, because she looked up.

Green eyes widened. Her whole face drained of color in the space of a single heartbeat.

"Charlie?"

His throat wouldn't work properly. Somehow, the sound came out anyway, strangled. "Sibyl . . ."

Without quite knowing how, he found her in his arms. She clung to him. She was weeping his name brokenly, again and again. He closed his arms around her back, crushed her against him, buried his face in her dark hair, still unable to believe she was alive. Wetness soaked through his shirt. For a moment, he wasn't sure which of them was holding up the other. Shudders coursed through both of them.

Charlie shut his eyes over stinging salt. For a moment, he was aware only of her warmth, the feel of her against him, the hiccoughing sound escaping her. He didn't know how, didn't *care* how. She was *here*, alive, and he was holding her. Nothing else mattered. Tension, fear, hatred, all drained out of him in that moment.

"Hey," he whispered wetly, "don't go all mushy on me now. . . ."

She shook her head mutely against his chest—and kept crying. He didn't think she would ever stop. Sibyl shifted in his arms, tightened her grip fiercely around broken ribs. Charlie gave a strangled cry and nearly went down.

Sibyl's eyes, wide and shocked and glimmering with tears, met his as she caught him.

"Charlie?" She sounded scared, *looked* scared. The look in her face hit him like a blow across the backs of his knees. He wobbled, then dragged himself up and braced himself against her.

"Sorry," he whispered, shaken more by the look in her eyes than by the pain. "Just busted a rib, is all." Charlie tilted her face up when she tried to hide against his shirt. Her eyes were dark, wet emeralds in a waxen face. Her lips trembled. Charlie wiped her cheeks with his fingertips. She tried to smile, but her lips were quivering too badly.

"Are you okay?" Charlie asked. He looked for signs of burns, found none. Another coil of tension unwound in his belly and drained away.

"Yes. I'm a little bruised and sore, but I'll be fine. You? Besides the rib?"

"In one piece, sort of."

"And—"

"Lucky's asleep in the next room."

Sibyl closed her eyes and started crying again. "Thank God . . . Thank God . . . Charlie, I thought you were both dead." She looked up.

"How—" they began simultaneously.

They halted and stared at one another. Then Sibyl beat him by a half-second with a glare in her eyes and a strangled, "Don't you *ever* die on me again, Charlie Flynn!"

From somewhere behind them, McKee's voice intruded.

"*Flynn?* Your name! At last!"

He glared at the lunatic. McKee was chuckling. "Should've known you were Irish," he said, shepherding them out of the sickroom. "With that hair and temper, what else could you be? Are you going to stand there all night, *Mr. Flynn*, or will you please enlighten me as to this young lady's name?"

He glanced with pointed interest toward Sibyl.

"My name's Sibyl Johnson," she answered for herself. "Who the hell are you?"

Charlie found himself grinning. That was what he liked about her.

"Logan Pfeiffer McKee, Ms. Johnson." He shook her hand formally.

She studied McKee. "So . . . were you the one who found Charlie?"

McKee rubbed the back of his head ruefully. "It was a little more the other way around."

"I hit him over the head with a rock and tried to shoot him," Charlie muttered. "Things were a little confused."

Dan Collins' voice came from the infirmary doorway. "I'm still confused."

Charlie glanced up. Collins and his son stood in the doorway. The colonel had aged ten years. He looked haggard in the harsh fluorescent light. The arm he'd wrapped around his son looked like a permanent fixture. He glanced from Charlie to Sibyl.

"You two obviously know each other. I take it this is the 'other Carreras victim' you thought had died at Herculaneum?"

Charlie just nodded.

"Hungry?"

Charlie's smile widened a little. "Hell, Collins, if it's

not moving, I'll eat it. Even if it *is* moving, I might eat it."

"Good. There's plenty of it."

Charlie glanced down at Sibyl, asking with his eyes if she'd join him. The way her eyes lit up lifted a load that felt like the weight of the entire earth off his shoulders. For the first time in how long he couldn't even recall, Charlie Flynn felt happy. Just plain and simple, happy.

Sibyl grinned and said a little too brightly, "Good. I think you could use some fattening up," she said, taking in the toughened scarecrow he'd become over four murderously tough years.

Sibyl spent the rest of the night on the floor, wrapped in blankets and Charlie Flynn's arms. She didn't sleep much. Charlie did, despite the fact that Logan McKee snored like a trumpeting mammoth. Despite the trickle of light coming from the bathroom, around the edges of the blanket they'd rigged for privacy. Despite worry for his little girl. Lucky slept nestled in blankets on the floor beside Sibyl's ear, looking utterly angelic. Janet Firelli, recovering some of her strength, had cooed over the little girl.

Danny had just rolled his eyes, earning Charlie's rusty laughter. Now Charlie slept so deeply she wasn't sure he'd ever awaken again. Despite everything they had yet to face, a smile tugged at the corners of Sibyl's lips. He'd looked so stunned when she'd invited him under the blankets with her. His weight and warmth felt good against her back. The arm he'd tucked around her waist hadn't moved even an inch. She wasn't sure which of them had needed the intimate contact more.

Right before supper, they'd managed to pry the slave's collar off his neck. His look as he'd hurled it outside had sent chills through her. Sibyl found herself almost pitying Carreras. She hoped he died as hard as Tony Bartlett had.

All during supper, he remained extremely withdrawn. He made certain Lucania had mashed up food she could eat and even managed to play airplanes with the spoon, drawing Lucania's giggles, but he avoided meeting anyone's eye. He flatly refused McKee's offer of first-aid attention after they finished eating.

So Sibyl took matters into her own hands. "Charlie, let me look at your back."

"I'm fine."

"No, you're not. You're white around the lips and swaying on your feet. Sit down. Now!"

He sat. Very gingerly, Sibyl eased off his shirt. Someone had wrapped cloth tightly around his ribs. It looked to Sibyl like a woman's stola—a cheap one.

"Who wrapped your ribs?"

"A fisherman's wife. We got out just—" He stiffened and made a ghastly sound.

Sibyl gulped. "I'm sorry. It's stuck to dried blood. Hold tight. I'll be right back. . . ."

She brought a pan of warm water from the kitchen and soaked the stuff loose with a wet cloth. *If I keep him talking, maybe this won't hurt so much.* "You were saying?"

He told her about the flight from Herculaneum, between little gasps and several sharp grunts. But the cloth came loose. His back was a mass of bruises, criss-crossed welts, swollen bands and lumps . . .

McKee, stepping past the sickroom, glanced in just as she finished unwrapping it.

"Holy Loving Jesus . . ."

Charlie snarled something under his breath.

"The way you've been moving, I knew it'd be bad under those bandages, but . . ." McKee's voice trailed off. "Sibyl, do you need any help?"

"No," Charlie grated. "We don't."

McKee shrugged and moved on toward the bathroom. Across the room, Dan Collins glanced up, but said nothing.

Very, very carefully, Sibyl washed Charlie's injuries. By the time she was done with the left shoulder, he was trembling. Quietly, Sibyl filled a hypo with a couple of cc's of Demerol. Without a little help, he'd pass out before she was done.

"Lean forward a little. That's good. Hold still."

He tried to crane around.

"I said, hold still! This is going to sting."

She jabbed the fleshy muscle and injected him.

He didn't flinch, but he did demand, a little sourly, "What the hell was that?"

"Synthetic morphine. Don't argue. Just lie down and let me deal with this."

Dan Collins glanced up from his own bedside vigil and tried to smile. "Take my advice. Don't argue. You'll be a happier man."

Charlie blinked, then swallowed sharply. "Okay."

Sibyl wanted to comfort the army colonel, too, but she couldn't lie to him and say, "Lucille will be fine." Lucille Collins' life was still very much in danger. At least Charlie had begun to relax under the influence of the medicine. By the time she finished washing grit and sand out of the welts, he was very drowsy and much more comfortable.

"Forgot how nice it is not to hurt," he mumbled into the army cot.

Sibyl turned aside, searching for the surgeon's medical kit. She found it on the floor and rummaged.

"What do you need?"

She glanced up. Francisco Valdez was awake. He looked a little pale.

"Something to prevent infection, something to deal with existing infection, and something for a broken rib."

Francisco eased up to a sitting position. "Let me see."

Sibyl helped the surgeon wobble over to Charlie's cot. Francisco's brows drew down sharply. He prodded cautiously, drawing a sharp yelp from Charlie.

"That needs to be set. It's out of proper alignment." He glanced around. "Where's that big lunatic, McKee?"

"I heard that," McKee said from the other room. He appeared in the doorway. "What's up?"

"I need some help setting a broken rib. If we don't,

he'll risk a punctured lung. We can't deal with that here."

McKee nodded. "Tell me what to do."

Sibyl scooted out of their way. She hugged herself and tried not to flinch too badly when Charlie yelled. *Thank God I dosed him first*. Sibyl learned more colorful curses during the next five minutes than she had during her entire academic career. New Jersey cops had *foul* mouths. In any language. The one time she dared look, Charlie was sweating down his mutilated back, fists tightened in the blanket. The wetness on his face wasn't sweat, nor did it look voluntary.

It took far too long, in Sibyl's estimation, but Francisco Valdez finally said, "Yes, that's better. Much better. Thanks, McKee. Hang around a minute, I'll need you again."

Francisco Valdez went to work on the welts, using a topical anesthetic, followed by antibiotic ointment.

"Normally," he told Charlie, "I'd want you on oral antibiotics, but I've got an appendectomy and a gunshot wound that take higher priority and we have a limited supply of ampicillin."

"No problem." Charlie's voice, muffled by the blanket on the cot, wobbled a little.

"We'll keep these scrupulously clean and apply topical antibiotics to the worst welts until we run out of it. Hopefully by then, we'll be somewhere to get these properly looked after."

While he talked, Francisco smoothed in the medicine.

"Ms. Johnson, would you find the large gauze pads, please, and the adhesive?"

Sibyl rummaged again. She handed over a whole box of gauze and the tape. "I can do that," she said. "Your hands aren't steady yet."

Francisco smiled ruefully. "Yes, my ribs hurt, but not as much as Charlie's. Relatively speaking, I'm fine. Place the pads like so, overlapping, and tape the outsides to one another. Yes, just like that. . . ."

They covered Charlie's whole back, from his neck to

his tailbone and partway around the sides. By the time they'd finished, Charlie looked more like the permanent occupant of an Egyptian crypt than a cop. At least he'd stopped wheezing like an asthmatic elephant. The wet trails down his cheeks had started to dry.

"Very good. Charlie, can you sit up?"

A sheen of sweat still glistened on his throat. "Sure, doc. No problem. Sometime next week, maybe."

McKee had to help him get there, then had to brace him once he made it.

"Now what?" McKee asked.

"We need to tape his ribs. Ms. Johnson?"

Sibyl handed over tape and helped hold Charlie up. McKee did the taping. Charlie compressed his lips and bruised Sibyl's wrist every few seconds. But he didn't yell again.

"Glad you . . . gave me that stuff," he said at one point. "This would'a been . . . murder without it."

Francisco lifted one brow. Sibyl explained. "I used only two cc's."

The army surgeon nodded. "That's all right, then. I'd have done the same. All right, Charlie, we're done torturing you for now. I prescribe plenty of rest and about twelve straight hours of sleep, followed by getting the hell out of here."

Charlie managed a wan smile that did amazing things to Sibyl's pulse. "You said it. When do we leave?"

"Right after you get some sleep," Sibyl said sternly.

Francisco caught her eye. "I think you need a little sleep as well, young lady. Off to bed. Now."

So Sibyl had ended up putting together two separate nests of blankets out in the main room, a small one into which she tucked sleeping little Lucania. She then offered to share the other with Charlie. The look in his eyes when she made that offer was one of the treasures she locked away in a secret corner of herself, along with memories of her parents and her grandmother's warm hugs and laughter.

Sibyl just wished she could sleep as deeply as Charlie.

Every time she closed her eyes, some newly remembered horror would present itself for reinspection. She stared into the semidarkness, watching dust motes in the narrow shaft of light from the bathroom, and listened to Charlie's heartbeat and soft breaths. She thanked God every few minutes he was alive, that he had a chance to recover. That Lucania was safe with him.

She hoped Charlie could afford some good reconstructive surgery. What kind of health insurance did a police officer have? And had he been missing, subjectively, long enough to account for the age of his injuries? *Not bloody likely.* . . . Some of those scars were four years old. She damned Carreras all over again. Maybe something could be done through Francisco Valdez. It was the least the Army could do.

Nothing was easy anymore. Not that anything had ever been *easy* in her life. When God handed out trouble, He seemed to keep a special eye out for the Johnsons.

She wondered what part of New Jersey Charlie'd grown up in. Where, exactly, *was* Jersey City? They'd had so little time to talk. Did he have family up there? Maybe even a wife and kids? The question left her stunned. Listening to little Lucania breathe, recalling a few things Charlie'd said, she didn't think there were any kids in his life as a twentieth-century cop.

And even if he'd been married, they'd have taken every physical clue from him at the time of his capture. She wasn't sure undercover cops who were married would even wear a wedding band. She had a feeling something like that would come under the heading of protective camouflage.

God . . . She didn't want Charlie to walk out of her life. She treasured his friendship and harbored a sneaking feeling she didn't *want* to settle for just friendship. Her thoughts jolted her. He was old enough—at least, *looked* old enough—to be her father. She barely *knew* him. All she really knew about Charlie . . .

He was tenacious. Infinitely gentle with those who

needed him, deadly to his enemies.. Loyal to a fault. Astonishingly resourceful. And the most honorable man she knew.

Her throat closed traitorously.

The only virtue she could lay at her own feet was stubbornness. *That* was something that got her into trouble as often as not.

She already knew how he felt about children.

Low voices from the infirmary sidetracked Sibyl from her own worries. Lucille was awake. Dan Collins' voice was a broken whisper in the darkness.

"Lucy, hon, I'm so sorry . . ."

"Shh . . . Dan, don't—"

"This is my fault, it's all my fault, you're hurt and I've smashed up all these innocent people's lives . . ."

Sibyl swallowed hard. As bad as her own situation was, Dan Collins was living in hell.

"No, Dan." Lucille Collins' voice was breathless from pain, but there was no compromise in her tone. "It is not your fault. You didn't put me here. *They* did. You didn't hold a gun to our heads. *They* did. You didn't pull the trigger . . . or order us marooned someplace horrible to die . . . *they* did."

"Lucy—"

"Dan, sometimes we have to . . . have to stand up to evil men, no matter what the cost. I love you even more because you did. Because you cared enough about . . . about what's right to risk us, to risk everything . . ."

The sound of a grown man crying like a child was too harsh, too intimate a sound to be borne. Sibyl wanted to stop her ears, but couldn't move without waking up Charlie. And if he woke up, he'd start hurting again. . . .

Sibyl must have moved, because Charlie stirred sleepily. His arm tightened around her.

"You okay?" he murmured.

She nodded, then turned over and looked up into his eyes. "And you?"

"Tired," he admitted.

The voices coming from the other room stopped, then resumed more quietly.

Charlie's eyes had gone dark, very nearly unreadable. "Sibyl, I—you're a wonderful girl, smart and sweet and . . . and *dammit*, you're a wonderful friend in a tight spot. But . . . there's . . . there's a lot you don't know yet about me. I'm not a very nice person, Sibyl."

She remembered waking up with ropes on her wrists and ankles, and no memory of herself. Remembered a battered man's whispered gentleness to a complete stranger.

"You don't know yourself very well, then, Charlie."

His glance was startled. She thought about marshaling all sorts of sentimental arguments. Settled for something he might be able to accept. "You could have chosen to work for Carreras, instead of hunting him."

His whole face closed, like a mimosa leaf that's been pinched too hard. "Yeah. Well. I could see where that got the rest of my good old buddies in the Thirty-Seventh Street Tarantulas. I didn't figure a coffin and a jail cell were all that much different."

Something in the way he wouldn't meet her eyes told her there was a great deal left unsaid. She wondered what had prompted him to become a police officer. She decided if he didn't want to share it, she didn't want to prod. Some things were too hurtful to share.

"Well," Sibyl muttered, having determined this was confession time, round one, "I'm not exactly the innocent you seem to think I am."

His glance was clearly skeptical.

"Charlie, I stabbed Tony and lied to him, then left him to die."

"Yeah, I know."

"And I was glad I—" A gasp of shock broke loose. "You *know*?"

"I found him. While I was looking for you."

"And you don't mind?"

"*Mind—*?"

"Jeezus H. Christ," Logan McKee muttered from

across the room, "keep it down, will you? Let a bum sleep!"

Sibyl gulped. These men had gone through hell to rescue her and the others, and they were being rude when Mr. McKee clearly needed sleep.

Meanwhile, Charlie's eyes reminded her of a little boy confronted by an abusive father after a Saturday night binge. *How many times has life slapped you to the ground, Charlie Flynn?*

She tried to explain how she felt in a way that wouldn't cause him further pain. "I don't rush into things. Generally, that is," she added ruefully. "Seems like lately, rush is all I've done."

"Does that mean you, uh, maybe want to get to know me better?"

She wouldn't meet his eyes for a moment, then, so softly he strained to hear it, whispered. "Yeah. Think I do."

His touch was so light she could barely feel his fingertips. He traced dark circles under her eyes. "You haven't slept at all, have you?"

She shook her head.

Across the room, Logan McKee grumbled into his blankets. Sibyl repressed the urge to laugh aloud at the black look Charlie gave McKee's back. She settled for a contented sigh as Charlie gathered her close. He tucked his arms securely around her again. For a long time, Sibyl lay with her eyes closed, more content than she'd believed possible, then drifted into sleep with Charlie still draped warmly against her.

"So," Dan Collins broached the subject that had been on Sibyl's mind since waking, "here we all are. Battered, bruised, but not quite beaten, in the year 28,000 B.C."

Seven of them sat around the makeshift table the guards had set up in the kitchen. Lucille still slept, drugged into painlessness, and Zac Hughes was still too ill to get out of bed. Lucania was asleep, too, having finished her breakfast then curled up like a puppy on her father's lap.

Logan McKee scratched his beard and merely looked thoughtful. Danny, looking more white-faced than any fifteen-year-old ought to, glanced toward his father for reassurance. Charlie said nothing, but gripped Sibyl's hand under the table. Dan Collins clearly had suffered a sleepless night. Purple hollows under his eyes met deep gouges that plowed down his cheeks from the edge of his nose. Francisco Valdez tried valiantly to look comfortable in the hard, straight-backed chair and failed utterly. Of them all, Janet Firelli was possibly in the best shape, and she'd been *shot*.

The condition they were in frightened Sibyl. *I've seen healthier people walk away from plane crashes. How can we possibly go after Carreras like this? He'd laugh himself to death.* She suppressed the urge to close her arms around herself. Carreras could send his people through at any time and catch them flat-footed. And just how did the recall devices work? Would they be reappear in the middle of Mafia Crime Central?

Sibyl decided someone had to start voicing doubts and questions and no one else seemed eager for the job.

"Colonel Collins—"

"Dan. Please." His eyes urged her to agree.

Sibyl shrugged. *Why not?* "All right. Dan, I don't really have any idea how this time-travel thing of yours works, except Tony told me you press a recall button on that little gadget he had with him and you get back home again." She frowned. "Where is it, anyway? I had it in a pouch . . ."

Francisco said, "All your stuff's in the sickroom. I didn't take the time to look at it. Your jewelry's in there, too."

For a moment she was nonplussed. "Jewelry?" Then she recalled the heavy gold ornaments Bericus had ordered her dressed in. She almost laughed aloud. She had a source of income, after all. "You know, I'd forgotten I came through dressed like the Queen of Sheba."

Charlie glanced up. "You sure were."

She cleared her throat delicately, aware of the heat in her face. "Anyway, Colonel—Dan—I don't know how this time-travel stuff is supposed to work, but a couple of worrisome thoughts have occurred to me."

Dan Collins nodded tiredly. "I expected them." He leaned forward and steepled his fingers. "Go on, please."

"I don't think Tony planned to end up here, in this time and place. What would be the point? And I can't imagine how you and Mr. McKee ended up in a position to rescue Charlie, although I'm eternally grateful you did."

"Hear, hear," Charlie muttered. He gave her hand another squeeze under the table.

She squeezed back. "It doesn't make sense you'd have known he was there at all, never mind knowing exactly where to look, when he was a couple of hundred miles from the place Carreras dumped him to die. Besides, you don't seem to have anything *with* you that would be appropriate to early Imperial Rome. So it couldn't have been a planned mission. The only explanation which makes sense is that you were up to something else altogether and something went seriously wrong. All of which tells me these jumps, or whatever you want to call them, aren't reliable."

Dan Collins' brows lifted silently.

"The other little problem I see is this. Even if the jump works just the way it's supposed to and we do get back, presumably the recall devices are set to return to the point and time of departure, or close to it. Which means we walk right into their base of operations. Where Carreras will presumably be waiting with open arms. Either that, or you have another recall device with you, something not even Carreras knows about, to take you to a place or time where you can strike safely at him, without him expecting it."

Dan shut his mouth. Then said, "Ever consider a career in military intelligence?"

Charlie laughed, one short syllable. "She's good, isn't

she? Told you she was the only reason Lucky and I are alive."

Her face flamed.

Logan McKee leaned forward and propped hairy elbows on the table. "She's also very right." The lines around his eyes deepened as he frowned. "Don't forget, Collins, there's still a traitor in your camp. *Somebody* talked." A brief silence followed that grim observation.

Janet toyed with a salt shaker and said nothing.

McKee finally broke the silence again. "How about it, Collins? That first jump you and I made screwed up big time. Apparently so did *hers*." He nodded toward Sibyl. "Back on that beach in whatever the place was—"

"Stabiae," Charlie put quietly.

McKee pressed his point. "Yeah. You said something about this, about how the whole time stream is coming unraveled. *Can* we get back?"

Sibyl shivered.

Across the table, Dan Collins' eyes darkened. "I don't know," he answered quietly. He glanced at Sibyl, at Francisco Valdez and Janet Firelli. "Probably. Maybe. The problem we're facing is called slippage. The more holes get punched through time, the more cracks radiate out around them. The more cracks, the more likely any given jump will slip into the wrong time or place. Or both. We know about one such crack. It dumped McKee five years into his future, from Florida onto my base. Another one allowed us to rescue Charlie, instead of taking us to Krakatoa to dispose of Carreras' goons."

He glanced at Sibyl. "You're here, Ms. Johnson, because of another one that diverted you into Alaska's remote past instead of the present where Tony was doubtless headed. What will happen when we try the next jump . . ." He lifted his hands, palms up. "I suspect a great deal will depend on what Carreras has running simultaneously when we try it. I know he's got something big planned. It's supposed to begin soon. At least the first phase of it, anyway. I don't know what it is."

He paused, lost in thought for a moment. Then he said, "Multiple jumps are always dangerous, whether they're the Firellian kind—like the one we made, McKee—or whether they're separate but simultaneous." A grimace tugged his mouth askew. "Firellian Jumps are worse, of course, because they're not simply straight-line progressions. They have sideways, nonlinear hops thrown in. Up until we jumped," he rubbed the back of his neck, "they were only theoretically possible."

McKee snorted. "Still a goddamned guinea pig."

Collins ignored him. "That's why I had no idea what to expect when we activated the second leg of our triple to jump *here*. Our jump may have been what messed up yours, Ms. Johnson, and vice versa. Or it could have been the slippage effect. I just don't *know*. I'm not even certain the physicists will know.

"When we do activate our recall, we'll be activating the third leg of a Firellian triple link that has already proven faulty once. Frankly, I don't know what will happen. I only partly understand what Sue and Zac and their teams are doing. I do know the whole fabric of what we conventionally think of as time is weakened every time a new hole is punched in it. Jumping out of here could kill us."

For a long, long moment, nobody said a word. Sibyl was scared all the way to her toenails, in a far quieter fashion than she had been on the beach at Herculaneum. Marooned in a Pleistocene winter?

Danny said, "So, like, we could be stuck here, hunh, Dad?"

Sibyl read signs of too much strain and sleeplessness in the man's face as he rumpled his son's hair. "Yeah, son. We could be. Either we stay here/now, or we try the jump out and potentially end up someplace worse."

"Like beyond Antares," McKee put in.

Francisco started to sit forward, grunted once, and sat abruptly back. "If it's all the same to you," he said stiffly, in obvious pain, "I'd just as soon try it. I think we all have a few scores to settle."

"Let me get the Demerol—" Janet began.

"No." He shook his head. "I'll be fine. Others need it worse than I do. And God knows, we might need it even more later."

The breakfast in Sibyl's stomach turned leaden. Charlie tightened his hand around hers.

"How shall we do this?" Sibyl asked quietly into the silence. "Vote? Or follow military command? Do lifeboat rules apply, or do we get to choose?"

McKee shook his head. "What's to choose? If we stay here, too chicken to try it, eventually we'll run out of food and diesel. And I don't think any of us could survive a winter in this place. Maybe not even a summer. I'm betting there's more than wooly mammoths out there."

Danny nodded. "There is. Zac, he's a nut on the stuff. There's saber-toothed cats, dire wolves, cave lions . . ."

Dan Collins smiled at his son. "Yes, we get the point. The Ice Ages weren't very friendly to humanity and we have too many wounded as it is to survive here."

McKee glanced at Collins. "How about it, Colonel? When do we leave?"

Dan Collins glanced toward the infirmary. "Not until Frank says it's safe to move Lucille and Zac."

They looked as one toward Francisco Valdez.

"Give them another couple of weeks, Lucille especially. Kids heal faster than adults. If she makes it that long, she has a good chance."

"Janet?"

She laughed harshly. "Do you have any idea how much I miss salad bars? Doors that actually have *doors*? My mother . . ." Her voice wavered. "Hell, yes, I'll risk it."

McKee turned his cool appraisal on Sibyl and Charlie. "That leaves you."

"You already know how I feel," Charlie said gruffly. "I'll kill Jésus Carreras with my bare hands, if I have to." He curled a hand protectively around Lucania's head. "I can't do that sitting on my butt in this icebox."

"I want the hell out of here," Sibyl said harshly. "No

way we can survive *here* for any length of time. Diesel and supplies'll run out eventually. So I vote we cut our losses and get away from this place. Soon."

"Well," McKee said briskly, "that leaves us with the question of how to deal with Carreras once we get there."

Collins swore softly. "Yeah. Except none of us knows a thing about him."

Sibyl heard Charlie draw breath. Felt him gather himself through the tightening of his hand on hers. He spoke like a man chopping through thick ice.

"I do."

He was instantly the focal point of their undivided attention. He kept his gaze on the table and seemed to have difficulty speaking. The hand that wasn't clasped in hers was clenched in a white-knuckled fist.

"A lot of this . . ." He paused. "I've never told anyone most of this." He glanced up, met Collins' gaze squarely. "I first tangled with the Carreras family a long time ago. I wasn't much older than your boy is now, Collins."

The colonel put an arm around his son.

"I don't kid myself about what I was back then. If you weren't in a gang, you were everybody's target. And the Carrerases of this world use gangs." He shook his head. "Most of it doesn't matter anymore. When I was seventeen, they shot my grandfather. They didn't know he was *my* grandfather and didn't care, either. He was just a witness that had to be silenced. After it happened . . ."

Nobody moved. Sibyl could *hear* the snow blowing against the concrete walls outside.

"I quit. Got a high school diploma so I could apply to the police academy. Worked my ass off, finally made detective. Found out *which* Carreras had given the order. Finagled a transfer from New York to Miami. For the first two years I couldn't get close. My captain had me working other cases hard as I could go. But we made busts, dug out more information. And then, when I was this close"—he held up thumb and forefinger almost touching—"I stumbled across this time-travel thing. Next thing I knew, Carreras was bending over me, laughing, while they pumped me full of drugs. I figured they'd make it look like an OD and dump my body in Biscayne Bay."

He paused. Nobody spoke. His eyes were haunted. His fingers trembled slightly in Sibyl's grasp. She pressed them and earned a slight squeeze back.

"Anyway, I woke up in chains, with Richie or Ricky or whatever his name was standing in front of me, explaining to some guy in a dress how I'd murdered some important friend of a Roman senator's. At least, that's what Richie told me he'd said. A couple of minutes later, he let me know they'd sentenced me to die in the arena."

His laughter was harsh. Across the table, Dan Collins actually flinched.

"A couple of days later, he came to visit me. I was in this hellhole of a prison, built out of solid rock underneath *another* prison."

Sibyl caught her breath. "The Tullianum . . ."

He glanced up. "Yeah. You know it?"

"It's under the Mamertine Prison. Jugurtha was starved to death in it and Vercingetorix was put to death there by Julius Caesar. It's . . . horrible. Sixteen feet high, maybe thirty feet long, twenty-two feet wide . . ."

"You know it, all right," Charlie muttered. "They drop you through a hole in the ceiling. Then, if they decide to let you out, they run down a ladder. Richie didn't bother with the ladder. He just shouted down the good news. He told me I was lucky. I was going to be the featured event of the day. The Emperor himself was going to watch me die."

The muscles on his scarred jawline stood out in high relief. "The Circus Maximus in Rome was really pretty, you know? All marble and gemstones and incredible bronze facings on the turning posts, gorgeous sculpture on the barrier. . . . They sprinkled ground-up mica flakes on the sand, to make it glitter. The first time I fought there, they used whips to drive us condemned slaves onto the sand. By the time my first fight ended, the place stank like a slaughterhouse. I was the last one of us left alive. God help me, I killed all the others to stay alive, even their goddamned champions, who were supposed to finish me off. That's when one of the schools begged the Emperor to have me sold to them, rather than execute me."

Sibyl leaned closer and slid an arm around him.

Nobody made a sound while he collected his composure.

"Well," he said heavily. "Now you know. What do you want to know about Carreras? His old man runs things, probably came out of retirement to set this up. Julio's got lieutenants in half the cities of the world. Most of them are cousins or in-laws. They control more money than the American budget deficit is worth and last I heard, they were planning . . ."

His voice trailed off. Dan Collins' head came up sharply.

"*What?*"

Charlie's eyes had lost their focus. "Collins, what do you know about this thing he's planning?"

"Not much."

"*Anything*, Collins."

"The only thing I've been told is, he'll be moving through a lot of men and equipment soon. Sue Firelli's lab notes refer to substantial disruption of the time stream from about fifty years back, in the general area of Alamogordo, New Mexico."

Charlie went white. "Jesus God . . ."

"*What?*"

Charlie looked up, but his eyes were nearly blank. "My sources . . ." He stopped. Cleared his throat once. "Julio Carreras plans to declare war on the Yakusa."

McKee started swearing.

"The what?" Danny asked.

Dan Collins was exceedingly pale. "The Japanese mob. And Trinity Site nuclear testing grounds is at Alamogordo, New Mexico."

Sibyl went cold all over. "Oh, my God. We have to stop him. He's mad . . ."

"Jésus Carreras would do it, too, damn him." Charlie swore. "Japan practically owns America—and what they don't own, they've driven out of business. Carreras can't make any money if Americans don't have disposable income, which they won't have if our economy's shot to hell. Eliminate or control the Yakusa—which owns Japan—and you'd have it all. That must be how he figures it."

Grim looks passed between Dan, Charlie, and Logan McKee. Unbidden, Sibyl thought of Athos, Porthos, and Aramis . . . An unlikely trio ranged against the darkness of eternity itself. Somewhere, somewhen, they would find a far edge to that darkness, just as Sibyl had found her way back from the far edge of her own personal darkness. She'd found her way back in the person of Charlie Flynn. Maybe a crippled cop from New Jersey, a frightened Army colonel, and an escaped lunatic could find the far edge of that darkness.

And if they did . . .

Maybe they could eventually try and put their lives back together again. Meanwhile . . .

"One for all, and all for one," she muttered to nobody in particular.

"What?" Dan Collins frowned.

Charlie stared at her, then began to laugh, very softly. "Who says watching old movies isn't educational?" He squeezed her hand and glanced at Collins and McKee, then said, "Gentlemen, 'tis our sacred duty to stop the evil Richelieu and save the Queen of France. Are ye with me, sirs?"

Dan Collins smiled slowly. "I was a collegiate fencing champion."

They stayed in the concrete bunker just long enough to get the most seriously ill and injured ready for safe transport. As Francisco had predicted, Zac Hughes III healed fast. Sibyl discovered she liked him a great deal, particularly when he felt well enough to gush on about the passion of his young life: construction and engineering methods in medieval cathedrals. Sibyl didn't know much about that period in history, but his knowledge—particularly for a twelve-year-old—was encyclopedic.

Lucille desperately needed surgery that Francisco was finally driven to attempt, just to keep gangrene from settling into the rotting meat around the hole through her chest and back, never mind the gunk that was rotting *inside*, along the path the bullet had traveled. She wouldn't survive if gangrene got into a major organ. So, with Sibyl and Janet assisting, Francisco worked over her for hours, the look in his eyes echoing a singular terror that he might kill her, she was so weak already. But the repair job he did, as he said, "Ought to hold until we get her to a real hospital. At least we've reduced the chances of gangrene by cleaning the entire wound track."

When Francisco said he was ready to risk it, they stripped the bodies of their warm clothes and redistributed them, moved all the food, blankets, fuel, the stove that had kept them alive, and anything else that looked remotely salvageable—including all the army cots and every knife and gun every guard had been carrying, not to mention every bit of spare ammo. Through some male chemistry Sibyl didn't understand, Dan Collins, Logan McKee, and Charlie Flynn just started hauling out boxes of loaded cartridges, without ever once discussing it.

With Logan driving, Sibyl beside him, Charlie squeezed in next to her. And—because (he'd argued) he'd missed all the fun the first go-round—Zac Hughes III rode on Charlie's lap. Logan hadn't objected. "Hell, with you up here, Sib, and little Zac there, we've got about as much historical expertise as we're gonna find around here, right in front where you can *see* what we jump into. Let's go. I'm freezin' my butt off."

Together, Charlie and Sibyl mashed the recall button. Slowly, the time storm gathered out above the incredibly long, blackened smear in the otherwise unblemished white ice, where Vesuvius had turned solid ice into steaming mud. The portal slowly opened, like the dilating lens of a good camera, with pink lightning sizzling out of it from every direction.

"Here goes nothing," Logan muttered. "Hope the guys in back hang on real tight." Charlie and Sibyl braced themselves as Logan stepped on the gas and roared into the puncture of blinding light. Sibyl *knew* she was still in the truck, grasping Charlie's hand, but the only sensation was that of falling down an elevator shaft.

They came out into a night so full of stars, Charlie gasped at the sight. Not the stronghold of the Carreras family, at least. Then Zac went nuts. "Look! There!" The bones of a two-towered cathedral loomed over them, off to the left; pink lightning struck the walls, the half-finished towers, the curve of flying buttresses visible in the stark flashes of semi-daylight. The impression was that of Satan slowly swallowing the cathedral down his gullet. "I know that one—it's Our Lady of Paris!" Zac stammered. "Before the masons finished her. Wow!"

Sibyl shot the excited kid a quick look. "Zac, isn't Notre Dame de Paris on the edge of the Isle de la Cité?"

"Yeah. Why?"

Logan yelled, seeing the reason for Sibyl's question in the steep dropoff now visible in the glare of truck headlights. Before he could even think of hitting the brakes or turning the wheel, they were airborne, falling like lead bricks toward the black water of the Seine.

Watch for *Unholy Trinity* by Linda Evans from Baen Books.